MW01122804

The Alexanders

Volume 1
1911 - 1920

ALLAN HUDSON

Copyright © 2020, Allan Hudson and South Branch
Scribbler Publishing. All rights reserved. The use of any
part of this publication, reproduced, transmitted in any
form or by any means, electronic, mechanical,
photocopying, recording or otherwise stored in a
retrieval system, without consent of the publisher is an
infringement of the copyright law.

This is a work of fiction. Names, Characters,
businesses, places, events, locales, and incidents are
either the product of the author's imagination or used
in a fictitious way. Any resemblances to actual persons,
living or dead, or actual events is purely accidental.

Cynthia Shannon – Editor
Mark Young Designs – Cover

ISBN
eBook – 978-1-988291-08-6
Print – 978-1-988291-07-9
First Edition

South Branch Scribbler
3469 Route 535, Cocagne, NB Canada E4R 3E5
www.southbranchscribbler.ca

ALSO BY ALLAN HUDSON

THE DRAKE ALEXANDER SERIES:

DARK SIDE OF A PROMISE

WALL OF WAR

A BOX OF MEMORIES – A COLLECTION OF SHORT STORIES

SHATTERED FIGURINE – A JO NAYLOR ADVENTURE

DEDICATION

To the memory of:

Maria Chiasson – 1918 - 2017

Paul Chiasson – 1943 - 2018

Denise Chiasson-Landry – 1954 - 2017

There are special people in our lives that never leave us… even after they are gone.

D. Morgan.

CONTENTS

ACKNOWLEDGMENTS

I would like to thank my wife Gloria who supports my writing and offers encouragement and inspiration.

Also, my family; Adam, Chris, Mark, Mireille, Georgette, Matthieu, Natasha, Damien, Eva, Mia and Leo.

Two special friends need to be mentioned for their support and companionship, Allen & Gracia Williston.

Thanks go to my editor, Cynthia Shannon. To my cover designer, Mark Young. To Jeremy McLean for formatting.

Special thanks go to the individuals that are always there, for their sharing, their words of encouragement and goodwill.

A special thank you to Eden Rogers for *Pearl*.

Gail Brown. Carol & Christine Beers. June Hebert. Pamela Cottrell. Shirley Arsenault. MJ LaBeff. Chuck Bowie. Bernie Blanchard. Susan Toy. Seumas Gallacher. Marc & Marthe Leger. Lynn Babin Fontaine. Irene & Lynn Fontaine. Linda Vautour. Eva Cormier. Stephen Shortall. Therese Leblanc. Linda Nilsson-Hall. Theresa Hachey. Elizabeth Roeding. Sheila Clark. Mary Hachey. Cynthia Murray. Susan Jardine. Julien & Lucille D'Astou. Lucille Robinson. Cover to Cover Books. John Roberts of Chapters, Moncton. Alyssa Lahaie of Chapters, Fredericton.

THE ALEXANDERS - DOMINIC

1911

Autumn   Near Glasgow, Scotland

Lucretia Alexander is about to abandon her middle child, Dominic. Poised on the wide front stoop of her brother-in-law's house, she is draped in sorrow. Her father waits in the cairt, which he has pulled to the side of the street. Her hand is raised to rap on the faded wooden door, but she hesitates. Looking at her eleven-year-old son by her side, almost as tall as her, she sees the uncertainty in his eyes. Like her heart, her will is almost broken. She yearns to hold him, to cling to him, to carry him away from the sadness they both feel. Biting her lower lip, her need for him to survive strengthens her resolve. She knocks firmly upon the door.

The sun is setting over the roofs along the street; detail is lost to silhouettes. A cool breeze whispers around the corners, it carries the scent of iron and oil from the shipyards Govan is famous for. The two horses pulling the cairt that brought them here, prance, unfamiliar with city sounds and the odd automobile. The River Clyde is deep and hosts an abundance of shipyards. It separates the municipality from its bigger brother, Glasgow. Ibrox is to the east and the borough of Renfrew is to the west.

Around back, Robert Alexander, Duff to his buddies, is leaning one-handed against his house, staring bleary eyed at the vomit on his new shoes, Florsheims he had paid 2 pounds sterling for yesterday. He had to work a whole day for them. The pansies at his feet are covered

1

with the frothy remains of a once damn-tasty haggis. It failed the taste test miserably coming back up.

He wobbles but stiffens when he hears a rapping at the front door. Straightening up, he guesses its Jacky Boy and Tubs, come to see if he has anything to drink. Pulling a wrinkled, stained hanky from the left front pocket of his trousers, he swipes the spittle from his bearded chin, flips the fabric over and honks his nose. He bellows with a raspy, slurry voice.

"Hold yer peckers, you dumb lads. I'll be along in a shake."

Lucretia stops rapping, a frown scrunching up her narrow face. Placing a hand on her hip, she turns to Dominic.

"The bugger is drunk."

Dominic is snickering. He only heard "pecker." His brother Tommy had told him what a pecker was last summer. Tommy didn't know why they called it that, but Dominic was certain his big brother wouldn't tell him a fib. Lucretia pokes her son on the shoulder with her free arm.

"Behave!"

Tugging on the fabric of his coarse shirt, she motions for him to follow her.

"Come along, I think we should forget this and…"

Her directive is interrupted by Duff staggering along the dirt driveway, coming from behind the house. He's trying to tuck his loose shirt in but can't get the edge around his ridiculously red suspenders. He stops two tentative steps towards the front walk of fieldstone sunken in the neatly clipped lawn. Forgetting the shirt, he closes one eye to focus on the two bodies on his stoop. They're about twenty-five feet away. Expecting a rotund Tubs and taller Jacky Boy, he is surprised when the image clears. The porch is in shadow, with the sun setting behind the houses across the street. He only sees the outlines. Both are thin; one is wearing a dress. The other is a step or two behind the dress. The dress has one hand on a hip. Why does he feel like he's going to be scolded?

"Robert Alexander! You should be ashamed of yourself. I know you're a man of an odd drink, but as long as I've been related to ya, I've never seen you this drunk. Look at ya, ya can hardly stand up."

Duff perks up, the lilt of his favorite sister-in–law is warmly recognized. He opens his eye and spreads his burly arms open.

"Lucretia, my dear, did you finally leave that no good brother of mine. Duff is here to rescue you…"

Motioning for Dominic to remain, Lucretia walks down the two steps to the walkway watching Duff shuffle along the flat stones. When he is halfway, he stumbles on the edge of a larger stone that frost has lifted and that has yet to be fixed. The unbalance causes his arms to flail about like a whirligig. His forward drunken momentum, powered by enthusiasm, propels him, head down, directly at Lucretia's feet. His temple and right ear are the first to connect with the stone in front of her. He loses consciousness upon impact. The thud of his bulky body causes the horses to stir. Lucretia's father, old man Watson tugs on their reins and whistles a rhythmic tune he had made up for them. The familiar trill calms the pair. Lucretia steps back one pace in shock, both hands on her face, and exclaims with a high, alarmed voice.

"Oh goodness, he can't be dead too!"

CHAPTER 2

Lucretia bends over the inert form of her brother-in-law, who is lying on his side, arms outstretched. She gently pushes him onto his back and places a hand on his chest. Finding the even rise and fall of his lungs, she sighs. She points to the front door, directing her son.

"Check and see if it's open."

Dominic turns to twist the knob and the door swings inward on silent hinges.

"Aye, 'tis."

"Get yourself down here then and give me a hand with this sorry sight."

Dominic joins his mother on the pathway and when he slides his hands under the shoulders of his uncle's supine form, Duff stirs and bats his hands away. Momentarily disoriented, Duff sits up, rubbing his scalp where flesh met stone. Lucretia backs off a little and Dominic stands beside her, facing the stunned man, their backs to the house. A welt grows on his forehead. His hand comes away with a drop of blood on the index finger.

"Damn, me head hurts. What did you hit me with, Lucretia?"

Clasping her hands in front of her, chin up as if insulted, she frowns at him.

"I didn't do a thing, you silly fool. You slipped on that cobblestone and landed on your face. You scared the life from me, man. Can ya get up?"

He asks about the boy standing in front of him.

"Who's this lad? Can that be wee Dom?"

"He's not wee anymore, Duff. Now, c'mon, let's get you into the house and I'll tend to that scratch on your head."

She waves to Dominic to get his attention. The two get their hands under Duff's arms and wrestle him to his feet. He wobbles like an infant that's just learned to stand up. Dom holds him under one arm, a smirk on his face, knowing better than to laugh. Straightening out his loose shirt, Lucretia helps him tuck the errant edges in when she catches a whiff of Duff's liquor-laden breath. She scrunches her nose and turns him towards the front door.

"You'll be wanting to gargle with something sweet and I'll be getting some tea in ya."

The two steps up to the porch and entering the house require Duff's full attention. Shrugging off his assistants, he uses the wall of the hallway that leads to the kitchen in back.

"Why would I be needing tea? S'better to have another tot of that whiskey inside."

Following him closely, she urges Dominic along with a gesture to get behind his uncle in case he loses his balance. Pausing while her middle child, the quietest and most obedient of her seven children, helps the man into a two-armed wooden chair at the table, she dreads what she must do. Trying not to cry, she clears her throat.

"You'll want to be sober when you hear what I have to ask you."

CHAPTER 3

Danny Alexander is buried on a hilltop not far from the Firth of Clyde, near the community of Saltcoats. He died three weeks previous by drowning. He and two drinking buddies in a stolen dory, none of whom could swim. Reckless fun turned deadly peril when the boat was swept asunder by a rogue wave. All three perished. Danny left behind a defeated wife, seven children, a legacy for drink and the cards, and no money. The rent was four months past due.

Unable to find work, with not enough food for her children, his wife, Lucretia, relented to the inevitable and moved to Kilwinning to live with her widowed father and accept charity.

The ancient farm provides a meager existence. Old man Brodie has two draft horses, Clydesdales named Charlie and Belle. The horses plow fields, haul fodder, yard logs and whatever else is needed for Brodie to earn a living. His parcel of land is just big enough for a small garden, a woodshed and his two bedroom house. Living alone for the last nine years, he welcomes his daughter to stifle the loneliness but is adamant that there is neither enough room nor food for eight more mouths.

The two youngest bairns, Paul and baby Sheila, could stay but the rest of her lot would have to find other lodgings. The two oldest boys, William and Thomas, went to live with Lucretia's brother and his wife in Newtongrange, where they would earn their keep by toiling in the coalfields at the Lady Victoria Colliery where he works. Her brother Robert is childless and the boys are most welcome.

Mary, the eldest girl, went to live with Molly MacDougall, her deceased husband's sister, in New Lanark. Molly's husband, Geoffrey, is the floor manager at the cotton mills and was more than willing to have Mary as a domestic to earn her keep until she is old enough to be employed at the mills. The second youngest girl, Lilly, went to live with Lucretia's sister, Victoria, in Dumgoyne. Victoria's husband, Willard, works at the Glengoyne distillery. They have a daughter the same age as Lilly.

Every time Lucretia leaves one of her children with a relative, she does so with a heavy heart. Her determination is a thin string holding a dead weight on each occasion when she turns her back to leave. Fortifying herself with the thought that each one will have a better life, the act nonetheless leaves a gap in her soul, an emptiness nothing can fill. She loves all her children but especially Dominic, and this will be the most difficult. She kept him until the last and decided that he will be better off with his uncle Duff.

CHAPTER 4

Duff, the cup of tea Lucretia made him sitting at his elbow, tries to focus on the pair that sits across from him at the table. The boy is looking around the kitchen, eyes wandering back and forth to the fishing rod leaning against the icebox. Lucretia is glaring and tsk-tsking at the empty crock on the cupboard, brown sauce drying on the top. Several errant beans are poised along the rim like sure footed bugs. She turns to stare at him directly. She speaks almost a whisper.

"Your brother Danny is dead."

Duff sits straighter, a bit more stable. Shock causes him to blubber loudly. Dominic stares at him with wide eyes, surprised by the outburst. He sits back in his chair.

"What! Little Danny! How? When? Why wasn't I told...?"

Lucretia has both elbows on the table when she leans forward and points a finger at him. It's no nonsense and freckled like her brow.

"You wouldn't have come anyway. You didn't even like him."

Accused, he relaxes back into the seat. One hand rubs worried fingers unconsciously through his beard.

"Well, I didn't hate him."

"You haven't spoken to him since your Da died. It must be what... almost four years now?"

Duff answers affirmatively by nodding his head. He's looking at the boy. He's not totally sober yet. The body glow from the liquor is still active but the head has cleared some. The lad looks intelligent, a disturbing image of his dead brother. From the corner of the table he picks up his mug, the tea Lucretia made still steams. Settling both elbows on the armrests, he cradles the cup in both hands.

"Tell me what happened."

"Him and his two mates…"

Lucretia relates the past 20 days of her life. There are tears, there is anger. Her voice raises in emphasis at points. Flat when in denial. Faint when she speaks of sorrow and loss, of which she has had plenty. A hard worker when sober, he always fed his kids, but alcohol, cards and other women were Danny's downfall. Dominic watches intently, fascinated by his mother's admissions. Both hands under his bum on the hard chair, he wiggles to get comfortable as he thinks about what she said, staring at the knees of his wool pants.

She tells Duff about the funeral, the dreaded landlord, her dire straits, the parting of her children. It goes on for forty-five minutes. He's had Dominic fetch two more teas in the telling. He's as sober as he's going to be. Watching the woman in front of him, he pities her but lets her speak. She pauses frequently, something personal arresting her thoughts. He follows her hazel eyes as they change from dark to light, perhaps a memory sweet. She finishes with the parting of her kin and the people who've helped her.

"…and they'll always be my angels."

Duff is sitting up, hands pushing the empty tea mug away. He knows what's coming. Tilting his head at his nephew, he sees his brother's eyes looking back at him. Same brownish center and green outer ring, same depth. Beginning to think of his lost freedom, Lucretia interrupts his thoughts.

"I need ya to help raise my Dom."

There's quiet now as everyone settles on the statement. Lucretia pulls her shawl tighter while fighting back her tears. Staring at the table, she only sees the blurry surface, wanting Duff to say no… needing him to say yes. Dominic is shy of his uncle's direct stare. The bushy eyebrows look stern. He glances back at the fishing rod in the corner. Duff notices where Dom's eyes travel.

"Do ya like fishing?"

The head bobs up and down in quick answer and he speaks to the rod, still shy.

"Aye, though I've never done it. I know I would though."

He chances a glance at his uncle, whose brows are unknitted. A slight grin makes the cheeks pudgier. He returns a weak smile, watching Duff push the teacup aside. One hand begins grooming the beard as he tries to grasp what raising a boy would entail. Lucretia knows she must remain silent while Duff considers her request. She understands how disruptive a child can be. She had brought Dom here because the boy usually does as he's told. A bachelor can be set in his ways.

Dominic had already shed tears over the parting, mostly on the wagon ride, but is warming to the idea of maybe his own bed, probably lots of food and hopefully a new pair of boots. His gaze returns to his hands, clasped in his lap. He goes red behind his ears because his uncle is still staring at him.

The ticks of the big clock in the entryway grow louder in the silence. Duff is wondering what Adairia and his buddies will think? He resents being forced into this situation. Breaking his gaze away from the boy, he looks back at the rod. He put it there last spring, promising himself he'd get out. He sees the dust bunny swirled about the end of the handle resting on the floor. It convinces him that a change might be needed. Sitting up abruptly, he claps his big hands, startling both of his visitors. Dominic jumps in his seat, Lucretia gasps and Duff waves a hand at Dominic.

"How old are ya, lad?"

"I'm... I'm eleven."

"Have ya had any schoolin'?"

Dominic squirms in his seat, the flushed cheeks, embarrassed at his lack of education. Lucretia attempts to speak for him.

"He's good with...."

Shaking his head at her, Duff keeps his eyes on his nephew.

"Let the boy answer."

Dominic may be pliant, an eager-to-please fellow, but he's never been known to back down from a challenge. He looks directly at Duff.

"I know my numbers and letters but have a hard time putting them all together. I... I don't know what to do with them."

Looking at his mother, the same Watson half-smile as her, as if they've had this discussion before. That moment Duff sees another facet of Dominic.

"Please don't ask me about fractions, or tell me I'm gonna like girls."

Duff chortles, slaps his thigh and breaks into a laugh and relaxes back into the chair. Lucretia, about to scold Dominic, is softened by the innocence in his eyes. She too begins chuckling, a rare occurrence of late. Dominic feels awkward and drops his gaze.

The revelry is short and quiet returns. Momentarily, Duff sits up in his chair, brushes his beard, and straightens out his suspenders. Looking at Dominic, his face is stern.

"You'll have to earn your keep. You'll have to learn how to arrange those numbers and letters properly and you'll do as I tell you. Is that understood?"

Dominic feels more confident in his uncle's words. He likes the bushy beard and bristly eyebrows, and eyes that looked like his da's. Trying to make himself look bigger, he straightens out from his slouch.

"I'm a good worker, uncle. You can ask Mr. McLaughlin. I worked on his farm for two summers. Isn't that right, Ma?"

"It's true, Duff. Lad may be skinny, but he's tough enough; good as any man. Gets that from you Alexanders."

Lucretia feels a warmth, thinking Duff has agreed to take Dominic. It is soon replaced by melancholy that she must leave one more child in the hands of a relative. Her emotions are a mixture of pain and comfort.

"You'll not be sorry, Duff, he's a good boy," she says.

Pushing her chair away from the table, she stands and waves to Dominic.

"Come along then, Dom, and get your bag from the cairt."

Dominic stands also and heads out the hallway to gather his belongings and say goodbye to his grandfather. Lucretia lags in the entryway, with Duff standing beside her. Looking up at her brother-in-law, she steps closer to hug him. Her voice is tiny, no more than a whisper.

"Take care of him, Duff. I don't know when I'll be back… and thank you."

She turns and hastens to leave. Duff stands at the doorway, watching the family say their goodbyes. The old man gets down from the wagon with a badly scuffed suitcase. Cheap cardboard, one clasp works. The other side is kept tight with a loop of twine knotted at the top. Belle and Charlie prance restlessly, eager to get moving.

Brodie Watson is a practical man but not mean, the parting bothers him as well. Dominic is the only one that shares his love for sketching and the feel of the charcoal in his hand. He'll miss the boy. He holds the case out to Dominic who is almost as tall as he is and looks him in the eyes.

"I put a couple of my favorite pencils in the case with your good clothes. Watch your shadows. And good luck, boy!"

Dominic drops the case on the roadway and hugs his grandfather. The act is so foreign to Brodie that he doesn't know how to react, red-faced from the embrace. He harrumphs and pats Dominic on the back. Stepping away he climbs back on the cairt, offering stern advice.

"Do as your uncle says."

Lucretia stands several feet behind the wagon, watching the exchange. The sun is lowering and she only sees their silhouettes. When her son approaches with her mother's old bag, she forges her will to bear their parting. Trying to smile, she doesn't want Dominic to see despair when she says goodbye. She tugs at her flowered shawl, wrapping it closer. She holds a small leather bag, worn with the burgundy dye faded. Grasping it with both hands, she holds it to her chest when Dominic stands in front of her. Neither know how to say goodbye; the loneliness each feel is the same. Lucretia knows she must be strong.

"I have something for you, Dom."

Undoing the draw string from a small velvet bag she takes from her purse; she removes a shiny jackknife and holds it in her palm. The side is opalescent, slim and four inches long. The letter A is embedded in the lacquered finish and gleams like polished silver. Tiny nicks and blemishes suggest it isn't new. A single blade is hidden on the right. She holds it out to him.

"This was your da's. And his da's before that, his wedding gift. The only reason we still have it is I kept it for one of you children. Lord knows your da would've lost it in a game of cards. You can sharpen the pencils Granda gave you."

Setting the bag down, Dominic takes the knife. Already overwhelmed with emotions, he is afraid to speak. He's never owned much before, other than his clothes. The knife's connection to his kin is not lost on him. Handling it tenderly, he looks up at his mother.

"I'll take good care of it, Ma, I promise."

Pocketing the knife, he hugs Lucretia.

"I wish it didn't have to be this way. I'm going to miss you and Lilly the most."

"She is going to miss you too, Dominic. We all will, but we all know tis better this way."

She steps to the side, not wanting to prolong their farewell any longer, certain she will not be able to contain her forced cheerfulness. Reaching once more into her bag, she removes two shillings and a farthing and hands them to Dominic."

"It's not much but it's all I can spare. Use it wisely. Now get back to your uncle. If anything changes, I'll send for you, Dom, but do the best you can here and make me proud of you. I love you, son."

She hastens to the cart heartbroken. She climbs up and before she is comfortable, Brodie flips the reins and the horses eagerly head home. Dominic watches until they turn onto Govan Road, heading west, and disappear. Turning back to the house, he sees Duff watching. The hundred feet he has to walk to the front door are the longest in his young life.

Duff scrutinizes the boy while he walks towards him, head down, staring at the roadway, the suitcase banging against his knee as he walks. He thinks the hair will have to be cut – too much on his forehead, too many curly ends. The face is a good blend of his parents, a handsome fellow with his mother's oval face, his da's wild eyes. The boots will have to be replaced, both heels missing. He needs a bath. Inhaling deeply, he wonders what he has gotten himself into. Dominic stands at the bottom of the stoop stairs looking up questioningly at his uncle.

"C'mon, lad, let's get you settled in."

CHAPTER 5

Just after sunrise Dominic is disturbed from his sleep by the delicate weight of four paws crawling up the quilt he is covered with. Slowly pulling the blanket from his head, afraid of what he will see, the movement stops and a Scottish Fold stares at him with orange mischievous eyes. The fur is soft and gray as fog. One front paw is raised, arrested in its advance by the appearance of the foreign head. Dom's pupils widen in surprise. Flaring its nostrils, the cat identifies the intruder. Dominic smiles at the small floppy ears and removes one arm from under the cover, offering his hand for inspection. A quick sniff and a direct look in the eyes cause the cat to relax on all fours upon Dominic's stomach. It's owl-like face almost smiles. Both are distracted by a happy morning voice.

"Ah, I see you've met Pearl. Your stay here will be much more tolerable that she seems to like you. Do you care for cats?"

"Aye, I do. We had an old tom, named Clancy, that died last spring. Ma said we couldn't have another for a while and then well..."

Duff waves his hand as if to never mind.

"Do you drink tea? Or milk? Do you fancy some bacon and cheese for breakfast? Bread's fresh two days ago from old Nelly across the street, best you've probably eaten. Makes some for her and the neighbors every three or four days. What do ya think?"

Dominic is trying to sit up without disturbing Pearl, who seems content to be jiggled around on the quilt, thinking it a game.

"Yes, uncle, that sounds fine, and I like tea. Can I have sugar in it?"

"Goodness, in my opinion you're not a true tea drinker if you take sugar, but sure you can. You introduce yourself to Pearl and then you can use the loo before you get to the kitchen. Join me in about twenty minutes."

Dominic is upright, the cover shrugged aside except over his knees, where Pearl is poised looking up at him. He moves a hand tentatively to stroke her back. Finding no resistance, he gently rubs the fur, soft as rose petals. Pearl warms to her new friend and begins to purr. Dominic checks out his surroundings while the cat basks in the attention. All the walls are light green, everywhere. The doors and trim are white. The couch he is on faces the stairway and a door to the right of the steps and the front door adjacent to him. The room has an open doorway to the left where Duff disappeared into the short hallway to the kitchen. The wall to his right has a large window where yellowish drapes are drawn, almost closed. A stuffed chair, in nondescript beige, sits in front of the window. Its twin sits to the left of the couch. Neither look much used. Several prints of running horses and seascapes are placed randomly around the room.

A polished circular table sits in the middle of the space. The surface is obscured from items placed hither and thither. A white mug, a folded newspaper, a pencil, a brass planter with a few dried stems sticking out, a flurry of tiny brown petals on the soil and around the planter make up a bachelor's palate. The floor is linoleum, brown and tan squares as big as a boot. A path is lightly tinted from doorway to kitchen. The clock in the hallway, a wooden Westminster pendulum, is on the wall facing him across from the door to the bathroom. The ticking fades as the sound of bacon sizzling grows louder. The scent of pork frying wafts into the living room.

Pearl is no longer interested in the newcomer. She rises and leaps from Dominic's lap, running to the kitchen. A low grumble in the pit of Dominic's stomach urges him from the couch. Folding the quilt, he places it on the flowered cushion, fluffs the pillow and places it on top. He slept in his cloths, except for the boots, which he had left by the door. His shirt is plain washed-out flannel, which was navy once but is now the color of an afternoon sky. The pants are wool, baggy kneed. They belonged to his older brother, Billy. The waist is still a size too big, and the legs, too short. Although they're a bit stinky, the socks are the only thing relatively new, black and knitted by his Ma three weeks ago.

Following the aroma, he finds himself in the five-foot hallway, a door ajar to the left. He can see his uncle standing at the cook stove, his back to Dominic. Wide of shoulders and hips, his stocky frame is like Grandma Alexander's family. His khaki cotton shirt is neatly pressed, sleeves rolled up over hairy forearms, and the hands are busy with the cooking. Trousers are dark brown and of fine wool, the one and a half inch cuffs trendy. His reddish hair has hints of gray surrounding a flesh-colored spot on the back of his head the size of an orange. The rest of his hair is thick and cut just over the ears. Some falls onto his forehead and the rest flows into his beard. Unaware that he is being watched, Duff, whistles a ditty from a bawdy song his friend Tubs made up.

"What are ya whistling?"

The spatula Duff was using flies in the air and falls to the floor, several drops of bacon fat splatter on the stove, hissing. The handle of the frying pan spins like a loose balloon. Duff jumps in the air several inches and grabs his heart. Coming about he bellows at a gape-faced Dominic.

"Jeez, lad, don't do that again. You startled me there. Phew!"

Breathing easier he pushes the pan to the warm side of the stove and settles his butt against the cupboard. Dominic has his back against the door jamb, his hands at his side and his head down. Feeling guilty, he is afraid of what his uncle will say. Daring a glance up, he sees Duff starting to laugh.

"I almost shat me pants."

Duff's laughter is easy and cheerful. Dominic can't help but join in. The next thirty seconds of glee set the tone for the rest of the day.

"You gave me old ticker a little jolt there, Dom. Try not to do that too often, all right?"

"Sorry, uncle."

"Never mind that uncle business. Call me Duff."

"Ma says that's not respectful."

Opening both arms, hands out, he says with raised eyebrows, "I don't see your ma anywhere. Do you?"

Not sure what to say, Dominic pouts, thinking hard about the possibilities of that simple statement. Duff bends to pick up the spatula and returns his attention to the meal. He begins cutting the bread already laid out on the cupboard he was leaning on.

"Go on lad and get washed up, there's hot water on the sideboard. You'll have to pump the upper tank full after you flush the toilet. Then we eat. Should be close to nine by then and we can go into town."

Dominic had never used a proper toilet before last night. Outhouses only. He remembers entering the loo curiously. Shutting the door behind him he marvels at the layout once more. There is an overhead cistern on the left near the ceiling. It spouts a dark pipe that leads to an odd-shaped porcelain seat. The opening looks like it can handle any size bum. The walls have wooden wainscoting, darkly varnished. The upper walls are whitish and need painting. A single window directly across from the door faces east and the sun streams in, brightening the room. On the right is a stand with a basin and a steaming kettle sitting on a divot. Under the window is a pump. He won't miss the outdoor plumbing.

Ten minutes later, Dom finds Duff sitting at the table. Same chair as last night. He waves to Dominic to join him at the other end of the table, opposite him.

"You sit at that end so we can see each other when we talk. Now dig in. We might not eat again until later this afternoon. Here's what we're going to do. After we clean up the breakfast dishes..."

They gorge on aged cheddar, crisp strips of meat, thick slices of bread and creamy salted butter, washing it down with tea. Between bites, Duff explains what they will be up to. New clothes. New boots. They're not a gift; Dominic must pay him back when he can. Find him work. Meet his friends and arrange for some schooling.

"... So that will keep us busy and we'll grab supper at Carmichael's. Tomorrow, we'll tackle that extra room upstairs so you'll have to spend one more night on the couch, Dominic."

Dominic is elated at the offer. The clothes and boots are a bonus, but the jewel is learning to read.

"That's fine uncle... I mean Duff."

"Change into those better pair of pants you said you had in the bag. That shirt looks clean enough for now."

"But those are my Sunday pants unc... Duff."

"Well, let's pretend it's Sunday already. It's only one day away."

CHAPTER 6

A sharp shadow looms over the doorway of Carmichael's Pub. At a little after 5 p.m., the setting sun hits the top of St. Constantine's, the Old Church seven blocks away, and points the tip of its spire directly above the door. Duff and Dominic stroll up the side of the street fifty feet away. October 1 is warmer than usual and Duff has his jacket folded over one arm and a bag in the other. Dominic is carrying two similar brown paper bags, an arm wrapped around each, holding them tightly to his side. Bright red ink on the bag says they come from Blossom's General Store. Shiny black leather boots tap a steady rhythm on the roadway. The beaming smile on his face displays his contentment.

Dominic's slim face looks fuller with the extra hair cut from his scalp. The sides are short and bristly. The forehead clear. The top of his head is untamed, with hair an inch long

The pub is on the left corner of a two-storey brick building a half a block wide. The outer wall facing the street has large framed windows for forty feet. The main entrance faces Underhill Lane and is in a five-foot recessed area on the right. Three other businesses share the downstairs of the forty-year-old commercial building. The upper level is Carmichael's Inn. Saturday's are paydays for the Carmichael family. It's far enough away from the shipyards to the north that not many worker's venture this far. Mostly local Scots from the borough. Older homes, here many years, stretch beyond the last of the commercial buildings. Removed from the overcrowding of foreign workers in other towns and boroughs. Peopled mainly by better paid, better educated than their lower-class neighbors Govan is noted for.

On Underhill Lane, Duff and Dominic reach the cross street directly facing the pub. A large elm tree grows on the corner of Underhill and Crescent. The lower leaves are dying in graceful reds and orange. The upper reaches stubbornly retain their summer green. Sweeping boughs provide ample shade and Duff waves a hand at Dominic and leans against the rough bole.

"Give me a second there, Dom."

The last of the sun is hitting the pub windows and the curtains will be drawn. Removing a handkerchief from the front pocket of his trousers, Duff wipes his brow, then swipes at his nose. Trading the cotton for a comb from another pocket, he grooms his beard while Dominic stares at his uncle, who is concentrating on the pub. Still overwhelmed by his good fortune and the day's adventure, Dominic retains a shyness and feels humbled by his uncle's generosity and seemingly unending money. His thoughts are interrupted.

"I know you must be hungry, lad. Well, let me tell you that Mrs. Carmichael makes the best mutton stew you will ever eat. I'm a tad dry from celebrating Tub's birthday yesterday, so I'll probably be having an ale before me meal. A little hair of the dog, ya know? But I'll get you set up, Dom."

Inside, Carmichael's Pub is long and narrow. The right side is a darkly stained bar extending along a mirrored wall for twenty-five feet. A brass foot rail gleams from the base. Bar stools of lighter wood sit haphazardly along the front. Several are occupied. A portly man, bald except for a fringe of peppered hair above the large ears, reddish cheeks and a perpetual smirk, doles out mugs of dark frothy liquid from behind the bar. The way he laughs with the patrons and orders around the other staff might make him Mr. Carmichael.

The left side of the establishment has low-backed booths lined up under the windows. Two by the front door, left of the entrance, and six down the side. Each is meant for four people, but on Saturday nights, they could seat six or seven. Three are already busy. Two men and a lady sit at the bar. Short waist high doors are on the back wall and people are going in and out. The other room is steamy, with wisps carrying scents of food being cooked drifting through the opening. The rest of the back wall is forest green to match the aprons and contains a scattering of photos, black and whites of men and women from years ago. Of the ten or so, it's eerie how they all look alike. A ten-by-ten-foot raised platform sits along the wall at the base of the last window on the left. A stool akin to the ones at the bar is alone in the center of the polished wood.

Dominic is introduced to the man tending bar, confirming his earlier assumption. Shuffled to the back booth where the bags are dumped in the corner, a bowl as big as a hat is slid under his nose, steaming with herbs and full of cubed potatoes and turnip and tender chunks of lamb. Dominic's stomach growls. A glass of cold water and a spoon wrapped in a linen napkin are delivered by a plain looking girl in glasses and short hair. The young lady is wearing a white cotton shirt, the same as the bartender, same reddish cheeks as him too. Same forest green apron, adorned with an elegant C in the center, tied about the waist.

"Names Shirley, most folks call me Shirl. What's yours?"

"Dominic."

After a thought he says, "Some folks call me Dom."

"Okay, Dom it is then. Duff tells me you're to be staying with him. It being Saturday, I'd keep an eye on that silly bloke."

Dominic can't stop staring at the steam coming off the thick broth, his hand tightly gripping the rolled napkin, not sure what he's supposed to do with it. Her warning makes him look up. The plain girl is transformed by the most delightful of smiles, wide and sincere. A pinpoint dimple appears on the right upper cheek adding some cuteness. The eyes tell him she is bluffing.

"Don't worry, Dom, I'll keep an eye on Duff. If you need something, give me a wave."

"Aye. Thank you, Shirl"

She turns to leave but espies Dominic's questioning gestures with the napkin, turning it about in his hands. Leaning over she removes the roll from him, unwraps the tucked-in edge, and with a little shake, the spoon rolls out into her hand and the napkin unfolds. Setting the spoon down by the bowl, she makes him sit back against the seat and drapes the linen across his lap.

"There now! Dab at your lips when you need it and keep it there when you're not using it."

She winks at him. His face is red. He doesn't care. He digs into the stew. The first bites are big and hastily chewed, but after the third, he slows down. He means to savor the flavor of the rich broth, the texture of fresh vegetables and the tenderness of the meat. He chews slowly while watching his uncle at the far end of the bar, who is fondling a frosty glass in one hand while the other rubs the back of the woman sitting on the next stool whose elbows are propped up on the bar. The other two occupants are men Duff's age.

One is rotund. On the bar stool, his scuffed boots barely reach the railing. The other is wide and not fat. His polished shoes touch the floor. Their laughter is light, with Duff seemingly conducting affairs, gesturing with his free hand between rubs. A drink and a joke it seems to Dominic. Relishing the stew he is slowly eating, his mind drifts off to what he knows about his uncle.

He loves Govan. He chatted continuously about what they saw as they walked from the house through narrow lanes and then wider streets with horse-drawn wagons and carriages and the infrequent automobile, which leave behind their burnt exhaust. Fresh manure was pancaked along the roadway, releasing its earthy odor. The Elder Park. The shipyards further north could be heard on the breezes, a clanging of metal on metal and warning whistles. Tall cranes rose skyward above the horizon. Even the smells were different than from the country, he exclaimed. Dominic remembers best Duff's promise to show him the keel of the Aquitania at the John Brown Shipyards in Clydebank, sister ship to the famous Lusitania.

He is a Liberal, capital L. The man Dominic met at the general store where he got his boots and pants was a true gentleman, gushing over them as if he'd known Dominic all his life, happy to help out, and so on. After the sale he mistakenly commented on the rising Labor Party and that Prime Minister Asquith would never survive another election. Dominic had to tug his uncle from the store, astounded by the crude remarks his uncle was making to the man. He decided he'd try to forget the comments.

They had met Adairia Gordon – the woman now sitting at the bar – around noon. As they were leaving Blossoms, she was about to enter, and in her haste, she bumped directly into Duff. Her arms were full of books and a cloth embroidered bag hung from one shoulder. The books were strewn to the concrete walk and Duff dropped the bag he was carrying. Dominic was puzzled when Duff's frown of consternation turned to a broad smile and the two hugged each other. Dominic set down his bags and picked up the books, none he could read. Introductions, her compliments, his fascination with her being a teacher and her thick wavy hair, and a promise to meet later at

Carmichaels kept him wondering about her during the day and how happy his uncle was when she was there.

During the afternoon he got an explanation of why he must work and cannot go to school. The need for him to support himself and learn to manage his money. But not to worry about learning because Duff has an idea for that.

His uncle works for himself, that's why he isn't working today. His workshop is behind the extra door at the foot of the stairs and to the right when you enter his house. He repairs clocks, which is not his main business. He's a goldsmith. He repairs jewellery for retailers in Glasgow. He has his own safe as well. Dominic is going to learn how to polish the gold and silver baubles, among other things, starting Monday and will work for Duff each morning until noon. Duff suggests that there could be a chance for Dominic to learn another trade from his friend Tubs. They'll know more tonight.

The last of the broth is spooned from a tipped dish and Dominic sets down spoon and bowl to see Duff and his cohorts bid goodbye to the stockier man who is about a half a foot taller than everyone else. The fatter man and the woman accompany Duff back to the table where Dominic sits. He feels uneasy when he notices that all three are eyeing him as they come near. He sees nothing mean in their gaze. Seeing Adairia's smile as she slides in beside him, forcing him closer to the bags at his right side, makes him relax. He thinks she's pretty with her wavy hair. Duff sits across from him and the larger man wiggles into the booth beside him with his belly tight to the wood. Duff sets down his quarter-full mug of ale and slaps a big hand on the table. He points a crooked thumb at the man beside him.

"This here is Cornelius MacGregor, more fondly referred to as Tubs for a reason you're too young to know..."

Duff pokes the man in the ribs as if to verify the comment. Tubs blushes and tips his mug at Dominic.

"It's settled lad, you're to start working with Tubs in the afternoons on Monday coming."

Shirley interrupts the foursome with a tray laden with three more bowls of stew and napkins. Another aproned girl stands behind her with two mugs filled to the rim. Duff points at Dominic.

"A piece of Mrs. Carmichael's famous apple pie for Dom there, Shirl. And a sweetened black tea."

"And a tea for me too, Shirl," says Adairia.

Dominic is ecstatic over the day's events. He politely listens to the trio, only speaking when spoken to. Exhausted and full of delicious food, the warmth and comfortable comradery soon see him nod off. An hour later, Duff wakes him, tells him to grab his bags and follow him home.

Duff heats a tub full of water, instructs Dominic that he needs to bathe and wash his hair. The new clothes are laid out on the living room chairs. Two pairs of trousers, two plain cotton shirts, socks, underwear including long johns for the coming cold months, a lined winter jacket and the togs he brought with him complete his wardrobe. His new boots sit at the door. He's never owned so many clothes, certainly nothing new. At 9:45 p.m. he dons the new pajamas, lies on the couch and pulls the blanket up to his shoulders. Duff turns off the lights and heads upstairs to his own bed. He stops several steps upward when he hears his nephew. The voice is low and sincere.

"Thank you, Uncle."

"You're welcome, lad. Now get some rest."

Dominic should be happy, but he misses his family. Only he can hear the quiet sobs as he cries himself to sleep.

CHAPTER 7

Pearl is like an alarm clock, if you're not up by 6 a.m., you're getting your face licked. She knows that Duff shoos her away so she tries the new guy. Jumping up on the couch, she lands on Dominic's chest, startling him awake. A few licks tell him she wants attention. Dominic strokes her fur, soon finding the spot behind her ears where she likes to be rubbed. A few more minutes and she's meowing to be fed. She leaps from the couch to head to the kitchen. Waiting at the hallway to see if Dominic is following, her plaints become anxious. A half hour later Duff finds the two of them in the kitchen. The bag of dry cat food is open on the cupboard, Pearl is at her bowl and Dominic is sitting at the table fiddling with the fishing rod.

By noon the Sunday morning rituals are in place. Duff makes breakfast; the two clean up. Pearl gets let out for a bit, finding amusement and prey handily in her master's messy back yard. Dominic wears new clothes completely for the first time in his life and they walk the half a mile to church. The service is over by noon. Dominic is introduced to the larger man he saw yesterday, Jack Beauregard Fillmore, hence Jacky Boy, his wife Esmerelda and several other friends of Duff's as well as Pastor Anderson. When they return home, Duff makes lunch, instructs Dominic to change into his other clothes, and afterwards they head upstairs to straighten out the spare bedroom.

The house is a storey and a half. The upper walls are perpendicular to the height of mid-thigh before slanting inward to follow the roof line. A few inches taller than the average man is a narrow ceiling. The landing at the top of the stairs is a small alcove with a white wicker two seater against the wall facing the stairs. Several dark brown cushions are stacked in one corner; on the other is a stained apron of a goldsmith, turned inside out and draped crookedly over one arm. Walls and ceilings are the same bargain green as downstairs. Books are piled everywhere: on the floor, against the back wall, under the chaise.

Dominic can see Duff's room on the right, and while cluttered, it is exceptionally neat. A plain white door is half open. He can see a bed against the lowest wall, a multi squared quilt of brown and beige covers the wide mattress and flows evenly with the polished pine floor, the boards almost a foot wide. A book lies open upside down in the middle of the bed.

"Over here, lad."

Duff is opening the other door across the landing. Standing in the doorway scrutinizing the room he places his arms akimbo and grunts. Dominic stands close to his uncle trying to see in.

"Goodness gracious. What am I gonna do with all this?"

Dominic steps back.

"With what, Uncle?"

With brow narrowed in question, Duff turns to face Dominic and stands aside to allow him entry.

"You don't want to call me Duff?"

Dominic looks down at the floor.

"I feel better calling you Uncle."

"All right, fine, Uncle will do."

He sweeps his arm around the room.

"Now, what do you think?"

Dominic takes three steps into the room and can't go any farther. Eyes wide, mouth open he stares at the clutter. A window at the end of the room, curtained by many years of dust, faces north and sheds little afternoon sun with a brownish glaze. He thinks there's a bed in the same position as his uncle's, head against the low wall, mid room on the right. The firm edge of a gray mattress is visible beneath wooden crates, several cardboard boxes, a stack of yellowed newspapers and a black wool coat draped over four picture frames of different sizes and styles. The floor between him and the bed is taken up with six matching dining chairs in various state of disrepair, the seating torn, a leg or two missing. The wood is ornate with delicate carvings of laurels and leaves. A rug is rolled up against the wall.

Under the window is a three drawer dresser with intricate carvings on the upper legs. The top is a receptacle for even more books, a scratched wooden box that might be for jewellery, an empty porcelain vase and a glass jar of nuts, small bolts and different size screws. A hall tree stands beside it draped with many coats, all navy or black, no fancy colors for Duff. A long dresser is to the left, six drawers; three aside. It too is covered with an odd arrangement. A buck saw is propped against the side, blaringly out of place. A wooden trunk sitting in front of the dresser, at the edge of the bed, cuts off the path to the window on the left. It has metal corners and a heavy brass clasp. The metal tries to be shiny, but a thin patina of dust dulls the finish. Paw prints are visible on the darkly stained slats.

As if to lay claim to the tracks, Pearl pounces onto the trunk and interrupts Dominic's scrutiny. She sits and looks around the room and back accusingly at Duff, who lifts his brows in silent communication. Ignoring him, she begins grooming with her front paw, a lick and a wipe. Duff harrumphs and shoos her off the trunk.

"Get out of the way, Pearl. What do you think, Dom, should we start with this old trunk of me da's?"

Dominic is overwhelmed by the thought of a whole room to himself. An earnest smile splits his face.

"Sure, Uncle, whatever you think. Where are we going to put all this stuff?"

"Oh, we'll find a spot; there's still some room in the cellar. We can likely give some stuff away, maybe sell a piece or two. I know Tub's been after these chairs, he loves fixing things up, but they were my nan's and the only thing I have of me grandparents. I dunno…"

Duff is scratching his beard, a habit he has when thinking.

"I can't keep them forever and not be using them. Aye, let's get rid of them. C'mon then, lad, let's get them downstairs and then we'll start on the trunk."

The rest of the day speeds by, with Duff and Dominic sorting the debris of days gone by. Pearl interrupts occasionally, looking for attention like a spoiled child. Tubs comes by mid-afternoon to pick up the chairs. The old clothes and odd trinkets are taken to Mrs. MacDonald's who, with several other ladies from the Catholic Church, will distribute them to needy folks. The trunk is emptied and in the cellar. The crates and boxes have been purged. The bucksaw is in the shed where it should've been all along. Duff had laughed when Dominic asked him why it was in the bedroom; he couldn't remember.

The dressers were emptied and the smaller one taken out to the stoop, where it will have a "for sale" sign put on it.

During the process the two chat. Both are curious and realize how little they know of each other even though they are related. Duff leads the conversation, probing the young man for news and history.

"Have you any friends?"

"What of your brothers and sisters?"

"What was your da like to live with?"

"Is there any of your Granddad Watson's family still around?"

While many of the questions provoke a melancholy for Dominic, they serve to get him over his shyness. The one he had trouble with was the one about his da. He was never close like his older brothers, but his da taught him some things and never did anything bad to him. He has his own curious posers too.

"How come you have so many books?"

"What was my da like when he was a boy?"

"Where did you learn to fix clocks and jewellery?"

"How did you meet Tubs and Jackie Boy?"

"How come you don't have a wife?"

"When can I start my schooling?"

The last question is just as they're finishing up, and Duff concentrates on the answer before speaking.

The bed has been made – clean sheets, a wool blanket and a patchwork quilt neatly spread. The dresser is under the window, with Dominic's clothes separated and stored. A promise is made for some curtains even though all you can see is the roof of the house next door. The rug has been rolled out in front of the bed. It has been cleaned, the floors swept and Dominic is cleaning the window when Duff stands at the door with hands in his pockets.

"Well, Dom, I'm still working on that one, and I think I'll have an answer tonight."

Dominic finishes up the window and turns to his uncle.

"Why tonight, Uncle?"

"Well, Adairia is meeting me at Carmichael's later on for that very reason. She does a bit of tutoring on the side and is a very busy lady, but I'm hoping she can spare some time to help you with your letters and numbers. When we hit the bench tomorrow morning, I should have an answer for you. Now let's get cleaned up and have a bite. I expect you'll be fine on your own tonight?"

"Sure, Uncle. I wish I could read some of these books, but I'd like to listen to your radio if I can."

Later that evening, Dominic is awakened by a repetitive squeaking of bed springs he thinks is coming from behind the closed door of his uncle's bedroom. There is a full moon outside his window, casting a bluish hue to his room. He can see a crack of dim light under his uncle's door. Muffled sounds escape the room across from his and he wonders what Duff is up to. He doesn't ponder the issue long before he falls asleep again. When Duff wakes him next morning, he tells him the problem of his schooling has been resolved and Fridays at 4 p.m. he can go to Adairia's house to start his schooling.

CHAPTER 8

The balance of 1911 passes quickly. Duff has discovered Dominic's skills with a pencil and marvels at his talent. Dominic has graduated from polishing jewellery in the mornings with Duff and has been providing artistic renditions of custom jewellery for clients, which Duff has always had a problem with. He has learned to carve waxes and the process of the lost wax method in producing jewellery. Duff has shown him how to attach the wax renditions to a wax tree and fit it in the proper canister made to withstand the high heat. He has learned how to mix the plaster and fire the kiln in the cellar. Duff has shown him how to melt the gold and fill the cavities left by the melted wax. When the gold or silver has hardened, he removes the plaster and presents a metal tree with rings and pins for his uncle to finish. By the end of the year he is doing all the plaster work, feeding the kiln and polishing the finished pieces.

Adairia has found Dominic to be a fast learner and when December ends, he is reading proficiently, has mastered, addition, subtraction, multiplication and division and even fractions. He has trouble with grammar and his writing is terrible and he cares little for history.

Tubs has taken a liking to Dominic and, like Adairia, finds he is quick to learn. By the end of the year, Dominic is not only responsible for keeping the work site clean but can cut wood in a straight line, use a hammer accurately at all angles, knows where a 2x4 will work better than a board and why 16 inches is so important in building things. He knows what a stud is, what a jack is, what a lintel is for and why you need headers over doors and windows. He knows the difference between a crosscut saw and a ripsaw, and why and how you need to keep your chisels sharp. He has purchased his own combination square, whetstone, a pair of pliers and two screwdrivers.

He knows when to leave his uncle alone and when he wants to chat. He knows his uncle's favorite foods and how to prepare a simple meal. He knows that when his uncle frequents Carmichael's and wants to go alone that he will have a headache in the morning and it's best to leave him with his tea. He has discovered that Adairia and Uncle have a monogamous relationship but neither want to be married or share the same house. He understands that he needs to keep his bed made and his room neat, his clothes washed and ironed and which chores he is responsible for. He pays his uncle a nominal sum for room and board. He learns how to manage his money and to make it last between paydays. He has a savings account.

The first Christmas together has gone by with him receiving a new tool belt from Tubs, a silver chain from his uncle, a hardcover copy of Robinson Caruso from Adairia, a new leather belt from Jackie Boy, a knit sweater from his mother and pencils from his Granda. In return for the gifts, Dominic has sketched a likeness of each, presented in frames he made himself, and sent a bag of hard candy for the wee ones. The frames are rough but the sketches are impeccable, catching each recipient with a beaming smile.

The year ends in sadness when his older brother William dies in a mining accident and Duff arranges for Dominic to return home for the funeral. It is then that he realizes how fortunate he is when he discovers the loneliness experienced by his displaced family, the grief his mother ails from that there is nothing he can do about. When he leaves to return to Govan, he never looks back, knowing he needs to live his own life.

1912

Being in the cooler northern region of Great Britain, Scotland is one of the windiest countries in the world, with higher than normal amounts of rainfall. Winter usually brings copious amounts of snow in the Highlands with lesser accumulation in the lower regions. The days are much shorter in winter months. This twenty-third of February is a Thursday and the last day of Dominic's work week is clear. A cool breeze chills from the southeast as he walks along Langlands Road. Bluish shadows from a gibbous moon accompany him home. Pulling his parka tighter about his face, he hurries his step, knowing Uncle likes to eat at six o'clock and he guesses it must be a half hour later than that. He's usually home by now, now that the days are not as long. But he and Tubs had to finish replacing the door in Danny Meek's bungalow in Ibrox.

He's tired, his shoulders are slouched. One gloved hand carries his still stiff tool belt. A well-used hammer Tubs gave him hangs from one of the side loops and bumps against his leg. The repetitive slap in the only noise except for the distant clanging of the Fairfield Shipyards, which go all night. The other hand holds the front of his coat tight at the neck. A well-used canvas lunch bag is slung over one shoulder. Dominic was up at six o'clock this morning helping Duff in his shop. The security men come every Thursday at noon, delivering the jewellery to be fixed and pick up the completed jobs. Dominic spent the morning polishing chains that Duff had repaired. There was a gold one he really liked and hoped to own one day. Turning onto Drive Road by Elder Park, he's thinking of how much he needs to put aside when he encounters three boys.

Two of them are pushing and shoving a smaller boy who is doing his best to hold his own, pushing and shoving when he can. The larger of the aggressors gets in close enough to grab the smaller one by his jacket collar and shove him against the wrought iron fence that surrounds the park. His companion steps closer and hits the smaller boy in the stomach. When the injured youngster falls to the ground, Dominic is close enough to hear them. Not liking what's going on, the fallen boy much smaller, he sets his tool belt and lunch bag down gently and creeps closer.

"We told you before Pestov, you stay in the Gorbals. You Russian scum need to stay in the tenements where you belong. We don't want you Pests around…"

The tall boy is interrupted by a blow to his left ear that causes him to stagger and cartwheel his arms before he careens into his helper, knocking them both down, the bigger one on top. Dominic steps up, his gloved fists in the fighter's pose his father had taught him, taught all his boys. His left foot is back for balance, both feet on their toes.

"Try someone your own size, ya bullies."

Dominic is a scary figure, only his silhouette visible to the downed ruffians, the partial moon shining over his left shoulder exposing his upraised defensive fists. The downed boy is surprised by the aggressive act of the stranger and sits up, trying to catch his breath. The two on the roadway are scrambling backwards. The bolder one shouts while rubbing his ear.

"What's it to you… and ya shouldn't sneak up on people."

They're standing now and may be street tough, but they're leery of this stranger. They strike their own poses, the shorter one a step behind and moving his head back and forth from Dominic to his companion, not sure what to do.

"Ya shouldn't be picking on people smaller than you, and you're obviously not brave enough to do it on your own, takes two of yas."

Dominic starts to bob lightly like a trained boxer.

"Step up now, you cowards, and let's finish this… or bugger off!"

Tall boy and Uncertain give each other a glance before deciding that buggering off is probably the best option. They turn and scamper away behind one of the apartment buildings on the other side of the street. Dominic relaxes and turns to face a bedraggled figure sitting with legs flat, holding his stomach and taking short breaths like a scared rabbit. The head is uncapped and hanging down. Even in the low light, Dominic can see the jacket is light and tattered. Gathering his tool belt and lunch bag, he wonders at the boy's silence.

"Ya could at least say thank you."

The voice is deep for someone so young and heavily accented from a foreign language.

"I didn't need any help."

"That's not what I saw."

No response. He reaches down with his free hand.

"C'mon, I'll help ya up."

Hesitant at first, the younger fellow offers a bare hand, small and delicate like a girl's. Dominic is startled by the uncovered limb. Grasping the hand, Dominic helps him to stand.

"Don't ya have any mitts?"

Tucking his hands in his jacket pockets belies the next statement.

"No, I don't, but I don't need any."

Stepping back, Dominic tries to see the boy's face, but the low light casts only shadows. He can see that it is wide, lots of stray hair. The chin is up. He's at least three or four inches shorter than Dominic.

"So, what was that all about? And do you really live in Gorbals?"

"They just think that all Russians are like the Ivanov gang and all we want to do is steal everything. And yes I do live in the Gorbals, and I do live in a tenement before you ask."

Dominic had heard about the squalid buildings that housed immigrants in crowded quarters, often four to five in one or two rooms, lured by work in the yards. A shortage of homes drives the rents upward. Sanitation is a problem. Many do not eat properly. He didn't believe it at first. He knows his family was poor, but they always had a roof that didn't leak, clean beds and food.

"What are you doing here? And at night?"

"I… I just need to get away from all the noise and dirty smells and…"

Dominic senses discouragement in the voice, a lower tone. The pitch changes, bolder.

"It's not your business. I should be going. My brothers will be home later and I need to be there."

Without any further comment, he set off towards the other side of the park. Dominic can see the figure shaking from the cold and stares at his gloves. He has an older pair at home, not as new but just as warm. Removing his gloves, he chases after the boy.

"Here, take these."

Surprised by the command, the boy stops and faces Dominic. He is affected by the offer.

"You'd give me your gloves?"

"Well it's two or three miles to Gorbals and I have another pair."

The boy can't say no. He can hardly grasp the gloves properly with his chilled fingers. He stares at Dominic while twisting them on.

"Why are you doing this? You don't know me."

"Not so long ago, I didn't always have mitts either, so I know what it's like. Now I'm working and can buy my own."

There was a moment of silence. Dominic puts his own hands in his coat pockets.

"What's your name?"

"Ivan."

It comes out in Russian, eeVAHN. Not I-van like Scots call him.

"Ivan Pestov and what's yours?"

"Dominic Alexander, but most people call me Dom. You can if you like."

"Why would I like, I'll probably never see you again. I doubt you hang around the Gorbals and I'm not welcome here."

"Sure ya are, ya can come home and have a bite with me and Uncle if ya like?"

Dominic is worried about his spontaneous suggestion, not sure how Duff will react to an uninvited guest; but he needn't be. Surprised by the stranger's generosity, Ivan waves him off and starts towards the Gorbals.

"Thanks for the gloves and for getting those jerks off my back."

Watching until the retreating figure is in darkness, Dominic hitches his lunch bag straighter on his shoulder and heads home, wondering what the surprise is that Duff said would be there.

CHAPTER 2

When Dominic enters Water Row, he can see Duff's house, which is the fourth one on the right, and stops. There isn't even a porch light on. The first thing he thinks is that something has happened to Uncle and he starts to run to the house, fiddling for the skeleton key that will open the front door. It's difficult to find the keyhole in the dark and he fumbles until he has the door opened and steps into the foyer. When he reaches for the light switch by the door, the light comes on in the living room and a cacophony of voices erupts as one from the crowd gathered in the hallway and living room.

"Happy Birthday, Dominic!"

Startled, he drops his tool belt and stares at the crowd flabbergasted, not knowing what to say. His birthday is not for two more days. There is a loud burst of applause and cheering while he stares at them dumbfounded. Duff moves to the front of the group.

"Well don't just stand there, lad, c'mon in and join the fun. It's a few days early, but this is the only time we could all get together, so happy birthday, Dominic."

Dominic is speechless. He's never had a birthday party. He's so overjoyed that tears glisten in his eyes. The group goes quiet, thinking him displeased. After ten seconds of uncomfortable silence, the front door opens and in walks Tubs, cheeks freshly shaved and duds dandied up. Expecting more noise, he scans the crowd, lifting his brows to say "what's going on?" Dominic turns, knowing there's only one person who just walks in without knocking.

"You knew about this all day and didn't say a word?"

Tubs moues with jowly cheeks and looks confused when suddenly Dominic steps up to embrace him. It's not common to be hugged and Tubs has never been huggy-huggy, but he likes the young boy and awkwardly pats him on the back. Dominic breaks away to slip over to reach his arms around Duff's ample chest.

"Thank you, Uncle, you are too nice to me."

Duff is blushing and shoos him into the living room. Deliriously happy, he is no longer the young man that toils among adults all day. He's a twelve-year-old. Amid the laughter and gaiety, he wants to hug everybody.

Adairia, who a shade taller than him, is slim and he feels bulky with his heavy coat on.

"Happy Birthday to one of my best students. So happy for you, Dom."

Dominic gets well wishes and many pats on the back. Jacky Boy is there with his wife, Esmerelda. He's only met her once before. Duff says her soft dark skin is because she's from Spain. He remembers the sweet scent of her perfume. The kiss on his cheek leaves a trace of red lipstick.

Shirl and her twin sisters, Carol and June, add more rouge to Dominic's gleeful grin. Behind the ladies is the only one he hasn't hugged nor seen because the last guest is shorter than the others. Shirl points at the young girl.

"This is Gloria, our little sister and the last of the bunch."

He's not prepared for what he feels when he stares at the girl's face. It's perfectly round, framed by full straight hair to her shoulders, the bangs cut evenly across the top of her eyebrows. Round eyes the colour of polished pine smile at him. She steps back, too shy to be hugged. Dominic's heart does a tumble and he stutters a hello. Duff breaks the spell.

"C'mon now, everyone to the kitchen. Let's eat and then we can have some of the delicious looking cake that Adairia brought."

Soon plates are piled with haggis, neeps and tatties from Carmichael's, compliments of the sisters. There are dainty sandwiches and potato salad for those that don't care for the mutton dish. People arrange themselves around the kitchen, with Dominic given the head of the table where Duff normally sits. The spillover heads to the living room with plates and linen napkins. The chatter is cheerful. Most of the adults are drinking ale that Tubs has brought, except Adairia and

Esmerelda, who are hovering over everyone like mother hens, making sure food and drink is adequate. Gloria is given a seat next to Dominic and is a chatty little lady warming up to the birthday boy. They're drinking Schweppes lemonade and ginger beer. Before long, everyone is full, the dishes have been cleaned up and stowed, the kitchen restored to order and the gang are standing around the table where Dominic sits in front of a double layered chocolate cake with twelve candles burning brightly. His grin is evidence of his happiness. Strains of "Happy Birthday" fill the air, the men slightly off key except for Jacky Boy who has a smooth tenor voice. Dominic is told to make a wish, an age-old tradition, and blow out his candles. Tea is served for those who want it and the group devour the sweet dessert. Duff sets his empty plate on the cupboard and turns to Dominic. He waves at those in the kitchen to be quiet.

"Let's join the rest in the living room. C'mon Dominic, we've something to show you."

Rising from the table, his face flushed, Dominic groans from a full stomach.

"I hope it isn't more to eat."

Duff, who probably ate the most, guffaws the loudest. Everyone is laughing. More pats on the back and the older sisters steer him into the other room. They direct him to the large chair near the front window and Adairia holds out one of her silk scarves.

"We have to blindfold you for a few minutes, Dominic."

Not sure what's going on, he just nods. Adairia folds the multicolored scarf until it is as wide as her hand. Wrapping it gently around Dominic's head, she ties a stout knot behind his head. The noise of the front door opening attracts Dominic's attention, but he cannot see. Whispers, soft laughter, shuffling feet make him curious, itching in the seat. He can't imagine anything better than the fun he just had. He hears the soft landing off something heavy in front of him. The crowd goes quiet. From the hallway Duff is behind the group, grinning, stroking his beard, happy with the young man he has adopted.

"Take off the mask now, Dom."

Dominic slowly pulls the mask away from his eyes and in the middle of the floor is a handcrafted pine desk. Only wide enough for a chair and a row of three drawers on the right, it has a raised top at a slight angle. He recognizes the drawing table. The joints and workmanship are impeccable – the craft of a master carpenter. Dominic knows that Tubs has made it, he's seen his work before. Staring dumbfounded, he can't believe his good fortune. He stands to rub his hand across the polished surface, the only thing brighter than the glee on the faces around him.

"I… I don't know what to say, I'm just so happy."

Duff moves closer.

"We all chipped in lad and hired Tubs here to make you something special. The kitchen table's not the best spot for all the nice drawings you do. Do you like it, lad?"

"Like it? Like it? I… I… I love it. Thank you everybody so much.

"Good then, let's get it up in your room."

Dominic gathers one end and Jacky Boy the other, and soon they have it beside his bed. The party only lasts for another hour. Dominic is profuse with his gratitude when he says goodnight to each guest. When he tells his uncle how much he appreciates his kindness, he is continually yawning, overcome with fatigue. Duff sends him off to bed saying he's going to gather up the last few glasses.

Into his pajamas, he pulls the one ancestral chair that Duff kept up to the new desk. Getting a fresh sheet of paper, he takes out his favourite pencil. Before he goes to bed, he's sketches a soft outline of Gloria's pretty face.

CHAPTER 3

By May 13 the people in Govan are not talking much of the Titanic anymore. The only comments of the tragedy are the huge loss of life. Where Dominic lives, the big news is the House of Commons Select Committee giving approval for the annexation of Govan by Glasgow. No one in Govan is for the idea, especially Duff and his cronies, who own their own properties and argue that they'll be paying more taxes for no improvements. It's always the same: cities get too big. Govan by 1912 is the seventh largest town in Scotland, desirable to Glasgow's expansion plans. The shipyards are busy. The Fairfield Titan, the largest crane on the River Clyde, was built, capable of lifting huge engines and sections weighing 200 tons. The keel has been laid for the British destroyer LaForey at the same yards.

Thousands of Russians have moved to Govan in search of the jobs. Not all of them are able to find work and some turn to crime. The older Pestov boys, Viktor and Anton, are brutes with quick tempers, the main reason they can't hold a job. They settle arguments with their fists. At present, they're arm-breakers for outstanding loans from Duncan Bell, slum lord. Desperate tenants borrow money from him at outrageous interest rates. If you don't pay on time, the Pestov boys will pay you a visit. They enjoy their work.

They want their younger brother, Ivan, to steal for them and are pulling him from the apartment building where their mother lives by the scuff of his neck. Anton is the biggest. At fifteen, he outweighs a twenty-year-old man. He has his mother's Slavic face and deep scowl. His cotton shirt sleeves are rolled up over bulging triceps. With little effort, he hauls his youngest brother through the wide doors to the street. The setting sun is directly in his eyes. Anton lifts his free hand for shade. Ivan takes advantage of the hesitation and wallops his brother directly in the groin. The strangling grip around his neck is instantly freed and he runs. Anton falls into a fetal position, clutching his jewels and screaming revenge when Viktor tumbles over him. By the time he's back on his feet, Ivan has disappeared. He runs west, into the sun and towards Govan.

*

Dominic likes watching his shadow move about in front of him as he walks home, heading east. He likes Wednesdays, especially a sunny one like today. Even when he is really beat, he always enjoys the quiet time as he walks from Tub's place to Duff's. It usually takes him a half hour. When he crosses the street beside Elder Park, he stares at the open greens and wonders if Gloria might like to go on a picnic this summer. He shakes his head at the idea; he'd never be brave enough to ask her. Hitching his shoulder bag straighter, tightening his grip on his tool belt, he watches the road where he is walking, lost in thought. He doesn't hear the footsteps behind him until they are just several feet away. The hairs rise on the back of his neck. He ducks.

A twisted two-by-four stud, the length of a baseball bat, slices the air inches above his head. Dominic reacts like his father taught him. With the momentum of the dropping motion, he swings his tool belt around behind him. The handle of the hammer strikes a skinny, unkempt youth directly on the kneecap. His shrieks scare the birds from trees nearby and freezes his companion. The two-by-four clatters to the ground and two middle-aged women on the opposite side of the road hasten their steps. Dominic leaps back, removes the hammer from its loop, chuck's the two bags aside and faces his foes.

It's the two boys from last February, the day of his birthday party. The one dancing around holding his knee is about his height, the other one is shorter, pudgier, and still uncertain. Same as the last encounter, he's looking back and forth from Dominic to his injured companion, his head like a pendulum. You can see in his face that this wasn't in the plans. Dominic steps towards him, ten feet away, smacking the flat side of the hammer in his palm.

"C'mon Fat Boy, you have something you want to settle with me?

I'm all alone."

A figure runs out from behind the brownstone building across the street towards them. Ivan hastens to Dominic's side, glaring at the ruffians, both bigger than him.

"You're not alone."

The pleasure in seeing the young Russian is evident in Dominic's smile. He acknowledges the offer of assistance with an affirmative nod. Ivan is bolder now.

"Step up now and let's finish this... or bugger off."

Exactly what Dominic said to them in February.

Three months later buggering off continues to be the best option. Fat Boy hustles over to his comrade, who is now leaning against the park's wrought iron fence, bearing his weight on his good left leg. Hitching an arm around his neck, the shorter boy is strong and helps him limp away. But not without the last word.

"We'll get you for this."

Dominic waves the hammer at him.

"I'll look forward to it."

Ivan can't help but laugh at Dominic's bravado. The hammer is a deadly weapon; why would they come back? Dominic relaxes and catches up with Ivan's chuckles.

"What's so funny?"

Ivan leans back on the fence. The sun is almost gone. His face is half lit in the last rays.

"I like that bugger off part, wasn't that what you said before?"

"Aye, it was, something like that. Well thank you for your help, but I didn't really need any."

"That's not what I saw."

Dominic is searching the ground next to the roadway for some nails that were scattered from his pouch when he swung it.

"Oh, yeah? What did you see?"

"Well, the piece of wood was only a step away from the fatter kid. If he'd a thought of going for it, he might a hurt you?"

"I doubt it or he would've done it. He looks to me like the type of person who always needs to be told what to do, not bright enough to think on his own."

Ivan drops to Dominic's side to help retrieve the errant nails because there is a horse drawn cart approaching from the east. The steady clop of shod hoofs grows louder with the heavy breaths of the horses. They aren't slowing down. Scooping several from the pathway, both boys move aside when the cart is behind them. Dominic straightens up, taking the nails from Ivan.

"What are you doing up this way?"

Ivan is dusting the knees of his wool pants off, one almost worn through. The legs end at the ankle bone. His feet are clad in worn boots. A faded red cotton shirt with sleeves rolled up is open at the front, all the buttons missing. The neck of his once white tee shirt is brown from the dirt of an unwashed neck. His short hair is spikey. Wanting to avoid that issue, he points at the piece of wood.

"I was watching you from the corner over there. I didn't have time to warn you. How did you know to duck?"

"I don't know. It was just a feeling that someone was behind me and I just reacted to what I felt was a threat. My da was a bit of a scrapper and got moody when he drank. He figured me and my brothers were going to be like him and made us learn to defend ourselves. I'm glad he did."

"Yeah, me too."

Dominic looks at the last rim of the sun slither behind the apartment buildings across the street. It shines back at his companion and the expression Dominic sees is of someone needing help.

"I should be getting home. Are ya hungry?"

The head falls.

"Yes… yes I am."

"I can't bring you into the house smelling like you do. Uncle is particular about being clean, but I can sneak you a bite. C'mon with me. It's only another fifteen minutes, and you can wait by our shed."

Ivan is thrilled with the offer to eat. Too proud to beg, he doesn't want to steal food, he doesn't want to be like his brothers. He hasn't eaten since yesterday. Brain and stomach are in tune, and the thought of food causes his tummy to almost purr. Both boys laugh at the rumble. Dominic starts walking.

"C'mon."

Duff had sliced up some boiled potatoes left over from last night and fried them in plenty of butter, some onions and fresh pepper. A bottle of pickled beets, open, with a utensil handle sticking out, is in the middle of the table. A bottle of chow is in the same predicament. A bowl, gaily flourished with wild flowers, exceptionally un-bachelor like, is full of boiled cabbage. Duff had just spooned it out, guessing

Dominic will be home soon. Finnan haddie waits on the stove, Duff's favorite fish. Glancing up at the big clock in the hallway, he sees its 7:15. He frowns at it as if it's to blame for Dominic being a few minutes late. The opening of the front door dissolves that thought.

"Glad your home, lad, me tummy is starting to complain. Go wash up and I'll dish out the vittles."

"I'm hungry too. What are we having?"

"Some fried up tatties and finnan haddie. I have a bowl of cabbage too, your favourite."

"That's great, Uncle, I'll just be a minute."

Dominic removes his boots at the door, places his tool belt against them and swings his lunch bag from his shoulder to fold it over the tool belt. Checking his pants for any sawdust or dirt, he sees they're okay and heads for the washroom. Duff spoons out the fish on identical plain white plates. Knife and fork parked on one side by a deep, heavy glass of cold water. A tall, old English, letter A is etched on one side of the glass. He lines the bare edge of the plate along the fish with crusty browned potatoes, leaving a spot for the cabbage. Just as he is ready to sit down, Dominic starts telling him about the ruffians he met, omitting Ivan. The whys and how comes absorb most of the meal until both go back for seconds.

Dominic stands in front of the remaining fish, the pan of tatties half full and begins to feel guilty knowing that Ivan is waiting outside. He stalls when he recounts what he has learnt on the brief walk home. Although they look after their alcoholic mother, Ivan's older brothers are very bad. His mother knows only how to drink; who's had so many men that the boys don't know who their father is. The brothers told him he had to support himself and want him to start stealing for them. Running away from them, he has nowhere to go. He'll be ten in another month.

His deep thoughts are interrupted with Duff standing just behind him waiting for more food.

"What's going on, Dom, are you not feeling good? What are you waiting for?"

Dominic feels he can't hide this from Uncle. Turning to Duff he indicates the abundant food with a crooked thumb.

"Thank you for the great meal, Uncle. We always have lots to eat."

Duff would like to smile at the compliment, but the look he sees in Dominic's eye gives him pause at its seriousness.

"There's a boy outside waiting by our shed who hasn't eaten since yesterday."

Duff's brow is beetled in surprise. He only harrumphs, not sure what to say.

"I said I'd sneak him out some food, but I don't want to be sneaky with you, Uncle. We have enough and I know he's really hungry."

Setting his plate on the cupboard, Duff begins to rub his beard.

"Who is it lad? Where does he come from?"

"Well, I didn't tell you everything about when the ruffians took off."

Sitting down at the table, he points to Dominic's chair.

"Before you go carting off food to strangers, it's best you tell me the rest."

It takes ten minutes for Dominic to recount the two events leading up to a nine-year-old hungrily waiting outside for a handout. The first on his birthday and the earlier one today.

"…and I can't bring him in, he's kinda dirty and doesn't smell so good, like sweat and sour milk."

Duff has both hands comfortably over his belly, fingers intertwined. He's impressed with Dominic's bravado, not thinking the boy had it in him. Also with his soft heart, but thinks him naïve. There's too many without food in some parts nearby, too many people looking for work and as busy as they are, there are never enough jobs. He's not friends with any Russians and only hears bad things about them. Sitting up straighter, he cocks his head, bushy eyebrows scrunched.

"Gorbals ya say? I've heard of a bunch from there, the Ivanovs, a rough crew with their little gang. You don't know anything about this fellow Dominic. You can't go around bringing stray dogs home. I know I don't have to remind you of the business I run here. The clocks are a good cover but we need to be careful."

Duff stands to take his plate once more, returning to the food. Digging at the potatoes, he offers with some reluctance.

"Go on then, get him a plate. Use the old yellow one and that fork with the missing prong, in case he tries to steal them."

With the spatula in hand he turns to Dominic who is digging in the knife drawer, to get his attention. Dominic sees the stern gaze his uncle uses when angry or making a point.

"Then you get him off the property. Make sure he doesn't come back. You tell him that if he starts hanging around here, I'll have the constable after him. I know you mean well, but I don't want you hanging around with this kind, Dominic."

Dominic gapes at his uncle's reaction, not expecting such finality.

"But, Uncle, we can't turn our backs on him, he's nowhere to…"

Duff interrupts and points the spatula at him.

"That's my final word on that, Dominic. You'll do as I say."

The glares are equal in intensity, both Alexander and deadly calm. Dominic lets his anger settle, uncomfortable with Duff's stance. He quietly gathers the yellow plate, dishes out a fair helping and with one final glare at his uncle, who is now sitting at the table eating and stewing, he takes the plate out to Ivan.

Duff finishes his meal. Puts the leftovers in a bowl in the icebox. Cleans up the dishes, which is usually Dominic's chore of the evening but decides to give the lad some time to get the message across to the unwanted guest. All in a sour mood. Blinded by the gossip he hears, certain Dominic will only pick up bad habits, he feels he made the right decision. It's best he find some good Scottish boys to chum with. Even though, he feels uncomfortable when he remembers Dominic's glare of defiance. He looks like his dead father with the rebellious eyes and set chin of Duff's younger brother. There is much to learn about this young man, but for now Duff's word is law.

Retreating to the living room with a copy of The Glasgow Herald, Duff sits in the chair nearest the window and begins to read the newspaper. It takes him forty-five minutes to get to the last page. Several times he reads the latest article of the Titanic. So many unidentified bodies, many taken to Halifax, Canada, for burial with only a small white headstone noting that no one knows who's in the grave. Folding the paper and setting it on the table, he realizes that Dominic has not come back in. Looking at the clock, he sees it's shortly after nine. He's usually lying in his bed with something Adairia gave him to practice his reading.

He shuffles to the front door, his left knee a bit stiff. Opening it, he steps out onto the stoop. In the light of the open door he sees the yellow plate is on the floor near the front step, not a grain of food remains. The damaged fork rests in the middle. There is no one around. Donning his shoes, he heads around back to the shed.

The night is clear, starry and moonlit, the peak of the shed stands out in the dim light. Duff gets his night vision enough to see that nothing is astir, there is no one here. He looks back to the street and starts to worry.

CHAPTER 4

Dominic and Ivan are standing outside of Tub's carriage house, hidden behind the large cairt used by the carpenter. The horses that haul it are inside. Both Highland ponies, the heavier one is named Jack; the friendlier one is Pepper. Tub's house is in the front, the only light in the kitchen, which faces them toward the back, fifteen feet away. Dominic peers around the foot board of the cairt to watch the un-curtained window to see if Tubs is around. There has been no movement for the last ten minutes. He guesses that Tubs is in the front room facing the street. Or asleep, as he sometimes leaves his lights on. Motioning for Ivan to crouch down with him, under the wagon, he points to the outline of a doorway visible in the star glazed night. His voice is low.

"You wait here until I keep the horses quiet. It won't be a problem with Pepper – he likes everybody – but Jack is funny, takes him awhile to get friendly, kinda snobbish. He loves vegetables, so when I bring you in, you hold out that piece of cabbage we brought. He's on the right. You know which your right is?"

Ivan waves a hand.

"*Da*. I'm not stupid, ya know."

"We won't be able to see in there, but the way in is easy. You watch where I go in and when I wave to you, just slink along the wall to your right. When you get to the doorway, I'll guide you along, don't worry."

Dominic darts for the entryway and hides in the recess of the door. He can hear the horses shuffling inside. They sense his presence. The click of the latch seems exaggerated in the quiet. Leaving the door open, he calls out to the horses.

"Hey Jack, hey Pepper, hey there boys…"

His low voice calms the horses when they recognize the bearer. Flared nostrils pick up his familiar scent. Pepper paws at the floor in content and Jack snorts as if he resents being interrupted. Strokes to their fleshy jowls and pats upon their chests quiet down the pair. Dominic tells them in whispers about his new friend. He leaves them to wave at Ivan.

After the horses are familiar with the stranger, Jack still standoffish and indifferent, Dominic leads Ivan through another door towards the back of the carriage house. It opens into a large storage room/workshop. A window faces northwest and the shrinking moon is rising over the treetops along the edge of Tub's property and casts enough light to distinguish large objects. To the immediate left is a rough ladder built on the wall leading to an open area under the roof and over the horses that serves as a mow. It is half filled with hay. Dominic shows Ivan where the handholds are.

"Crawl up there and at the top move in away from the edge. I'll follow soon."

Ivan is careful on the wood with his worn boots. The rung is narrow and digs in his foot through the thin soles. Making it to the top, he creeps onto what feels like wide boards, mostly worn smooth except for the odd spot still coarse like un-planed wood. There is chaff and loose strands of hay scattered about the floor that clings to his body. Without warning he is struck with the edge of a heavy blanket, almost a quilt. The shadow of Dominic's head rises above the loft edge. He stops when he is chest high to the opening.

"Take that horse blanket and slide back a bit and you can curl up in the hay, should be good for the night. I have to get back; Uncle will be worried."

Pulling at the blanket, Ivan wraps it around himself.

"Why are you helping me like this? Especially since your uncle told you to have nothing to do with me."

Dominic is not sure himself other than he feels drawn to help Ivan; he enjoys having him around.

"I don't know really. You seem like a nice fellow and maybe we could be mates. There are not many boys around here my age. My family don't have much, but I've been kinda lucky and Uncle is good to me. We just need him to see that you aren't like the Russians he's heard about."

Both boys are startled when a heavy breeze blows the front door against the back wall. The horses shuffle and snort. Ivan shuffles back towards the hay mound. Dominic chuckles.

"It's only the door swinging open. Hope Tubs didn't hear it. Now, listen, I've got to get going. Tubs might be out to feed and water the horses in the morning, but I know he's not taking them out tomorrow and he gets down enough hay for the next day before he goes in. So, stay here and be quiet. I'll meet you at Elder Park when you see the sun over the trees in the window. "

"What if the owner is around?"

"Naw, he won't be here because both he and Uncle are going to a funeral in Ibrox. One of their drinking buddies they play cards with on Tuesday nights had a heart attack a couple of days ago. You'll be okay. Now I have to go. See ya in the morning."

He starts to climb down and as an afterthought.

"Oh, and I'll bring you some better boots."

Dominic hastens from the coach house to head home. It'll be another half hour, shortly after ten when he gets there. Ivan has crept back to lay in the soft hay and with the blanket tightly around him is soon asleep.

Duff is sitting on the stoop, his feet two steps down. Crouched forward with elbows on his knees, hands clasped, he stares up the street, waiting for Dominic. Other than returning to don a cardigan with the evening cooling off, he's been watching the street since he discovered the boys were gone. Worrying over what Dominic might be doing is making him feel guilty. He's not sure how to respond to this act of defiance. The lad has never been a pinch of trouble. If it was someone else besides a Russian kid, he might not be so adamant. He's sure the boy will be nothing but trouble. He decides that Dominic must see his way.

A porch light at the corner of the street is the only illumination other than the stars with their frosty glow. A shadow appears at its edge and grows longer as Dominic comes into view. A flush of relief tingles his skin when he sees the familiar lope. As glad as he is that the lad is back, he stands and frowns at the oncoming figure, ready for battle.

Dominic sees the silhouette of his uncle rise from the front step. It is too dark to see his face but the arms akimbo mean he's upset. His disappointment at Duff's demand is equal to his discomfort at being at odds with his uncle. Not wanting to be disobedient, he must do as Uncle says but let him know how he feels. A tad nervous, he turns into the walkway and stops close enough to see the scowl on Duff's face.

"Where have ya been?"

"I did like you said and got Ivan… that's his name… off your property."

"And that took you two hours?"

Duff is standing on the bottom step and Dominic has to look up at him.

"I'm sorry, Uncle. I should've told you, but I was scared you wouldn't let me go. I couldn't just send him off. I had to help find him a place to stay for the night. He really can't go home."

Duff just stares at his nephew. He's touched by the kindness in the lad but thinks him gullible.

"Where did you take him?"

Unable to lie, Dominic remains mute. Duff lets his arms relax and the light from the doorway crosses Dominic's face. He can see that he's not going to find out. Rather than being stern, he reminds Dominic of their earlier conversation.

"You remember what I told you. I don't want you hanging around with the Russians."

"I understand Uncle. I'm not hanging around with them. I'm just trying to help one of them that doesn't seem so bad. I already told him he can't come back here, and he said he wouldn't. I won't have anything to do with him after tomorrow."

"Why tomorrow?"

"I want to give him my old boots; they're still in the shed."

"And then what?"

Dominic hangs his head, torn between two emotions.

"I'll… I'll tell him I can't be his friend."

Before Duff can respond, Dominic moves around his uncle and heads into the house.

CHAPTER 5

With the scuffed boots tucked under one arm and a brown paper bag under the other, Dominic is hurrying up Langlands Road towards Elder Park. With both Duff and Tubs away to the funeral, he asked for the morning off. When he reaches the southeast corner, he can see Ivan sitting on the grass by a young oak tree inside the park. The buds have opened and green shoots begin to unfold. The sprawling limbs will soon be filled with leaves, but now streaks and shards of morning sun dapple the boy under them. It rained briefly in the night and the air smells like new growth – until he reaches Ivan.

"You need a bath. You don't smell so good."

Ivan shrugs and points to the bag.

"What's in there?"

Dominic chucks the boots in front of Ivan.

"Take these. You'll find out soon enough what's in the bag. Let's get going."

Ivan scrambles with the boots, no laces or heels but they beat his poorer ones any day.

"So where we going?"

"I'm going to save you from going to the poorhouse. I understand it's not so nice there, but better than nothing maybe. Anyway, c'mon, we can get you cleaned up at the public baths on Summertown Road."

Ivan stops.

"That costs money. I don't have a towel or even any soap."

"What do ya thinks in the bag, dummy. And I got you a clean shirt too. Now c'mon."

The public baths are administered by the government to provide sanitation for the hundreds with no such amenity. Built in the late 1800s, the building the boys hurry out of a short while later is solid, crafted stone for two storeys. Marble arches cap wide serious windows. The square glass panes have a yellowish glow from the first rays of the rising sun.

By the time he had soaked and soaped and changed clothes, the boys had decided to hang out until noon, when Dominic has to return home. When they had entered the baths an hour ago, they overheard two older men say that there was a British Submarine in the graving yards across from the Plantation Quay that might've hit something. Came in during the night. The yard is going to drain the lock this morning. They're hoping it hasn't been done yet.

Ivan is almost at a full trot by the time they reach Town Hall on the corner of Govan Road. Dominic catches up to Ivan at the chain fence that separates the yards from the public. He can't help but laugh at the oversized shirt on his friend. It is the faded shirt he was wearing when he first came to Govan. It's a size too big for Ivan and the sleeves hide his hands. He tries to roll them up, but when he runs and swing his arms, the cuffs unfurl. He is staring intently at the strange boat. It's the first time either of them has seen one.

"I wonder what's that big round part sticking up in the middle."

Dominic has his hands up grabbing the fence and his face pressed against the small rectangular openings. Marveling at the smooth lines, he tries to remember what it is called.

"It's… it's called a fin, I think."

Ivan turns to look up at Dominic with a surprised look.

"How do ya know that?"

"Well, last winter I read *Twenty Thousand Leagues Under the Sea*, and when I talked to Adairia about it… that's my teacher and Uncle's girlfriend… she showed me some pictures and I asked her the same thing. I'm pretty sure that's what she called it."

Now Ivan is wide-eyed.

"Wish I could read?"

Dominic backs away from the fence to look at Ivan. The wire left an impression indented in his skin. Forehead, chin and one side of his face has been precisely divided in sections. The crease on the upper lip is deepest and emphasizes the fuzz that is beginning to grow there. Ivan can't help but laugh and loses his balance from wild chuckling.

Clutching his stomach, gasping for breath between snickers, he can't stop. Dominic is staring at his friend, bewildered. He doesn't see anything funny. Ivan's glee begins to taper off, he rolls on his side and tries to control his breathing.

Dominic waves him away and returns his gaze towards the submarine. Ignoring the giggling boy, he sees movement on the fin, someone climbing what must be a ladder. He is amazed by how small the person seems. His curiosity is interrupted by the quiet. Ivan is soon standing beside him.

"Well how come ya can't? Doesn't the schools make ya go?" Dominic says and is struck by a brief thought of when his Da took him out of school, said he had to be working. He knew the answer to his own question if your folks didn't want you to go.

Ivan watches the action on the fin, where several people are milling about, while he speaks.

"I started school, but the first time I got punished, my brothers beat the teacher up and I was told I could never come back. The boys made me stay home and watch my mother, keep her inside, clean up her mess, get her another bottle."

They both stay quiet. Dominic reflecting on the kindness of his own mother. Ivan indifferent, more interested in the yards. Starting to run along the fence line towards the water, Ivan wants to avoid further discussion.

"C'mon, I know a way in."

CHAPTER 6

Going through an opening only a foot wide in the fence is difficult. The knees of their pants are scuffed with green grass streaks and dry dirt from crawling through the field that separates the warehouses and the street. The sun is midway through its morning arc and the shadows are long in front of the building they are hiding against. They are perched beside a huge anchor, twice as tall as them, crated in rough lumber. It stands alone at the bay doors farthest away from the water. The submarine is only a hundred feet away, with its black hide gleaming. They are near the front. There are other crates, and coils of thick rope, and men along the sides. The air is thick with industrial smells: diesel fuel and oil, galvanized sheathing and raw steel. A din of hurried voices, whirring cranes and hammering heightens the boys' curiosity.

Ivan is laying on his stomach at edge of the crate, one eye peeking out. The wooden planks that form the envelope for the anchor are uneven and provide viewing slits as well as a hiding spot. Dominic is ten feet away, kneeling at the opposite side, his eyes glued to a three-inch opening. Ivan scoots beside him and shares the same portal to study the boat. He points to the taut cable and stays that line the upper deck.

"What do ya think those are for?"

"The cables?"

"Yeah."

"I'm not sure, but maybe it could be to hang onto."

Ivan looks at Dominic with eyebrows raised.

"I wouldn't want to have to walk out there when it's underwater."

Dominic sees that Ivan is serious and starts to laugh, cupping his mouth so as to not make any noise. Ivan imagines himself clinging to the wire and trying not to breath. He too has to cover his mouth to contain his giggling. The boys glance at each other. That moment of covertness and shared laughter feels good and a bond is formed. They don't have to say out loud how much they like each other. Ivan has never had a close friend and is shy. He points to the boat.

"The lock still has water. I know where we can watch it drain. C'mon."

On all fours, he creeps back to the other side of the crate, glances to see that no one is near and darts for the end of the warehouse. Dominic is right behind him. They are soon at the rear of the building where empty shipping crates are stacked. The yards repair many ships that require huge replacement parts, so the crates are abundant. There are several spots where the rough wood reaches the lower back roofline, making access quite simple. Ivan begins to climb on a route he seems familiar with and Dominic apes him on the way up.

The sun is directly on their backs and the galvanized metal that covers the roof is getting hot. They're standing on the last crate, balancing its wobbly placement, the eaves at their waist. Dominic is staring at the vertical ribs that form the edge of the panels and rise to the crest of the roof. Every second one is dotted with dozens of small rubber rings with a fastener in their center. They are evenly spaced apart. A frown expresses his bewilderment.

"How do we get up there? I don't see anything to climb up on."

"It's not steep. Watch me."

Ivan tugs himself over the edge and, placing each foot on one of the protruding nubs, uses the small projections, with hands flat on the roof, to propel him to the top, where he lies down to peek over. Turning to look at Dominic, he sees his friend's hesitation. He waves at him and keeps his voice low.

"Hurry, the water is starting to go down."

Dominic has never been much of a climber and is leery of the small bumps. Not wanting to miss the draining, he overcomes his reluctance and cautiously follows Ivan's route. The metal is getting warmer, with the rubber washers attracting the most heat. The nail in its center is hot. Almost to the top, Dominic places his palm on one of them and pulls back his hand in response. The action throws him off balance and he loses his foothold. The slide to the bottom is twenty feet of momentum, and when Dominic plunges into the air, his body is pointing feet down. His legs are splayed, and the left one goes through an opening in a wider crate halfway to the ground. His right leg and upper body are on the outside and continue to fall. The snapping of the two lower leg bones can be heard over the clattering of the disrupted crates. Dominic's painful yell can be heard in the yards.

Ivan is frozen, dumbfounded, as he watches Dominic fall. When he hears Dominic's wail, he scurries to the bottom. When he eases himself back onto the planks, he sees his friend upside down, his head almost touching the ground, his leg jammed in a crate stopping his fall. Scrambling down to the bottom, he rushes over to help. He's uttering reassurance amidst anguished cries as he tries to lift Dominic up. At 125 pounds, Dominic outweighs Ivan by 25. He can only get some weight off the injured leg. Dom is too heavy for Ivan to lift high enough to free him and he realizes he needs help.

"I'm going to find somebody, Dom. I have to leave you here."

Dominic braces himself for more pain and hisses through gritted teeth.

"Hurry, please hurry, it hurts so much."

Just as Ivan is about to lower Dominic, a coverall-clad worker comes running around the back corner. The man is stocky and his face and hat are smeared with dirt. He sees the fallen boy immediately and hastens to the crates. His voice is scolding.

"What are you boys doing back here?"

Ivan ignores the question.

"Please help me, my friend is hurt."

The man gets a moaning Dominic under the shoulders and lifts him up high enough for Ivan to lift out the leg. Just below the knee, the calf and booted foot are at the wrong angle. When Ivan tries to hold the broken section, Dominic passes out from the pain.

CHAPTER 7

Duff turns the corner at the end of his street. Tubs had let him off on Langlands Road. He had offered to drop him off closer, but Duff had wanted to walk the quarter mile home reflecting on his friend Brice and the many times he had carried him home. A terrible card player, he rarely won any pots. Duff's face is softened with memories, and a satisfied smile crosses his face. It only lasts seconds until he sees a young boy sitting on his stoop. Displeasure creases his brow. He recognizes the pale blue shirt and guesses it to be the Russian boy. He's about to shout out when he realizes Dominic is not around. Sensing something's amiss, he hurries to his front walk. Ivan has spied Duff as well and runs towards him.

"You've got to come quick Mr. Alexander. Dominic has broken his leg."

Duff gapes at the boy wide-eyed. Thinking such a thing unimaginable, he sputters out questions.

"What do ya mean, a broken leg? What've you boys been up to? Where is he?"

Ivan is not much for explanations and hastens around Duff to head back up the street.

"C'mon Mr. Alexander, he's at the hospital across from the high school. Ya need to sign some papers."

Duff is walking so fast, he's almost running. Ivan is trotting a ways ahead of him. He's been answering Duff's queries as succinctly as possible. Yes and no answers. It happened about three hours ago. Brief details. What is normally a half hour stroll takes the two of them fifteen minutes before they enter the main hospital doors. It's a few minutes past noon and the central concourse is alive with activity. Flowing white jackets distinguish the professionals; moans, limps and wheelchairs identify the stricken. White uncomfortable looking chairs on the right with people here and there identify a waiting area. A large desk on the left is armed with several busy women. Most of them are serving someone.

Duff has his handkerchief out, rubbing the sweat from his brow when he approaches the darkly stained counter. Ivan waits by the front doors, rolling up the long sleeves. A middle-aged lady, dark rimmed glasses and short wavy hair, is talking on a phone. A name tag on her white cardigan tells people her name is Irene. Duff is impatient and waves at the lady. Holding up a finger to wait, she ignores Duff's glare. Worried too much to be still, he turns and points Ivan to the chairs. Ivan acknowledges it with a nod. Duff turns towards the hallways, picks the one on the right where he sees more hospital staff. The lady on the phone has turned her back to retrieve a note pad and doesn't see him hurry away.

The first door on the right is an examination room, brightly lit. An orderly is attending to the aftermath of the last person treated and is placing odd utensils in a shiny metal bowl. The smell of iodine still pervades the warm air of the room. The white neat uniform is spoiled by two drops of blood on his right knee, turned burgundy where it has dried. The man is short, has to look up at Duff when he's startled from his duties by the gruff, portly intruder.

"Excuse me, Mister, where would they take a boy with a broken leg?"

The orderly steps back, sets the tray down on the desk, and points towards the front.

"You have to check in at the front desk. The ladies there will help you."

Duff steps closer, hands on his hips.

"Never mind the ladies. You work here. Where would they take a broken bone to be fixed?"

The small man is back against the wall, waving his hands at Duff, who looms over him.

"Aye, aye, aye… I'll tell you where to go, just back off a little Mr. Please?"

Duff is at half scowl and gives way several feet towards the door, watching the orderly straighten his comb over. He again points to the front.

"Go down the hallway until you come to another hallway going left and right. Go right and through the white doors. There's a waiting area and desk on the left. Someone there will help you."

Duff is gone, uttering a "Thank ya." He's turning the corner and even though there are few pedestrians, and mostly staff, no one seems to pay attention to him. He walks firmly and decisively. No attempts are made to get in his way. Doors everywhere, people bearing stethoscopes or mops. The nurses in their stiff pinned-on hats. Swinging the wide door, he is in a ward that is curtained off. Those coming and going are all in medical uniforms, none are idle. Peculiar antiseptic aromas dominate the air. Chatter makes an even hum. Duff sees a counter on the left and hastens to the front. A young man in a long white jacket is bent over, dictating something to another clerk who looks like Irene, only in different colored cardigan. Duff slaps his hand on the counter

"Where can I find Dominic Alexander, the boy with the broken leg?"

The two staff are disconcerted with Duff's outburst. The woman is about to reply when the man with the jacket waves her off. Before he can respond, Duff points at him.

"You there, young man, do you know where I can find my nephew. He broke his leg down at the graving yard. Do you know if there's doctor around so I can find out what is going on?"

The man smirks at Duff's impatience. He returns a pen to his chest pocket and tucks a clipboard under his arm.

"Well, I'm Dr. McInnis and I'll try to help. Who is it that you are looking for again?'

Duff pauses at the admission thinking the man too young to be a doctor and much too happy. Red straight hair with a sharp part on the left covers an average head. Several strands fall over his much-freckled forehead. The protruding Adam's apple bobs like a cork on water. His white shirt is open at the collar and the McInnis Tartan decorates his tie. Duff thinks he should be on a stage telling jokes not fixing broken bones, but when he speaks, he is calmer.

"My nephew, Dominic Alexander, has broken his leg, and I was told they brought him to this hospital. Young man up front said he might be here."

Dr. McInnis nods knowingly, and with a gesture to follow, he starts down the aisle.

"Aye, Dominic. I examined him myself when they brought him in earlier. Both fibula and tibia broken quite keenly. Good news is that we were able to set them properly. The skin is bruised of course but will be fine. The cast is on and he'll need to…"

By the time they've reached the end stall of tall curtains dividing the emergency beds Duff has learned that Dominic will be laid up for at least six weeks. Reassured that all will be well, when he sees Dominic asleep under a crisp ruffled sheet, the leg with the fresh white plaster propped up and uncovered, he sighs with relief. The doctor talks in a whisper.

"He'll be asleep for a bit, and we'll keep him overnight. I'll discharge him tomorrow morning at eleven o'clock if he seems well enough. If you have any questions, have one of the staff call for me. G'day."

Duff thanks the young man and turns to walk to the bed, staring at his nephew. His hair is in disarray, cowlicks front and back, some falling on his forehead. His mouth is open and each intake of breath is regular and audible. A green hospital gown covers his shoulders and disappears under the sheet. There is movement beneath the closed eyelids and Duff wonders what Dominic is dreaming of. Relieved that the boy is okay, Duff looks around for a chair. Finding one by the head of the bed on the opposite side, he pulls it over beside Dominic and sits to wait until he awakens.

Except for a stern heavyset nurse who stops by to check on her patient, there is no traffic at this end of the aisle. Duff has his hands clasped over his belly, one leg crossed over the other, the foot swinging, and contemplates Dominic's convalescence. His eyes are closed in thought. The couch will have to be his bed again for a short time until he can get around, there will be crutches and long days for him. He might get Gloria to come keep him occupied. They seem to get along well enough. He'll dig out some of his favorite books to share with him now that he likes to read so much. Duff's thoughts turn to the young Russian boy in the waiting room and he ponders what he's to do about him. His musing is interrupted.

"Hello, Uncle."

Duff's eyes pop open at the sound of Dominic's weak voice. He stands and holds the rail on the side of the bed. Dominic's face is drawn and remorseful.

"I'm sorry, Uncle."

"What is there to be sorry for lad?"

"I shouldn't have been trespassing."

"Yes, you're right, you shouldn't have. I told you that chumming with that boy would lead you into trouble. Never mind that for now. It's good to see that you are okay. How do you feel?"

Dominic props himself up to rest on one elbow, facing his uncle. He uses his free hand to brush his hair out of his face.

"My leg hurts, but I can stand it; and I feel like I want to sleep some more. I'm kinda hungry though."

Duff looks at his watch.

"I'm sure there will be something coming soon; it's not much after twelve. I expect you feel drowsy from the pills the doctor told me they gave you. He says you can come home tomorrow."

The two discuss the coming days and how they will handle this alteration to their lives. Dominic worries about going up and down stairs with crutches. Going to the bathroom. Leaving Tubs shorthanded. How he'll be a burden. Six weeks seems like forever. Duff assures him that the time will go fast and he's not to worry about his jobs. They'll manage. Their conversation comes around to Ivan.

"Yes, okay then, I'll bring him back before I go and you can say goodbye. I'll send him off after and that's to be the end of your association with him. You understand, Dominic?"

"But, Uncle, how can you just send him off when he has nowhere to go. I told you what his family is like. He doesn't want to be that way. Where they live, they have to share a bathroom with five other families. Please, Uncle, can't you help find him a place to stay?"

Duff is moved by the compassion in his young charge's eyes. He strokes his beard, undecided.

"Aw, Dominic, how am I going to find a spot for a boy we're not sure we can trust?"

Dominic looks directly in his uncle's eyes. His own are hopeful.

"You did it for me."

CHAPTER 8

Not only do the six weeks go fast, but 1912 passes in a blur. Duff houses the Russian boy for several days until pastor Anderson intercedes on his behalf. Ivan stays in an orphanage until the end of August. None of his family members come looking for him. Now he is living in Whiteinch, across the River Clyde. Arthur and Pamela Guthrie have opened their home to him. Their little boy died more than two years ago, and unable to bear more children, the couple sought the help of their pastor to find a suitable replacement. Pastor Budge, who the Guthries worship with and Pastor Anderson are brothers-in-law.

During the time it takes for his leg to heal, Dominic is on it too much and the leg heals with a slight curve. He will have the faintest of limps the rest of his life. Teaches Ivan to read when he is at the orphanage. After a couple of weeks back from the hospital, he is able to work at his bench with his uncle. Tubs manages on his own, most jobs taking a bit longer. Gloria drops by occasionally with a deck of cards. The day Dominic has his cast removed, they go to the park for a picnic. It's Gloria's idea, insisting they celebrate his new freedom. He only works on her sketch after he's seen her in person, remembering the finest details of her presence. The eyes are the hardest; he can never duplicate the happiness he always sees in them. The dimple high on the left cheek is the easiest, a slight mischievous curve. He finishes the drawing at the end of July, two days before her eleventh birthday on the thirtieth. He asks Tubs for the afternoon off early that Tuesday and he gives it to her when he walks her home from school. It is the first time she kisses him. A quick peck on the cheek. He doesn't wash that side of his face for a week.

The submarine is repaired and sails to the North Atlantic in the middle of June. Duff accompanies the boys to watch it leave. Gustav Mahler premieres his Ninth Symphony in Vienna shortly after.

Ivan and Dominic have become terrific buddies. Using the Whiteinch ferry, they take turns hanging out on Saturdays when they can. One time in Govan, the next in Whiteinch and so on. They learn to play cricket. Ivan is a tricky and natural pitcher; Dominic, an exceptional batsman. They play sometimes on pick-up teams near one of the parks. Ivan is going to school and having trouble with his grammar. His foster parents are not rich, but he is well fed and properly dressed. He loves his new boots and has a pair of shoes too, for "good." Mr. Guthrie works as a butcher at the slaughterhouses. Pamela cleans houses in the mornings, mainly on Broomhill Drive, and cares of her men in the afternoons.

Edgar Rice Burroughs publishes *Tarzan of the Apes* and Dominic buys Adairia a copy of the *All-Story Magazine* for her birthday in October. Harriet Quimbly is the first female to fly over the English Channel. Dominic cuts her photo out of the newspaper, uses it for a bookmark and tries to imagine what flying is like. Fenway Park opens in New York and he cuts that article out too. A scrap book begins: events and mementos that spark his interest begin to accumulate.

Tubs shows Dominic how to miter joints. Sometimes Dom helps with the trim work. The frames he is making this year for the Christmas sketches he is doing are of finer detail and craftsmanship. All the drawings are of something meaningful to the recipient. The two horses working for Tubs, the rose bushes Adairia so tenderly cares for, a close-up of a pitted dart board with three darts stuck in the center for Jackie Boy, two butterflies hovering over petunias for Gloria, and a front view of the #12 tram that Duff says has the best seats. It's the one he usually waits for. He finishes them by the end of November and they are all wrapped in paper in the bottom drawer of his dresser.

Duff and Dominic go fishing ten times, mostly Sunday afternoons. Dominic has bought himself a bamboo rod. Same loch, same spot; they don't catch too many fish and let the little ones go, but several times their day ends with the frying pan full of their catch. Crisp skins and mouth-watering flakes of brown trout with mashed potatoes is one of Duff's favourites. The hours idle by often in silence, the cork floaters of their lines the only movement. It is also a time for private "man talk" when they feel the need for conversation. Dominic's finances. His developing skills. His developing puberty. Gloria. His saving to buy a set of chisels.

Duff talks about Adairia sometimes, often fondly or sometimes in frustration at her stubbornness. He loves his card night with the "boys." As much as he misses Brice, he enjoys the companionship of Tubs, Roy, Dougie and David and their mutual friend "Lagavulin." Youngest of the bunch, Mr. Lagavulin is ideally twenty-two years old and the leader of the gang. He's to blame for most of their silly antics, which Duff will sometimes relate. Their hearty laughter echoes off the hardwoods behind them and his belly jiggles. Dominic finds comfort in his uncle's jollity and laughs more at him than at the stories. Duff begins teaching Dominic to solder precious metals, starting with broken chains, a chore Duff doesn't like. And he doesn't like the new Unionist party; the Liberals are the only answer.

He apologizes a dozen times for embarrassing him at Carmichael's in the spring. The dart tournament had started at noon and so did the drinking. Duff was so hammered he was trying to put ice cubes, stolen from the back of the bar, down the back of different ladies' tops. At the insistence of old man Carmichael, it was best that Dominic get him home before he did anything worse. Dominic had to bear the weight of his uncle on his slim frame to keep him moving. Trying to counteract the stagger was difficult with Duff's extra bulk. Halfway home he puked on his shoes again, no big deal anymore; they were getting used to it. Dominic tells him a dozen times that it doesn't matter anymore and if he has to, he'll do it again. Duff reassures him it won't. Neither believe him.

Dominic's scrap book is growing with cut outs from the newspaper.

The Beverly Hills Hotel opens in California.
The British Admiralty recalls all their warships from the Mediterranean to station them in the North Sea due to the German expansion of their maritime fleet.
August 25 records the first time an airplane has recovered from a spin.
The Aswan Dam begins operations. 2500 US Marines invade Nicaragua.
While campaigning in Milwaukee, Theodore Roosevelt is shot by a saloon

keeper. The bullet passes through a steel eyeglass case and his single folded 50 page speech and lodges in his chest muscle. He continues to deliver his 90-minute speech.

A south-westerly gale hits Scotland, ten people die. The town of Troon is heavily flooded.

By the end of 1912, Dominic is as tall as Duff and weighs fifteen pounds more than when he arrived. He has sketched fourteen custom rings for Duff's clients. He is taking Gloria to the cinema for New Years. Adairia notes his proficiency in arithmetic, especially multiplication and division, and has decided it is time for algebra. His grammar and handwriting are still poor but he loves to read and bought himself a dictionary that cost him a day's wages. His Friday afternoons are still his until 4 p.m., when he meets with his teacher for two hours of instruction. Having purchased most of the tools he needs, he has started to take on small projects on his own that Tubs sends his way, mainly repairs: a splintered door jamb, a broken windowpane, damaged house shingles, malfunctioning doorknobs and such. People pay him in cash.

Dominic is earning more than his keep with Duff in the mornings. An increase in higher paying commissions from his sketches, his attention to detail and care when polishing fine jewellery, mastering the skills to properly cast gold, he has a feather touch on the torch when he helps out on the repairs. Duff has begun to pay him ten pence each day, for forty pence a week. Tubs pays him an hourly wage of two pence. Altogether a better-than-fair salary for a working adult. Lucretia, his mother, receives fifty pence every month and is able to bring Lilly back home. He has saved over five pounds sterling since Duff helped him set up his account and has never felt so rich. In the New Year, he'll be at zero again.

1913

The *Royal Zoological Society of Scotland* begins work on the Edinburgh Zoo early in 1913. It sits on 82 acres on the south side of the Corstorphine Hill, with a view of Scotland's capital city. The news is exciting to animal lovers everywhere, and kids plead with their parents to be able to go once it is open. Dominic is fascinated by the mention of wild animals, but what intrigues him the most is the news of penguins coming the next year. Edinburgh is near enough to make a visit possible.

The story is on the inside of the first page of the *Herald*. The paper is two days old: Friday April 2. Dominic has the paper spread out over his knees, the article – on the bottom left of the page – sitting in his lap. The upper half of the paper flops down over his legs. The setting sun is only a whisper over the housetops and the light coming in over his shoulder from the large front window blossoms from yellow to orange. He holds the paper up higher to catch the soft rays. Duff is asleep on the couch behind him, the last page of the paper pulled up over his head. The grunts and odd breaking of wind from his uncle are the only noises in the house, until a loud rap disturbs the tranquility.

The knocking at the front door startles Dominic and his reaction causes the paper to rustle to the floor. Jumping to his feet and looking out the window, he sees a black buggy and a sweating horse in the roadway. Turning, he looks at his uncle, who is undisturbed, almost comatose. Heading to the entryway, he remembers to heed Duff's instructions of "don't let any strangers in," turns the skeleton key and pauses by the door.

"Who's there?"

"It's Tommy. Open up, Dom, hurry."

Recognizing the deep bass of his older brother, Thomas, he pulls the door open. His sibling is built like their grandfather Watson, wide and strong of body. Even though he is 13 months older than Dominic, he is two inches shorter. The large ears are his grandfather's too, but the smell of booze makes him more like their father. He has green eyes, like Dom and Lilly. A gray outlander covers his short hair. His jacket clings to his frame, a size too small. The pants and boots are dusty and worn.

Mouth agape, Thomas stares at his younger brother, who is well dressed and bug-eyed. Surprised by the changes he sees in his sibling – who is taller and possesses a confident stare – he almost forgets why he came.

"Dom, get your coat on. You're to come with me. Mam's missing."

Dominic is aghast at the news. He steps back, shaking his head as if he heard wrong.

"What happened?"

"We don't know. She left Paul and Sheila with Mrs. MacDonald on the farm next to Granda's to go into Kilwinning yesterday morning and no one has seen her since. When she didn't show up last night, Granda went to the Flewelling's this morning to use their phone and left me a message to get you and come as quickly as possible."

"Well, what do you think is going on, Tommy?"

The eyes tell the story before the lips do. Thomas lowers his head.

"We just don't know, Dom. You're best to hurry."

Dominic can't believe what he's heard. Never in a moment had he ever considered his mother not being around. Tommy sees his indecision and his deep voice is commanding.

"Go on and get your coat and gloves, and a hat; it's damn chilly. I've a blanket on the buggy. Tell Duff you're going."

The conversation was loud and Duff is rousing from his slumber when Dominic touches his shoulder. The newspaper covering his face slides to the floor as Duff rises into a sitting position, rubbing the sleep from his eyes. After explaining the situation to him, Dominic rushes around to gather his things. Even though his grandfather's place outside of Kilwinning is only about twenty miles, it will take four of five hours to get there and will be after midnight when they arrive. Thankfully the night is clear and visibility should be good.

Duff assures his nephew that he will let Tubs know that he will be absent for a time and tells him not to worry about the sketch he was supposed to do for the banker's wife's anniversary ring. While Dominic heads upstairs to fetch a light bag and some clothes, Duff invites Tommy to step inside and shuts the door. He gets a brief outline of the situation from him, frowning at the unfortunate news. As he is offering any help the family may need, Dominic joins them at the door, pulling a hat down over his ears. When he speaks, his voice is confidant but the glazed eyes say something different.

"I don't know how long I'll be. There'll be a phone in town, and I'll leave a message at Carmichaels."

Duff reaches out to shake his hand, seeing the uncertainty in the lad's eyes. Reaching for Dominic's shoulder, he gives it a squeeze.

"We'll hope for the best, Dom. I'm sure there's a logical explanation."

The tears are close. Tommy shuffles by the door. Duff worries his beard. A few seconds lapse until Tommy leads the way out.

"Thank you, Uncle."

The covered buggy belongs to their uncle Bobby Watson in Newtongate, where the two oldest boys had gone to live. The mines offer work – tough labour. Deep pits and tunnels offer danger and low pay. Yet men line up for jobs. The troughs cut into the earth demand a much higher compensation and takes the lives of many young men. William Alexander was one. Tommy has always been assertive and easily assumed the role of the lead male in the family.

The Highland pony pulling them is only four years old and called Bonnie, a whitish figure in the half moon night that will work until she is told to stop. The steady rhythm of her sure-footed trot fills the empty roadside. Occasionally the creaking of the forest that borders the path on one side or the warning calls of some panicked nocturnal creature interrupts their conversation. Fifteen minutes out of the city, Dominic is huddled under a thick quilt listening to his brother.

"...so last week the wheel came off the wagon and Ma was sitting on that side. When it went over, she was chucked to the ground and the load almost landed on her."

"What were they hauling?"

"Logs."

Squinting and sucking in a deep breath, Dominic tries to imagine the fright she must've felt.

"I don't understand why a wheel would come off; Grandpa always takes the best care of his wagon. You know that. He was always doing something to fix it up."

"Aye, you're right, we'll know more when we get there. But I don't know why she would have been in the wagon when he was working."

"Likely to handle the horses. Belle only takes orders from Grandpa and her."

Tommy is leaning back on his seat, thinking about that. The dark quilt is up over his lap, the outlander pulled over the right side of his face. The reins are laying in his lap, Bonnie following the twisting road on her own, already having set the pace. When he talks, his breath frosts in the air.

"Aye you could be right. She's left the little ones next door to help out before. Speaking of the little ones, what's to become of Paul and Sheila if something bad happened to Ma?"

Dominic is shaking his head.

"No, don't say that."

Tommy turns to stare at his brother. He is enduring the same feeling of despair, but he remembers his grandfather's message.

"Face it, Dom, she's been gone for two days. I think we should be prepared for the worst."

Dominic is lost in thought, his eyes glued to the swishing tail of the pony.

"I hope she's all right."

Many miles pass in uncomfortable silence. Each brother considers possible outcomes and their accompanying difficulties. Passing through Uplawmoor, they are still a couple of hours away. While they head south, the shrinking moon stares directly down on them, casting its bluish glaze upon the fields bordering the roadway. Black silhouettes of bushes, stone fences and trees cut a crooked line across the horizon. Unturned ground, nourished with winter's runoff and compost from last year's crop yields a pungent earthy smell. Only the sounds of the horse's hoofs can be heard when Tommy speaks up.

He relates how and when he was alerted. They discuss Mary, their oldest sister, expecting that she will be there already or on her way. She'll know more what to do about the bairns. They can't get over the misfortune that their family has experienced over the last two years, what with their father and oldest brother gone and their mother missing. By the time they pull the wagon onto the dirt lane of their grandfather's home, they agree that the first place they need to look is at the hospital. Even though their grandfather has already done that, they speculate that perhaps she's had an accident and can't remember who she is. It is the only explanation that makes sense to them without knowing more.

Brodie Watson does not have electricity at his home yet, but the downstairs is aglow, with pale yellowish light outlining the kitchen and sitting room windows. Wavering light flickers from kerosene lanterns. The open back door where their grandfather waits faces the driveway. Stopping the pony, Tommy and Dom jump down to approach him. The back light does nothing to hide the worry in the man's worn face. Dom is as tall as his grandfather now and hugs him one armed.

"Is there any more word, Granda?"

Brodie only shakes his head, staring out at the empty drive as if expecting someone else.

"Nae Dom, not a thing. I'm terribly worried; this is not like your mam."

Tommy stands opposite Dominic, his hand on his grandfather's shoulder.

"We'll find her, Granda. Have you told the authorities yet?"

"Aye, did that early this morning, having given her the night to return, right after I got a hold of Tommy here. They're not doing much, saying she'll turn up. Wrote it down that she was missing. Me, Peter MacDonald, Sammy Goethe and Jim Pederson looked everywhere to no use – the hospital, the shops, the surrounding fields, even the old Brown Yard gravel pit, fearing the worst."

Dominic can see the despair in Brodie's furrowed brow, the gloss in his eyes.

"What of the little ones and Lilly? Is Mary here?"

"I had to leave them with Lilly today and Paul gave her a hard time. She's abed. Mary arrived a couple of hours ago and after getting both the boy and Sheila asleep, she walked over to Peter and Molly's place to stay the night. They have an extra room. She said she'd see you boys in the morning."

Bonnie is pawing the dirt, tired of the rigging about her body. Snorting at the trio, she tries to get their attention. Tommy responds and goes to pick up the reins. Brodie points to the barn in back.

"Put your horse in the back stall, Tommy. Leave the buggy there for now. The lantern is just inside the door. The bucket is hanging on the pump and you know where the feed is. Come in after. The teapot will still be warm, and I'll tell you and Dom where she was last seen."

It's close to 2:30 in the morning when the teapot is empty and the three of them are sitting around the oak table in the center of the kitchen, each lost in thought. A black and polished cook stove is behind them on the outside wall giving off a comfortable heat and the faintest aroma of smoke. Sitting to its right is a box of rough boards half full of chopped wood. To its left is a door to the back woodshed and against the wall is a cot with a thick mattress used for sitting and the odd nap. A grey wool blanket is pulled haphazardly about its length. Boots and galoshes of different sizes are lined up on a rug underneath. On the opposite wall are cupboards up to the unadorned window that faces the drive. In front of the window on a lower counter is a hand pump. A tin mug hangs from a hook on the end of the upper cupboard. From a lantern hanging over the stove, a flame flickers with every wisp of moving air. Shadows waver about the room.

Brodie has told the boys of the fruitless search. Their mother had walked the mile and a half into Kilwinning after seeing to the children. He had already left with the horses and wagon to haul firewood to Saltcoats. The last person to see her was Isabel Macready at Pearson's general store. Mrs. Macready is their closest neighbour to the north, the two farms abut in the fields behind the houses. The lady that served her remembered her and told Brodie she had bought a new comb and few toiletries. After a brief chat about the ailments that chilly weather and slushy snow bring, Lucretia's parting words to Isabel Macready were, "Maybe I'll go somewhere warmer." Dominic has been concentrating of what she might've meant. Sitting up straighter, he pushes his empty cup away.

"Do you think she might have just got up and left? It sounds like she already had leaving on her mind."

The possibility of Lucretia walking away from her family and responsibilities is unimaginable. Tommy is leaning forward with a troubled brow. Brodie waves at the thought.

"Why would she do that? She has a home here."

Tommy offers his opinion.

"Well, it hasn't been very easy for her the last year or more. It was bad enough when Da was alive and having to fend for us with whatever earnings he didn't drink. Then he up and drowns himself, she loses her house, has to find us all homes, and only five months ago Willie dies.

You remember how haggard she looked then, even the blush she used on her cheeks didn't hide her sad face."

Nods of agreement. Brodie pushes himself away from the table and rises, stifling a yawn.

"Even so, it's not like your ma to quit. Something has happened to her. We need to keep looking. And you boys can help in the morning."

"What are you planning?" says Dominic.

"We only covered the most traveled parts of the town. I think we have to search through the back streets and talk to people. We can use that sketch you did of her for Christmas last year, Dom. Show it around. But look, its late now, boys. You two can bunk in Lucretia's room. The girls are in the other one. Be quiet when you go upstairs because Paul is on the cot in her room. He's usually a sound sleeper, but don't get him up now or we'll never get him back to bed."

Both boys stand, putting their chairs back against the table. Exhausted from the long buggy ride, they are more than agreeable to calling it a night. Reassuring their grandfather that he's probably right, they ask him to wake them as soon as he is up.

To the east of the Watson farm is a half mile of fields before the next neighbour. A copse of trees in the distance, barren hardwoods, surround a small pond. The edges of the fields are lined with stubborn brownish snow. Early the next morning, opening his kitchen door, Brodie is usually greeted with the tip of the sun skimming the still water, turning it morning pink, but today the pond is pimpled with large droplets of pounding rain. The water seems to boil. Grey clouds own the sky. Puddles everywhere. Water drips from all black surfaces of the buggy. The galvanized metal that covers the roof of the barn offers a rhythmic cadence from the pelting shower and obliterates any other sounds. The scene before him is fitting for his mood, lost and unsettled. He fears for his daughter if she is lost somewhere in this. Tiny arms envelope him from behind and he is shaken from his somber thoughts.

"G'morning Granda."

"Ah, good morning to you too, Lilly. What are you doing up so early, it's not yet 6 o'clock?"

He turns to behold the gem of the Alexander family. He has to look down at her as Lilly, at twelve years old, only comes up to his chest. An ever present smile melts his old heart. Long bangs, the color of sand, fall almost to her faint eyebrows. The rest of her long hair is tied back, with a thin ribbon of royal blue holding it in place. A tiny mole graces her left cheek; otherwise the skin is rosy and smooth. She is wearing her mother's apron over her wool navy skirt.

"I know they boys will be up soon and I bet they're going to be hungry. I'm going to make some pancakes; the little ones love them. Do you remember where ma puts the skillet?"

"I lit the fire in the parlor stove, too. Even though it's raining, it's nippy out. The skillet is in the corner cabinet under the bottom shelf where she keeps the pots and pans. It's hidden in the back. I'll get some more wood while you round up some breakfast then."

Lilly busies herself with bowls, spatula, flour, baking soda, milk and eggs. Even though there is some wood already chopped, Brodie is splitting some the bigger blocks to take his mind off Lucretia. Four-year-old Sheila is sitting up at the table, brown curls tucked behind her ears, nothing shields her eyes. A half-eaten pancake is drooling rich dark molasses on a plate in front of her. Stuffed cheeks undulate with her vigorous chewing. One hand holds a fork like she's going to stab somebody. The other hand is playing with Miss Molly, her Raggedy-Ann doll. A droplet of syrup sticks to the cotton freckled nose where Sheila has pretended to feed her breakfast partner.

Upstairs, pajama-clad Paul is staring at his sleeping brother, their faces only inches apart. Dominic senses someone near and assumes it is one of the younger ones. He gapes wide-eyed at the room, saying "Boo." Paul is startled and back pedals in shock until he crashes into his mother's armoire with a whack to the back of his head. He rebounds and falls to the floor, the front of his head meeting linoleum.

Tommy sleeps like a larvae, he might squirm if you poke him but don't expect any action until he's ready. He doesn't even flinch at the commotion – he might as well be made of stone. Dominic on the other hand is quick to react. Tossing the covers aside, he swings his feet out trying to reach for his receding brother but misses the outstretched hand by fractions. He sees Paul bounce off the clothes press and smack his head on the floor. Kneeling down to help him sit up he softly rubs the red spot forming on the boy's forehead. Seeing the eyes glaze, Dominic knows he wants to cry. Tears come hard to Paul, so it must hurt.

"You're not going to let a little bump like that make you blubber like Sheila are you? You're an Alexander, you're tougher than that."

Paul is rubbing the back of his head. When he stands up the other hand is straightening his pajama bottoms. Same height now with Dominic on his knees he steps into his older brother's embrace. A hug and a fake knock to the chin put a crack in his pudgy face as he attempts a smile.

"Yeah, but you scared me."

"Aye, I did and I'm sorry. I didn't know you were that close."

"How did you know I was there at all?"

"I don't know, it's just a feeling I get sometimes. It's saved me neck a few times too. Hope I don't lose it whatever it is."

Bumps forgotten, Paul's next priority is breakfast.

"Do ya think Lilly is making pancakes? It smells like it."

"Aye it does, and if you listen you can hear the sizzle when she adds fat to the griddle."

"I like molasses on mine."

"Me too. Okay, go get dressed and wash up. I'll wake Tommy and meet you downstairs."

Paul steps back. A twisted grimace adds to the puzzled look.

"When's Ma coming back, Dom? Where did she go? Mary says she went visiting."

Paul may only be seven but he's keen on his surroundings, the coming and goings of the family. Dominic dare not share his worst thoughts but doesn't want to lie to him. A wee one doesn't need an adult worry. He adds a half smile for support.

"That might be, Paul, but I think she might've bumped her head and forget where she lives. All we have to do is find her. And we will, right?

"Aye. I don't sleep so good when she doesn't tell me a story."

A voice from downstairs calls out to them. The pancakes are ready. Dominic is glad for the interruption.

"Don't worry, there'll be more stories. Go on now, Paul, get dressed and go eat."

Appeased somewhat, Paul skips into the other room. Dominic sets about to wake his brother safely, with a broom handle that has been beheaded and left wherever Tommy sleeps. He doesn't respond well to verbal commands or pleas. Sometimes he might strike out at the probing instrument, or kick. Experience has taught them to stand back. Three or four pokes to the shoulder while reminding him of the search for his mother has a groan coming from under a covered head. A tousled mop slides from under the covers, cowlick first. The eyes are slits as if the low light hurts. The voice is not pleasant.

"Aye, aye, aye. Leave me be for a few more minutes."

Thinking that's as good as it's going to get, Dominic replaces the prod next to his mother's dresser. Pulling his workpants over his long johns, he is struck once more by the same thought that woke him many times in the night. What if his mother just left? It seems inconceivable. He hopes dearly it is not so, but admits that as much as it would hurt, he dreads finding her dead.

During breakfast, Mary arrives and sets about helping Lilly with the chores and the young ones. She scolds and bosses, making sure everyone is busy. She's built like their grandfather, wide of hip and straight shoulders. When she's not frowning, she's almost pretty if you like plainness.

Brodie apologizes to the boys that he has to pick up the first of three loads of lumber for the Reid's new granary as the carpenters want to work on Saturday. The mill is an hour each way. With loading and unloading, he won't be able to help until after supper. Regardless of his daughter's plight, the family still needs to be fed. On that note Mary reminds him that there is very little flour left if he's going by the grist mill.

He is fast to proclaim his pleasure that Tommy and Dom can go looking and offers a few more suggestions. Rousting the men from the table, Mary demands they not waste any time going to look for their mother. Tommy heads for the barn to feed and water the horses before Brodie leaves. The rain has abated, but the gray clouds promise more. The weather is acting like it's in a bad mood, with a steady breeze from the southeast making the morning frosty. Dominic found his old raincoat in the back porch and is preparing the buggy by drying off the seat. The first place they intend to go is to the farm behind them to speak with Mrs. Macready themselves. Granda doesn't always hear well and may have missed something from their conversation. If she doesn't offer anything new, Dominic has a list of possibilities he wrote this morning. He remembers Lilly's comment when she was helping him look for his coat.

"I caught ma crying a couple of times last week."

"Crying? That's not like Ma."

"Aye, tis true. The first time was when I had to use the loo in the night and she was sitting at the table. She didn't hear me and I watched from the hallway. It was the saddest thing I ever saw, Dom. She was weeping and so quiet. I saw the tears fall."

Lilly is alone in her thoughts for a second, poised over an open wooden trunk, its contents half on the floor. Dominic is fascinated with this revelation, and goosebumps claim his skin.

"And what happened, what did she say?"

"I couldn't walk in on her sorrows. I went back to bed. I lie awake until I heard her come up the stairs."

Not having any luck with her digging, she returns the folded goods to the trunk. Dominic's raised brows urge her on.

"The second time was the day before she left for Kilwinning. After supper she was in the barn brushing down Belle. I ran out to get her when Paul was trying to lift Granda's sledge hammer and dropped it on Sheila's foot. She only had rubbers on, but she's okay. Oh here, here's your jacket."

Passing him the navy slicker, she continues.

"I surprised her and she said she missed the kids, especially Willie. I started crying too, until she shushed me, dried up my cheeks and hers, and made me promise to not tell anybody… but I thought…"

Lilly is almost in tears, eyes glistening like a marble. Dominic reassures her that they will do what they can and today might well be the day they find her.

Tucking the damp cloth on the floorboard, Dominic watches Tommy hitch up the pony. Knowing nothing of reins and rigging himself, he stands out of the way. Tommy hooks things up as if he does it every day. A few minutes before nine, Dominic is standing on the front porch of the Macready's home. Tommy waits in the buggy. Having seen the boys approach, Isabel Macready answers his polite knock. She's a big woman, her bosom is the first thing out the door, followed by wide hips and arms akimbo. There's a touch of pleasure in her eyes.

"Good morning, young Dom, my goodness but you've changed, as tall as a man. And a darn fine looking one too. The lasses must be lining up to have a look at ya. You got your dad's mischievous eyes, but I hope you're more sensible than him. Never mind, step inside and tell me what I can do for you, Master Alexander. But you're here about your ma, I'm sure. How can I help?"

Dominic's cheeks are still flush from the compliments, but he gets right to the point, asking Mrs. Macready about her last encounter with his mother. Aside from his mother's odd comment of "go somewhere warm" when she left the shop shortly after ten, the one thing that Granda missed was what Lucretia had purchased. Mrs. Macready ended her conversation with a description of the bag.

"… it was plain white paper, not the smallest one but the one just a bit bigger with the store name across the middle. Whatever was in it wasn't much. If I remember correctly, it was the Portuguese lady that was at the till. She's usually there in the morning. You might want to ask her."

It only takes ten minutes to reach Pearson's General Store. Tommy waits with elbows on his knees, the reins ready in each hand. Only another ten minutes goes by before Dominic walks slowly out the main door, a heavy glass and oak portal. His face is scrunched in confusion, the picture of his mother hanging from one hand by his side, he shuffles in his brother's direction. He's oblivious to the sounds of people coming and going, the snorts of working horses, the thump of hammers down the street. Tommy sees the faraway look in his brother's eyes as he approaches the buggy.

"Well? What did she buy, Dominic?"

"A tube of lipstick. Bright red."

Tommy jerks upright in his shock. The pony prances from the sudden action until Tommy tightens the reins. Eyes locked, each brother contemplates the incredulity of the purchase. Dominic tries to reason the makeup with the disappearance of his mother. He's afraid of the answer. Tommy sees no connection whatsoever.

"Ma never wears lipstick, Dom. Did you ever see her ever wearing any?"

"Nae, never. She always told the girls lipstick is too expensive and only uppity-ups and tarts wear it. Only a little rouge on her cheeks sometimes."

"Well, she's neither so this tells us nothing."

Dominic climbs into his seat.

"She bought something else a week ago."

"What?"

"Some writing paper and one envelope."

Tommy is shaking his head looking down at his feet.

"This is getting stranger every minute. What could those things mean?"

Dominic goes stiff. A rash thought strikes deep. He yells out to a patron leaving the store, an elderly lady, laden with bags.

"Can ya tell me please where the Post Office is?"

The old lady has a tsk-tsk look on her face as she points with her chin in the direction the pony is headed.

"Take a left at the next street and it's on the next corner."

She doesn't wait for an acknowledgment and hastens away. Dominic elbows his brother.

"You heard her. Go!"

The postmistress is portly, pleasant and practical. Her perfume is not.

"I'm sorry, lad, but there's no mail for the Watsons."

Too busy for chatting, she returns to the mail she is sorting. The disappointment is evident in Dominic's drooping shoulders. The not knowing is weighing him down. Turning to leave, he is uncertain of what to do next. Opening the door to leave, he can see Tommy waiting in the buggy across the street, the same question in his look. The door is almost closed when the lady calls out.

"Hold on, lad, there's a letter here in this new bunch for…"

The door shuts, cutting off the rest. Dominic re-enters the post office and hastens back to the desk.

"Who's it for?"

Her glasses are at the end of her nose when she holds up the envelope.

"Mmm… posted three days ago. It's for Dominic Alexander in care of Brodie Watson. Know him?"

"It's me!"

Looking over her glasses, she is skeptical of someone she doesn't know. She is leery of the expectation in his eyes. She knows Watson's daughter is an Alexander as she sometimes picks up the mail. It's only a few seconds before she thinks of something to test the young man with.

"A lady picks up mail here sometimes for Mr. Watson and the odd letter for herself. What color is her winter coat?"

Anyone else and the logical guess would be black, winter's mandatory color – but not Lucretia. She might not have worn any make-up or adornments, but she loved the color purple, especially plum.

"Dark purple!"

She hands him the envelope unemotionally and returns to her work. Dominic stares at his mother's handwriting. Dread prickles his skin, and knowing she's not dead does nothing to alleviate his fear of the contents — something she couldn't say to him personally. He returns to the buggy feeling like a man walking to the gallows. The springs creak when he steps up to the seat. Tommy is about to inquire what he has when Dominic asks him to leave him alone for a few minutes until he reads the letter. Tearing it open, he silently thanks Adairia. Lucretia, unlike Dominic, is a beautiful writer with even letters that sweep to the right.

My dearest Dominic.

Only you would be able to understand what I am about to tell you. You've always been the logical one, the quiet one, my wee Dom. You'll have to tell the rest the best you can.

I can't go on, Son. I can't bear it any longer. Both Danny and Willie gone in less than a year. I lost the rest of you, and even with your wonderful help, I can't keep Lilly any longer. Da does his best, but there is not always work. I'm forever scraping for food. We don't have any more credit at the grocer's. I don't have the patience any more for Paul and his antics.

I have been offered a way out of my misery, Dom, and I'm going to take it. I know you'll all hate me, and I'm so so sorry to hurt you. I'm going far away and I'm not alone. Don't come looking for me

(Instead of a period, the page has a blot on it at the end of the sentence)

I know you'll see to the little ones, Dominic. Get Mary to help you. As much as you may think I don't, I do love you all.

Mam.

Help Tommy quit the liquor before it's too late.

The paper falls to his lap, the envelope to the floor. He slumps in the seat. Disbelief shields Dominic from outside influences and he feels as if he's falling into a void, sinking. His mother's gone. It's too late for Tommy. His brother's angry demand startles him.

"Who in God's name is it from, what does it say?"

Tommy can't read or he'd be reaching for the letter himself.

Straightening up, Dom looks to his brother. The silly hat he wears covers half his head and face. The eyes are shrouded by shadow and questions. Folding up the letter to place it in his side pocket, Dom asks for his brother's forbearance.

"I can only tell you it's from our Mam and she's okay. I need to have everybody round to tell you what she says. Please, Tommy, can we wait…"

Too young to be a man, the middle child remains a boy. Tears still come easy. Tommy's too embarrassed to tease like he used to and gives the leather a light snap to get the pony going.

"Back to the house then, Dom?"

With no sobs, just a quiet sorrow, Dom merely nods his hanging head. He doesn't want this responsibility – to be the bearer of such sad news. The ride home is not so fast; Tommy keeps the pony at a lazy gait, wanting to give Dominic time to stiffen up. He offers him a mouthful from a pint he keeps inside his jacket. Waving him off, Dom ignores Tommy's large gulp, not caring that it's not even noon yet. All he can think of is a comment from the letter "*I'm going far away and I'm not alone.*" Who was she with? He tried to ration the why: what his mother was going through; where she was going. Thoughts were tripping over themselves in his mind, none an answer.

When they pulled into the yard, Dominic was sitting straight, his head up, the blanket pulled up over their knees. The ride was mostly under a grey umbrella, with a drizzle for the last five minutes. Everything dripped. Brodie's heavy wagon full of lumber was in front of the barn, no horses hooked up. The lane was solid underneath, but the top was mushy and brown dirt covered the wheels and splash guards of both carriers. Tommy directed the animal to the right of the wagon and halted her there.

"Go on in. I'll get Bonnie inside and dried off. It's odd that Granda's here, and it's good that he is. And don't start anything until I get there."

Removing the heavy covering, Dominic steps out into the mist. Watching Tommy hasten to unhook the pony, he's surprised at his brother's dexterity considering the five or six "drops" he had on the way home.

"Ay, tis. See ya inside."

Twenty minutes later, when Tommy enters, he is surprised that the kitchen is empty. The only thing left is half empty plates, still at the table. The cabbage is evident by its aroma, the liver is evident in the chunks yet to be eaten. Mary calls from the front room.

"We're in here, Tommy. Grab a tea, and come join us."

"Aye, I'll be there in a spit when I get rid of the wet coat and me hat."

The front room is rarely used. Through a wide archway opposite the stairs you can see two couches older than any of the kids, in the right corner, arm to arm at ninety degrees. Not often sat upon, they look as if they were delivered last month. They abut a dark square table camouflaged in doilies. Perhaps the now deceased Mrs. Watson had a hobby. An empty vase, a crucifix and a portrait of a comely couple from a few generations past collect dust. Another dark table, much lower, more rectangular, equally laden with doilies, is in the center of the room. A stove is on the opposite wall. It glows and flickers from its smoke-stained glass. Close by is a heavy rocking chair, nicked with decades of use. A soon as Tommy enters the archway, the window over the farthest right couch yellows with an unexpected sun. He's smiling while he rolls up his sleeves, and fresh from yet another "drop," he's starting to be tipsy. By the end of the night he'll be teetering.

Seated on the couch facing the opening is Mary, next to her is Lilly with Sheila and the ragdoll on her lap. To their left on the window couch is Dominic and Paul close beside him, who for once is sitting still. Tommy figures he's been bribed with a promise of chocolate. Brodie is in the rocker and going like a madman. It's the only movement, the only sound the rhythmic squeak of a loose leg. The rocker seems impatient, like its occupant.

"Grab a seat there, Tommy, and get on with it, Dom."

Tommy ignores the command and leans against the archway.

"What are you doing here, Granda, I thought the lumber had to be hauled. We thought we'd have to get you."

The rocker picks up a pace, Brodie's anger propelling it.

"That damn Benjamin Reid. I had the first load in his yard and reminded him of our agreement that he's to pay me when I drop off the third load. The bugger said he didn't have the cash until Monday. I turned right round, ran over the Mrs. flower bed, and yelled out that I'd see him on Monday. The miser has to hang onto his coin as long as he can."

Tommy loves the old man's spunk and claps him on the shoulder.

"Are you trying to wear that chair out today?"

"Never mind, go sit down. Let's hear it, Dominic."

All eyes are on him. He gulps visibly.

"Mam ran away with someone and she's not coming back."

The rocker stops. Tommy straightens up, eyes bugged out. Mary gasps. Lilly starts to cry. Sheila sees her crying and joins her. Paul is shocked right off the couch and confronts his brother.

"What do ya mean she's not coming back?"

Everyone starts speaking at once. Dominic sinks back into the couch, ignoring the pointed fingers, the raised fist, the disappointment and pain evident on their faces.

"Who is the bastard? I'll break his bloody neck!"

"She wouldn't leave the bairns!"

"Who's to mind the house?"

"Why didn't she tell us herself?"

It's Paul's query that quietens the group.

"Who's going to tuck us in at night? What about my stories?"

Sitting up again, Dominic hugs his little brother, the tiny shoulders heaving. How do you explain to a seven-year-old that his mother would rather be somewhere else? Dominic wants to hate her right now, wills himself to hold her in contempt. He looks each of the family in the eyes, their own dismay felt in Paul's boyish sobs. They're quieted by their own thoughts. Most look away, except Lilly rocking Sheila gently on her lap, the little girl at the edge of sleep. She felt this, expected it and can't explain why. Dry-eyed now, she nods understanding. It's Tommy who breaks the moment of grief.

"Aye well, we're better off without her then if she feels that way. I can't lose work over this farce. I'm gathering my things and heading out. There's plenty of time to make it back before dark. Are you coming with me, Dominic?"

The girls frown at him. Brodie is about to growl at him, but Dominic cuts him off, not needing any confrontations.

"No, Tommy, we have too many decisions to make. I'll stay for a bit and find a way back."

Mary offers her opinion.

"You're probably in need of another drink, I imagine, Tommy, or you wouldn't be off in such a hurry with news of Mam running off."

Tommy won't back down, but wants to avoid a fight with his sister.

"Aw, listen Mary, she's gone. What can I do here to bring her back? We said goodbye once already. She left us back then, even you. I can't miss any more work if she ain't hurt or dead. I'm to find a flat with a couple of me mates and I need the money."

Tommy doesn't wait for an answer. He gathers his jacket, boots, floppy hat and raincoat. Before everyone is settled, he's gone out the door. They won't see Tommy again for many years.

The conversation is dominated by the whys, merges into the problems they face, and by suppertime – when Mary and Lilly clean up the kitchen and prepare the evening meal – they talk of their fates without their mother.

In the end, it is decided that Mary will return to New Lanark and give notice to her aunt and uncle MacDougal, pack up her possessions and return to care for the household. She'll try to get her mother's job as a domestic with the Clancys. It has been agreed upon that Lilly should return to her schooling. The issue of money comes up, or rather the lack thereof. Mary mainly worked for her room and board with a few extra coins for her personal spending, which didn't go far for a fifteen-year-old girl bordering on womanhood. There is money owed at the grocers. Brodie had to borrow money to fix his wagon.

Brodie can't understand a woman abandoning her children, and after informing the group at the table that she is no longer a relative of his, will not discuss it further. Whatever they decide on with regard to the young ones will be fine with him.

To Brodie's relief, he answers a knock on the door to find Ben Reid with some coins and a benevolent grin, lamenting that he needs the lumber today. Brodie leaves to hook up the horses once more, saying he'll return late.

*

Early the next morning heavy grayish clouds are moving west, the sun following in their wake drying up the puddles. Roosters from the adjoining farm finish up their reveille. Crows add their caws to the wake-up calls. Dominic is in the kitchen with Lilly, Mary and Brodie saying goodbye. He arranged to return to Govan with Brodie's brother-in-law, who drives a mail wagon. He only has to walk into Kilwinning to meet the carrier in an hour, before seven. Mary joins him to the end of the driveway.

"Dominic, I can't thank you enough for sending us some money when you get back to see us through this rough period. I hope this doesn't put you in a bad way. We can't really repay you."

"It's okay, Mary. I saved up a little and it's for the family. There's lots of work, so I'll be okay."

Mary's like Brodie and not much for hugging, but before he goes she rests her hand on his shoulder.

"Do ya think we'll ever see Mam again?"

Dom looks away from his sister, a lump in his throat. Afraid to speak, he stares towards town, the peak of the Catholic Church, visible over the horizon, catching the early sun, perhaps offering a smidgen of hope. He scrunches his shoulders and turns once more to leave.

"There's something else, Dominic. I haven't told anyone else yet, but when I return, there will be someone coming with me. His name is Pascal Brun, and he's from Canada; and we're getting married in the fall. He's a hard worker and it'll not be hard to find him work. For now, we can make something suitable in the mow for him to sleep, but he'll need a place to stay until the wedding."

Mary is blushing. Dominic raises his brows as Mary is not a prude but is particular about who she shares her intimacy with. The eyes tell him how happy this makes her.

"Well I hope he's worth it, Mary, and will be kind to you. Let me know when you have things worked out and I'll be here. Wouldn't want to miss my big sister's special day."

Paul interrupts their conversation, yelling out to Mary that he wants more pancakes and Lilly says he's had enough. The siblings part with Mary kissing him on the cheek.

CHAPTER 2

All through the summer and into the fall, Dominic's scrap book is filled and a second one purchased the first week of October. He loves the texture of the brown unmarked paper. The long pages allow him to post several complete headlines. Some have photos, sometimes he pastes in only the article. He's fascinated with cars, ships, airplanes and American baseball. Those and world events, female suffrage, assassinations, the threat of war and a few silly things fill his memory book.

The Royal Flying Corps builds the first military airfield in Montrose, Scotland.
Suffragette Emmeline Pankhurst is sentenced to penal servitude for three years.
In protest, Emily Davison steps in front of the king's horse, is trampled and dies four days later.
The first sedan-style car, a Hudson, goes on display in New York City.
Tiny Broadwick is the first woman to parachute from an airplane.
King George I of Greece is assassinated.
The Woolworth Building, the world's tallest, is completed.
Walter Johnson of the Washington Senator's pitches 55 consecutive scoreless innings.
The Reichstag's massive buildup of defensive weapons.
The HMS Aquitania is launched in Govan on the River Clyde.

The pages are rumpled from the homemade glue he uses, comfortably thick. The passing of summer is marked by the timing of each event, Dominic is particular about the proper chronology. Usually pasted the day he cuts it out, often several may accumulate. A rare lazy afternoon will find him working on his scrapbook, trimming the paper to precise and even lines, the layout on the page just so. Dominic's inherent attention to detail serves him in his hobbies as well as his work. He sketches a few of the many ships that come into dry-docks, especially warships. His collection of drawings of Gloria grows slowly, and he keeps them in a drawer in his desk, only sharing them with Ivan.

Duff has taught him to size rings and he does so with precision. His ability to solder the gold properly has him doing most of the repairs while Duff does the custom work. Tubs has shown him how to hang a door and finish the inside trim, how to glaze glass and repair broken window panes and how to install siding shingles and keep them straight. His Fridays are still his and filled with his own projects until 4 p.m. when he visits Adairia and continues his schooling. He can find the area of squares, rectangles and triangles, but circles with pi, radii and circumference continue to stump him. He knows the differences between you're and your as well as their, there and they're. But he's still confused by past and present tense. Saturdays are for household chores and free afternoons with friends.

He continues to see Ivan every other Saturday, each switching weekends to visit. They continue to haunt the shipyards building war machines, fascinated by the armor and sleek lines of the fighting craft. Duff joins them when huge ships are launched on the River Clyde if it goes out on a weekend. Each of them go silent when the mass of fresh steel embraces water for the first time. It always seems as if the ship might flounder, but like a bloated cork it bobs with buoyancy to the thrill of the crowd.

During a late summer mid-afternoon, the boys hiked to the docks to watch the Fairfield Titan, the largest crane in the world. Ivan takes to numbers like a bee to pollen and boasts that the crane can lift 500,000 lbs. Dominic argues over how big something would be to weigh that much, saying a whole ship is less than that. Ivan laughs at him, proclaiming that the ship's weight would be in the millions. Suggesting Dominic is *dumbscot* is only meant in jest, but Dominic feels slighted and heads home.

"You can go to the ferry yourself!"

Ivan gapes at his friend, unbelieving. His head droops when he rethinks what he said. He didn't mean to hurt his friend's feelings. He thought *dumbscot* was funny. He needs to apologize. Dominic is hustling along and quite a ways ahead when Ivan tosses the stick he is fiddling with aside and takes off. There's more to name calling that bothers Dominic. Yesterday he was replacing a pane of glass in a neighbor's window and broke the new one. He had to pay to replace it and didn't make any money. Ivan's remark was just a spark to a bad mood.

Turning up Elder Street, Dominic crosses the train tracks. There is an alley to the right, outlined by elderly birch, their leaves silvery in the western light. Brick buildings line the opposite side, mostly delivery doors along the back. The entrance to the alley is dark and hides two troublemakers looking for things to steal. When they see Dominic alone, head sagging, hands shoved deep into his pockets, no one around, they jump him when he nears the building. Caught unaware, his mind occupied by other matters and his defense mechanisms turned off, Dominic is easily knocked to the ground by the weight of the bullies. Fat Boy took him at the knees and Skinny at the chest. When they smack the dirt, Dominic's head hits hard, he passes out. Thinking they might've killed him, the two bullies drag him back into the recesses of the building.

Ivan crosses the tracks just as a pair of feet disappear behind the Kroft Warehouse. He recognizes the boots, scuffed around the toes, with different colored laces. Suspecting the two they have clashed with before are the culprits at hand, Ivan is fuming. He's not the same boy he was. He's more confident now and Dominic is the best friend he's ever had. Returning to the tracks, he looks around for a weapon. Several ties twenty feet from the road have been replaced recently and construction debris rests at the base of the gravel bed away from the tracks. It's a quick scoot down the short embankment to fetch a piece of broken board. It's split across the width to the length of a broom. The end is six inches wide before it tapers to a point. The edge of the split is uneven but works handily as a handle.

Rushing back with the sword-like lumber, he has no concern for noise. He just runs. Bursting from the edge of the trees, he sees the two hoodlums behind a pile of pallets, bent over the inert body rifling the pockets. A slavish yell and a full swing catch the tall boy's forehead when he looks up in surprise, toppling him over onto Dominic's motionless legs. Fat Boy jumps up only to receive the butt end of the broken board in the gut. Doubling over from the blow, he gasps for air and starts to cry. He staggers to fall at the base of a tree, dead limbs crunching under his bulk. Ivan sees red, wanting to keep pummeling him but knows he's made his point.

Turning to Dominic, he kneels at his friend's head, setting the board down beside him. Drool escapes Dominic's open mouth and Ivan can feel his chest move. Grit, dried droplets of blood and fine scratches decorate his forehead, bulging to the size of an orange. Not sure what to do, he rolls the other body off, flipping it over. He grins at the red welt on the bugger's head. Propping Dominic into a sitting position, the motion brings him back to consciousness. With much difficulty, Ivan gets Dominic up on his feet. Dominic grimaces when he rubs his forehead, mumbling incoherently, and Ivan props him against the brick wall at the edge of the building.

Ivan turns his attention to the two aggressors – the fatter kid is staring at him, pleading not to be hurt. His partner lies face down, starting to moan awake. Ivan picks up his weapon, the pointed end forward. He walks close to the younger boy, who now crouches near the tree trunk, trembling, eyes darting from Ivan to the wooden sword whose point is only a foot from his face. Ivan's voice is deep, not that of a young boy.

"If this happens again, I promise you, neither one of you will be able to walk away. This is the last time. You understand?"

He calls him a few unkind Russian names as he chucks the wood aside. The fatter boy is nodding, his "Ayes" convincing. Ivan backs off. The fallen boy crawls to his cohort's side. Ivan gets Dominic away.

They laugh many times into the fall whenever Dominic makes Ivan recount the startled look on the taller boy's face just before the flat of the board hit him. The bond is tighter now, the boys almost inseparable. Dominic has saved almost two pounds Sterling since helping out the family in the spring. Even though he is too young to be served at Carmichaels, Dominic likes the taste of ale but remembers what liquor did to his father so stays away from it. The many visits to Carmichaels have him tend to his gleeful uncle, who is fond of the spirits. He and Gloria have gone to the moving pictures twice. They go for walks and she tells him stories she makes up. His favorite is about a princess who is very beautiful but can't see. Gloria tags along with the boys on some Saturdays. She doesn't like it when Ivan teases her about liking Dominic, who just blushes.

October is unusually warm this year, the leaves late in turning colors. The days grow shorter. Dominic's scrap book grows thicker.

Jim Thorpe relinquishes his 1912 Olympic medals for being a pro.
Serbia and Greece declare war on Bulgaria.
An explosion in the Universal Colliery in South Wales kills 439 miners, the worst mining accident in the history of the United Kingdom.
The Royal Navy launches HMS Queen Elizabeth, the first oil fired battleship in the world.
The Philadelphia Athletes defeat the New York Giants to win the 1913 World Series.
The Panama Canal is finished.

CHAPTER 3

Duff and Dominic receive a simple invitation to the wedding of Mary Agnes Alexander to Pascal Joseph Brun, November 8, 1913, at 1:00 p.m. Wedding & Reception at home of Brodie Watson, Kilwinning. Dominic asks if he can invite Ivan to come with them. Duff agrees to be responsible for the lad, and everything is arranged with the wedding only three weeks away. What would be the proper attire causes all the males to fret. Duff hates to get dandied up and the boys have never been to a wedding before. Making it tougher is that Pascal has no relatives or friends in Kilwinning so Mary and he would like Dominic to be the best man. Ivan doesn't bother because he knows that he'll be wearing what the Guthrie's provide for him. Dominic arranges a phone conversation with his sister and she tells him she'd like to see him in a jacket and a tie wouldn't hurt. Not a hint of color, design or style is suggested; he's on his own.

Duff's wardrobe consists of eight pairs of pants, the same color navy, and one kilt. Eight shirts; here he ventures a bit on the bold side: four tan, three light blue and one white. The *best* shirt is the white. As the garments get older, the worst three are worn in the shop. He doesn't own a tie. Refuses to wear "a noose." His silky beard serves as an ascot to his open-necked shirts. The only jacket he owns is over twenty years old with a discolored neck and saggy pockets. When Dominic points out the flaws, Duff complains that the weather will be fine and a new jacket won't be necessary, not wanting to spend the money. Dominic is not the best with matching things up. They get Adairia involved. The first thing she points out is Duff's jacket.

"You are definitely not wearing that rag to a wedding, and especially with family."

Walking out of the kitchen with a small basket of rolls and several plates, the scent of fresh cinnamon precedes her. She had brought them along when they invited her for dinner that Saturday to help them with their clothing dilemma. Duff is twirling around with the jacket on to the amused audience of Dominic and Tubs. He stops to question her with chin and brows up.

"And why not?"

Both audience members lean their bodies forward to hear what she has to say. Tubs sees nothing wrong; his wardrobe is almost the same. Dominic agrees with Adairia.

"You look like old man MacIver that begs down at Elder Park, only worse. That coat should've been cut to rags ages ago."

Duff opens the lapels, eyeing the worn lining along the bottom, checks the pockets with their exhausted openings. He can't button it anymore.

"It's not that bad."

"Yes, it is. Take it off, empty the pockets, and throw it away."

Bumping him aside with her hip, she offers the rolls. Dominic waits impatiently for Tubs to decide if he wants one, says he's quite full. Dominic decides for him and plunks one onto a plate.

"Go ahead, Tubs, you know how good they are. You'll not be able to watch me eat one."

"Aye, you know me too well, lad. If you insist."

He's laughing when he sits ahead to stretch over his belly, curling his eager fingers about the plate to relax and savor the pastry. Turning around to offer Duff a roll, Adairia sees him rifling the pockets of the coat, placing what he finds on his chair. Pleased with his decision, she smiles inwardly before helping herself to dessert too. Sitting on the couch with Tubs, she mumbles between bites.

"As soon as we finish these, Duff, and you're done, we'll take a run up to your room and see what we need. I'll go shopping on Monday."

Tubs thanks his friends for the meal and leaves. Only the faint aroma of his pipe tobacco lingers. They sort Dominic's things out first. Most of his clothes are stored in the old dresser. Each drawer has its own purpose. Socks and underwear. Shirts. Trousers for work and a pair for good. Sweaters. Taught by his sisters to fold and his own fussiness at his good fortune, he even sorts things out by color, darks on the bottom. He too has a white shirt, normally worn to church. No tie and no jacket. No shoes.

Adairia gestures to Dominic to get off the bed where he has sat watching her make her selections. He frowns each time she says he needs something. She won't talk him into a kilt.

"Get over here young man and let's see what size you are. And when are you going to stop growing? You're as tall as your uncle."

Dominic stands with his back to her as she touches each shoulder, thinking she'll look for a large.

"How much is this going to cost, Adairia? "

"Oh a bit, Dom, but I think you can afford a new tie. Seeing how this is special day for you, I'd like to buy you your jacket, and Duff can pay for your shoes."

Duff has carried his mug of tea upstairs with them, sipping while she hums and haws. He's taking a sip when he hears her comment and sputters half a mouthful into the air. Catching the dribbles off his beard with his handkerchief, he scowls.

"I can, can I?"

"Yes, you can. How often does a young lad get to be a best man?"

"Well, with me new jacket and all…"

"Oh, hush, Duff."

Waving him off, she writes her estimates and objects in Dominic's note book on his desk. Dominic is back sitting on the bed anxious to be away. The feeling among the three is mutual. Her back is to Dominic when Adairia sees the discontent in Duff's eyes.

"We'll do yours next, Duff."

Duff looks at her and sees the seductive wink. He forgets about the shoes. Not knowing what his nephew's plans are for the rest of the evening, he steps around Adairia and with his own man to man wink, nods Dominic towards the door. He needs no coaxing. Gloria said she would help him with his scrapbook. He won't see Duff until breakfast, and by then his uncle will be satisfied he's a few shillings the poorer.

CHAPTER 4

Duff borrows Tubs' four-seater trap on the morning of the wedding. It's still dark when Duff hitches up Jack and Pepper, and he, Adairia, Dominic and Ivan are off. Duff is half correct in his estimate of the weather. With the sun rising at their backs on the road, the sky is clear as a bell jar. On the other hand, the fall temperature made them glad to have a jacket. By the time they arrive at the Watson farm, the hamper sharing the back seat with the boys is empty. Sandwiches and fruit, water and fresh donuts served as breakfast and lunch. They won't eat again until mid-afternoon.

Looking for a place to park, Duff slows the team. There are already two traps lining the driveway and the wedding is not for another two hours. Horses are tethered beside the barn and being fed by a man with a limp. Duff suggests that one of them belongs to the MacDougall's, Duff's sister Molly, where Mary was living. Knowing Molly, she'd be wanting to help decorate. The paper bells will be out and strung inside the door, he bets Adairia.

"She uses them for birthdays, Christmas, New Year's, you name it. Those bells have done a lot of celebrating."

"I'm sure they're nice," says Adairia.

She's sitting up front with Duff, wrapped in a shawl of black and white swirls. Her hat is also black, wide brimmed and low, adorned with a white ostrich feather, suitable for the fall and a happy occasion. Her skirt is dark gray and the delicate boots are black. A white, high collared blouse caresses her neck with silk ruffles. The pleasing aroma of musk follows her closely. She holds onto the seat when Duff maneuvers the trap through a shallow ditch in the field bordering the house. A section has been mowed short where there will be lots of room for the guests' transportation.

Ivan has never traveled much and even though the distance from Govan is not great, it's like an adventure to him. The boys are each hanging on to an armrest, interested in the few people coming out of the house waving at them. Dominic recognizes three of them.

"There's Uncle Geoffrey wearing his kilt and Granda and Uncle David, but I don't know who the other one is. He's wearing a red bow tie, maybe it's the groom. I can't wait to meet him"

They all agree on that. Duff stops the trap nearest the barn where the ground is more solid.

"Jump down there Dom and give the lady a hand. Ivan you go with them and I'll settle the wagon with that gent tending the horses. I'll meet you in a bit."

Out of the trap quickly, Dominic offers his hand to Adairia. She pauses for a moment, admiring the young man. The black jacket and tartan tie add polish to his innocent face.

"You look quite dashing, Dom. Don't be breaking too many hearts today."

He looks away with reddened face when she takes his hand to alight from the trap to join the men in the front yard. Ivan elbows Dominic as they follow her, his voice low enough only they can hear.

"Yeah, lover boy, don't break too many hearts..."

Dominic pushes his friend away and tries to suppress a laugh as they approach the group. Everyone is paying attention as Brodie introduces Adairia to the groom.

"And this young man is Pascal Brun."

"Pascal Brun" comes out in a heavy brogue, *Passkull Brun* (sounding like Bun with an r, not the rolling fluidity of its French origin).

"You'll have to pay attention, he talks a bit funny."

The young man's laugh comes easy. The wide smile and gleaming eyes are infectious. Liking him right away is not difficult. When he speaks, his English is tinctured with the accent of the mother tongue of his Acadian father.

"I talk funny? This whole country talks funny. I've been called a *bampot* a few times."

Recognizing the expression for an idiot, everyone breaks out in laughter. Brodie grins with delight at his granddaughter's choice, patting him on the back. He points to Adairia's escorts.

"The taller of those two is Mary's brother and your best man, Dominic. This other lad, I think, must be Dom's friend from Govan."

Stepping up to Pascal, Dominic extends his hand and best face.

"Thank you for asking me, Pascal, I'm honoured. Welcome to our family."

Everyone is talking at once and to each other, greetings and introductions abound, Dominic referring to his friend "Eye-van." Adairia breaks away from the group to head into the house to see if she can help. Duff joins in the goodwill and wedding jokes. David and his wife Beulah had arrived last night, coming early to help with the food preparation. It's discovered that Mary is getting ready at the Macready place and will arrive fifteen minutes before the ceremony. The couple will be staying at Sunnybrae Inn tonight, a wedding gift from Molly and Geoffrey. Pascal has been working at the Budge Bros. Warehouse for the last three months. As well as being introduced to a few off-color wedding jokes, Ivan and Dominic are being teased that there will be plenty of young ladies attending.

When asked how a young man from eastern Canada ended up in Kilwinning, Pascal explained to the group that his grandmother on his mother's side was born in Mayfield, a community south of Edinburg, not far from Newtongrange, where Tommy and William had gone to live. Three years ago, when he was only seventeen, he had hired on to a Norwegian freighter out of Bouctouche, New Brunswick, a coastal village not far from where he was born. The ship was being laden with pulpwood harvested from the surrounding forests. He had been hired to load the wood from wagons to slings hanging from the ship's cranes. Three days it took to fill the cavernous stomach of the freighter. The last night at dock, several of the ship's crew shared a few beers with some off the workers at a pub. Too many of them got drunk and when he awoke the next morning, the ship and he had already been at sea for several hours.

"...so the captain offered me a choice, either sign on as a crew member for the duration of the trip or walk the plank."

A ripple of laughter from the listeners. They are enthralled by Pascal's tale and the way his hands always move when he talks.

"The ship docked in Liverpool to unload its holds. I left with the lumber, deciding to find my grandmother's headstone. I wanted to see where my roots are. And to make the story shorter, I decided to stay."

Dominic likes Pascal, wondering if all Canadians are like him. The country seems so far away.

"How did you meet Mary?" he asks.

"I worked at the colliery in Newtongrange with your brothers Tommy and Willy."

With the mention of the deceased brother, a murmur of recognition interrupts the flow. Pascal frowns. He looks to Dominic.

"Sorry about your brother, Dominic. I really liked him. He told me about your family, where they all were. I have relatives in New Lanark and when I visited them last year, I stopped in to see Mary to offer my condolences and well…here we are today."

The men are surreptitiously passing flasks, an early sip. Glancing over their shoulders at the windows to see if the women are looking. Pascal receives a few claps on the back and some manly advice. Dominic and his uncle David engage in conversation. His mother's brother and he have similar traits. With the sun directly overhead offering no shadows, it is easy to see they are related. David is forty years older than his nephew and hasn't seen him for several years. He is impressed with Dominic's development. The unlined face of youth, the growing body and the open mind of a young man. Tall like his father. He can see concern in Dom's eyes when he speaks.

"What of Tommy?"

David frowns. He's looking down, kicking at some pebbles in the driveway. Not liking to be the bearer of bad news.

"He's in with a bad bunch back home, Dominic. Moved out when he got back last spring when we found out about Lucretia. He was terribly upset when telling us of her letter, swearing he'd be happy to never see her again. He's taken to drink and won't listen to common sense. We haven't seen him since then."

"Do you know where he lives?"

"Nae, he went to stay with a buddy of his from work, one of the Fergussons. They're a rough crew. He said something about getting their own flat in town."

Dominic absorbs the news, looking off into the roadway and the fallow fields across the way. He has promised himself he wouldn't let regrets over his mother's disappearance ruin Mary's day. Over the last six months, Brodie has made it quite clear it's a subject he'll no longer discuss. Knowing it will be a topic during the day nonetheless, mostly in whispers, he glances at Pascal, who is chatting with Ivan. He hopes the arrival of a new relative will bring some happiness that has been missing. He's not going to start worrying over his brother now.

"Well, Uncle, there really is nothing we can do. Tommy will have to take care of himself."

A trap came over the rise towards them followed closely by another heading in their direction. When he notices them, David pulls a pocket watch from his vest.

"It's just after twelve. Folks are starting to arrive. I'll go tell the ladies."

When you enter Brodie Watson's home from the side door, there is a vestibule for hanging coats and leaving boots just off to the right while a large kitchen opens up to the left. The first row of spread out paper bells, the accordion pleats stretched taut, tacked close to the ceiling, announce a celebration. Ribbon bows lead the visitor towards the living room. Teasing aromas escape from the crocks and pots covering the wood stove, a fire dying inside. One end of the kitchen is split by a hallway that ends at the rarely used front door, where a large red ribbon is centered on the window. A stairway on the right takes you to the bedrooms. More paper bells. Everything shines, including the faces.

When Mary arrives in a covered trap, everyone is gathered in the living room and hallway, with Lilly with the younger ones sitting on the stairway to peek through the rails. A buzz of hushed voices fills the empty spaces. Wooden chairs borrowed from the church are added helter-skelter. The couches are full with mostly ladies, so is the rocker with Mr. Watson himself. Gent's line the entryway, the over spill peeking over their shoulders in the kitchen. Dominic and Pascal are standing in the living room archway, hands folded at their front, both bashful at being the center of attention. An Anglican priest, shallow cheeked and long of face, with happy eyes and a patient smile, stands with them, his back against the archway. Molly is watching the arrival, peeking through the curtained window.

"Quiet everyone, she's coming in the front door. Oh my goodness, she's so lovely."

Pascal has a glow of light perspiration on his upper lip. Anticipation is in his eyes, in his flaring smile. He watches the front door and everything goes quiet. His heart almost stops when he hears the clicking of the door latch. He's never felt such happiness. A sunbeam enters first before Mary steps into the room. Not even the glow of the afternoon sun matches her radiance. The women sigh and the men stare enviously.

Her thick hair is swept up to buns on the side and wisps stylishly pinned in the back. A tiara holds a glossy veil made of lace and chiffon doing nothing to hide her contentment. Full smile, both dimples deep. From a high waist, the bodice covers her shoulders, arms and soft neck with a simple lace pattern over a satin jacket. The dress is layers of the same lace pattern but in three tiers, the last ending only inches from the floor. A white skirt is outlined beneath. Stopping in front of her future husband, her maid of honor, Gwen Rees – her best friend from growing up in Saltcoats – lifts the veil to drape it back over her hair, and moves to stand beside Dominic. Bride and groom face each other. Their love is palpable, something you could almost reach out and touch. They face the priest as he steps forward.

"Dear friends and family, we are gathered here today..."

When it comes time for the rings, Dominic removes a burgundy velvet box, curved on the top corners, large enough for two rings. His gift to his sister and new husband, he had made them himself. Hers is a polished yellow gold band, narrow and ornate with a cluster of tiny hearts etched into the shank. The top of the band has a rectangular sliver of onyx set inside the metal. Two 1 point diamonds highlight the black and yellow gleam. His is slightly wider, without the scroll work. The onyx and diamond placement are the same. Mary touches her heart when she stares at her younger brother. Her eyes tell him how much she's touched, a poignant moment between siblings.

A few tears are shed during the ceremony, not all by women. When instructed to kiss the bride, the small crowd begins to cheer. Over the happy noise The Reverend John Biggs raises his voice a few notches.

"I present to you Mr. and Mrs. Pascal Brun."

Everyone rises from their seats, the crowd in the hallway back into the kitchen to give the newlyweds more room. Everyone is talking at once. The first to hug Mary is Brodie – she's always been his favorite. Next in line is Paul, asking when they can eat. Pascal is engulfed in handshakes and merry hugs. The rings are admired, as is her dress. Flasks and pints are shared once more, not as furtively as before. The party has begun. After warmly embracing the bride, Aunt Molly, Aunt Beulah and Lilly escape to the kitchen to arrange the food and refreshments. Men are already moving outdoors, where a made-to-order, perfect fall day awaits them. Several are rolling a cigarette and a couple lighting pipes. Uncle David owns a camera, a Kodak Brownie. He coaxes the couple to walk the short distance to the pond, where he will photograph them. Dominic and Gwen are invited along.

The afternoon passes quickly. Once people have eaten, the dishes and utensils are washed and put away. Small groups form in the house and in the yard. Pascal and Mary have spent most of the time in the parlor, where they shared the meal and received their guests. Brodie is getting tipsy, and so is Uncle Geoffrey. Ivan follows Lilly everywhere. Gwen would like to follow Dominic everywhere even though he is two years younger than she. Adairia has more fun chatting with the men and attracts jealous stares from some of the spouses. Duff knows better and doesn't pay any attention to her merriment. The sun starts to set on the gathering when Brodie makes a suggestion.

"Go get that fiddle of yours, David, and your mandolin, Geoffrey. Let's gather in the house, friends, and see if we can get some feet tapping."

Furniture is rearranged in the kitchen and the music plays on. Duff adds his harmonica. Adairia sings several Highland ballads of lost warriors and forgotten love. Everyone wants to dance with the bride or groom. The music continues late into the evening until Mary and Pascal decide to head to the inn. The little ones have fallen asleep in the living room and many folks are munching on sandwiches that the aunts prepared. Tea is being served and that is a signal that the celebration is coming to an end. David has offered to drive the newlyweds to the inn and heads out to hitch the trap they will be using for the night. While Mary changes clothes upstairs, Dominic asks Pascal to join him outside while he waits for his new bride.

The moon is waxing and almost full. A bluish glow causes night shadows and the open yard looks ghostly. A breeze from the north adds a coolness to the air but the weather has been extraordinary for the time of the year and the men are in their shirt sleeves. Pascal has his jacket over his arm, his bowtie in his pocket. Dominic has been itching to ask Pascal about his home in Canada.

"What's it like where you grew up, Pascal?"

"Well, the village is called Cocagne and it is not far from a major center called Moncton on the east coast of Canada. There's lots of farms around and many fishermen. It is surrounded by a bay of the same name. The province I lived in is New Brunswick and if you look it up some time, you will see that the Atlantic Ocean is our biggest neighbour."

Pascal's smile is evident as other thoughts cross his mind when he continues.

"It's a beautiful place, Dominic. There's a small island off shore with a thick forest, plenty birds, a heronry and wild animals. My parent's house is right on the water facing the tiny piece of land. The sunrises are magnificent, full of blues and reds and oranges when the skies are clear and with the land low to the west, the sunsets are equally amazing. The waters can be as calm as a mirror one day and the next morning you'd thing they were angry with crashing and rolling waves. Ah, I miss the bay."

Pascal stares at the lantern light by the barn, the silhouette of David, moving about getting the pony hitched wavers in the dark. A smile warms his oval face with remembrances of home. Dominic is intrigued and interrupts his musings.

"What of the winters?"

"*Oui (yes), oui*, the winters."

Pascal turns towards the house to face his new brother-in-law, amused by the young man's intelligence and stature; he can't believe that Dominic is only thirteen years old. From the moment they met, just that day, he regarded him as he might a seventeen or eighteen-year-old man.

"Well, they can be a bit tough. There's lots more snow there and not near as much rain as this area. But still, winter brings its own kind of beauty. A new snowfall covers everything in white, pure white. The trees hang with the weight, snowbanks sometimes eight or nine feet, the bay turns to snow drifts and ice. If it melts some days and freezes overnight, you should see the trees, the whole forest, the buildings, all glazed with rime."

"Rime?"

"A white frost with tiny crystals that grips everything, it's very pretty. Except when you have to work outdoors I suppose. Oh look, there's Mary waving in the window. The raised finger must mean another minute."

Pascal acknowledges his new bride by blowing her a kiss. Dominic grins, a little embarrassed by the Frenchman's affection, always hugging the women, pecks on the cheek, two-handed handshakes.

"Look Dominic, we'll get together soon and I'll tell you about

Cocagne and all the pretty Acadian girls that live there."

The trap pulls up just as Mary comes out with a gaggle of ladies surrounding her, Molly carrying a lantern to light the way. The ladies have donned shawls. Mary's is borrowed from one of her aunts, the beige and dark brown complimenting her dark brown features. They're still hugging and going on; the men that haven't passed out are looking for something to lean on and waving with loud cheer. Brodie had stopped the liquor an hour ago, replacing it with strong black tea, not wanting to embarrass his granddaughter on her wedding but damn he had had fun. He parts the crowd of ladies as Pascal is helping Mary into the trap. His tie is askew on an unbuttoned collar

"Whoa there, little lady, ya can't be off without a word from your Granda."

The Watsons grew up with parents that didn't love each other, hugs and fond caresses were uncommon. Brodie has been softened by wee Dom's eagerness to embrace. Enough moonlight glows that he sees his own mother in her glassy dark eyes. He engulfs her in his brawny arms, his voice only for them.

"Thank you for helping an old man out. I don't know what we'd do without you, Mary. Pascal seems like a good man. I want you to have this."

His hand grasps hers as if to shake it and the open palm presses the object into hers. Stepping back, she unfolds her fingers. The opal is as large as a shelled walnut, encased in a delicate and ornate filigree of polished silver. The blue and green fire shifts across a dark background from the flickering of the lantern light. Brodie steps back as others crowd in to see the marvelous gem, especially Dominic, who is standing beside his sister, wide eyed at the brilliance. The ladies all gasp at its splendor.

"Where did you get this, Granda? It's beautiful." says Mary.

Brodie looks down for a moment, rubbing his chin.

"Let's see now… it'd be twelve years ago when I took it as partial payment from the jeweller in Kilwinning when I did some hauling for him the time he moved his shop closer to the town center. I had intended to give it to your grandmother for our anniversary that fall but that was when she took sick, and with everything happening so fast I never had a chance to give it to her before she passed."

Mary looks over at Molly to see how she is reacting to the news. Molly just smiles knowingly and nods at her niece. Brodie catches the gesture.

"It wouldn't have been fair to either of my girls to give it to just one and not the other so it's never been worn. I'd like you to be the first, Mary."

Mary is teary-eyed. The women are purring, the men are bobbing their heads in agreement. Hugs follow. The newlyweds are soon silhouettes in the moonlight as they head out the lane with David and Beulah, who will carry on to the Macready's where they have been invited to spend the night. Folks decide to go home. Brodie and Geoffrey open another bottle of scotch. Ivan is asleep on the couch. Lilly is getting the small children to bed. Molly takes down the paper bows.

Dominic is still awake from the excitement of the day. Finding one of his grandfather's drawing pencils, he sits at the kitchen table, now pulled back to the middle of the floor, opens the small note pad he carries and starts to sketch the brooch from memory, in awe of the delicate twisting and shaping of the fine metal as well as the fiery gem.

CHAPTER 5

There are no ripples in the remaining days of 1913. The sketches he gives everyone that Christmas are four by six, the thin frames handmade of highly polished pine. Duff gets a profile of Adairia and she receives one of her lover. Gloria brags about her sketch of a yellow pansy, her favorite flower. Ivan hangs his beside his bed where he can see the likeness of Lilly whenever he wants to. Tubs has his on the old rolltop desk where he keeps his stamp collection. The drawing is of his rare King Duncan issue as seen through a magnifying glass. Jackie Boy and Esmerelda have one of their four-year-old daughter, Silvia.

Dominic's favorite gift is the backsaw that Tubs and Duff chip in for. Manufactured by Jacob B. Hamlin & Co of Sheffield, England. The handle is beautifully formed, with sculptured leaves etched within the grip. The brass backing holding the thin blade is rigid and unblemished. Adairia gives him a hardwood miter box. His angles will be precise. Ivan gives him a kite he made, Mr. Guthrie helping him with the wood. Its four quadrants are different colours and bright, only needing a clear sky. A shirt from Jacky Boy and Esmeralda. What he treasures most is the Sampson Morden mechanical pencil he received from Gloria. Made of solid silver, the sides are adorned with artistic scroll work. She told him he could use it to write in his scrapbooks.

Dominic's second scrapbook is half full when he and Gloria get together on New Year's Eve day and fill in the accumulation of headlines for the last two months. They're sitting on the couch at Duff's house. Duff has joined Adairia and Tubs at Carmichaels and won't be home until suppertime. The fire is on in the kitchen stove, the heat emanating through the house. A coffee table is pulled close to them and filled with the opened book. A pile of newspaper clippings between them, glue and brush on the edge.

Holding up a photo of the *HMS Queen Elizabeth*, the Royal Navy's first oil-fired battleship, he glues the edges carefully and adds the article to the page. Gloria helps to sort articles out.

Mahatma Gandhi is arrested for leading the Indian miners march in South Africa.
Jack Johnson battles Jim Johnson to a draw in ten for the heavyweight championship.
Ford operates the first moving assembly line, a car every two hours and thirty-eight minutes.
The Mona Lisa is recovered after missing for two years.
An exposition baseball game in Tokyo sees the Chicago White Sox defeat the San Francisco Giants 9-4.
Charlie Chaplin begins his film career at Keystone for $150.00 a week.

When they are finished and nothing stirs in the house, only the ticking of Duff's wall clock reminds them they're alone for a short time. Their kisses are young and unpracticed. It is the first time she allows him to touch her breast. Only for a moment, pushing him gently away. She reminds him a young lady shouldn't do such things. He tries to hide his disappointment, and the sound of the back door opening causes them to sit up straight, adjusting their clothing and bending over the scrapbook. As Duff comes in, they're talking about the fun it is and wonder what the future pages will hold. Many of the articles in 1914 will be of aggression. War looms.

1914

The new year is extremely cold, colder than many of the older folks remember and talk about. Freezing rain seems to be the norm for most of January. Ice covers everything. The roads are slick, as if they've been greased. Tubs doesn't have as much work, so Dominic spends more time with Duff. In February, one of his birthday presents is a pair of ice skates. They tie on to his boots. Ivan gets a pair as well and the frozen ponds become a delight. Awkward as a new born foal, Dom's first skating ventures are an experiment in balance. Ivan has caught on much quicker and teases his friend, who falls on his butt more often than he likes. Gloria is a keen skater and helps him, to his embarrassment, but it's not long before Dominic gains his footing and Ivan has a hard time keeping up with Dominic's long strides when they race around the edges of the pond.

March brings more snow, more than usual. Investing in his own shovel, Dominic earns extra money by clearing people's driveways and walkways. Duff admonishes him that he's not charging people enough for his work, but Dominic explains that the old people who hire him don't have much money and he enjoys the exercise. When he explains to his uncle that it's not always about the pay but about helping people, Duff just frowns at him but is full of pride and boasts of his nephew's good heart at Carmichaels, explaining that he must take after his uncle. The guffaws from his drinking buddies suggest otherwise.

By the time May rolls around, Dominic is helping Tubs build a new coach house for one of his more affluent customers in Renfrew. The mornings are still chilly, but by noon the men are working with sleeves rolled up. Dominic learns how to build trusses with their complicated angles, how to shingle a roof and the proper cap to prevent leakage. By the end of the month the project if finished and both Tubs and Dominic are on hand when the owner brings his new automobile to the carriage house. A gleaming 1913 Buick Model 31 imported from America. The brass headlights, horn, lamps and hood ornament shine like miniature suns. The wooden spokes are white. Shiny black leather covers the four seats, two in front and two in back. The body is so polished, their reflection is mirrored in the deep green paint.

Tubs thinks it's a noisy contraption. It leaves Dominic speechless. He can't imagine ever owning one. Tubs grumbles at his fantasy.

"They're a smelly thing, always getting stuck with those spindly wheels. They spook my horses and are not near as dependable. Nae, you'll not be needing one of those, nothing good will come of them."

Dominic waves off his boss, grinning at his old-fashioned opinion.

"You'll see Tubs, they'll be everywhere some day. There's more and more all the time."

Tubs harrumphs at the suggestion, glancing at his team, Jack and Pepper. Their deep chests, powerful quarters. Jack a bay dun with a flowing grey mane and distinctive zebra marking on his lower legs; Pepper an uncommon fox dun, a dark dorsal stripe down his back and shaded face. He loves their big intelligent eyes. He pats both on their jowls before continuing to put away their tools.

Because the job is all done, they have to load up their sawhorses and scaffolding, leftover lumber and waste pieces. Dominic had disassembled the staging earlier and the lumber is all stacked in the back of the heavy wagon. They really should make two trips, but the owner wants his property clear of building materials, workbenches and such by noon. With everything tied down, a little lopsided on the right, Tubs and Mr. Crombie, the owner, settle the final bill. Dominic waits on the seat with his tool belt in his lap. Tubs comes back with a pocket full of cash, and is glowing, a thick smile across his pudgy face. Doffing his hat at the owner, he flicks the reins and the horses head home.

A quarter mile from Tubs place, they hold up for the trolley that crosses the street with its clattering bell. The street is narrow and it sweeps to the left on the other side of the tracks. He can see several cairts on the other side when he stops, realizing he'll have to pull his team to the right in order to pass. It causes him a bit of concern because the street borders a shipbuilding yard and the field near is fallow and separated by a wide ditch. He's glad Pepper is a right lead; he responds better to the leather and Tubs urgings.

When the trolley passes, Tubs eases the pair across the tracks and tight to the right. They pass the other cairts with only a few inches to spare. Passing the last wagon, Jack decides to empty his bowls and with tail raised drops a couple of stinky bombs on the ground, passes a gush of gas. Dominic pinches his nostrils and speaks in a squeaky voice.

"You've got to stop feeding him so much oats. He's worse when you do"

Tubs' heavy body is shaking with glee, a loud bellow causes Dominic to smirk.

"Aye, it's a stinker. But you should see your face laddie. It's..."

A roaring sound interrupts his comment. An automobile is heading directly at them, startling Tubs and the two horses. They can't see a driver. When the vehicle gets closer, they realize it's a young child at the wheel, barely able to see over the dash. The auto weaves back and forth, the driver unable to control it. The horses recoil from the moaning threat and rear their forelegs. Tubs panics as he has nowhere to divert the team, and when the vehicle is almost upon them Pepper shies to the right and pulls the wagon over the edge of the road toward the ditch. When the front wheel loses traction, it slips sideways into the trough and the load shifts, pulling the whole wagon and tethered horses with it. Dominic and Tubs jump from the seat. Tubs lands on his backside at the edge of the ditch and rolls onto the road. Dominic's young legs propel him forward, away from the falling wagon, and he lands on his side before rolling down into the trench.

The wagon topples down the embankment, coming to rest on its side. The horses are strapped into the traces with harnesses, collars, back straps, hip drops and breaching. Connected to the falling tongue of the wagon and chains reaching to the double trees of the wagon, the momentum pulls the animals with it, flipping Pepper and Jack. Pepper's on the right and falls easily to his side, but Jack is whipped over and falls lopsided on the far right. The loud crunching sound is the simultaneous snapping of Jack's front and back leg.

Pepper is struggling to right himself and whinnying in fright. Jack is unmoving and bleeding from both legs, as well as his head where he's hit it on a large rock. Tubs rushes to the animals, yelling to Dominic to calm Pepper down and unhook him. He falls to his knees at Jack's side, holding his head. He bellows at the horse to wake up.

The blood trickles to a stop. Jack is dead. The auto never even stopped.

Dominic unhooks Pepper and calms him down, until he hears a grief-stricken wail from Tubs. Looking over he sees Tubs kneeling at the horse's head, shoulders heaving, rubbing the broad neck of the animal. Dominic blanches at the scene and his heart breaks at Tub's reaction. He can feel Pepper shaking, he strokes his neck and offers calming words. Holding Pepper's long reins, he kneels at Tubs side.

"Is he dead?"

Tubs wipes his eyes with the sleeve of his jacket, nodding.

"Aye, he is lad. He's gone. He was contrary sometimes but such a hard worker, a good animal. I'm gonna miss him."

Dominic touches Tubs on the shoulder. Trying to take his attention away from the fallen animal, he gestures toward the overturned wagon. A few people stand at the roadside, wagons and an auto parked close by. Several scramble down the ditch offering help and condolences.

"It's an awful mess, Tubs. What are we gonna do?"

The question brings Tubs to his senses. He rises and looks around.

"Aye, aye, tis a mess is right. Damn automobiles. Look Dominic, it's not far to my place. Can you take Pepper to the barn? Get back here as soon as you can and we'll have to empty the wagon and get Jack..."

A lump in his throat causes him to pause. He's not sure what to do about the horse, not sure what to say. Dominic sees the confusion on his face, the regret.

"Tubs, maybe it's best you take Pepper home. I'll start unloading what I can. Get a hold of Duff to help. We'll have to take care of poor Jack. We'll need a team to pull the wagon upright and back on the road. Get a message to Fred Banting; he can bring his horses."

Tubs is nodding.

"Aye, that's probably best. Poor Pepper, must be still shaken up."

Tubs turns from his dead horse and takes Pepper's reins. Leading the horse up the embankment, the two head home. Watching Tubs go through the onlookers, silent, with slumped shoulders, it's the saddest sight Dominic has ever seen.

A heavy-set man, bushy beard and a deep voice people obey, points out the man in the auto, telling him to go get the police. Yells at his two strapping boys sitting on his own freight wagon, laden with goods for the shipyards.

"Get down here boys and we'll give this man a hand."

Turns to Dominic and steps closer with outstretched hand.

"Names Maurice, people call me Moe. Sorry about your horse there, lad. Poor animal. From the look at those legs, it's a blessing you not having to put him down."

Dominic shakes the man's hand, thanking him profusely. Doing their best to ignore the dead animal, they all start on the wagon. The boys, both over six feet tall, start on the mess of the load strewn about the ditch. Moe and Dominic unload the wagon. The police arrive about the same time as Fred Banting with his Clydesdales. It's late afternoon by the time the wagon is back on the road, reloaded properly by the kindness of a dozen strangers. Banting's strong animals are yoked to the load. Duff has helped the police with Jack and the carcass is taken away.

Tubs has to replace Jack but waits several days before going to visit the breeder where he bought him. Returning with a two-year-old mare, the same color as Jack, different spots on her coat, different stripes on her lower legs, the same rebellious nature, he names her Jackie.

Dominic neglects his scrap book over the summer; working, frolicking, sneaking kisses with Gloria, going on picnics and to the movies on the weekends. It's the end of July before he gets back at it. Duff is off to Carmichaels for Esmerelda's birthday party. Ivan is away with the Garfields visiting family in Dundee, Gloria is suffering from girl sickness, and he's all alone. Taking out the cut outs and making some glue, he adds a butter and jam sandwich to the necessities and settles own on the couch.

Early in the New Year HMHS Britannica, sister to the Titanic, is launched from the Harland & Wolff shipyards in Belfast.

In February Charlie Chaplin stars in his debut movie, Making a Living. Five days later his character, The Tramp, is introduced to moviegoers.

March sees the invention of green beer to celebrate Irish festivities.

In April the United States occupies the port city of Veracruz, Mexico, with over 2000 sailors and Marines to enforce an arms embargo when Germany attempts to unload weapons.

In May the RMS Empress of Ireland, an ocean liner, collides with a Norwegian collier and sinks in the Gulf of St. Lawrence with the loss of 1012 lives.

In June Archduke Franz Ferdinand of Austria is assassinated, initiating the July Crisis and World War I.

CHAPTER 2

Duff and Ivan are sitting on the stoop at Duff's house, chatting. Both are wearing light jackets, the sun is at its zenith and the rays that penetrates the oak trees in front can't coax the temperature any higher than 59 degrees even though it is the middle of August, the fifteenth actually. Ivan's hands are telling a story and Duff rubs his beard while listening with amused wonder. A few birds, mostly wrens and bullfinches, dart in and out of the branches, their trills and calls sounding bossy or plaintive. Water still drips from the inner leaves when disturbed. The last drops of the previous three days of intermittent rain and gray clouds are hidden from the sun. Everyone is outdoors to bask in the rare sunshine. The earth's perfume escapes from the drying lawn.

Ivan had come over on the ferry earlier today to meet Dominic for the matinee at the theatre only to have Duff tell him that Dom had an emergency with Tubs that morning but would be back soon, probably by dinner time. Duff invited Ivan to sit with him and wait and asked him about his kites. After the latest kite story, they are quiet for a few minutes. Ivan has his face in his palms, elbows on his knees. Duff is leaning back on one of the posts that hold the porch roof. Pearl jumps up from the side and places a dead mouse at their feet. Duff grimaces in disgust.

"Get that outta here now, Pearl, go on!" says Duff.

"Yuk," says Ivan who jumps up as if the mouse will rub some of its deadness on him. Pearl has other things on her mind and runs behind the house. The humans can deal with the dead rodent; it's a gift after all. Duff lifts the mouse by the tail, flings it across the fence to his left where it lands in the middle of his neighbour's lawn. The cantankerous old Miss Abigale can have it. Ivan knows of the ongoing feud with the old lady next door and chortles at what Duff did. Ivan sits back down.

"Have you talked Dominic out of signing up?"

Duff's happy face changes to a disgruntled look and he starts to rub his beard again.

"Ach, I've got him thinking, and I threatened to tell the recruiters his real age if he tries anything."

"Aye, but you know how stubborn he can be."

"True, but he's too young, too young to go off to war. War's crazy anyway. Austria, Germany and Serbia are all a boil and he thinks he can defend the kingdom's honor. He's agog at the call for volunteers to make up Kitchener's Army, the new British Expeditionary Force."

Ivan is nodding in agreement. He leans back on the post opposite Duff. He's not worried about signing up and they're not making people go. He's too short anyway, not that the army or navy is looking for twelve-year olds who look as if they're still ten. Not old enough to know the gory side of war, he thinks only of soldiers shooting guns and fighting bad guys.

"Still, though, it must be exciting to be part of something so big… so important. Will we be safe here, Duff?"

"Oh yes, Ivan, we're way up north on one of the greatest nations in the world. Our navy is at least as big as France's or Russia's, certainly Germany's. The army is another question though, with most of our regular army posted in our colonies. That's why the government is calling for volunteers. I just wish he wasn't so eager."

The two are interrupted by Tub's large wagon turning the corner at the end of the street. Ivan runs to the picket fence that lines the front of Duff's property with the trees.

"Here he comes now."

Duff sits forward, elbows on his knees, hands clasped, smiling at Ivan's zeal to see his friend. He thinks of how wrong he was in trying to keep them apart, proud of Dominic's ability to see good in others.

"What movie are you two hooligans off to see?"

Ivan turns to look at Duff.

"It's a Charlie Chaplin movie, and I bet its real funny."

"Well good then. I'll go get lunch ready. I expect he'll be hungry;

they left early this morning."

After washing up and a shave, since Duff told him the fuzz on his chin doesn't look good and that women like a clean-shaven man or a beard of course, a bite to eat and an explanation of the broken door they had to fix that morning at the drugstore where someone broke in last night, Dominic and Ivan set off for the theatre in Govan. Heading for the trolley, Ivan is yakking but can see that even though Dominic is trying to be enthused about the movie, his friend has something else on his mind. He notes not just Dominic's freshly shaved face but also his new jacket normally reserved for Sundays. Equally as odd is that there has been no usual banter of armies or Germany, which is all he talks about. And Dominic has that look on his face when he thinks really hard, his mind is busy.

"What's going on Dominic, you're not listening to me."

Dominic regards his companion with a sheepish grin. Hands shoved in his pockets, he stops and stares at Ivan with questions in his eyes.

"I've just got a lot on my mind, Ivan."

"What? What's going on?"

Dominic puts his hand on his friend's shoulder.

"I have something to tell you, Ivan, and I need you to keep it a secret, at least for the next few days."

"Sure, Dom, you know I wouldn't say anything you didn't want me to."

"I'm not going to the movies. I'm going to the recruiter's office in Glasgow and I'm going to enlist. Anyone who's not working and some who are, are being taken. The feeling is that we will be at war soon, I want to do my part."

Ivan shrugs the hand from his shoulder, upset and worried.

"Why would you do that? Everything is fine here. Some say the war won't last. Why give up all the good things you have to go get killed. And you're not old enough anyway, so why bother? You know Duff will be against that, said he'd tell on you if you're too stupid to save your own skin."

Dominic starts walking towards the trolley stop and Ivan reluctantly follows.

"Be that as it may, rumour has it that the recruiters are turning a blind eye to young men. Besides, it'll be too late once I've signed the papers."

"What about Gloria? Won't you miss her? What if you get killed?"

"I already told Gloria and even though she says the same thing, she knows I need to do this. There's more to an army than soldiers, Ivan. I know how to build and fix things. The army will need people like that. I can help."

Ivan's jutted chin and sarcastic voice express his opinion.

"Aye and sure, the Germans will see you with your hammer and not bother shooting at you, knowing you need to build things. Well I'm not going with you!"

Ivan stretches his steps to hurry away from Dominic, not wanting him to see the puddles in his eyes. Dominic is surprised by the flurry and tone of the words.

"Oh c'mon, Ivan, I want you to come along. I'd like to have a friend with me. I'm a bit nervous. Please?"

Ivan swallows, tries not to blink and turns back to Dominic, who has stopped. They stare at each other. Hanging his head, Ivan doesn't want to let his buddy down even though he doesn't agree with his actions.

"Okay, then, but I'm not happy about this."

"I understand, and thanks," says Dominic.

It takes them almost forty minutes even though Glasgow is only a couple of miles from Govan. A trolley through Govan and Ibrox lets them off a hundred feet from the river crossing. They walk the Albert Street Bridge across River Clyde towards the Glasgow Greens. Dominic knows from the small talk at Carmichael's that the recruiter's offices are near here. The boys ask a passerby and are directed three streets to the east and one up. The glass front on the office has a poster of a British soldier dressed in uniform: green, multi-pocketed, leggings, black shiny boots, a rifle at his side, short hair and a stoic face. Dominic lights up when he visualizes his own face in the same uniform. Ivan is shaking his head. A glass and wooden door on their left has a large red sign that says "Enter."

They are standing in front of the large window when Dominic turns to his friend and passes him several coins.

"Go get yourself a copy of Comic Cuts and a soda at the drugstore across the street and I'll meet you there."

"You don't know how long you'll be."

Dominic stares through the large window at the few people milling about. He can see three desks occupied with army green on the inside and brave men on the other. Two people, from the same crooked nose and freckled faces – obviously brothers – are sitting in the waiting area.

"There's no line-up today and only a couple ahead of me. I don't think it will take too long."

Ivan pockets the change and starts to cross the street.

"I still think you're dumb to do this."

Dominic only grins, watching Ivan turn his back and slog across the street. Heading towards the closed door, Dom gulps down his nervousness and enters. Men are being processed as quickly as possible. Dominic only waits for fifteen minutes before he's sitting in a hard backed chair in front of a plain wooden desk. The recruiter has a waxed moustache, large ears and a friendly smile that makes Dominic think about magicians. He nods at Dominic while pulling a sheet of paper from one of his drawers.

"Full Name?"

"Dominic Daniel Alexander."

"Birth date?"

Dominic falters, he forgot to figure out what year he would've been born in if he is eighteen years old but recovers soon enough.

"February 25, 1896."

The recruiter never even pauses as he asks the remaining questions, Dominic has passed the first line of questioning. The man adds a red check mark in the top right corner.

"Take this sheet young man and go through the side door to my left. Check in with the corporal at the desk and one of the doctors will examine you, won't be too long."

Dominic heads through the office all grins, imagining what Gloria will think of him when he has a uniform. He feels a quickening in his chest, thinking of her pretty face and how much he'll miss her, especially when she smiles. She always makes him laugh with her silly jokes and naïveté. A prickling of doubt steals along his neck. Mind flashes of the faces he could possibly never see again if something happened to him: Duff, Ivan, Adairia, Tubs, all his friends. His reflections are interrupted by a brisk, lets-get-this-over-with voice.

"Your paper, please!"

Dominic steps close to the desk, same dull brown as the others, filled with a typewriter and papers, to pass the acceptance form to the clerk. The man is quite plump, lazy eyes and a strip of greying hair curls about his ears and just above his neck, otherwise the head is totally void of hair. Black braces over the olive shirt that has to be extra, extra large doesn't appear in posters. Eyeing the document, eyeing Dominic, the rotund officer points with his chin to a waiting alcove opposite them.

"Join the others, young Alexander, it won't be long."

There was emphasis on the word *young*. Dominic is aware that the man thinks him not old enough and stands straighter.

"Thank you, Sir, just want to do my part."

The corporal waves him off. He's heard it before.

The alcove is a recessed area opposite the clerk's desk, three boring pea green walls open to the reception area. The area smells like ink and tobacco smoke. Two posters calling for heroes face each other to create a little colour. Hard-backed wooden chairs right, left and centre, maybe fifteen or so, hold four occupants with only the brothers sitting next to each other. They're sharing something funny and the other strangers are listening. They all go quiet when Dominic approaches the uninviting chairs. He takes in all the faces when he tries to decide where to sit. The two men are directly in the middle along the back wall, an older man is in the first chair on the left and a surprise is in the first chair on his right. Floppy bangs and an untrusting stare make him think of a piece of wood whistling in the air. The boy that tried to knock him in the skull and the fink that bullied Ivan. Dominic falters as he draws near, talking low.

"What are you doing here? Where's Fatboy? Don't you need him to back you up?"

Dominic's uncharacteristic aggression is met with aggression. The chair slides into the wall when the young man jerks to his feet, meeting Dominic eye to eye. Dominic rears back into a defensive stance, his fists ready at his side. The older man scrapes his chair when he rises to get out of the way. The brothers elbow each other and grin like hungry foxes eyeing a rabbit. The corporal stares bug-eyed at the pair, startled by the furor. Trying to wrest himself from the chair that is too narrow, he wants to control this situation. It takes a moment before he can waddle into their midst. The standoff is a show of dominance, neither wanting to back down from nor begin a confrontation. Large hands push them apart and the voice is almost a boom.

"Get your arses back in the seats. Save that spit for the Huns."

Glaring at Dominic he points at the seat in the back corner.

"You, sit there and watch your mouth. You act like that in the service and you'll be doing garbage detail for the duration of the war."

The other hand points to the displaced chair.

"And you Mr. Sensitive, get that chair back in place and sit."

Obeying the officer's commands, both are leery and regard the other with aloofness. A nurse stands just behind the corporal and calls out a name. James Arthur MacIver is next. Still eyeing Dominic, his rival stands. He speaks directly to Dominic though everyone can hear.

"Some people change you know. I just want to do my share."

The magic words. The compulsive feeling that speaks to many men when their home is threatened. Dominic frowns, feeling guilty as he watches MacIver follow the nurse. His previous encounters don't leave him prepared for what he sees. It does, however, fortify his reason for being here. They share a common bond. His thoughts return to the poster and him in uniform.

*

Ninety minutes later the longest face exits the building. Dominic holds a paper in his hand with large letters stamped in black across the middle of the page. Rejected! Ivan is leaning against the brown brick façade across the street, from where he can watch the front door. Even from there, he can see disappointment etched upon Dom's brow. He guesses things didn't go well and a smile takes up most of his face. At the edge of the street, Dominic just stares off into the west where the sun is setting and the light magnifies his frustration, the curled brow and scrunched lips. Ivan takes his hands out of his pocket, brushes his bangs from his forehead and saunters over.

"So what's up? You look like a kid that lost his favorite toy."

Dominic hangs the paper at his side and starts walking back to the river. His long legs are almost running. Ivan hastens to catch up to him.

"I failed the medical. My limp. Doctor says the injury didn't heal properly, and would be easier to break again. Said I wouldn't be able to finish basic training. Told me to go home."

Ivan has a difficult time not expressing his delight. He is slightly behind, intentionally lagging, and yes, he sees the limp, ever so slight. He remembers the broken leg and how Dominic walked a little different at first but it seemed to go away. The sagging shoulders and following silence make him feel bad for his pal. Wanting to cheer him up, Ivan catches up to remind him of the positive things.

"Gloria and Duff will be glad, don't ya think? And you'll be able to build that arbour you designed for Adairia and her flowers. Didn't Duff say he's going to teach you how to set diamonds? And you can make me a bigger sketch of Lilly."

Dominic stalls when they turn the last corner halfway to the bridge. This street is busier, with stores and offices and apartment buildings. Traps and an automobile, carts and wagons clutter the roadways. People are shopping and hurrying everywhere. The buzz overhead is a cacophony of humanity. Stepping aside to let two men pass, Dom places his arms akimbo to glare at Ivan, who rears back from the sudden anger. Dom's almost a head taller and looks down at Ivan's silly smile.

"What are you grinning about? I wanted to be a soldier. They tell me I'm not good enough. I'm upset. I want to be upset; there's nothing to be happy about. I'm just as able as anyone else!"

Ivan stares up at his friend's eyes, the bravado in his voice is not evident.

"You're better than good enough to us Dominic and that's what count's, right? I know you're disappointed, but maybe you can help in other ways."

Dominic exhales sharply, trying to control his feelings. The building they are in front of is a bank and on a corner. The left side is all red brick with an extra door and many windows. It stretches back to a warehouse. Facing west, the sun is half set and people moving to and fro have long shadows. He leans back against the warm brick. Even knowing Ivan is right he still feels sorry for himself. Ivan steps off to his side, letting him sift through his thoughts. Several minutes go by. Dominic sighs and pushes himself off the wall.

"There's nothing I can do about it, so let's go tell Duff. Guess who I saw in there?"

Ivan is off the wall in a flash, the square face beaming.

"And after can we talk about that sketch of Lilly?"

CHAPTER 3

The only Hallowe'en decoration at Duff's house is the two jack-o-lanterns sitting by the porch uprights bordering the stairs. Yellowish light flickers from the wicked smile and triangle eyes carved through the thick rind. Tallow candles burn inside with black smoke escaping from vents in the top. The neighbourhood is quiet, no masked children about, only pranksters at this time of night. The celebrations won't be over until midnight, yet an hour away. Only a few stars and the aura of a half-moon escape the scattered clouds. The darkness around the house is teased by the wavering flames in the pumpkins, a thin breeze causing them to frolic. The inside lights are off, there is no one home.

Earlier Duff and Dominic had passed out cookies they made that day for the trick or treaters. They didn't need many; most of the youngsters that visited were the neighbours, kids they knew. They each wore cloth masks with eyes and mouths crudely cut out. Using his pencils, Dominic had colored them up with funny brows and oversized noses. The silly faces and gentle teasing made the children laugh except for a few of the wee ones who started to cry. When the sun finally gave up, nighttime sent them all home to gorge on the collected sweets. Two hours ago Duff and Dominic locked the door and walked to Carmichaels. Tonight, regulars receive their first drink on Mr. Carmichael as their treat. Duff would have to be dead to pass on a free drink. He hurried his nephew out of the house.

Three shapes slither about the oak trees in front of Miss Abigale's house. The old lady has been in bed since sundown. Not a light is evident. The porch, much like Duff's, only wider, is darker than the night around it, a deep recess that hides any movement. Paddy O'Connor, his two cronies, Spike and Geraldo, use Hallowe'en night as an excuse to do mostly tricking. Far from their home turf in Ibrox, it's the first time they've cruised in Govan. No one knows them here. Their idea of fun is disrupting dried up flowerbeds or a fire and debris in the middle of the street, something silly and senseless.

They can see no lights on in the house and are trying to figure out what they can do. A parting of the clouds causes a sliver of moonlight to glare at the ceramic pot beside the front door. Dried stems of some type of plant are all that remain sticking out of the dirt. Geraldo, the skinny Italian kid, says he can sliver up the sidewalk where there are leafless bushes lining each side. Paddy tells him to wait for the moonlight to disappear. He comments on the wavering light from next door, commenting that they should douse those lights first. He sends Spike, the smallest of the bunch to go see where the light is coming from.

Five minutes later, Spike tells them of the two pumpkins with grinning faces and candles burning inside with no other lights on anywhere. Candles, pumpkins, darkness are all the ingredients needed for mischievous boys. Paddy sends Geraldo to overturn the pot on the porch but to wait while he and Spike get rid of the candlelight. When the two culprits are crouched by the trees in front of Duff's, Paddy tells Spike to take the one on the left and toss it in the yard while he goes for the one on the right.

In a rush, the two boys race to the front steps. Spike grabs his pumpkin and heaves it on the dried grass in the yard. The pumpkin splits in half and the candle flies from the center with its flame being extinguished as it tumbles about the yard. A wisp of dying smoke follows Spike as he runs back to the safety of the trees. Paddy grasps the smirking pumpkin and espying small rocks at the corner of the house, he sidesteps to the side, raises the gourd to shoulder height and slams it to the ground. The impact causes the orange head to split in three large pieces that fly against the side of the house and into the flowerbed. The candle rolls among dead stalks of the tall flowers planted in the spring. The tiny flame clings to the waxed wick and does not die. Crisp brown leaves, dead and dry are clumped about the bases of the hollow stems. They invite the tiny flame to join them.

Paddy, Spike and Geraldo race on to the next street. At Duff's place, one after the other, crumpled leaves, baked in the southern sun, burst into flame to race up the stalks. Lower leaves feeding the upper ones and the soft hairs on the stems send them even higher. The hollow stems are excellent fodder for an enthusiastic fire. The ten or so that lie crumpled against the shingles on the house are soon burning eagerly. Cedar shingles on this side bear the hottest sun and the paint is curled and worn along the bottoms of the first half dozen rows. The sudden heat grips the lower shingles as the flames nibble at the dried wood. Finding a foothold in the old cedar, they get a taste of the curled paint and the fire feasts.

*

Dominic has his uncle propped up with the man's arm wrapped around his neck. With his other hand behind Duff's back, he steers him toward the tram to get him home. It's the last one of the night. It'll be close to midnight before they get there, with Duff so wobbly. Old Carmichael isn't stupid, a free beer lures some coin when the boys decide to drink up. At least, Dominic thinks, his uncle can walk; he just needs a bit of direction. Duff sings his favorite old song, aloud and off key.

"Let's drink to our next meeting, lads…"

When they get to the stop, they only wait five minutes before they can board. Swinging Duff into the first vacant seat, which is at the front fortunately, Dominic flops into the seat beside him. Duff goes limp and hangs his head, which is soon rolling to the rhythm of the streetcar. It's not often he gets in this condition; most times he can stagger home on his own. Dominic sits up with a groan, looking back at the retreating street. He forgot Duff's jacket at Carmichaels. The weather has been oddly warm and he had left it in the booth. It is likely one of the Carmichael girls will put it away for him. He'll have to get it tomorrow.

Before he sits back, he looks out the front window to see a wavering light in the horizon. The man sitting behind him notices it too.

"Something burning, I think. Hope it's not anyone's house."

Dominic eyes the stranger, a shorter, worried looking man with a missing tooth, his stare fixed on the light over the roof tops.

"Me too, that would be terrible."

Aye."

Dominic tries to pinpoint the location of the fire by orienting himself to their house, another five minutes on the tram and a fifteen-minute walk north. His flesh goosebumps when he guesses the two are very, very close. Scared now, he shakes his uncle on the shoulder, wanting him more alert. They'll need to hasten.

"Duff... Duff, get ready to get off, we have to hurry."

Lifting his woozy head and trying to focus is difficult. Duff grips the seat with both hands to prop himself up straighter.

"What did ya say, lad?" Rubbing his head now. "And talk gently."

Pointing to the horizon, now on their left.

"The gentleman behind me says the light flickering out there could be a fire and I think it is near our house."

All Duff hears is "fire" and "our house." A few blinks, rub on the beard while trying to concentrate on the glowering in the darkness to the northeast. It brightens and fades, rises and falls, something on fire for certain. He's not too far gone as to not recognize the location. He's several steps ahead of Dominic when the tram stops. Sober enough to keep upright on an uneven path, he heads to the next street up. Two over to theirs.

"C'mon Dom, that might be near our place."

They are rounding the tip of the street knowing the fire is close, they could smell it hundreds of feet away. Duff is fueled by alcohol, outrunning his nephew by several paces and the first to come to the realization of what is burning. He is stunned to a standstill. Eyes agape, unbelieving. Hands waving at it to go away. Dominic pants at his side, catching up. Overcome by shock at what he witnesses, he can hardly catch his breath. He leans close to his uncle, looking for and giving support.

The back and the further end of Duff's house and the front corner are all ablaze, flames lick at the roof. Smoke rolls from the heat, visible in the firelight. Twenty or so people mill around the front. Everyone is watching the house burn. Men in uniform keep the crowd away. A team of horses stand patiently in front of a bright red tank, ladders attached to its side. A hose lies coiled on the ground, its nose dripping to form a puddle where it lays. A statuesque man, wide of shoulder seems to be directing people away from the house. All Dominic sees is the sketches he made of Gloria, his own private horde and his scrapbooks. Duff sees his whole life and cries out running towards the house.

"No, no... not me home, not my wee house."

120

Dominic hustles along, breaking through the crowd behind his uncle. Neighbours eye them with pity and sorrow. Disbelief shades many brows. Eyes are fearful and glued to the tragic moment. Duff reaches the tall man to tug on the shoulder, startling him from his directing. Miss Abigale, John and Donna from across the street, and the Blacks from next door crowd in around him murmuring their collective regret and consolation.

"Why aren't you fighting the fire, man? Why is no one throwing water on it?

The man with the chief's insignia on the front panel of his hat looks down at the bearded face, places a firm hand on his arm. His voice is full of sorrow.

"It's too far along, Mister, there is nothing we can do, the back and side are burning, and it's inside now."

Duff is barely listening, he's imagining the family photos, his papers upstairs, his clothes, and his furniture all burning, all in flame. He attempts to move to the front door, which is not afire. Nor is the left side of the house. Before he can get two steps, both Fire Chief Polansky and Bertrand Black get a grip on him, one by the shirt and the other by a black wide brace, to yank him back. Everyone is scolding him at the same time. He wrestles with them to no avail, subdued by strong arms. He hangs his head and moans out loud.

Dominic is standing off from his uncle staring at the flames, not able to imagine what it will be like with everything gone, only the clothes they are wearing left. People talk around him but he blanks it out. He thinks of his desk, the one Tubs made and his friends paid for. Again, the many sketches he drew of Gloria, the moments he captured her pretty likeness in his mind. His heart breaks when he watches his uncle relent to the horror in front of them, his head hanging, the men each holding an arm. He moves to Duff's side, offering the big man an arm over the shoulder. Dominic has grown a few inches taller than Duff. He doesn't know what to say. Duff looks him in the eye and shakes his head, no hope there. Before either can say anything, someone shouts out.

"Oh no… look up there."

All eyes go to the dormer in the middle of the roof. The one at the end of the hallway where the stairs enter the second floor. On the window sill is Pearl. Her grey paws scratch at the window, her wide toothed mewl can't be heard through the glass. Out of the knowing silence comes a scream.

"No, not my Pearl too. I've got to save her; we can't let her burn."

With the words hollering in the night, startled onlookers gasp as Duff tears free of the crowd to rush towards the front door. Dominic tries to follow, to turn his uncle away but is restrained by many hands with admonishments to not be insane. It's too late to halt Duff and he barges through the front door and runs into the burning house. Women go on their knees to pray. Several men attempt to run after him but they also are held back from their madness by one of the fireman or others from the crowd.

When Duff breaks through the door, smoke rolls out to greet him, blinding him momentarily, invading his lungs, causing him to cough. Reaching for his handkerchief, he holds it to his mouth and tries to see where the stairs are. A wisp of fresh air from the open doorway pushes back the smoke and the stairway is briefly visible ahead of him. Flames leap through the hallway from the burning kitchen. Duff rushes for the stairs, going by memory. He stumbles on the first step, reaching out to hold his hand against the wall and is shocked by the heat.

The other room is engulfed in flame, not yet broken through the central walls of the house but it has caught between the floors, the upstairs beginning to ignite. Pearl has already died from smoke inhalation and Duff's efforts are in vain. The floor supports have been totally eaten by the flames — dried wood and sawdust for insulation burn rapidly with intense heat. The main support on the right side is mainly embers when it snaps in half. Duff is halfway up the stairs when the upper floor and wall collapse directly upon him. The weight breaks his neck and he dies instantly; the fire will claim his already dead body.

CHAPTER 4

Duff's funeral is a week later. Closed coffin. The rain starts early in the morning, dropping like pellets of sorrow over the crowd standing around Duff's final resting place. Dominic is the only one without an umbrella, not caring that the rain is soaking his new suit. Drips of water run down his face indistinguishable from the tears that run freely. He didn't realize how much he loved his uncle until the moment the two workers began lowering the coffin in the ground. All he can think about is Duff laughing at his own jokes, how much he loved good food, how much he cared about those close to him.

After the mass, the pallbearers carry the polished wooden coffin from the vestry to the cemetery behind the church. Many of the mourners elect to stay in the church hall to talk about and grieve over their friend. Lunch and refreshments will be served soon. Adairia, Tubs, Jackie Boy and Esmerelda, Dominic, Geoffrey and Molly, David and Beulah, Shirley and Edwin and Carol and Terry, June, Gloria, Ivan and the Guthries, Mary and Pascal and Brodie accompany the coffin to the empty hole in the ground, along with Reverend Anderson to say the last words during the internment. The women are sobbing; the men are watery-eyed as well.

When the Reverend finishes his benediction, he moves to shake hands with the people gathered around. A boy holds a wide black umbrella over the reverend's head and follows him from one mourner to the other. The last to receive his sympathy is Dominic.

"Remember, Dominic, that I will always be here if you need to talk. I know how much he meant to you."

Dominic brushes the damp hair from his forehead and nods at the minister, afraid to speak, uncertain still of what to say.

"Also Dominic, I am very aware of how much you meant to him. He often spoke of how proud he was of you and what a fine young man you are becoming. He loved you. Dominic, don't ever forget that."

Adairia moves to Dominic's side. She can see the turmoil in his young face, the sagging of the shoulders. Bearing her own lose, she holds her umbrella so that it covers both of them. Dominic is still wordless, unable to understand why his uncle is gone. She directs her comment to the minister.

"Thank you, Reverend Anderson. Thank you for your kind words and the beautiful sermon. Come Dominic, we should go to the hall and be with our friends."

He gently pushes her away.

"No, no I can't do that. I can't be around anyone right now. This hurts...it hurts too much..."

Dominic tears from her side and runs towards the street. The mud in the lane slops around his shoes and water from the puddles sloshes behind him. The group watches him as he hastens from them; their hearts go with him.

After lunch, the rain stops. Tubs is concerned about Dominic, who hasn't returned after his sudden departure. He remembers watching the lad run off heading towards Duff's house and decides he will try there first to find him and bring him back to his house, where he has been staying since the fire. Tubs catches up to Dominic, who is standing in front of the picket fence staring at the rubble and ashes that were once his home. When he gets nearer, he can see the glistening in the lad's eyes, the sunken cheeks and pale skin. Tubs has a hard time dealing with the loss of his best friend knowing that Dominic's feelings run deeper than his own. He remembers the shy boy from three years ago when he came to live with Duff. Unsure of himself, no family around. He was able to witness firsthand the bond that developed between the two. He knows he needs to be tough if he's going to be able to help Dominic through his time of grief. Approaching from Dominic's left, he stops close by to stare at the burnt timbers and the skeleton of the wood stove that lies crookedly in the middle of the debris.

"It's no good coming here so soon, Dominic. It's nothing but a pile of bad feelings."

"I... I know, Tubs, but I can't help it. I miss him so much. I don't know what I'm going to do and what's going to happen with this mess. Who's to look after it?"

"I don't know all the answers yet either, Dominic. We have to give this a bit of time and have our heads straight to see what can be done. I'm sure Duff has likely made arrangements; it'd be like him to think ahead. We should head home now and you can get some rest."

Dominic nods, knowing Tubs is right. They turn to head back up the street when a carriage pulls into the lane in front of them. A man is driving a covered trap and a single bay horse pulls him hurriedly along. Raincoat, white shirt and navy tie suggests someone of importance. Pulling up alongside the pair, the man slows the trap to a stop. Eyeing Dominic, he directs his comment to him.

"Are you Master Alexander? Dominic Alexander?"

Dominic is baffled by the appearance of a well-tailored man he doesn't know but recognizes him as one of the members of the congregation during the funeral service.

"Yes, I'm Dominic Alexander, and who might you be, sir?"

The man has a look of authority in his countenance. Wisps of greying hair cover a balding head. A goatee claims his chin; round black-framed glasses shelter the deep-set eyes. He speaks with a heavy brogue with his words sounding educated. Getting down from the trap, he loops the reins around a hook on the front panel. Extending his hand, he walks over to Dominic.

"My name is Godfrey Young. I am an attorney-at-law and I have been directed specifically to ask for you in the event of Duff Alexander's untimely death. I waited until what seemed like an appropriate time, but with the funeral over, it is imperative that I speak to you as soon as possible. I looked for you earlier only to find you absent from the reception, but Adairia suggested you might be here."

Dominic takes the hand; the grip is solid. Dropping his own to his side, he eyes Young suspiciously and then at Tubs questioningly. Tubs has his own hands in his pockets and just shrugs his shoulders. Dominic points to his companion.

"This is Cornelius MacGregor, a good friend of my uncle's."

"Aye, but you can call me Tubs."

Young looks Tubs up and down as if his girth is evidence of the nickname.

"Pleased I'm sure…ah, Mr. Tubs."

"Nae, just Tubs, I'm not much for that mister business."

"Yes, certainly."

Turning his attention once more to Dominic, he points at the remains of the house.

"Terribly sorry about Duff and the house, of course."

Dominic is curious why he or Duff would need a lawyer.

"Thank you. What's this about Mr. Young? How do you know my uncle?"

"Well to answer the last question first, your uncle Duff has been an acquaintance of mine for some time. Many years ago, my wife inherited a rather large diamond from her parents and Duff designed the ring that carries the stone and which she wears to this day. We, of course, have all our precious jewellery cared for by your uncle's skilled hand. But I also know him as his attorney and this is the reason I am visiting you today."

Young pauses for a moment, taking off his glasses to wipe the dampness from them with a handkerchief from his coat pocket. Dominic moves back to lean on the fence.

"For what purpose, Mr. Young."

"Well it's rather a private affair, and I suggest we meet at my office at your earliest possible convenience. Would tomorrow morning at 8:30 a.m. be acceptable?"

Dominic knows that there is nothing stopping him from the appointment but feels weary and lost over the events of the last week since the fire. Arranging for Duff's funeral, buying new clothes, finding a place to stay. He's not sure of his own future and doesn't want to have to make any more decisions. Young notices the hesitation.

"It's regarding his will, and he's made you the executor. There are items that need special attention and should be acted upon as soon as possible. I must add that it is in your best interest to see that Duff's wishes are carried out. Shall I see you in the morning?"

Dominic is surprised by Duff's instructions. He doesn't even know what an executor is. More curious now he nods affirmatively.

"I'll be there Mr. Young."

"One other thing. Do you have any form of identification that may not have been lost in the fire?"

"Yes, I have a copy of my birth certificate that I carry in my wallet."

"Excellent. Be sure to bring it along when you come to the office."

The lawyer smiles, passes Dominic his business card, jumps back on his trap and flicks the reins.

"Good day then, gentlemen."

Dominic turns to Tubs.

"Wonder what that's all about?"

"Well, you'll know more tomorrow, won't you? C'mon now, lad, let's get back to the house."

CHAPTER 5

The law offices of Young, Young and Pollack are in Glasgow. At 8:15 a.m. Dominic is standing in front of the large frosted glass doors with gilt script proclaiming what is behind them. Wearing the same jacket and pants he had on yesterday, he decided to skip the tie. He tossed and turned all night like a landed fish, worrying what this visit would entail. Over a late snack and discussion, Tubs assured him it was only a matter of settling Duff's estate and that Dominic should be flattered that he was chosen with the trust to do what needed to be done. It didn't make him sleep any better.

Dominic's Adam's apple bobs a couple of times as he pushes open the wide door to step into a brightly lit foyer of darkly stained wainscoting and cream walls. A reception desk sits near the back wall with a stodgy faced lady commanding it. Her hair is neatly arranged in a bun and her glasses cover eyes that look as if they don't trust anyone. Another gulp and Dominic approaches. She looks up with the weakest of smiles, eyeing the young man before her.

"Welcome to Young, Young and Pollack. How can I assist you today?"

"My name is Dominic Alexander and I have an 8:30 appointment with Mr. Young."

"And which Mr. Young would that be?"

Dominic has forgotten the man's first name but retrieves the card from his jacket pocket.

'Um…Mr. Godfrey Young, ma'am."

She points to the upholstered chairs in the corner to her left.

"Please have a seat and I'll tell him you are here."

"Thank you."

At exactly 8:29 a.m. a comely young lady, the exact opposite to the barrier at the front desk, approaches Dominic, asking him to follow her as Mr. Young will see him now. Dominic is more than eager to follow her after she flashes him a very large and welcoming smile. They proceed along a hallway decorated with the same wainscoting and colored walls festooned with lawyerly art of judges and robes until they reach an open door at the end with more gilt announcing the occupant. She stops and points to the portal.

"Please, go in and have a seat and Mr. Young will only be a moment."

Dominic nods his thanks and enters. There are two identical chairs in front of a large oak desk. Both are burgundy leather with creases around the seat. Dominic takes the one on the right and sinks in. He only waits a few minutes until the click-clack of shoes on the hardwood floors announce someone approaching. A voice enters the doorway behind him.

"Good morning, Master Alexander."

Dominic attempts to stand to greet the lawyer.

"Good morning, Mr. Young."

"No, no, young man, remain seated and I'll just get your file here."

Godfrey Young removes his navy jacket to hang it on a dark hall tree to the left of the desk near wooden file cabinets. His shirt is starched and gleaming white. The black suspenders and red striped tie fall over a round belly. Digging in the top drawer of the closest cabinet, he removes a manila file folder that contains a wad of papers and lays it flat on the desk. The only other items are a silver fountain pen and a pot of ink. Taking the seat behind the desk, he swivels it into place while opening the file.

"Well I must say, Dominic, that this is certainly a first for me. There has never been another estate that has been left to manage by one so young. You're not yet fifteen, are you?"

The question is rhetorical and he continues.

"I had to apply for a special dispensation so that nothing could be contested due to your age. Judge Farwell has kindly signed off on this and there should be no problems with the division of your uncle's estate. Now as the executor..."

Dominic's confusion is evident in his face when the lawyer looks up at him while he speaks.

"Do you have a question?"

"Yes, thank you, but I don't know what an executor is."

"Ah, yes, well an executor, simply put, is a person appointed by a testator which is a person making a will, and in this case your uncle, to see that the terms of his will are carried out. Do you understand?"

"I think so. I have to make sure that what Duff wants done gets done after he dies?"

Young smiles at the simple version.

"Yes, that is exactly what it means. Now let's carry on. It really is very simple and all laid out in black and white so that there are no mistakes. The only problem, if it can be called that, is that a few physical objects he wanted given to specific individuals have perished in the fire so those items will not be available, of course, and can be eliminated. So let's go over the details."

The next half hour changes Dominic's life. Duff Alexander was careful with his earnings. He could've stopped working on his fiftieth birthday three years ago and lived off the funds he had saved even if he made it to a hundred. The Bank of Scotland has an account made out to Robert Alexander that contains a balance of 5,366 pounds sterling, a small fortune. Dominic is flabbergasted and speechless. During the explanation of fees and disbursements of a share to his friend Adairia and the church, Dominic asks intelligent questions and shows great insight, impressing the lawyer. In addition to the property, he would be left with 4238 pounds. He stares open-mouthed at Mr. Young, who slides several documents to his side of the desk and offers Dominic his fountain pen.

"The new deed will be drawn up shortly and seeing as how this is Tuesday, you can pick it up at the end of the week. So, all you have to do is sign on the line at the bottom of the top two sheets and I'll witness them. You can take one and the death certificate I've obtained on your behalf to the bank and they will set up your new account. I advise you to use this wisely young man. This is a chance at a good life that not many of us have been given. I would also, if I was you, keep this sum to yourself or you will suddenly have more friends than you bargained for."

Dominic sits straighter, taking the pen and staring at the blank line on the document. Overcome by his instant wealth, he is astonished by both his uncle's inheritance and that he loved him enough that it would be coming to him. He wants to cry but stifles his feelings, too embarrassed to be so childlike in front of Mr. Young. With the words swimming in his vision, he places his neat signature along the lines pointed out and passes the pen back to the lawyer. Still speechless, he slides back into the seat to stare at his feet.

"Excellent! Do you have any questions?"

Dominic shakes his head. Rising from behind the desk, the lawyer shuffles the papers, separates two sheets from the pile and asks Dominic to follow him. Walking to an open area at the end of the hall where several ladies and young men sit at desks in an open area, he hands the papers to the young lady who had escorted Dominic in.

"Bonnie, will you please fold these and place them in an envelope for this gentleman."

Turning back to Dominic, he once more offers his hand and speaks low.

"During our short time together young man, I can see why your uncle decided to trust you with his legacy. If I can be of further service at any time, pleased don't hesitate to drop by. Good day, Dominic."

Finding his tongue once more, Dominic grips the proffered hand tightly.

"Thank you, Mr. Young."

Tucking the envelope in the side pocket of his jacket, Dominic leaves the law offices a very rich man.

CHAPTER 6

The second week in November is chilly. For several days a steady drizzle hangs in the air like an invisible barrier, cold and clinging to clothes and skin alike. Stubborn gray clouds curl about the sky over Kilwinning threatening rain, the people hoping it would come and be over with. The lane up to the Watson Farm is muddy and rutted when Dominic approaches it in Tub's trap. Dusk is close. Dominic's stomach complains, not having been fed since breakfast. He hopes he's in time for supper. He chose Pepper to bring him here, the horse more docile and friendly. There is no one in the yard when he approaches, but he sees Lilly in the window, beaming and waving. The front door opens when he stops the trap close by. Mary's delight at seeing her brother causes a wide smile. She wants to be positive, knowing how hard he is taking losing Duff.

"Oh Dominic, I'm so glad to see you."

"Me too, Sis. I should've let you know I was coming, but I'm hoping you can put me up for a few days."

"Of course, Dom. You can put the horse in the last stall. Granda is gone overnight with the wagon. Pascal should be home soon, and you can join us for supper. Hope you're hungry!"

"Aye that I am. I'll be in shortly."

Dominic gets Pepper out of the rigging and leads her into the last stall near where Brodie's horses are kept. He places fodder from the mow into the trough and fills the water bowl. Using the old curry comb, he whisks the dampness from her hide while she feeds. After placing a heavy blanket over her flanks, he heads to the house. A blast

132

of warm, welcoming air hits him when he enters, as does little Paul, with Sheila doddering right behind to greet their older brother. Sheila moves around her brother with her arms up, wanting to be hugged. Paul wants him to watch him spin the top Pascal bought him for his birthday. Both are talking at once. Mary is setting the table and Lilly is stirring something in a large pot on the stove, provoking a delicious aroma of herbs and vegetables. Hellos and hugs follow.

After he hangs his coat up, Dom removes two brown paper bags from the pockets. He gives one to Paul and one to Sheila. Together the three move into the living room while the ladies prepare the evening meal. In Paul's bag, there is a wooden boat with a house sitting on top. The roof is removable and underneath is a bible verse about Noah's ark printed in black ink. Paul is all excited by the painted window and bright red roof. Sheila's bag contains small wooden animals that will fit inside the ark. An elephant mother and a calf, a cow, a pig, a giraffe, a tiger, a dog and a cat, and a man and a woman. All three are lying on the floor in their new pretend world. They play undisturbed until Pascal enters a half hour later. Dominic joins the three in the kitchen after Pascal has changed and cleaned up.

The conversation around the table varies, Pascal's new job at the sawmill, what Brodie is up to, Mary's cleaning work, the miserable weather, politics and the Labour Party, who is sick and which neighbours are in trouble, but they never talk about Duff. Lilly asks about Ivan and the three older ones tease her playfully. The smaller two are silent at the table, eating their meal quickly so they can get back to the ark. After the meal, the ladies clean up while Dominic and Pascal chat. Soon Mary and Lilly join the two men with cups of tea and a plate of gingerbread cookies. When there is a lull in the conversation Mary asks what all are thinking.

"What are you going to do now, Dominic?"

No one has brought the subject up, but all three wonder. Dominic is looking down at the teacup engulfed in his hands. He thinks for a moment before replying. Tired of decisions, he can't bring himself to the most important one. Looking up at his sister, she sees the wavering in his eyes.

"I don't really know Mary. I miss Duff terribly."

Pausing, he takes a deep breath, waits out the lump in his throat. The nodding of their heads say they understand.

"I can't go back where the house was. It's too painful to see everything gone and be reminded where our uncle died. I've already sold it."

Dominic pushes the cup away and sits straighter. All are sitting forward, concerned and curious.

"Perry's Jewellers has offered me Duff's job, and the money is quite good. Tubs said I can work full time with him if I want and has offed me a room in his house. I could start my own handyman business if I wanted to. The Carmichaels have offered me lodging, as has Adairia. Everybody has been so kind."

Lilly and Pascal are deep in thought, shy of offering advice. Mary's about ready to burst with pride and pity for her younger brother, smarter than the older ones, so much kinder. She wishes she could carry some of his sorrow.

"What does your heart tell you to do, Dom?"

Dominic ponders that. A burst of childish laughter erupts from the living room, the wee animals, the boat and their imagination create an amusement and the glee infects those at the table. Dominic smiles at the merriment. Lilly smiles also while she regards Dominic. Her voice is honeyed and hopeful.

"You could come back and stay with us again, Dominic."

This strikes a funny chord with Dominic who has never even considered such an event. He laughs easy, causing the others to giggle too.

"No, I don't think so, Lilly, but you're so sweet to offer... even without asking Granda first."

They all know as loving as he may be, there isn't really enough room for Dominic, and Brodie wouldn't be averse to telling him so. That gets a round of hee-haws. The laughter feels good for a moment, but the weight of the future summons them back to reality. Dominic frowns, and the others wait for him to speak.

"I'm not even sure if I can go back to Govan. There are too many things that remind me of Duff. And I..."

Dominic cannot hold it in anymore. Too embarrassed to let them see him cry, he thrusts his chair back to rush from the kitchen, not even closing the door when he hastens down the lane.

Lilly gasps. Pascal stares at the empty chair not knowing what to say. Mary rises and moves to action.

"Pascal, get up, grab his jacket and go after him."

"Me? What would I say. I don't know your brother as well as I should."

"Don't say anything. Just take him his jacket; it's still raining. Now go on. Lilly, make some more tea. I'll get the little ones to bed."

She watches Pascal don his own jacket before grabbing Dominic's off the peg. Her eyes are kinder than her voice.

"Just be a friend, Pascal"

He nods and leaves. He sees Dominic's silhouette halfway down the lane, leaning against one of the fence posts. Walking briskly, he looks up at the sky, which has finally opened to cast a faint light. He's glad the rain has finally stopped. A southeast breeze is moving the mist away and the air feels slightly warmer. It's still cool and he can see Dominic shivering as he approaches him.

"*Tiens, mon amie*. Put your jacket on if you want to stay outside."

Wordlessly, Dominic takes his jacket, rubbing at his eyes with his inner elbow. He puts it on and buttons it in silence. Pascal regards Dominic with respect, trying to put himself in his place. He waits. Pulling the collar tightly around his chin, Dominic stares off at the night light from the split in the sky, a few stars visible now. He stands to the right of his brother-in-law.

"I suppose you think I'm a small kid crying like that."

Pascal is looking at him directly.

"*Non*. I think you are a man. It is nothing to be ashamed of. I know how much he meant to you. It only makes sense that you should mourn."

Dominic warms to Pascal, finding comfort in his presence, having the same feeling of enjoyment as when he met him for the first time at their wedding and the few times since.

"Thanks, Pascal. Yes, he meant a lot to me. I remember going there with my mam and was worried about living with a man who had no kids of his own, but he welcomed me and I learned so much from him. Now I'll never be able to repay him."

Pascal is shaking his head.

"That's not true, Dominic. If he was a good man like you say, then you can be a good man too. That is all the repayment I'm sure he would want. No one can take the good memories away from you… not even a fire."

Both are quiet for a moment. Dominic has his hands in his jacket pockets and leans back against the post. Pascal tries a half smile, hoping he has said the right thing. He can't help but worry about the sad face he sees. Dominic stares at him.

"I still don't know what to do. I can't really go back, Pascal."

"I understand, Dominic. Hey, maybe you should go to Canada."

The remark is meant as a joke, something to perhaps lighten the moment, but Dominic looks back at his brother-in-law with a serious mien, surprised by the suggestion.

"Why would I do that, Pascal? What's there for me?"

Pascal grins.

"Well I was only joking, of course, but you know, Dominic, if you could afford it, my home town is a beautiful place and perhaps a vacation is all you need. I remember when you told us about being rejected from the army and how bad you felt… and now you have this to deal with. The war is raging in Europe. Canada is involved and sending many men, there will be many jobs available if you decide to stay. I mean look at me. I came to visit and fell in love. Who knows what a different shore may hold for you."

Dominic's interest is piqued. He hasn't considered moving away, but the lure of a new beginning has him all ears.

"Tell me about your home, Pascal."

"Ah, Dom, if you could see the sunrises over the Atlantic, the long sunny days of summer…"

Pascal is smiling and the hands are going as he describes the shores of eastern Canada, the cities of New Brunswick and especially his hometown of Cocagne.

"…and the people are genuine and friendly, Dom, and the girls are so beautiful, all dark-eyed brunettes with a little native thrown in from their ancestors."

"Does everybody speak French?"

"*Non mon amie*. Everywhere there is the English. Only small communities and most of the older people in them speak only French. Not sure if anyone would understand you anyway with the way you silly Scots talk."

Their laughter is genuine and comfortable. Dominic is imagining the life in another country, watching the sun rise over the water all pink and orange like Pascal described it. He likes the image.

"Thank you, Pascal, for being my friend. I'm going to take a little walk and nothing personal but I'd like to be alone to think."

"*Oui,* Dom, take all the time you need. Mary will have the couch made up for you when you are ready."

Pascal pats his friend on the back, winks at him and returns to the house. Dominic walks slowly towards the road. He spends an hour walking and thinking. Getting comfortable with the idea of heading to Canada. He worries about leaving Ivan and Gloria, especially Gloria. By the time he returns to the house, the sky is clearing and a near full moon is exposed to light his path. He has made up his mind. His rushes the last steps towards the house to burst in on Mary and Pascal sitting at the kitchen table.

"I know exactly what I'm going to do. I'm going to Canada."

CHAPTER 7

There are many tearful goodbyes. The news of Dominic emigrating to Canada has swept through the small group of his friends, at first in disbelief and amusement as a young man confused, but when confronted, he assures them that this is what he wants and needs to do. He wants to visit the east coast first before he decides where he might live and start over. Especially when he shows them the ticket he purchased for a berth on the *SS Missanabie*. The ship was built in Glasgow and is owned by the Canadian Pacific Line. Her maiden voyage was in September from Liverpool to Montreal. Her last trip of 1914 would call on the port of Halifax, Nova Scotia, before carrying on to New York, and Dominic would be on it. He was tempted to buy a first-class ticket, but Duff scolded him in his mind that a third class would get him there just as well and he'd save the difference.

The ship is set to sail on December 28 and will take almost a week to make the voyage across the Atlantic. Dominic has purchased a steam trunk, which is packed with his new clothing and mementos collected by those saying goodbye. He's decided to buy new tools when he arrives in Canada. Christmas is spent at Tubs' house, where Dominic has been staying until he leaves. He has already said farewell to his family in Kilwinning. Pascal has written the names and addresses for a couple of his friends and his parents in Cocagne. He left them a cloth bag of shillings before he left. The money, which equals a year's pay for either Brodie or Pascal, is to be divided by six, with an equal share to be given to his Granda, Mary and Pascal and Lilly, with the last two shares kept in the bank until Paul and Sheila are older.

There are no sketches this year at Christmas but modest gifts to remind them of him. The gifts he receives are small personal things. On December 26, a small going away party is held for him at Carmichael's and the only one of his close friends who is not there is Gloria. She doesn't want him to go and refuses to be part of the celebration. Ivan arrives early with his adopted parents and sticks to his side all evening. Dominic promises him they will spend the next afternoon together at one last movie before they part. He also plans to see Gloria in the morning if she will let him. She was not pleased when he told her his plans and had stormed off in tears. When the night ends a collection is taken up for him and the pot of money is considerable. People guess, but no one knows of Dominic's windfall.

The last evening he is in Scotland, he spends with Tubs. Long into the night the two of them talk of Duff and their ups and downs for the last three years since they've known each other. Before they go to bed, Tubs brings from his bedroom a large gift box with the J P McInnis Haberdashery logo of a hat and umbrella on the top. Tubs happy eyes express his pride as he passes the box to Dominic.

"Got you a little something to remember me by, Dominic, and a place to put your papers. I'm right proud of ya… and I know Duff would be too. I'll miss ya lad, but I wish ya all the best."

His flushed face portrays how touched Dom is. Unable to speak, he lifts the cover to expose sheets of white tissue. Gently lifting the folds, he finds a hand-crafted leather satchel. The embroidered edges and stitches are precise and the leather dyed a soft tan. A braided strap and brass clasp are the only adornments. Profuse with thanks, Dominic promises Tubs he'll keep it forever.

Rising early, he washes, shaves and dons his best clothing, black wool pants, white shirt and the new winter jacket and boots he purchased because Pascal has told him to expect snow, more than he is used to here. He has to be on board the ship by midnight and Gloria is the only one he hasn't said goodbye to. His heart is heavy. He tells himself that he will return for her someday; and as difficult as leaving is, he is determined to go. He thinks he has to let her know how he feels. All the time they've spent together has mostly been in the company of Ivan as the three have grown close. There have been only a few brief moments when they've been alone, usually with the scrapbooks. Their kisses and groping have been immature and uncertain.

The Carmichael's home is on a slight rise overlooking River Clyde. Today is Wednesday and there is no school. The weather has been typical with little snow, but this year alone there have been eighteen days of rain. Today the temperature hovers around six degrees Celsius but with a clear sky. When he knocks on the door, he is holding two gift-wrapped packages. One is for Mrs. Carmichael and the other is for Gloria. He made them both. Celia Carmichael has a deep-seated faith and her gift is a polished, simple cross made out of silver. The bale that will slide over a chain he knows she wears is engraved with her initials on the front and his on the back. All the family work in the business and Gloria is the only one home when she answers the door. Surprised at his appearance, she is inwardly pleased but doesn't want to show it.

"What are you doing here? I thought you were leaving today."

"No, I only have to be aboard the ship by midnight and I wanted to say goodbye."

She tries to close the door so he won't see the tears that are forming.

"Well, goodbye then!"

Jamming his foot in the door, he pleads.

"Please, Gloria. Just give me a few minutes. You know how much I care about you, and I can't leave with you being mad."

She regards him with new interest.

"If you really cared about me, you wouldn't go. And you've never told me you love me."

Red faced, he admits what is on his heart.

"I do Gloria, very much."

"Well then say it."

"I… I love you."

"Then why are you leaving?"

"Let me come in, please. I can explain it all to you and I have something for you."

She stares at the eyes that are soft, the long bangs hanging on his forehead that are always there even when he brushes them away, and his lopsided smile that melts her heart. Seeing the gifts in his hands, she is curious. Opening the door wider, she gestures at him to enter.

"Come in then and I'll make some tea."

They spend the next hour on the couch in the living room, a brocaded hard back sofa that is not easy to get comfortable on. She remains misty eyed as he shares the loss he is experiencing, the reluctance to return to his former life without Duff. He finishes the conversation with Pascal's words of the new country and what it could mean for him. He promises he will write often and hopes that she will too. Thinking he should go soon as he still has to make it back to meet Ivan at the theater, he tells her what is on his heart as he passes her the gift.

"I'll get settled, Gloria, and if you will still have me, I'll return for you. Here, I made this for you."

She is wide-eyed both at the hope of his return and the small package tied with a red ribbon. Undoing the neat knot, she keeps the silky cord in her palm. The precise folds of the shiny silver paper, when untethered, open like a paper flower on each end. The box is made from oak, carved by Dominic's own hand, the cover tightly fit. The lining inside is black velvet and upon it lies a gold locket. A perfect heart. Delicate swirls are etched around the edges. Gloria's initials, in French script, are in the centre, GC. The clasp and hinge are strong but feigning delicacy in their creative design. Gloria holds it tenderly in her palm, only her smile is grander than her gaze.

"It's beautiful Dominic, it's the most beautiful thing I've ever seen... and you made this for me?"

Dominic can see she's pleased. Basking in her sincerity, he colors and nods. Coaxing her on, he points to the narrow slit in the side of the trinket.

"Open it. Just poke your thumb nail in the groove."

Lining her nail properly, she applies pressure and the locket opens. She gasps at what is revealed. Inside is a starfish carved from a silver ingot. The five points fit precisely inside the open heart. Gloria loves starfish, feverishly collects pictures and stories about them. Glancing inside the front portion she sees his initials, DA. Looking up at him, she feels overcome and faint from this gift of love and how hard he must have worked at it. Dominic sees her falter and reaches to wrap her in his arms. Still clutching the box and gift she rests her head on his shoulder, her voice barely a whisper.

"Thank you, Dominic. Thank you so much."

She wants to tell him what she really feels but holds back because he is leaving. That she now knows for certain. She had hoped to dissuade him but sees the hope in his face, the way his eyes shine when he speaks of a place called Cocagne. As much as she hates the feeling, her heart tells her he will never come back. She can only give him one thing. Urging herself up, she shifts on the couch to face Dominic. Leaning in to kiss him, she playfully bites his lip before snuggling closer to his ear.

"Hold me tight Dominic. Kiss me."

Dominic and Gloria are almost fifteen. Both have been mistaken for youths much older than they are, both physically developed, both on the border of adolescence, both on the fine edge of first love. Their hearts are pure, their desires undefined, their actions inexperienced. Leading him to the couch in the back parlor, in a fit of wonder they grope awkwardly at each other. Dominic is already erect from desire. He draws her close and she responds to his hardness by pushing herself close. Their kisses are sloppy and needy. Dominic can barely contain himself. He slides a hand toward the hem of her skirt, wanting to touch her. The motion stops when the slamming of the front door ruins everything, including his erection.

"Damn!" is all Gloria says as both scramble to arrange their clothing. A voice from the entryway calls out. It's Carol, home from the bar.

"Gloria, where are you? I brought dinner. Mam wants you to come help because I twisted my ankle and I can hardly walk on it. Terry drove me home."

Adjusting her waistband, Gloria shouts out.

"I'm in the far room Carol, showing Dominic my new Eleanor Potter book. He wants to borrow *The Lost World*, is that okay?"

"Aye, for sure. Bring him out, there's enough food here for him too."

Quieter now, she holds Dominic close.

"I'm sorry, Dom, so sorry."

"It's okay, Gloria. Probably better this way. I might not have been able to leave."

"I was hoping for that. Dominic, before we go out, do you really love me? Will you come back someday?"

"Yes. Will you wait for me?"

"Forever."

They kiss deeply once more. Grabbing the copy of *The Lost World* from the shelf she hands it to him.

"Leave this at Tub's house and I'll pick it up sometime. Write as soon as you can with your address."

The lovers join Carol in the kitchen. Dominic politely refuses the food and reminds them he has to meet his friend Ivan. Holding Gloria's hand tightly he says good-bye, watery eyes and silence make the parting poignant.

The movie goes fast, the buddies spend time joking and roughing each other up, ignoring the finality of their time together. They talk about Lilly and Ivan gushes at the very mention of her name. When they finally must part, Dominic promises to write and expects Ivan to do so as well. He returns to Tubs and joins his mentor on the carriage with his trunk locked up on the back. Dominic boards the ship at 9:20 p.m., has his luggage stowed, presents his ticket, is guided to the third class rooms. He's asked his friends to not come and see him off, says it would be too emotional, so he's alone but not sad. He is carrying a book he bought about the English colonies and the Canadian section is marked with a dog-ear. Going to the railing he views Govan from on high, the lights twinkling in the frosty air as if saying farewell. He can't wait to step on shore in a new country.

*

War rages in Europe on the last days of 1914. The Germans have taken Lodz and the Russians retreat to Moscow. Neither force obtains a decisive victory at the first battle of Ypres. The Royal navy defeat a German Squadron at the Falkland Islands. Australian and New Zealand troops arrive in Cairo, Egypt. The *Christmas Truce* on December 25 takes place on the battlefields of Europe when the Germans and the British stop fighting and exchange gifts and play football. It will never happen again and the event becomes legendary. The *SS Missanabie* sets sail for Canada.

1915

Dominic shares a third-class cabin with two boys and their father. There are four bunks, a washbasin, four towels and four hooks on the wall for their jackets. He has the bottom bed on the right. There is no privacy. Only the youngest of the three speaks English. During conversations over the time it takes to reach Canada, Dominic learns that the family are Russian Jews who refuse to don the uniform of the Russian Army. Many of their relatives live in Germany. Trying to remain neutral while the country is at war causes backlashes resulting in the deportation of many families. Unable to acquire a room together, the mother and daughter are in another cabin on the level above. While the Zaslavsky family spends most of their time together, Efim befriends Dominic. When Efim is not needed as an interpreter, he and Dominic spend part of their days on deck or roaming the ship.

The *Missanabie* had left port at 7:00 a.m. sharp. Once out of the River Clyde, the ship sails through the Firth of Clyde with little disturbance, but upon reaching the Atlantic Ocean, the seas are in an uproar from strong winds out of the north. Huge swells rock the ship and batter the hull like mad spirits for most of the night. Dominic's first twenty-four hours are mostly spent in bed, frightened by the motion and bouts of seasickness. Besides missing Duff, battling with his loneliness and wondering whether he made the right decision, he worries about the large amount of money in the belt under his clothing. While in bed he keeps his shirt on, and changes it every other day in the privacy of a locked stall in the shared loo. It doesn't take long for him to realize that the Zaslavsky family are not thieves. By midafternoon of the second day, the sea levels and remains calm for the duration of the sailing.

Eating, sleeping, playing cards with the Zaslavskys, wandering the decks with Efim, all relieve the monotony of the cruise; otherwise, Dominic keeps mostly to himself, not venturing in unfamiliar quarters. Occasionally the older brother, Naum, joins them. The days are long and uneventful in most cases, until the day before they arrive in Halifax, when they sail through a field of icebergs in the early afternoon. People are out on all decks. The sun is the brightest it's been, with wavelets glimmering towards the horizon. He likens the sparkle to diamonds he's seen while working with Duff.

Ever since the *Titanic* hit an iceberg almost three years previously, every captain that sails these waters reduces speed, taking every precaution to steer clear of the bergs. One of the sailors tells him if he looks northeast and imagines fifty miles in a straight line, he'll be roughly where the *Titanic* sank. Dominic is enthralled and will tell the story many times of the blinding white mountains floating in the endless sea and of having sailed near the deep graveyard of the largest ship in the world.

SS Missanabie's first voyage broke the speed record for an Atlantic crossing but this trip was delayed by the icefield. Reaching the east coast of Canada, the massive ship bypasses McNab's Island with its two lighthouses and sails towards George's Island, directed by another lighthouse on the eastern shore. The guiding lights on the islands will soon be blacked out by the threat of German submarines. Having picked up a pilot, she enters the port of Halifax on Sunday, six days after it left Scotland. Situated on the southeast shores of Nova Scotia, the city grows around a deep, ice free natural harbor. Entering the narrows that separate the cities of Halifax and Dartmouth, the ship docks at a wide wooden wharf.

The third of January is promising. No wind but frost clings to anything not moving. With the news that they would be arriving roughly around 5 a.m., Dominic has already packed the new trunk he had purchased before he left and is standing on the upper deck watching the coastline. In the east a ribbon of light hints at clear skies. The stars fade behind city lights that line the shores. Dominic tightens his collar to keep out the cool air and pulls his new hat down tighter. Tall silhouettes of grain elevators can be seen on the Halifax side close to a brightly lit rail yard that is bustling with activity. The movement of men and material needed in Europe does not regard nighttime as any reason to slow down. Many ships can be seen at anchor as Canada equips for war. On her return voyage the *SS Missanabie* will carry Canadian troops.

When Dominic's feet touch the rough tarred planks of the wharf, the tip of the sun blinks over the horizon, casting a sharp light hitting him directly. Stepping aside, he turns his face into the glow, head back, and closing his eyes he takes a deep breath through his nose. A mishmash of scents: brine of the water, creosote from the thick boards he stands on, leather bindings and shaggy hides of the horses waiting with wagons, and slightly above it all is the aroma of bread baking. He listens. Hissing locomotives from a train leaving the city, porters and sailors securing the ship and accommodating the many passengers, neighing and snorting of impatient horses, the clatter of their hooves on the wood. He hears birds screeching as gulls drift overhead, laughter from the welcoming relatives and the clang of a porter's bell. His feelings of melancholy dissipate. He knows he made the right decision.

Opening his eyes, he directs his gaze towards the ringing from a hand drawn wagon holding passenger's trunks. He can see his in the middle of the pile. Two young Negro men in Canadian Lines uniforms are assisting the passengers in claiming their possessions. Their stiff round hats are as black and shiny as their skin. The larger man lifts and shifts the heavy chests as if they are mere suitcases. The smaller fellow is checking identification and searching for the claimant's property. A wide smile that exposes the whitest teeth Dominic has ever seen greets him along with an outstretched hand.

"Good morning, sir, welcome to Halifax. Could I have your ticket please?"

Dominic gives him his claim stub. His conversations with Pascal have familiarized him with the Canadian accent and odd words, and he understands the man clearly.

"A good morning to you and all, sir."

Only it comes out, "A guid morn tae ya an aw, sairr."

The porter stops for a moment to stare at Dominic, who spoke with a rolling brogue, which to the porter sounds like he's talking with a mouth full of food. The porter doesn't understand what Dominic said, but being accustomed to foreigners getting off ship who are unable to speak English, he nods his head and continues to smile.

146

Dominic notices the bewilderment in the man's eyes and realizes he didn't understand him. A moment of doubt creeps and he wonders if he'll be able to communicate with anyone. He decides he'll talk slower. The porter scans a group of trunks and finds Dominic's.

"Yes sir and …uhm, here's your trunk right here. Do you have a way to transport it, sir?

"Nae, I do not."

The smiling porter catches that and points to a group of men near the back entrance to the customs offices.

"Those men have buggies for hire. Door to the left of them is where you can get your paperwork done."

Dominic scratches his head at the word buggy, but when he sees what he thinks of as a trap he nods vigorously, thanking the porter who, with a salute, moves on to another passenger. He heads for double doors on the front of the building called Shed 21, smiling at the large sign hanging over the doorway – Welcome to Canada. At the Customs Examination and Waiting Rooms, three rows of people, five or six deep, are lined up in front of desks, moving snail-like but not stalling. Reaching to an inside pocket, he withdraws and unfolds a copy of his birth certificate. The people who sold him the ticket told him he would need it when he arrived in Canada. The one he carries is a lie.

When he decided to come to Canada, he took Tubs' trap to Saltcoats, where he obtained a birth certificate from the parish priest of the church his mother and father had attended. It has been artistically altered by Dominic so that the birth year reads 1896 rather than 1900. The customs people are swamped. A mere look at the birth certificate, a quick check of his luggage and all the forms are processed rapidly. He leaves the building an hour later with all the necessary papers to enter Canada.

Approaching the men with the buggies, several call out to him offering their services. Dominic catches a hint of his homeland in one of the voices. A middle-aged man is one of four, wider than the others, a bit shorter with red curls hanging below his tweed newsboy hat, much like the one Dominic is wearing. Focusing on the man's words, he recognizes the edge of the Scottish burr that, no matter how long a person has been assimilated, will never leave a native's tongue. Dominic grins as he talks loudly, doing nothing to disguise his heavy accent.

"Ah'll hire anyone yon can un'erstn me."

When the other three men hesitate and frown at the strange words, the gentleman with the curls steps up smartly, doffing his hat at Dominic.

"Ah can kin ya!"

Confirming that he was right, Dominic waves at the man, asking him to help. The two chat – introductions and where-ya-froms – while loading the trunk. Dominic pulls himself up beside the man named Seamus. Thick neat blankets cover the leather seat, very comfortable, and the transport is led by a sleek black stallion. The first thing he asks is when the next train leaves for Moncton.

"Ya just missed that one, laddie. Won't be another until five this afternoon"

Pointing to the west, he indicates the vaporous trail.

"If you look towards the basin, over them apartments, you can see the smoke from her engines, and she won't stop until she gets to Shubenacadie to take on passengers if there are any."

The driver sees the young man's face expressing disappointment.

"So, where are we off too?"

"Just give me a moment then, please."

Frustrated by having been so close, he is rubbing his chin, tapping the heel of his boot on the floorboard while he thinks. Part of him wants to stay in Halifax and explore for a bit, but he really wants to visit Cocagne first. He remembers the passion of Pascal's details, the rising of the sun, the mystery of Cocagne Island, the sting of the salt air, the abundance of seabirds.

"How far is it to Shubenacadie?

"About 40 miles."

"Can you get there before the train?"

Seamus lets out a breath through pursed lips, eyeing his horse.

"No, laddie, that's for certain, but I knows for sure that she waits in Bedford until the freighter from Montreal arrives, and that won't be for another hour. You could get a ticket and catch her there if you wants to take a chance."

"How much to take me to the station and then on to Bedford?"

Seamus looks Dominic up and down, clean clothes, nothing torn, not some refugee or stinking curry lovers he's carted out of here. Figures he must have a dollar or two.

"Ya look pretty young, you got enough money for this trip?"

Dominic sits up straighter.

"I'm not that young. Take after me mam and her side of the family; they all look young. I've got a bit of coin. So how much?"

"You carrying pounds sterling or Canadian dollars."

"Quid and pence and I've a wee bit of Canadian money I changed on the ship."

As much as he likes the Scottish lad, he's in business and watches for a way to make a fast buck.

"A quid then."

Dominic is brighter than the man gives him credit for and knows that a pound sterling is a little better than $5.00 Canadian. One of the stewards in the dining room is from Canada and during many of their conversations told him that good wages is New Brunswick are about $15-$20 a week.

"A quid? I'm not after buying your trap…I mean buggy. How about fifty pence?"

Seamus frowns at his passenger but realizes for an hour's work, fifty pence is a good sum indeed. He flicks the reins to get the horse moving.

"Well, no need to be smart about it, young man, but seeing as how you're from me homeland, I'll do it for that."

It's not far to the station. Pulling up in front Seamus gives Dominic directions to the ticket counter and tells him he'll wait for him. The agent suggests he should wait until the next train tomorrow but even though Dominic hates to lie, he explains a need to be in Moncton as early as possible for a pretend funeral and the agent reluctantly sells him a ticket on the train that has already left. He tells Dominic that he best hurry as he only has a half hour before the train pulls out.

The road to Bedford is dirt and well rutted, making the ride uneven and bumpy. It follows the railway tracks for a good distance as it heads around the basin. Traffic is heavy as this is the main artery leading in and out of the city, but Seamus looks for openings to pass the slower moving carts. The odd automobile scoots around also, looking for openings and scaring the horses. Seamus curses at the wheeled vehicles, suggesting nothing good will come from having too many of them on the roads. They smell bad and make far too much noise. Dominic grins as he remembers Tubs' similar statement last year when Jack was killed.

The sun has risen to coat them in its early rays, warming their backs and Dominic's spirits. He marvels at all the ships collected in the basin, which is a half a mile wide. Steamers and freighters are at anchor.

"What are those ships waiting for Seamus?"

"Well with news of German submarines being a possible threat, they sail in groups. These ones are likely waiting for a warship to take them across the Atlantic."

"Have there been any submarines sighted hereabouts?"

"Not yet but there is lots of talk of them. The news we hear is that the German Navy is tied up at their home ports by the British and that she has a fleet of submarines that can get in and out undetected. There's a lot of goods and men leaving here to help the people of England so I figure the thinking is that it won't be long before they make themselves known. The gov'ment is even rigging up a big net with bombs and such to string across the harbor at night to keep the pesky U-boats out."

Dominic is swallowing the new information, wondering if he might've been safer to stay in Scotland until this foolishness of war is over. The rest of the ride is quiet other than the clop of the heavy hooves on the road, Seamus whistling a ditty and talking softly to his horse. The sun is getting warmer, with clouds forming in the west. Dominic is perplexed by the lack of snow that Pascal had warned him about. He eyeballs pockets of brownish snow piled in corners of buildings and in the bottom of the ditch.

"I thought there'd be more snow here, Seamus."

"Aye, well, there is not a much right now as usual cause Halifax is right on the coast and we gets quite a bit of rain. There was a fierce amount of snow just after Christmas but there's been several days of rain lately so it doesn't stay long, but if its snow you're wanting, you'll be in for a treat when you get inland as Moncton gets its fair share."

Getting closer to the end of the basin, the road and tracks turn north and soon the caboose is visible not far from them. Within minutes, Seamus has stopped near the engine and Dominic has gone to see if he can find a conductor, seeking permission to get aboard. Maritime hospitality and a bogus dead uncle soon have the conductor and Dominic marching back to the buggy to fetch Dominic's trunk. Everything is stowed on board and Dominic is directed to an empty seat in the coach. Their timing is perfect for as soon as Dominic is settled a large engine pulling twenty shaky freight cars passes them so close that the trains are almost touching. The turbulence from the moving cars shakes the passenger train like a big bully and when the last of the cars pass, the train he is on is already moving. The rhythm of the rocking car and clacking of the breaks in the tracks lulls Dominic to sleep all the way to Truro.

CHAPTER 2

It's midafternoon when the train pulls into Moncton and Dominic takes in the view with the train cutting directly through the middle of the city before coming to a stop at the station. Waist high snowbanks define the roads and staging spaces. Fences, empty trees and electricity wires are shadowed in white from a light snowfall overnight. Crystals of ice sparkle from the lowering sun. Many buildings are posed at the edge of a river that looks like melted chocolate. Two tall ships with candlestick masts are tied to piers along the bend in the river where a large shipyard and other wharves jut out. Factories and brick smoke stacks score the horizon to the east. Many businesses line what seems like a busy street. The passenger the next seat over tells him it is Main Street.

During an earlier conversation, the gentleman had informed him that Moncton is a very busy city and growing faster than people can keep up with. If a young man is looking for a place to settle and to find a good job, there are fewer cities with as much opportunity. Dominic has not shared his plans with anyone, not even family back home, but he wants to be like his uncle and fix jewellery. But he is going to work for himself. Remembering to speak slowly, he reminds the gentleman a job won't be necessary.

"I've got plans all lined up, sir, and won't be needing to look for one."

Once Dominic disembarks from the train and collects his trunk, he leaves the station to be confronted with another clamor of men and buggies for hire. He eyes a fellow he guesses to not be much older than

151

him standing in the background with a weathered cart and a dark brown horse. He notices the dark wool pants that are baggy at the knees, the plaid jacket with a frayed collar, a felt hat that might've been a fedora when it was new, all of which tell Dominic the driver waits in the back with hopes for a much needed fare. Favoring the underdog, he waves to the young man, ignoring the bustle of the better dressed men with the fancy buggies. Something about the boy's bright eyes speaks to Dominic. A huge grin splits the round face when he sees Dominic trying to get his attention. Remembering the porter, he speaks slowly, but there's nothing to be done with his accent and he has to repeat himself three times.

"Hey there, can you give me a hand with my trunk?"

"*Oui* mister, I can."

Dominic is all smiles when he hears the Acadian lilt much like Pascal's and feels a welcoming relief similar to when he met Seumas that morning. The two return to the station to retrieve Dominic's things. They're not as chatty right away, with neither comfortable in Canadian English. Once on the wagon, the young man secures the reins in his left and extends his other hand.

"*Je m'appeal Dominic Bourgeois.* What's yur name?"

With his mouth a round O of surprise and a raised brow, Dominic Alexander pushes his hat back off his forehead and starts laughing. Unsure if he is being laughed at, Dominic Bourgeois glares at his passenger. His eyes are not friendly.

"You *tink dat's* funny?"

Dominic realizes the other Dominic thinks he is laughing at him.

"No, no… I'm sorry. My name is Dominic too. And that's funny."

Surprised and realizing he was wrong, the first Dominic breaks into a cheerful laugh.

"*Bein oui*, that is funny. Small chance of that, eh? But the better news is that folks call me Nick. That's easier, eh?"

The two share a chuckle over the coincidence. A good feeling flows between the strangers.

"So then, where would you like me to take you on this chilly day?"

Tightening up his collar once more, Dominic waves to the surrounding buildings. His curiosity piqued by the many shapes and styles of architecture. Large homes are mixed in with buildings housing businesses.

"Well, first off I'd like to go to a bank, and then I need a place to stay for a few days. I don't want the fanciest hotel in the city, but something nice. I'll pay you to wait for me, and if you're for hire for a time, I'd like you to show me around. Would that be okay?"

Nick's pleasure is evident in his rosy-colored cheeks. He rarely gets any passengers, and there isn't much work this time of the year for his transport so an all-afternoon passenger is good news. He points to a blanket neatly folded on the seat between them. Puffs of vapor escape from his lips when he talks.

"If you're cold you can use that. The Royal Bank and Wesley Hotel are close by. I'll wait behind the hotel and then we can do a bit of look-see."

"Good then."

Turning east on Main, the horse clops slowly through the muddy street, carefully stepping over the shiny trolley rails. In the distance, Dominic is admiring the arches on the train station and large columns when his attention is drawn to a grand three-story building to their left.

"What's that building?"

"That's the American Hotel, stayin' there a night can cost ya."

"It's a fine looking place, must be nice inside."

"I couldn't say, never been."

The wagon slows for the main train tracks that cross Main Street. Dominic stares down at the shiny rails as they traverse them.

"Are there many trains coming through here"

"Ah oui, there are as many as eight or ten a day. Some go to Shediac, Bouctouche, which are not too far, but they mainly take freight to the ships that moor there and then there's the ones from Nova Scotia and Montreal. Just this year, the line from Winnipeg reached us here in Moncton. Lots of stuff to help out in the war goes through here. If you look to your right where the foundry buildings are, you can see other tracks. The old repair shops used to be there too, but they burned down in '06. There are new shops out of the city to the west."

Dominic is bobbing his head in understanding.

"These tracks that we just went over must be a nuisance then?"

"Oh yes they are, but next year the city and the railroad companies are going to be building a subway and the trains will pass right over the road, can you imagine that? The railroad is sending a huge steam shovel to dig the hole and I can't wait to see it."

Dominic is thinking of the business he hopes to start and lots of work means money to spend.

"There must be many people working then?"

"Oh yes, lots. There's *beaucoup* industry here in Moncton. There's a cotton mill that I'll show you later. There's Salters shipbuilding behind us at the end of the western portion of Main. Two sawmills along the water. There are five wharfs, and they're all busy. There's a Lock company on Church Street. The new sugar refinery is almost finished. The railway. And much more."

A grand home with a wrought iron fence along Main Street catches Dominic's attention.

"Who lives there?"

"That'd be the Lutes family; they got some money for sure and the street beside the house is named after them. And across the road is the Minto Hotel. That red stone building down the street a stretch on the left is the new bank and the Wesley hotel is just a bit farther. I'll let you off and meet you at the hotel. Will that be all right?"

Dominic just nods, thinking of the money belt under his shirt and how he'll be glad to get it off. He doesn't completely understand Canadian dollars and cents yet, but the bank will set him straight. The rig halts across the street from the Royal, Dominic jumps down and waits for Nick to pull away. He has to wait for the trolley to pass as the bell clangs for the right of way. Lots of people are going about their business. The long dresses of the ladies are held up to avoid the red mud. The odd car puffs on by, and many rigs are transporting logs and other goods. Once on the other side, he enters the glass door and walks into the bank.

CHAPTER 3

It's a beautiful building. Dominic recognizes the coffered ceiling with patterned tin squares – which he estimates to be twelve to thirteen feet tall – that he's seen in other grand buildings. There are tall doors with hinged transoms filled with frosty glass. A short wall made of stained wood and topped with clear windows and openings separate the entry area from the rest of the offices. Tellers are standing behind the openings busy with customers. Dominic notices an empty space and walks up to the counter. A young lady with a flash of freckles smiles at him. Her curly hair reminds him of Gloria. He experiences a dull pang.

"Good afternoon, sir, how can I assist you today?"

When Dominic speaks of his money, he talks low, worried about privacy. He's a bit nervous and talks too fast.

"I'd like to open an account and deposit some money."

"Oh my, that's a pleasant accent you have, sir, but could you say that again a bit slower."

Red-faced now, Dominic feels the eyes of other patrons on him. He repeats himself slowly. The pretty lady nods in understanding.

"Oh certainly, if you'd like to wait a moment, I'll have someone help you."

Locking her cash drawer, the lady turns to one of the desks behind her and speaks to another woman. Pointing at Dominic, they both smile at him and he blushes again. When the teller returns, she tells Dominic that it won't be long.

"Miss. McKay will help you. If you'd like to go through that half door to your right, there is an empty office on the right. Just have a

155

seat in there and she'll join you shortly.'

Noticing there is nothing on her ring finger on the left hand, he nods.

"Thank you, Miss."

He moves through the short swinging door and finds the vacant office. The woman named Mackay is gathering some forms from her desk and nods affirmative when he points to the open door. Dominic enters and takes a seat in front of the plain wooden desk. The chair is wood also and not designed for sitting at great lengths. He only waits several moments before Mrs. Mackay enters and shuts the door. She has a welcoming smile, seemingly genuine. Her hair is short, revealing a high intelligent-looking forehead. The pink cardigan she wears complements her fair complexion. She reaches out to greet him with a well-manicured hand.

"My name is Linda. Mary, the young lady that served you, said that you would like to open an account with us. What is your name, please?"

Dominic takes off his hat and stands to shake her hand. Worried about his brogue, he hesitates between words.

"My name's Dominic. I know I speak odd to you so I'll not talk as fast. I'm not real sure what kind of an account I'll need to open."

Linda doesn't pause, understanding him clearly. There is no smugness in her voice, just a merriment in her eyes.

"Don't you worry about that, last name's Mackay, my Dad speaks just like you. He moved here before I was born and he still has the homeland in his speech. Well, let's get seated then Dominic and see how I can help."

After a brief explanation of Dominic's recent trip across the Atlantic and plans to move to Canada, he needs to change his money for Canadian funds and have an account he can access anytime and write checks on. She offers him several options, depending on the amount of his deposit. Some cost a nominal fee while others, if the deposit is substantial, the fees are waived. She skims over those, naive to his needs. She's aware of his youth, uncertain of his exact age. No worry lines trouble his eyes and they're bright with anticipation. He's taller than her, thin but not skinny. His callused hands suggest he's worked hard.

After several intelligent questions from Dominic, they decide on a checking account and a savings account.

"How much would you like to deposit, Dominic?"

Dominic waves a give-me-a-second finger at her and stands with his back to her. Unbuttoning his shirt around his middle, he tugs the linen money belt over his stomach. He opens the two snaps holding it closed. Retrieving the carefully folded 100-pound notes, he holds them away and one-handed, buttons his shirt up. Returning to his seat, he offers the wad to Miss Mackay, who regards it with an uncertain stare. She takes what she immediately sees as a large amount of money, the 100 note is enough to catch her attention. She recognizes and knows what a pound sterling is worth.

"I have more."

With raised brows she watches Dominic pick up his satchel. Opening the large flap, the leather squeaks. He removes a handful of coins followed by a loose selection of notes from the bag, more notes from his wallet and coin from his pocket. In a change purse from his jacket pocket he takes out folded Canadian bills and a dozen coins. Placing it all on the desk, he sits back, eyes agleam, a hard grin on his face. Pointing at the collection he says, "That's it."

Linda has unfolded the 100-pound notes while Dominic was digging the rest of his money from the bag and his pockets. As she did, she counted them as well. Doing a quick calculation of the exchange to Canadian funds, she is awed at the amount of cash the young man is carrying, so amazed in fact that she wonders where it came from. That, of course, is none of her business, but it is a rare occurrence to have someone she deems shy of twenty years old, an immigrant recently off a ship from Scotland, to possess such a large amount. When he lays the last of the coins on her desk and sits down, she doesn't want to be deceived by the innocence in his youthful glee. When Dominic takes his eyes off the money and looks up at the lady serving him, his smile disappears when he sees the questioning look on her face. Her earlier cheerfulness is replaced with a frown. Dominic waits a few seconds until he speaks.

"Is there something wrong, Ma'am?"

Linda forces a smile, Dominic notes that it is strained and worries he's done something wrong. Before he can ask again, she rises from her chair. With the flat of her hand she gestures for him to remain sitting.

"Just a moment, Dominic, there's someone I'd like you to meet."

Closing the door behind her, her hurrying footsteps fade back towards the other offices. Dominic sits back, staring at the money, and scratches his head. Only a moment goes by when the growing tap of footsteps approach the door. There is more than one set, the second is from someone heavier. Sitting up straighter, the thuds cause him some concern. He glances at the money, thinking he should stuff it back in his bag, when the door opens smartly and announces a portly, barrel-chested man in an impeccable vested suit. The look in his eyes does not say welcome to my bank. Even his moustache looks serious – stiff and curled on the ends. Approaching Dominic with hands clasped at his chest, he eyes the pile of money on the desk before speaking.

"My name is Leopold Van Geist. I'm the manager here at the Royal Bank. Linda tells me that you wish to deposit a large amount of money. While we value your future business, we are regulated by laws to verify the origin of larger deposits. It is also required that such a large amount be reported to the local police because of recent banking irregularities from profiteers. I will also..."

The rest of his diatribe is interrupted when Dominic rises to confront the man. His chair creaks out of his way. He's an inch taller but eye to eye. Dominic looks at Van Geist askance. The brogue is thick and full of disbelief.

"Are you saying my money is illegally gotten?"

Van Geist steps back, bug eyed and cowed from the unexpected aggression. He didn't catch the whole sentence but the word illegal caught his ear as did the tone of the request. He waves his slim hand in the air.

"No... no, I didn't say that."

"Sounds to me like you did. Don't know why it's your business where it came from. If my money and my future is not wanted here, I'm certain there are other banks in Moncton."

Seeing the manager is confused by Dominic's excited speech, Linda steps to the forefront. She sees that Dominic is astonished, misunderstanding the manger's precautions. She calms him by placing her hand on his forearm.

"Dominic, no matter which bank you go to, you have been in Canada for only a day, and it is a large sum of money. We have to follow the proper banking procedures. I'm sure there's a logical explanation."

The manager is happy to have Linda's input. Regardless of his usual gruff manner, he doesn't care for confrontations. Normally his position of authority carries him through most instances. Lacking that, he can't understand the young man anyway. Dominic nods at her and the bank manager too. They both see the shift in his countenance. A downcast look betrays Dominic's sorrow at the flash in his head of how the money came in to his possession. All he sees is the look on Duff's face when they sat at the table that night with his mother. He was eleven and Duff asked him if he liked to fish. It was the first time his uncle smiled when his mother was scolding him and trying to sober him up.

Reluctantly, he reaches down for his bag and places it on his chair. Upon opening it he retrieves a large white envelope that has worn edges and one narrower side has been cut open. Curled lips of different size documents poke out. He takes out a yellowish copy and searches for another one, thicker and folded in half. Taking it out, he unfolds it and passes it to the bank manager. It is the last will and testament of his uncle Robert Alexander.

"Look at the third paragraph on the second page, please. And here's my birth certificate."

Linda takes the identification and knowing he'll want her to, she eases to her manager's side to read the other document too. He turns the top page over, and they both read Duff's final wish. A red-faced manager refolds the document, scans the birth certificate, surprised Dominic is only nineteen. He clicks his heels and passes both back respectfully.

"My condolences, Master Alexander. I apologize for my unseemly approach. I meant only to maintain the bank's integrity as we are watched carefully by the banking commission. I'm satisfied that you are indeed the rightful owner of these funds. I welcome you the Royal Bank. Please call upon me personally for any financial advice. I'll leave you with Linda."

Gesturing for him to sit, Linda returns to the desk.

"I'm sorry about your uncle, Dominic. Why don't we sit down and start over? If you don't mind, I'll need to see your identification so I can fill out the forms. Would that be all right?"

Dominic understands she is only doing her job. He likes the way she makes him feel safe when they talk about money.

"Aye, let's do that then, please."

Thirty-three minutes later, Dominic is paused at the sidewalk in front of the bank. Replacing his hat, he gazes west along Main Street.

Earlier clouds have separated, letting rays of errant sunshine mark several of the storefronts. A sawmill across the street catches his eye. It has tall precise letters, P.N. LEBLANC, painted across the rectangular roof line propped in back by wooden braces. In front a horse waits with a four-wheeled wagon. Two men are standing in one of the open doors, shaking hands. The familiar smell of wood shavings and sawdust can be detected from where he stands.

A loneliness had followed him out the door after the reminder of Duff, but as he gazes at the people hurrying about, most smiling as if they know some happy secret, and as the ray of late afternoon sun shines on his face, he thinks of the new bank book he has in his bag. Besides the fifty-three Canadian dollars he carries, the little black book has a balance of $21,477.83. He can hear Duff admonishing him in his head to "be wise." He smiles at the thought and heads to the Wesley Hotel.

CHAPTER 4

Dominic hurries the two blocks to the hotel, a tall brooding building, across Main Street from the sawmills. The lumber yards are filled with bustling men, with heavy sleds and wagons pulled by teams of strong horses, with rough logs still covered with snow, and with finished lumber. Looking east, he can see a bridge that crosses a mid-sized gulf of reddish mud. There are a few buildings on the horizon, but the view is mostly empty space, dull in winter's clothing. Turning the corner, he sees Nick standing at the head of his wagon, whispering to his horse. The animal responds with soft snorts and head bobbing as if they're sharing a joke. He almost hates to disturb their rapport but Dominic is anxious to see the city and find a place for the night.

"Hey there Nick, I'm going to get a room for a night or two and then you can give me a tour."

"*Ah oui.* But you know, if you are going to stay here for a time, you will pay dearly for a couple of nights in here." He jerks his thumb at the building beside them. "I know a nice lady that has a room to rent and a week would cost you less. My buddy Donald moved out this past weekend. Clean house too. Only thing is she's kind of nosy, talks too much sometimes, but she's nice if you're nice. And she doesn't look too bad either. Interested?"

"Be wise," echoes again in Dominic's head. It was what he was planning on doing anyway.

"Aye, if you think it's a good place. I don't know anyone here of course."

"You'll like it. We'll go there after as it is not too far, only up Lutz

161

Street where we saw that nice house a while ago, the one you asked about. It's just up from there a stretch. It'll be dark early, so we can do a roundabout through the city first."

They climb up on the wagon; Nick stirs the horse to action, turning right on Main Street. Nick assumes that Dominic wants to know about the city and proves to be a knowledgeable source, talking about each business as they pass. A variety of businesses carry the name of the owner, W.F. Fergusson's, J.D. Creaghans, Peter McSweeney Company, R.L. Colpitts, and Henry Kirsch.

Continuing west, they avoid several autos that spin mud from their skinny wheels while belching foul-smelling odors. Dominic keeps the cart at an even pace, pointing out the larger structures or commenting on what he thinks is important to a newcomer. The Ford Dealership they pass with three identical black vehicles parked out front is owned by the mayor, Frank Robinson. The Lantic sugar refinery is supposed to be finished and operating this year. The company is even going to be making their own barrels at the factory next door, explains Nick. Driving to the edge of the city, they turn north.

It's not long before they're in front of the giant repair yards owned by the Intercontinental Railways. The hissing of an engine shunting cars can be heard in the background. Large buildings face them with tall doors that swallow the railroad tracks leading up to them. The clanging of large hammers and the high voices of workers can be heard even from where they sit. Nick has pulled the wagon over to the side of the street.

"They built this yard after the other one burnt in 1906 down by the Foundry. They only deliver freight there now and the station where I picked you up. This one repairs engines and boxcars and stuff from around the country. It's big, eh?"

"Aye, tis. Back home we got shipyards and they're very big like this too and many different kinds of ships, but I've never seen so many trains." Dominic thinks once more of his business intentions.

"There must be a lot of men that work here?"

"Oui, there's hundreds."

Flicking the reins, Nick signals for his horse to set a quicker pace.

"I'll show you our own castle."

"A castle, really?"

"Well, not really but it looks like one. It's a place for orphans the church built out on Mary's hill. It's got the same name, Mary's Home.

Don't know why they put it out of the city."

The journey has less stops as the sun sets. The air is getting chillier and Dominic has wrapped the blanket around his knees. With his earflaps down, his wool jacket and leather mitts, he keeps warm. Turning down Church Street takes them past The Lock factory, closer to Main Dominic points out the many churches. Turning left on Main, they continue to King Street, pass the Cotton Mill and its smoke stack and turn the wagon around at the hospital on King before going west again on St. George past the Aberdeen High School. It is mostly residential, but there are some businesses. They take a left turn on Lutz and stop in front of a two-story home with a wide veranda, the house is white with dark blue trim. A walkway is cleared through the snow and muddy footprints mark the four steps up to the front door.

Nick points to the small sign to the left of the door.

"That says O'Bannon's Rooming House. Just use the knocker, that shiny thing on the door. I'll wait for you and give you a hand with that trunk. Being Monday, Mrs. O'Bannon should be there. Her first name's Rosie."

Dominic jumps down from the wagon to hasten up the steps. He is almost overwhelmed with content. The city is bustling. People are friendly. He grins when he looks down at the large woven mat by the doorstep. The last *e* in *Welcome* and one corner are crusted with dried mud. The door is quite wide, solid wood with ornate panels and painted blue like the rest of the trim. A brass knocker shaped like a small hammer is in the center, a bit below eye level. Handling it with confidence, he raps three times. He waits only a few moments until it swings open to reveal Rosie O'Bannon.

Dominic has never seen so much red hair. Loose curls, thick with a few streaks of gray fall to the nape of her neck. They surround a face so perfectly round with reddish cheeks, Dominic thinks 'apple.' Only up to his chin, the next noticeable attribute is her full breasts, demonstrated by the button on her linen blouse straining at the threads. The next is the sweetness of her voice.

"Hello there, young man. Is it a room you be seeking?"

The eyes are not as sweet as the greeting and scrutinize him closely. She nods approvingly at the quality of his clothing. More welcoming is the look she sees in Dominic's eyes, the eagerness in his youth. Sensing the smile is genuine, she relaxes her defenses. Dominic remembers to talk slowly and try to straighten out his words.

"Aye, ma'am, I'd like to rent a room for the next month, maybe longer, if you have one available."

Rosie likes his Scottish tongue.

"A month, you say?"

"Aye, ma'am."

She looks over her nose at him. She doesn't want to seem too eager, and normally she like folks to stay for longer, but she hates an empty room. He looks decent enough and the Lord knows she gets some odd characters here. Seems a bit young, but so long as he's got money. Dominic likes the house, the inviting hallway and the warm, feminine scent of Mrs. O'Bannon, something like flowers. He reassures her with a broader smile and takes off his hat, holding it by his side.

"Could you tell me please what the rent would be?"

"I've a nice place here. You'll find the rooms and facilities quite clean, supervise it myself, I do. The rent is $2.50 a week, with the first two weeks paid in advance."

"Be wise." Dominic's more than happy to pay the ten dollars for the month but learned from Duff that money is not to be wasted and not to be flaunted it if you have it. Everybody's first offer is usually high.

"How about I give you the whole month in advance for say, nine dollars."

Now Dominic looks like an Alexander, the brown trust-me eyes, floppy bangs like his father he has to keep brushing aside, the set chin. He can pose all he likes, but Rosie would've taken two dollars a week and felt she got one over on the young Scot. Pretending to be offended, she waves him inside to follow her.

"Come along then and please take your boots off at the door. I hope you feel good cutting into my profits but I'll let you have it for this month. Goodness but it costs a lot of money to run a business these days, why just yesterday…"

She rambles on as she moves into a hallway with stairs on the left. Leading him to the top she takes him to the last room on the right and flicks the light switch. Dominic peeks inside to find a double size bed, a dresser painted white and an armoire with mirrored doors against one wall. There is a tall narrow window in the room and the white curtains are open. A stiff backed, wood and velvet chair is under it. The floor is brown linoleum with beige squares, and it shines. The walls are light and the trim is all dark wood. She points out a shared bathroom directly across from his room. She never stops talking. He nods approvingly and passes her a five and two two-dollar bills. They return to the front door. He gets his trunk; she gives him a key to the house, informing him she will write him a receipt and he can pick it up in the morning.

The two Dominic's are standing at the cart after setting the chest at the end of the bed. Rosie has returned to her rooms, the first door on the right when you enter the hallway. The last light of the day is only a glimmer behind the neighboring houses. Shadows cover the street. The frosty air wisps from their lips when they talk.

"Aye then, how much do I owe you for the hire of your wagon today?"

Nick climbs up, talking over his shoulder.

"I think a dollar fifty would be good."

He normally hires out for 3 to 4 dollars a day. He likes the stranger and it was fun showing him around. He feels that's enough.

Dominic is looking up at the driver, enjoying the wide grin. He too likes the stranger. Taking out his wallet, he digs out another two-dollar bill and passes it over with a satisfied smirk.

"Take this then. I liked the tour. I've a good feel for the city."

Relieved because he doesn't have any change, Nick gladly accepts the money. Pleased that he had a profitable afternoon.

"*Merci,* Dominic. I hope we will have a chance to meet again."

Dominic Alexander yearns to see the coast and has formulated a plan.

"Are you familiar with a village called Cocagne?"

"*Ah oui,* I grew up in Grande Digue and it is not too far from Cocagne."

"How long would it take to get there?"

"'By wagon?'"

"Aye, this wagon, unless you have another."

"It would be quicker by train to Bouctouche and hire a buggy or a sleigh there. It takes about three hours, its fast. This time of the year, there are some very bad spots in the road to the coast. If we are fortunate, it would take us five or six hours. Depends on the weather too; some says we're in for a storm soon. Halo around the moon and silly stuff. Suppose to be colder so it will be better if the road freezes. There's been some good weather lately though. Road might not be in bad shape. When did you want to go?"

Encouraged by the possibility of easy transit, Dominic doesn't hesitate.

"How about tomorrow? Unless you have other plans."

Nick responds with raised eyebrows and a hopeful smile.

"There and back tomorrow? We'll be all day in the cart. Wait, I could borrow my uncle's buggy. It has a roof. He hardly uses it now that he has a car. It would save us some time."

He points at the horse, more at the broad, dark brown hips.

"*Clementine* here, don't ask her to run a lot but the sweet lady can walk at a nice clip all day with the lighter wheels. She's a sweetheart to the reins. *Oui*, it could be done."

"I was thinking a couple of days or more, get there tomorrow afternoon and rest. Is there an inn or hotel in Cocagne?"

Nick's head's bobbing, one hand is pointing several places

"*Ah oui.* There is some. Near the bridge. Across the bridge. Mostly empty in January. I don't know how much they charge. Or you could stay at my sister's place in Cote d'Or, a short ways from the village center."

Dominic is impressed with Nick's familiarity of the area and is pleased that he has family nearby. He is touched by the offer of lodging.

"Would she have room? I would be happy to pay for a bed."

"She lives by herself. Her husband passed on almost four years ago. She doesn't get out much. She'd be happy to see us. What time do you want to leave?"

Reaching up to shake the driver's hand, Dominic is warmed by the sincerity of the eyes.

"What about day break? Do you live far from here?"

"*Bien*, first light of day I'll be here. And no, not too far, I have a room at *mon oncle Albanie*. A short way out Union Street, he has a farm. He lets me keep my horse and wagon there. No longer than fifteen minutes from here."

Stepping back out of the way, Dominic doffs his hat at his new friend.

"First thing in the morning then!"

With a wave and a snap on the leather, Dominic the carter heads up Lutz Street, barely stopping at the corner when he enters St. George. Dominic, the immigrant, is tired. Wanting nothing more than to be under the brightly patterned quilt on his bed, he heads into the house. He leaves his boots on a rug in the entryway. He stops at the washroom before going to his room. Turning on the lamp that rests atop the dresser, he places his jacket and hat on the chair. Removing a key from his trousers pocket, he opens the trunk they put by the bed. On top is a canvas portfolio. A flap is held by a brass button on one side. He lifts the flap to expose a collection of sketches. The first one is of Gloria. He removes it and places the case back in the trunk. Setting the drawing on the blanket, he removes pajamas from his travelling bag.

Lying in bed staring at the image, he feels melancholy, lonesome for his friends and family. He misses Gloria the most. Worried over the conflict in Europe, he prays for their safety. He vows that he will see them again when the war ends. He reminisces about the people he left behind. Of the events that brought him to this strange and comfortable room. Of the voyage on the ship and the rattling of the train. He thinks about his new home. His mind drifts back and forth. The light is still on when he falls asleep. The drawing is on his chest.

CHAPTER 5

The temperature fell in the night. Shortly before sunrise, Dominic opens the door to see how cold it is. The moisture in the air has crystallized and there is frost on everything, pure white and it shimmers even in the gray dawn. His breath turns smoky. A soft pink hue in the eastern sky suggests sunshine coming. Expecting it to be cold in the wagon, he is not put off with his excitement to see the country Pascal spoke so fondly of. He's glad he decided to wear two pairs of long johns and bring extra socks. About to close the door, he sees Dominic turn onto Lutz. He hurries back to his room to grab his things. A small linen sack contains a few sundries and an extra set of clothes. It closes with a drawstring. Hefting it over his shoulder, he leaves the room.

The trip takes them just over five hours. They arrive at the south end of the bridge that crosses to the center of the community. It's banked by massive logs on each end and filled with gravel, making a raised road to the wooden span that crosses the bay. The sun has crested and polishes the frozen surfaces with glistening shards of light. The trip was mostly uneventful and full of chatter as the two young men became better acquainted with each other – one talks about growing up in Canada, and the other, about living in Scotland. Nick wants Dominic to call him Nick because that is what everyone else calls him. The day after Christmas past, he turned eighteen. He has a sister and two brothers. He bought his horse and wagon last summer, and depends on his wagon to make a living. Dominic says to call him Dom and talks about his family, learning his trades and his hopes for the future. The frozen road was cleared of any snow and rutted in many places, making the covered buggy rock side to side but otherwise the ride was smooth enough. They met many other wagons and a few cars on the way. The only two stops were once to help a stranger get his car out of a snowbank and the other was when they had lunch in Shediac, a community about halfway to their destination.

Nick pulls the buggy over to the side of the road and points across the bridge.

"The center of the village is over there. The building on the right there is a hotel. My sister lives on the other side to the right."

"There's not much to see is there? Only farms and fields. Is the ice thick in the bay even though it's open by the bridge?"

"It's thick enough to walk on for sure. Can you see the edge of the island over there?"

Nick is pointing to a jut of land sitting a half mile away with thick trees and spiky branches pointing into the air.

"Aye, I can."

"There's a house over there, and in the summer, they get back and forth with a boat; but now they have a road cleared over the ice. We can have a look if you like?"

"Go across the ice?"

"Sure. Let's go around the village first and then we can visit the island before we get to my sister's place."

Dominic is all aglow. The land is covered with snow and ice, but yet he feels something different here. He wishes it were summer.

"Aye that would be fun. You never told me your sister's name? And you're sure she won't mind?"

"*Ah oui*. Her name is Sylvie and *non*, she won't mind, likely glad to have a bit of company."

The next two days go by quickly as Dominic is enthralled with the country and the icy shores. Sylvie welcomes them with open arms and a happy face. She gives the new visitor the upstairs spare room and her brother sleeps downstairs on the couch. Their first evening is spent around the kitchen table with the teapot refilled several times. Dominic learns about the history of Cocagne and that it had been incorporated in 1757, 110 years before Canada even became a country. He hears tales and gossip of many families that have been here for decades if not a century or more, the Goguens, the Bourques, the Despres, the Melansons and many others.

They spend the next day touring the surrounding shores, visiting people Nick knows and listening to stories of local lore. Most of the people speak French and English but at first it is difficult to understand the young Scotsman, with the strange words causing many smiles. Dominic tries a few words in French much to the others glee. People along the coast are warm and inviting, Dominic has never felt so comfortable.

When they follow the coast towards Sylvie's house, there is a farmhouse for sale. A handwritten sign stuck in the window suggests the house and land are available. It tells the viewer to contact the law offices of Cormier & Flewelling in Bouctouche. Nick stops the buggy at the edge of the road to view the bay that is colored by a kaleidoscope of pale blues and pinks from the setting sun at their backs. The rough ice and snow scattered the changing light over the frozen vista. Dominic gapes wide-eyed in awe. Looking around, that's when he spies the house across the road from them and comments.

"It must be nice to live here, especially in the summer."

Pointing to the colored sign in the front window, Nick says, "Well it's for sale. The folks that lived there are dead now. They only had one son and he lives in Montreal, not interested in coming back as I understand. Lots of open land and woods in the back too. Maybe you could be a farmer."

Dominic laughs at the suggestion as he doesn't know a plow from a harrow and can't imagine being a farmer or raising animals, but he is swept up in the idea of owning such a property. He arranges for Nick to bring him back in the morning so he can watch the sun make its appearance over the horizon before they return to the city. The field of ice glistens like shards of glass. A repeat of the previous night with the changing colors occurs until the sky becomes blue. Shadows shrink along the island as the sun rises over the forest. A satisfied smile and wide eyes express his delight. By the time they get back to Moncton on Thursday, there is only one thing stuck in Dominic's head.

All he can think about is owning that view.

CHAPTER 6

The following day, he rises early. Dressing in his finest clothing, he has two very important things to do today. He ventures out under a cloudless sky, the sun hovering on the rooftops. Off he goes to a diner that Rosie suggested for breakfast, not far from the rooming house. The waitress is an older woman, tired eyes and short grayish hair, who offers him a proper smile.

"Need a menu young man?"

"Nae, I'll be having a tea please with sugar. If you have biscuits, I'd like two with butter and a bit of grape jelly if you have it."

"Love your accent, *laddie*. We make the best biscuits in the city, but there's no grape jelly. How about strawberry jam instead? The cook makes it himself and it's quite good."

"Aye, that'll do. Thank you."

She sticks her pencil over her ear, nodding at him.

"Good, I'll get your tea. The sugar is in that covered bowl beside you, by the salt and pepper."

Dominic sips on the hot tea as he looks around the diner. He takes notice of two men in a booth just inside the door on the same side as he is. One is wearing a topcoat and suit, which makes Dom think of a business man like the manager at the bank. The other man is in uniform, but his left sleeve is folded and pinned to the side. They laugh at something. Three young men in coveralls and heavy work boots sit at the counter. The lightning bolt logo on their chests probably indicate where they work. They all seem like friends. It makes him a bit lonely, and he wonders what Ivan is doing.

171

Patting his pocket, he remembers the letters he wrote last night. He must mail them right away. One to Gloria, one to Ivan, one to Tubs and one to Adairia. While he's thinking of what he wrote, the biscuits arrive and there is steam coming from them.

"Be careful, love, they just come out of the oven. Can't get fresher than that now, can ya? More tea?"

"Aye, it's good."

She likes the boy and winks at him before she turns to other patrons that have just arrived.

"Of course it's good."

The biscuits are the best he's eaten, dripping fresh butter and sweet jam. Refusing the offer of more tea when the waitress returns for his plate, he looks up at her.

"Pardon me, ma'am, but I'm new here...."

"Oh, really?"

They both chuckle at her sarcasm.

"...and anyway, can you tell me where the post office is, and can you recommend a reputable advocate.

"Ya mean a lawyer?"

"Aye"

Her cousin's a lawyer and had recently opened an office on St. George Street. Working for the largest law offices in the city, he acquired a reputation for service and pleased clients. She remembers him telling her how nervous he was about going out on his own.

"Well, the post office is on Main Street, know where that is?"

Dominic nods affirmative. As she talks, she gather's his plate and utensils.

"Across from the train station, know where that is?"

Another nod.

"When you're done there, walk north on Highfield until you come to St. George and I know you know where that is."

Benny's Diner is on Archibald Street on the corner of St. George.

"Walk west until the city starts to thin out, it's not far, and there's a brick office building, fairly new. Brass sign on the front says Foster Building. In there, upstairs, is the office of my cousin, John Bannister. He'll treat ya right. I'll get your bill."

The building is reddish bricks and the brass plate has bold dark letters. An arch of stone adorns the front top of the building, three stories up, with large letters proclaiming the name FOSTER, carved in the façade. A vacant lot filled with snow and crusted drifts sits to the left of the building, a short way to the right an older farm house awaits the inevitable progress. The juxtaposition of new and old defines the changing landscape of Moncton. Sensing many opportunities, Dominic's excitement can hardly be contained and his persistent smile is either frowned at or reciprocated by passers-by. Straightening his jacket, hitching his trousers up, he checks his reflection in the glass doors. He likes what he sees and enters.

A hallway leads to a central stairway that switches back and forth to each upper level. A duplicate hallway on the second floor goes right and left. Uncertain which way to go, he looks both ways for a sign. When his search goes left, towards the back of the building, a gentleman enters from the office on the right. Dress shirt open at collar, necktie loosened, I'm-in-a-hurry crease on the brow comes toward him.

"Excuse me, *Sair*, can you tell me where I can find Mr. Bannister's law office, please?"

The man stops short, checks his watch to see it's only nine o'clock. He has no appointments this morning. He eyes the stranger in front of him, right away envying the mop of hair sticking out of his hat.

"That'd be me. How can I help you, young man?"

Dominic frowns at "young man." Everyone calls him that, making him wish he could grow a beard. He's pleased that they use the word *man*, though. He speaks a bit deeper, hoping his voice will belie his true age.

"I'd like some help buying a property."

Bannister perks up. Every new account is a bonus. The potential client seems quite young to be hiring a lawyer, so he will establish his ability to pay right away. Checking his watch again, he offers Dominic his only free time today.

"I won't be able to see you right now, but if you could return at three o'clock today, I can squeeze you in then.

Disappointment registers on Dominic's face. Bannister almost feels sorry for him, but he's much too busy preparing for court in one hour. Shaking it off, Dominic nods.

"Aye, I'll see you at three."

He was going to do it later, but given the circumstances he walks Main Street and St. George Street searching for a spot where he can open up his repair shop. Every time he calculates how much money he

173

is willing to spend to open a shop, uncertain if he should rent or buy, he hears Duff scolding him to be smart. The memory of his uncle, bent over his bench, showing him the secrets of his trade comforts Dominic.

After a hot lunch back at Benny's, he wanders west on St. George. Nothing on Main offered him any frontage except for two that were much too big for his needs. He looks in windows at any empty space, which there is not much of. Paying attention to the traffic, he notes which cross streets are used the most. The busiest ones, of course, have nothing vacant or for sale. There are offices for rent. He might have to take one of those. At one-thirty he is at the west end of the street, back at the Foster Building. The exertion causes him to loosen the top button of his jacket. Asking a passer-by for the time, he realizes he still has a good wait before his appointment and with the thought he must purchase a watch of his own soon, he decides to walk down to Main and head west. The main throughway is used frequently as it joins other roads towards the country. With lots of time before his appointment, he walks out of the city.

There is not much past the wharves except a few houses. The warm sun makes the center of the road soft and brown sludge adheres to horses' hooves and wheels of the passing wagons and cars that putter noisily. Over the fields he can see the roofs of the car repair shops at the railyard and hear the clanging of the shunter engine. He pauses at the side of the road, visualizing all the activity in the huge yards, all the men working. That makes him think of all the industry. And even though he wants to live in Cocagne, he must have his shop here in Moncton. Cocagne will have to wait. He needs to do another walkabout and perhaps not be so fussy.

The countryside is barren except for a vacant house and a barn about a quarter mile from the edge of the city. Looking around at the edge of the city and the fields, he knows that when Moncton expands, it's coming in this direction or going north. Perhaps he should find land and build something. He's so uncertain regarding some things. Kicking a chunk of ice out of his way, he stares at the empty house. It's a two-story cube. Only one thing saves it from total ugliness, a wrap-around porch. It may've been elegant at one time but the broken rails and peeling paint are the result of neglect. Dominic sees beyond the surface defects to the straight sides, the even rooflines and the strong beams supporting the porch, thinking the house has a proper skeleton. He wonders why it's abandoned, boards nailed over the windows. Walking around, he can see it is quite large, 28 x 28 he guesses, plus a second floor. The lawn is bare in spots where wind has rearranged the snow into drifts along the porch. Brown stringy grasses from last summer are visible and Dominic surmises no one's been taking care of this property for a while. A quick look at the barn, not too big, solid, same complexion as the house, needs someone to take care of it. But right now, he knows he should head back.

Across the road is the Petitcodiac River, the muddy walls containing it visible with the low tide. Stopping at the end of the driveway, he sees how far he is from the edge of the city, a poor place to set up a new business, nothing else out this way except more fields and farms to the west. A gentleman he questioned earlier tells him the road leads to the village of Salisbury. He remembers Duff telling him how important it was to own your own property as it was the only thing that you could depend on during hard times. Maybe he'd ask Mr. Bannister about it.

Dominic arrives back at the law office a few minutes before 3 p.m. and announces himself to a lady who occupies a desk in the reception area. Several inviting chairs to her right are empty. A coat rack stands by the door, adorned with the latest fashions. Light gray walls and white trim invite you to stay.

"I've an appointment with Mr. Bannister at three."

Dark glasses look up at him, the smile makes him think she's glad to see him, but she's actually grinning at his foreign accent.

"Yes, he mentioned that this morning. I believe he said it was regarding a house purchase?"

"Aye, that's it."

She's writing on a pad in front of her and speaks as she makes a notation.

"What is your name, please, and where is the property located?"

"Name's Dominic Alexander and the house is in Cocagne."

She looks up at him, eyes widened with surprise.

"My grandfather grew up there; it's a lovely place."

Professionalism keeps her from being nosy.

"Well good luck. Please have a seat, Mr. Alexander. I'm certain that Mr. Bannister won't be…"

She's interrupted when an elderly man huffs his way from the inner office, hat pulled down boldly over his forehead, hands crunched into fists at his sides. Yanking open the door, he bellows.

"We'll just see about that!"

Bannister stands at his door, disappointment on his chin, embarrassment on his cheeks. Dominic stands with his hat in his hands, amused by the man's hasty retreat. He looked very angry. The receptionist goes to shut the door and introduces Dominic, reminding Bannister of his three o'clock appointment. Waving to Dominic, the lawyer beckons for him to come in.

"Sorry about that. Lois, if Jack Whalen shows up early, tell him I won't be long. Now come in young man."

Dominic scratches his head at his title and follows him into the office. Same décor, different desk, more chairs. Bannister points to the one nearest him and sits down behind the desk burdened by papers and files. Tearing off the top page of a writing pad, he places it on top of the pile. Picking up a fountain pen he nods at Dominic.

"What can I do for you Mr. Alexander. You mentioned purchasing a property."

In a clear voice, he asks the lawyer to call him Dominic and tells him of the house he discovered on a recent trip to Cocagne and his desire to own it.

"The sign in the window said to contact a law office in Bouctouche and to be quite honest, *Sair*, I've no experience with lawyers and was told you could be trusted."

Bannister reddens at the compliment, even across his hairless dome.

"Well thank you, Dominic. You can be assured I will only act in your best interests. There is one matter we should be clear on before we begin. From my own experience, a house in Cocagne can sell as high as two thousand dollars. There will be legal fees and other expenditures regarding ownership of the property. I mean you no offense but my regular clientele is not quite so young. Do you have the means for this transaction?"

Dominic straightens his back, brushing the bangs from his forehead as his eyes go serious.

"Certainly, Mr. Bannister, I'd not be after seeking your services if I didn't have the money to pay you. Perhaps you could contact Mr. Van Geist at the Royal Bank. I expect he would vouch for me."

Bannister sees no guile, only a face that wouldn't know how to be dishonest. There's also the certainty in the voice. Nonetheless, he knows Van Geist personally and will inquire.

"Yes, yes of course. Let's get the details then, shall we?"

Twenty-five minutes later a plan has been formulated. They agree to meet next Friday, a week from now, January 15 at the same time as today. Dominic is expected to bring a retainer of two hundred dollars. Dominic stands, as does Bannister.

"I have one other request before I leave. Can you find out who owns the vacant house to the west of the city on Main Street?"

"I already know that. Belongs to the railroad. They bought the MacDougall farm when they were building the shops. For whatever reason, it never was used. They had folks living there for a while, renting it, but it's been boarded up for over a year now."

Replacing his hat Dominic smiles at the lawyer.

"Can you inquire if it is for sale?"

Bannister's raises his brow, misunderstanding Dominic's plans.

"You're interested in farming?"

"*Nae, Sair*, just curiosity at this point. Thank you."

A nod at the busy receptionist and he leaves.

Totally satisfied with his day, Dominic heads back to the boarding house, a tired man. After a late supper at Benny's, he decides that buying his meals every day is going to be too expensive so he asks Rosie where the nearest grocer is. She directs him to O'Connor's Market on St. George. Going in he's confronted by the comforting scent of the many offerings on the cramped shelves: salted pork, the iron used in new nails, fresh bread, jute ropes, gun oil. Not to mention the human beings. He loosens his scarf, tucks his gloves in the side pocket of his jacket, sweeps the bangs back and takes note of what he can eat that won't spoil. Only two aisles have food stuffs. From those he gets a loaf of bread, a bottle of grape preserves, a package of cookies and two cans of meat. He'd have at least one meal, maybe two at the room, buy a decent supper maybe. The store is busy, women dragging kids, rough men in work clothes carrying brand new shovels, men in suits buying tobacco and confections. It takes him twenty minutes to get back to his room. Putting the preserves on the windowsill where a little cold air circulates, he hangs his coat, hat and scarf. Plunking down on the bed, he falls on his back. Fully clothed, he's asleep in two minutes.

For the next week Dominic rises every morning, begging the time to go fast, hungering for an answer to his query with Bannister. Trying to forget the house until Friday, he busies himself with exploring the city more closely, stopping to talk to people as everyone is so friendly. Some folks can't understand him when he's excited or in a hurry so he remembers to be conscious of his foreign tongue. There are two jewellery stores in the city, Murphy's and Allain's. He visit's each, asking if they repair jewellery. At Murphy's he is regarded as competition by the owner and not well received, but at Allain's he is greeted with enthusiasm. The owner's son has recently taken over the business and is not a craftsman. Dominic is offered all the equipment, goldsmith's desk and tools for a very modest price. After the purchase is completed, Mr. Allain agrees to keep the items stored in his back room until Dominic finds a place of his own. This is on Wednesday; Dominic can't believe his luck. And yet he has nowhere to hang his shingle. Unable to find a suitable location in the city, he keeps thinking of the house owned by the railroad and how he could have his business and live there too. Excited as he is, he will have to wait.

On Friday, he is at the office at 3 p.m. sharp but has to wait for a few minutes until Bannister finishes with another client. At a quarter after the hour, Bannister comes from his office preceded by a portly man in his late fifties, busy brows and red cheeks. Bannister touches the man's arm and points to Dominic who rises to greet the two men whose grins match, both enthusiastic.

"This is the gentleman I was telling you about, Dominic Alexander. Dominic this is Mr. Campbell, agent for Intercolonial Railways."

"Trickit to meet ye, lad."

"Aye, me as well Mr. Campbell."

Campbell shakes Dominic's hand and steps back to study the young gentleman before him. He sees the innocence of youth in his eyes, but yet there is something more confident about his bearing. He wonders why he is not in uniform.

"John here tells me you are interested in the old MacDougall farm. You couldn't be more fortunate in the timing of your inquiry. Forgive my boldness but tell me, please, is there a valid reason you are not in uniform Dominic?"

Dominic raises his brow, surprised by the question. His cheeks blush and regret underlines his voice.

"Aye, I tried to enlist back in Glasgow, but they wouldn't have me. I broke my leg and it never healed properly and I still have a limp. Doctor that examined me said I'd never make it through training."

Satisfied at the explanation, he nods at Dominic, offers farewell to both Lois and Bannister, dons his fedora and leaves. Bannister loosens his tie and removes his jacket as he returns to his office.

"Come in, Dominic. Lois, do you have the documents ready?"

Lois follows Dominic into the office and places several sheets of paper on the desk. Smiling at Dominic, she shuts the door as she goes out. Bannister hangs the coat on the hall tree near the filing cabinets and returns to his seat. Dominic is on the edge of his chair, hat in his hands folded over his lap, straight-faced waiting for the news. Bannister shuffles through the pages until he finds the one he wants. Offering it to Dominic he fills him in on its contents.

"The house in Cocagne belongs to Geoff Leblanc of Montreal, and he is very anxious to be rid of it and is willing to sell the contents as well if you are interested."

Dominic's head is up and down. He'll agree to anything now.

"Yes, certainly, Mr. Bannister."

"Call me John, please."

"All right, John"

"The sheet you are holding is an offer to purchase. You can decide how much you'd like to pay and we will get it off right away. We can hurry things a bit by telephone now, a wonderful invention by the way. The property has over a hundred acres of mostly woodland, five acres across the road along the water. They're asking eight hundred and fifty dollars. I checked around and last summer houses were selling between a thousand and twelve hundred, older houses, not so much, so this seems like a pretty good deal. What do you think Dominic?"

As bad as he wants it, Duff's voice trails through his thoughts. "Be careful with your money...."

"Let's offer him six hundred and fifty."

Bannister smirks at what he thinks of as naiveté.

"I think that might be a bit low Dominic."

"Didn't you say the owner was anxious to be rid of it?"

Looking down at his notes, Bannister agrees with him. Dominic sits back in his chair.

"Let's see how anxious he is then."

The lawyer jots down a few lines and takes the paper back from Dominic.

"Okay then. I also inquired regarding the old house west of the city. You met Mr. Campbell of course, who was kind enough to come to my office with the details of the property. It was only last Wednesday that he was instructed to vest the Railway of properties they were no longer interested in. Bids for the properties will open on Monday and will remain so for one week. Again, I've been inquiring about properties outside the city and I feel I have a reasonable figure for your bid. Let's go over the details of the property first Dominic."

When Dominic returns to the rooming house later, he is beyond happy. A bid is in on the house in Cocagne and he'll know Monday if it has been accepted. He declined the idea of looking at the house outside the city before bidding on it. Dominic assures the lawyer he'd had a good enough look and knows what to expect. Although John suggested twenty-two hundred dollars, Dominic had a bid drawn up for fifteen acres of land, the house and a barn for one thousand eight hundred dollars. He'll only know next Friday whether on that one. Monday comes, the bid for the property in Cocagne is accepted and Dominic instructs Bannister to proceed. He delivers the money for the transaction as well as a retainer to be held by Bannister for his services. The rest of the week creeps by. To relieve his boredom, he sketches a profile of Gloria from memory, writes and posts letters to Mary and Lilly, and buys a new scrapbook.

A German spy attempts to bomb the Vanceboro International Bridge between Canada and the U.S.
Princess Patricia Canadian Light Infantry are the first Canadian troops sent to the front line.
Enemy battleships bombard the English ports of Hartleport and Scarborough.
"Christmas Truce" takes place on the battlefields of WWI.
An earthquake in Avezzano, Italy, kills over 29,000 people.
The Yankees are sold for $460,000.00.
A Model T Ford Runabout at the mayor's Ford dealership sells for $390.00.
German planes drop bombs on Dover, England.

CHAPTER 7

On February first, Dominic is the first customer at Benny' Diner. The younger waitress, the one with the wide hips and open heart, gushes over him as usual, making it obvious that she's interested. But Dominic is in love and not in tune with the wiles of young ladies. In his satchel he has all the papers he received from John Bannister yesterday. He now owns the property west of the city as well as the one in Cocagne. The bank account at the Royal is now $3236.28 lighter than when he opened it. He removes a note pad from his bag and while he eats his biscuits, he makes a list of the things he must do and in what order. Two cups of tea later, he sets out to take care of number one. Nick is waiting at the station because a train arrives from Montreal at 6:45 every Monday morning.

The walk to the station takes him about ten minutes. It snowed in the night and the intermittent clouds overhead are trying to regroup for possibly some more later in the day. An inch of new snow makes most things white except the brown mud of the roadways. When the sun is exposed by the passing clouds, the crystals along the buildings blaze and it matches Dominic's mood.

When he walks along Main Street, he can see Nick's wagon pulling out with something strapped to the back. When the wagon turns onto Main Street, Dominic hails him down. He's greeted by a "*Bon Matin*" when Nick pulls over as close to the side of the road as possible.

"*Braw morn* to you as well, Nick. Where ya heading?"

"Got a load of goods from Montreal for Creaghans downtown, mostly new clothing I suspect. What are you doing?"

"Well I'd like to talk to you for a bit. Can I jump on?"

"*Oui, oui*, get up here."

Dominic climbs on and the wagon pulls away after letting a car pass that makes the horse jittery.

"I was wondering, Nick, if you have any carpentry skills?"

"Well, Dom, I know which end of a hammer to use, but I wouldn't want to try building anything on my own. Why do you ask?"

"I've purchased a property west of here and I need help fixing it up. And I need a wagon for supplies and stuff like that. I'd like to hire you for the next two months if you're interested, maybe longer because there's lots of work to be done. What do you think?"

Nick has a wide forehead and it creases as he considers the offer. He likes the idea of steady employment, though he's not sure about his skills with a saw and tools. He likes Dom. Impressed that he seems to have money to spend and he doesn't look any older than himself.

"You'd have to show me what to do."

"It's mostly labor work and helping but there's lots of things you can learn to do, I'm sure. You seem like a smart guy."

Nick grins in response to the compliment, not having many, and reddens a bit.

"Well *merci* for that. How much would this work pay?"

Dominic has a serious face for not having set a budget for that yet. He knows he can't do all the work alone, and he wants to be in business as soon as possible. Nick is the perfect choice; he feels he can trust him and his wagon will be handy. Before he starts this project, he must decide how much of his inheritance he can spend. He would be a fool to waste even a penny. He recalls the conversation he had on the train with one of the passengers. "An average wage is ten to fifteen dollars a week…" He knows on a good week Nick can make up to twenty dollars, but he has to pay his uncle for space for him and the horse and the feed as well so he would have about fourteen or fifteen left. He was honest enough to admit that he averages less than that, normally about twelve to fifteen a week and he has to pay the same things. Dominic wants to be generous but Duff's words are imprinted in his skull.

"What if I give you twelve dollars and an extra five for the wagon and horse and I'll pay you every Friday?"

Nick's first thought is seventeen dollars every week for a couple of months is a good deal. Summer will be here after and that's always busier for him.

"*Tres bien*, it's a deal. When do we start?"

They shake mitted hands and laugh at the awkwardness of it. Dominic pats his knees in glee.

"Well today is Monday. Do you have any other jobs to do this week?"

"*Oui, oui*, I have boards tomorrow and furniture from a law office to move on Thursday. I could start on Friday."

"That's just grand, Nick. Pick me up at Rosie's then at seven in the morning if that's not too early for you.

"That will be good."

When Nick stops at the back of the department store, Dominic pats him on the shoulder, both smiling at the agreement, and alights from the wagon.

"Until Friday then, Nick."

CHAPTER 8

The fifth of February is cold. Roiling gray clouds shift across the sky like tumbleweeds in the southern wind. When either Dominic talks, their vaporous words escape into the chill. Their first day on the job could be interrupted by snow. Pulling into the driveway, they have to wheel through small drifts that cross the path. Soft snow from earlier this week wisps around the porch and the building. Both men are bundled for the cold. Scarves tied about the throat; hats pulled tight. Outer mitts of leather protect the woolen ones inside. Dominic is grinning from ear flap to ear flap. In the back of the wagon are two snow shovels, enough lumber to build a decent ladder and a chest holding Dominic's new tools.

"The first thing we should do is open the barn for a place for Clementine away from the cold After, we'll take a look inside and then we can pry the boards off the windows but we need to be gentle until we see what is under them. Okay?"

"*Bon idée*, Dom. It's damn chilly."

After prying the door open to the barn, the two men find empty stalls in the front section, dust and cobwebs everywhere. Cleaning out one section, Nick unhitches the horse, brings her inside and covers her with a heavy horse blanket. There is old hay in the mow that is as dry as when it was put there three years ago and Nick fills a trough in front of Clementine. They unlock the door to the house with the key Bannister gave Dominic and enter a dark and cold domain.

The door opens into a foyer that has a set of stairs in the center with a hall on each side. There is a large room to the right and one to the left, possibly a living room and dining room. The front room on the left is bare except for a battered couch that has springs sticking out of the seat and a rip across the back. Other than dust and spiderwebs filling the corners, several empty boxes, scattered newspapers and mouse tracks, the house is empty. They go from room to room on both levels, with Dominic doing a quick scan of what needs to be fixed and finds the interior in better condition than he expected. There is no dampness on the second floor and everything is dry except the smaller room at the back right, which has water stains on the wallpaper near the outer corner of the house.

The floors in the bedrooms, hallways and kitchen have linoleum of different colors and patterns – none match. The edges have curled in some places and there are tears where something heavy, likely furniture, has been dragged. The floors on the main level are hardwood but badly scratched. Wallpaper, like the linoleum, is many colored and curled in some corners. The whole house has an aroma of forgottenness.

After checking the premises, they find a door to a cellar and venture down. Dominic has purchased a flashlight and they use it to explore the lowest level. A musty smell hangs in the air, larger cobwebs have to be pushed aside. The walls are rough stone properly fitted to create weather tight support. The floor is packed dirt. In the center is a huge stove with pipes coming from the top heading in different directions, and Dominic comments that it looks like Medusa. Nick scratches his head at the comparison, wondering who Medusa is. Dominic finds a pile of split wood in one corner. He flashes his light towards the stairs.

"Go bring the two-by-fours and the tool chest, Nick, into the living room and we'll build a ladder so we can get up on the roof to check the chimney."

After the ladder is built, they can see that the stove pipe is clear and Nick builds a fire. Within a half an hour the main floor is toasty, but the upstairs is still frigid, telling Dominic that something needs to be done about the circulating heat. Venturing in and out of the house to warm up occasionally, the men soon have all the boards removed from the windows, which are still intact except for the ones in the back of the house near the kitchen. Those have been smashed. Dominic tells Nick to leave them boarded up for now.

The biggest surprise is that the front windows are beyond words.

Large panels are topped by smaller panes that are beveled and even the low light bends in the prism-like channels. There are two in each large room facing the front. Both Dominics stand in what was likely the living room watching the wind curl the snow round the front porch. Nick has his mitts under his arms and is rubbing his hands to warm them. Dominic is in a daze and doesn't hear Nick talking to him.

"… so, there's lots of work to be done."

"Oh, sorry Nick, what did you say?"

"I can tell you are happy Dom, but I was saying you still have a lot of work to do."

Nodding his head, Dominic smiles at his friend. "Yes, we do. So let's get started."

CHAPTER 9

Dominic celebrates his first birthday in Canada alone. He's much too busy to be sad or even to reflect on becoming fifteen. Spring arrives early that year. The robins come when the ground is warmed up enough so the worms will come to the top. By the end of April, the snow all but disappears except in the deepest reaches of the forest. The men work long days often but Dominic insists that the weekends be free from work. Nick proves to be a quick learner and helps with all the woodworking except the finish work, which Dominic does. Nick's wagon is put to good use throughout the renovation. Fetching supplies, lumber, doors and windows, topsoil and furniture. Removing garbage and debris. The barn alone took five trips to clear.

Dominic lives upstairs since moving from Rosie's in March. He's watching every nickel and some things are costing him less than he thought but not everything goes smoothly. There was work that Dominic had not accounted for when Moncton Gas, Light and Water Company installed electricity and the cost of converting his heat to gas. Always something or someone stalling the work at times. He had trouble with not being a citizen yet and had to turn to John Bannister for advice when dealing with government agencies and municipal regulations for businesses. The large doors to the barn could not be repaired and had to be replaced. The roof in the back had to be re-shingled.

On the other hand, he sold the wood stove, sold the two buggies that were stored in the barn, sold an acre of land to a coal dealer, the last section closest to the city. So far, he's ahead of his costs by $78.48.

The house is built rugged, he was right in his assumption of the main structure being true. It will stand for many years.

When Dominic turns to the outdoors and the yard, he is uncertain of what to do. There was never time for flowers or trees back home, or anyone interested in landscaping. Only the rich folk had proper yards. In May he hires a gardener, they haggle over wages and the budget but the middle-aged man gives in to Dominic's pleas and says he'll do it all for twenty-five cents an hour and no less. They shake on the deal. He decides to build a fence around his dwelling.

Dominic works relentlessly but relishes the Sundays when he vows to not work. He reads the first letters he's received. Adairia writes for her and Tubs because Tubs never learnt to. The words try to be cheerful but Dominic reads the pain of missing Duff and how they are carrying on without him. They're happy for him and his new home, missing him so much. Mary and Lilly both write back, the two letters making the envelope bulge. Lilly's filled with adolescent thrills of being in love, gushing over Ivan and learning to make bread. Missing him. Sending love. Mary's tells of life with Pascal, how their grandfather is getting old and Tommy's in trouble, likely to go to jail. Missing him. Sending love. Ivan tells of new friends and newer kites and when he went to visit Lilly and how much he likes her. Misses his best friend.

Gloria's is longer, full of pledges for the future. Full of questions. Scented, filled with kisses.

Some Sundays Dominic works on larger drawings that he will build frames for and hang in his shop. Three hold designs for ladies' rings, one for a gentleman. Other Sundays he attends movies at the Empress, learns to drink Moosehead ale with Nick, visits people he meets when they invite him over. But mostly its work. Passers-by notice the changes and the nosier ones ask what is going on.

CHAPTER 10

Alexander's Jewellery Repair is born on June 30, 1915 when John Bannister hands over all the legal documents required for doing business in the County of Westmoreland, in the province of New Brunswick. Dominic opens July 1, a Thursday. He has posted flyers he had printed all over the city, he and Nick stuffing them in mail boxes or handing them out, tacking them to hydro poles.

Rosie O'Bannon wants to be the first customer, but when the buggy she hired pulls up in front of the building, there are already several people there. Dave Ingersoll and his wife, the nearest neighbors and occasional helper, Don Melanson, the foreman of the crew who installed the electricity and gas, and his daughter and an elderly lady, fashionably dressed and straight backed who arrived in an elegant automobile that awaits her. It's parked to the right of the driveway. All of them are early for the opening at 9 a.m.

The group gather at the bottom of the stairs that lead to the porch and front door. The ladies are in a clutch waving hands and pointing fingers at the landscaped property. The newly planted shrubs along the front, young and green, evenly spaced for growth. Yellow, purple, many blue and bright orange flowers color the ground along the length of the porch. They comment on the dark gray trim around the windows and along the porch, how striking it is against the white shingle siding; the sparkling light from the beveled glass over the windows; the tastefulness of the light gray curtains. How handsome the young owner is.

The men are saying Dominic is clever with having the picket fence

189

surrounding his buildings; how painting the barn the same colors as the house makes it welcoming and the new doors look good in red; there's lots of room in front of them to park their buggies; the fine stone that lines the driveway and parking area is hard to find, must've cost him a pretty penny. The house never looked this good. They gossip about Dominic too: so young, has his own money, talks excitedly, is hard to understand when he's upset, which isn't too often – he's a nice young man. Seems smart, and a goldsmith too. Not sure about such a small sign by the door although the detail is the sign of a good carpenter and a keen painter.

Dominic is peeking from behind the curtain. He sees the group gathered at the foot of the stairs. Glancing at his new watch, he sees that he has another ten minutes before he unlocks the front door. He wants today to be perfect. Rubbing his hands together, he's glad to see Rosie, her reddish curls and happy face. Thinking about all the work coming together, coming to this point, he wishes Duff were here. He knows his uncle would be proud. He wishes all his friends were here and he experiences a brief spasm of loneliness and yearning for his homeland. The movement of a young girl up the steps towards the front door disrupts his melancholy moment. Stepping back, he checks his reflection in the window, straightens his jacket, brushes a piece of lint off his blue cotton shirt, brushes a few loose hairs from his forehead and goes to unlock the door. A large smile appears when he sees the sunlight streaming through.

When the people enter, they pause in the foyer, enraptured by the décor. The sanded floors gleam, the dark wainscoting with clear finish shines like new wood. The upper walls are papered in solid silver lines and tiny crowns with hints of burgundy. Stairs to the second floor are sealed off at the bottom with a burgundy velvet rope. The archway to the left where Dominic will run his operation is open to a large room with the morning sun making prisms along the ceiling. A leather couch and several chairs surround a small table upon which a vase of clear glass holds fresh flowers. The sketches of jewellery Dominic drew are placed upon the walls and have the visitors gawking, oohing over them in the case of the ladies. After hugging Rosie and asking her to wait so he can show her around, he moves behind a hip-high counter where he will serve his clients.

"So, welcome to Alexanders Jewellery Repair. Who's first please?"

The Ingersolls are his first clients and have a ring that belonged to

Mrs. Ingersoll's mother that it is too small. How much will it cost to enlarge it? Using his new mandrel, he checks the size and then with a ring sizer that came with the tools and desk from Allain's Jewelers, he checks her finger. He thinks about how much material he will need and how long it should take him and some pricing suggestions from Mr. Allain to come up with a figure. Even though he paid Ingersoll, Dominic wants to be generous to the man who helped out last spring when he needed a third hand, and settles upon half the price with a wink at Mrs. Ingersoll, who flushes. He writes the instructions down on a sales book he acquired at Colpitts Stationers. The header is blank for now as Dominic spends as little as possible. He writes in a description of the ring with a quick rough sketch and what needs to be done and the price. He gives them a copy and keeps the carbon copy in the book telling them it will be ready later today and they can pick it up tomorrow. Thanking them, he replaces the carbon in the next page and turns to his visitors.

The elderly lady is Mrs. Van Geist, the bank manager's wife. She wishes him well after complimenting him on the good taste of the decorator and the exceptional artwork of the drawings. Dominic explains that is was a friend's sister from Cocagne who helped him with the decorations and colors. Making an innocent face, he professes to having done the sketches. She shows him her husband's wedding band. The filigree pattern that encircles the ring is worn in the center, only the scrolled edges can still be seen. It's bent and out of shape, almost an oval.

"Hope Mr. Van Geist's finger is okay, something heavy must've fell on this."

Mrs. Van Geist still has the accent from her mother country of The Netherlands. Her voice is low and quite charming as is her short laugh. Her hands hold a pair of black gloves and rest upon each other on the counter.

"Yes. He caught his hand in the safe door at the bank. The ring saved his fingers. It's a good time to have the scrollwork redone as well as reshaping it. Can you do this sort of work?"

A serious brow watches him as Dominic contemplates what needs to be done. The scrollwork is no problem, but with his loupe, he can see the fine cracks at the far edges of the oval. It could break when he tries to straighten it. This will have to be fixed first. Explaining what he must do, he names his price. The opening of her eyes makes him think it is too high, but he reconsiders given how long the scrollwork will take and remains silent. He tries a little charm and salesmanship.

"The scroll work is quite complicated and needs special tools and skills. When I am finished, it will be like the day you got married. The day you placed it on his hand. The cost is a lot less than purchasing it new."

"Well yes I expect so, but it's more than I paid for the ring thirty-three years ago. But I do like your suggestion of it being new again. I'll do it for our anniversary and present it to him then."

Dominic wears his satisfaction well, trying to hide his pleasure using his best smile.

"And when is that Mrs. Van Geist?"

"Saturday. Could you possibly do it for then?"

He can do it tomorrow first thing. He fills out his sales book.

"I'll have it ready by closing tomorrow night. Will that do?

"Oh yes, thank you so much, Mr. Alexander."

"Please call me Dominic. And thank you for your business."

Don Melanson and his daughter, Ginette, have a genuine ruby of a rich red, like a ripe tomato, almost flawless, a very rare stone. It is rectangular and multi-faceted, the size of a kidney bean. They want a new setting for the gem so Mrs. Melanson can wear it as a pendant. It's her birthday in two weeks and the ruby comes from her father, obtained when he was a missionary in Brazil thirty years ago. The stone was a gift to her mother but there was never enough money to do anything with it. When her father passed away last year, she was given the stone by her mother with wishes it could be put to use. Mr. Melanson wants something nicer than just a simple setting.

"We'd like something surrounding the stone to make it stand out and it has to have something to hold it on a chain. My daughter here, Ginette, has a sketch she did and it could look something like that. She's clever with a pencil and paper."

The little lady takes a folded paper from her coat pocket and places it on the counter, where she unfolds it. On the page facing up, she pushes it towards Dominic who picks it up to study the drawing. The stone sits in the middle of a frame much like a photo with half circles crisscrossing between the frame and the stone.

"She is indeed clever. I can see exactly what you mean, Ginette. I will have to make the circle sections a little heavier to form the center basket which holds the stone but I can do that. Just give me a moment and I can give you a price."

Dominic does his calculations on a notepad and when he tells Don the price, he can detect from the man's expression that it is more money than was expected. He makes a counter offer.

"Or I could make it in silver for quite a bit less."

Now the girl is elated and moves excitedly up and down on her toes.

"Oh, that would be better Papa, her chain isn't yellow like your rings."

"Yes, you're right, Ginette. Okay then, Dominic, please do it in silver. When can we pick it up?"

"Hmmm, I'm closed Sunday and Mondays so how about Tuesday afternoon?"

"Excellent."

They shake hands and when Dominic gives Don a copy of the sales order, he offers Ginette her choice of a yellow or a red lollipop from a bowlful he keeps under the counter. When they leave, Rosie rises from the sofa and approaches Dominic. She's been watching the negotiations and is quite impressed by Dominic's confidence and professional manner.

"You enjoy this don't you, Dominic?"

"Aye, Rosie, very much. It's all about love and heirlooms in this business and I can't wait to start creating these wonderful pieces. I'm thrilled that so many folks showed up. I hope it continues. Now c'mon, I'll show you around. There's no one waiting so I'll just lock the door. He writes a note on the top page of his pad and with sticky tape attaches it to the glass of the front door telling anyone he'll be back in a few minutes.

Gesturing for Rosie to follow him, he removes the velvet rope from its holder and re-attaches it to the opposite side, leaving the entrance to the stairs open.

At the top of the stairs is a landing wide enough for two small chairs and a narrow table in one corner and a vase with tall dried flowers in the other corner. Dominic has built a wall across the front of the stairs and added a door to allow him entry to his living quarters. When Rosie follows him in, she discovers a small living room on the right and a bedroom on the left where the blankets are askew. Dominic apologizes and pulls the covers up. Rosie waves it away.

"You think I never saw an unmade bed before, Dominic."

There is a new kitchen at the end of the hallway with an area off to the left for a table and four chairs. The wall behind the table has a narrow door where a bathroom has been installed and on the opposite wall by the kitchen there is a door leading to a landing and stairs descending to a short walkway that leads to the parking area.

The furniture is all second-hand, only the table has been refinished and two of the chairs. There are no adornments on the walls, which at this point are all the same basic white, making it look like a typical bachelor's home. But the apartment is neat and orderly.

"Very nice, Dominic, but I think it needs a lady's touch, don't you? Some decorations and knick-knacks."

"Aye, that it does, Rosie, but I've been working so hard to get the place ready and presentable that I haven't had much time to bother with up here yet. But I'll get to it by and by. Let's go back down and I'll show you my workshop."

At the bottom of the stairs, he replaces the velvet barrier and unlocks the door. Carrying his makeshift sign to the back, he goes around the counter with Rosie following him and enters an open space separated from the main area by half doors that swing inwards.

"I left this door this way so I can see whenever anyone is here. I've yet to get myself a bell for when the front door opens and lets me know when there is someone coming in. I'll try to get that this coming week."

The work area is designed around a bench in the center of the floor that faces the half doors. There is a side table with tools and a polishing wheel with a treadle. A filing cabinet is in one corner and off to the left is what is left over from the old kitchen, the sink and hand pump even though he has a new pump for the upstairs, an icebox, several up and down cupboards that are a glossy white. The walls over similar wainscoting are light grey, staying with the color motif of the main area and outdoors. There are pencil sketches on the walls of the people close to Dominic that he has sketched over the summer when he had some free time and drawing helped him to relax. One each of Gloria, Duff, Adairia, Tubs and Ivan and directly behind his bench so that it can be seen from the open doorway is a group sketch with people sitting or standing at the bar at Carmichael's, Carol, June and Shirley, Jackie Boy and Esmerelda, Mr. and Mrs. Carmichael behind the bar.

Hands clasped at her chest, face beaming, she faces Dominic.

"Did you do the portraits?"

Looking at his shoes, he replies.

"Aye."

She walks over to the group sketch to study the figures.

"My goodness, Dominic, they're marvelous, so real. You chose lovely gestures with their mouths and each set of eyes tells me something different, I feel like I know these people. Well done!"

Not much for compliments – they make him shy – he changes the subject.

"Thank you, Rosie. Do you have jewellery that needs attention?"

She takes a small cloth bag from the side pocket of her dress. Returning to the counter she empties the contents upon it. Two rings and a bracelet.

"Well not just one piece Dominic but several. And I want it all to become one piece. I have an idea of what I want. Instead of..."

On it went throughout the fall as more and more people tell others about Alexander's and the fine work that is being done. By October, if a customer comes in the store, Dominic stops taking off his apron when working in the back to greet them, he has to do it so often. It will become his trademark – the goldsmith's apron. By December he stops taking repairs and orders for Christmas on the twelfth. There is too much work. He is tending the counter so much during the day that he works most of his evenings in the shop. He promises himself that in the first of the year he will close up for a week to take some time off, answer letters, sketch a few new designs for ladies' rings, sleep in late. Grateful for all the work, he worries he may need some help in the New Year – and what the extra expense will cost. He remains open Christmas Eve until six o'clock, staying open for a young man to pick up an engagement ring he had resized.

He spends Christmas in Grande-Digue at Nick's parent's place. Silvia is there and Nick's brothers, one with a wife and two boys, and Nick's new girlfriend, Joanne. They started dating in October and are all gushy around each other. He likes Nick's relatives a lot and enjoys their company. They are eager to hear about his work and how fascinating it is. He makes jokes of being too busy to sleep and thinks he might need help. He sleeps over and after Nick drops him off in Bouctouche, where Joanne lives, he takes the train back to Moncton. Loneliness sets in about noon on Boxing Day. Dominic has never felt so low. He reads over the letters he's received since he's been in Canada so he feels closer to the ones he misses. Filling time by scanning the stories from his collection of newspapers, looking to cut out articles or pictures for his scrapbook. On New Year's Eve day, he calculates his expenses and income. The business is making money and if it continues, in another year, he will have back all he invested. He sold the hay on his property in the fall and added that to his savings. He rents a section of the barn to a carpenter who stores his tools, ladders and material there. After a turkey sandwich and a glass of Moosehead that evening, he pastes the new stories into his scrapbook.

The war dominates the news, stories and stories of German victories, how the Allies are being pushed back and frustrated by not being able to breach the Western Front.

In April, the Easter Rebellion, an armed uprising takes place in Ireland. Lord Kitchener dies when the HMS Hampshire hits a land mine and sinks off the coast of Orkney Islands, Scotland.

In May the HMS Lusitania is sunk by a German U-boat with 1198 passengers and crew members.

Italy declares war on Turkey.

Woodrow Wilson is the first president to attend a World Series game.

Ford Motor Company manufactures it's one millionth Model T.

Ku Klux Klan receive charter from Fulton County, Ga.

Boston Red Sox win the 12th World Series.

1916

The fifth day of March is overcast. Sprinkled across the belligerent blue of the skies are clouds stretched thin by shifting winds; they yellow from the promise of sun. Snow clings to the edges of buildings and lies brown and crusty in the ditches, knowing it's no longer wanted. Last year's stubble of brown grass is visible and people talk of an early spring. The air carries an odd scent, seasoned by the surrounding industry of railways, a busy river and the melting earth. Dominic can smell it when a cool breeze ventures through the window he keeps open at night.

The morning whistle blows at the repair yards, telling everyone that it's 8 a.m. This, a Sunday, is the only day Dominic sleeps late. He loves his new home and ponders for a moment how fortunate he is. Stretching and tossing the bed covers aside, he sits at the edge of the bed rubbing the night from his eyes to gaze out his window. He'd hoped it would've been nice today but the skies look mean, as if it might rain. That'd be okay too, get rid of the last stubborn snow. Either way, he's off today – the only time he gets to himself. He has plenty to do with the business, but he keeps this day to himself to do whatever he wants. The only plan he has right now is to fry the rest of the ham that Nick's mother sent him with some eggs and fresh bread from Bailey's Bakery. While he's eating, he's going to paste the last five entries he collected since the beginning of the year in his scrapbook.

While he washes up and shaves, he decides to grow a moustache. He likes the way the stubble looks under his nose as he imagines it thicker. Freshly polished, dressed in his everyday dungarees and brown flannel shirt, he sits with a plate of steaming vittles at the table where he's left his open scrapbook and loose cut outs. While he chews between bites, he dabs some glue on the newspaper sections and pastes them on different pages.

The Yankees buy Frank "Home Run" Baker from the Athletics for $37,500.
Canada's original Parliament Building in Ottawa burns down.
The first bombing of Paris by German Zeppelins takes place.
Military conscription begins in Britain.
Germany begins to attack ships in the Atlantic.

While he dabs the bread crust in the molten yolk on his plate, he considers the last news story. Ships being sunk in the Atlantic. It must be scary to travel cross the waters that are rife with U-boats. He's glad he has no need to travel, although he yearns at times to return to see his family and friends. It's not as often now, but missing everyone remains as intense. Popping the last bite into his mouth, he closes the scrapbook and finishes his tea. He pushes his plate aside and plants his elbows on the table while holding his mug in both hands. Staring out the window in the kitchen, he studies the barren field next to his house, looking forward to the new plants sprouting. In the distance he notices activity in the yard around the hansom hitched to the horse at the Ingersoll's farm. He expects the family are getting ready to drive into the city to attend church. Reflecting upon his own spirituality, he feels that he should be attending church too. He knows they go St. Bernard's Catholic Church on Botsford Street, and even though he is Protestant, thinks he might visit one day. But not today.

Thinking of what he might do, he decides to work on his latest sketch of his new home that he will send to Gloria. Now that he thinks of her, he hasn't had a letter from her for quite a while. He answered her last one in February and she is usually quick to respond. He guesses she is busy at school and helping her parents at home or at the bar. One thing he must do is compose an ad for the Transcript to find someone to help in his shop. Part time for now at least. In fact, he'll do that first.

He cleans up his dishes and the frying pan and puts everything away. Digging a notepad from a drawer in the kitchen and a pencil, he returns to the table to write the ad. While he thinks of the right words, he's pushing the hair out of his eyes, which reminds him he needs a haircut soon. Twenty minutes later, after a few attempts, he comes up with what he feels is the right wording.

> *Help wanted. Alexander's Jewellery Repair is looking for a part-time clerk to assist with the public. Must have retail or office experience. Please apply in person before March 15.*

Satisfied, he sets the paper aside. He will take it to the newspaper offices tomorrow during his lunch, leaving a sign on the door stating when he will be back. Donning a light jacket and his boots, he ventures out to the barn where he has set up an area for his sketching. He and Nick have installed a wood stove on the main floor and he will light a small fire because even though the weather has been milder, the air still holds a chill.

Entering through the main door, set in the larger door, he walks into a wide common area, open to the top lofts and enclosed by wooden walls on each side. Nick and Dave Ingersoll had hauled away old hay and debris from inside by the wagonful and the place is spotless. The rooms to the left are the old stables and storage, which Dominic has left for the same purposes. The carpenter keeps his things in one of the rooms on the right, and the other two are empty. Five feet from the back wall is a pot-bellied stove, sitting on a metal plate which rests upon a wooden floor comprised of heavy beams on their narrow side, strong as steel. Along the back wall away from the stove is a pile of split wood and sawmill tailings. Using old sections from newspapers, he soon has the dry wood ablaze.

He's tired when he finishes the sketch. Only stopping for a quick sandwich at noon and a couple of short breaks. From the two windows in the back wall, he's noticed the faint light move shadows across the floor as the day passes and he knows it is close to suppertime, his growling stomach is telling him the same thing. Putting away his pencils and things, he stops to admire the drawing. From the perspective of standing at the end of the driveway, the drawing is finely detailed, each shingle meticulously placed, the flowers of summer decorating the base of the porch, the small sign by the door, the sparkle of the beveled glass on the windows. The barn is half visible behind from this angle but the detail is the same. The edges of the sketch fade out to empty fields. He likes it. He straightens out a few things on the old desk he uses and remembers to dampen the stove.

He opens the iron door just as a gnarled knot in one of the wood pieces boils inside with sap. Becoming steam, it bursts, shooting sparks out upon the metal plate. Startled, Dominic jumps back from the stove. Seeing the sparks on the floor, he starts stamping them out with the sole of his boot. There's a half dozen pieces smoldering and they are soon extinguished. Dominic is sweating from the scare. Looking around to see if he got them all, there is no sign of any errant embers. He closes the stove door, takes his sketch and leaves.

One spark, however, remained. It had rolled off the edge of the metal plate and lodged in a crack between two beams. It went unseen by Dominic. As hard as the men had worked to clean the floor, there are still remnants of old hay that have been pressed through the cracks over the decades. The hot ember finds some and there's soon a gathering of flame and dry wood. Dominic's barn catches fire.

After supper Dominic settles in the living room, curled up on his couch with his new book, *The Grizzly King* by James Oliver Curwood. He's fascinated by bears and found this one at the stationery store when he was recently there. A chapter and a half in, twenty minutes later Dominic is nodding off. He's almost into a deep sleep when a pounding on the back door awakens him. The heavy knocking doesn't stop and he rushes to see who it is. He has to go through the kitchen and out the back way, whose steps take him to ground level. He is stopped short by the wavering light caught in the upper windows. Looking out he sees flames curling along the edge of the new barn doors they built last summer.

Dave Ingersoll is at the back door when Dominic throws it open and rushes out, almost knocking him over. Dominic pauses only for a few seconds, panic in his eyes. Ingersoll recovers as Dominic runs towards the barn and quickly yells out to him

"Dominic, it's gone, it's all aflame. Don't go in there. You need to call the fire department. Stop it from spreading and save the house."

Save the house! The words bring Dominic up short twenty feet from the barn. Ghastly images of Duff's house all aflame, Pearl appearing in the upper window pawing at the glass, Duff fighting off the men holding him and running into the inferno to try and save his beloved pet. The charred bones of his uncle claimed by the horrible grayness. Buried among the rubble. Rapid flashes of painful memories.

Ingersoll grabs him by the shoulder to pulls him away. The flames have eaten a hole through the roof and lick the dry shingles. Flames are visible around the large doors and in the window. Something explodes and both men fall backwards. Dominic is still in a daze when Ingersoll gets him to his feet.

"Go, go call the fire department. I know you have a phone, Dominic. Hurry before it's too late."

Dominic grasps reality, nodding his head up and down as he runs towards the house.

"But… but I don't know the number."

"Just call the operator and she'll put you through. It's an emergency."

It's almost midnight when the barn is nearly extinguished. Fire consumed the mighty beams, which collapsed several hours ago. Knowing they can't save the building, the fire team concentrate on watering the back of the house. Earlier the intense flames threatened to catch it as well. Two horse drawn wagons with water tanks rush back and forth alternately from a brook nearby. Men in soot covered uniforms scurry about containing the pile of embers and dousing the timber that still burns. The air contains the stinging scent of drowned ashes no matter where you move.

A crowd had formed when the light from the fire filled the dark skies, those coming to help, other strangers lured to tragedy. Nick, who upon noticing the odd light in the skies had realized there was a fire and surmised it was close to Dominic's property, has come as well. Dominic sits on the back stoop staring at the loss. Too exhausted from the night's torment, he hangs his head when Mrs. Ingersoll approaches him.

"Here, I have taken the liberty to make you and the men some tea, Dominic. There's a little of the Mr.'s brandy in it."

Dominic takes the cup, barely able to register her words. He is fraught with sorrow, not so much at the barn, because he's already considering replacing it with something smaller, but of the burdensome reminder of the fire back in Scotland, the event that had changed his life. It's a terrible memory that sticks in his mind. Looking up he sees a man approaching him with smoke smeared cheeks and responsibility on his jaw. When the man gets closer, he realizes it's the captain of the fire team. A tall, gangly man whose lips are pursed in regret.

"I'm sorry for your loss, Mr. Alexander. I'm sending my men and teams back to the station for there is naught we can do now. I'll leave a couple of the fresher men here for a few hours to make sure nothing spreads. We're damn lucky the wind was away from the house or it could've gone too. I'll be back at my office in the morning if you need me."

Dominic has stood to meet the Captain.

"Thank you for all you've done, Mr....I 'm sorry but I've forgotten your name."

"Kent, Captain Joshua Kent at your service. Just doing what the city pays us for. By the way, there will be someone out to do an inspection once this is over to be sure there was no arson involved. You understand?"

Dominic shakes the proffered hand.

"Aye, I understand and please tell your men too, Captain Kent, I much appreciate the hard work they did and am so thankful for still having the house. I don't really have the right words to express how grateful I am."

"Well I can certainly understand that and I'll be sure to pass that on. Good evening then."

Nick approaches Dominic. Black soot covers the hem of his pants and bottom of the legs. Several other men helped him beat down the burning stubble in the field behind the barn. An early melt left brown dried strands of grass throughout the field, excellent fodder for hungry flames.

"Oh, Dominic, I'm so sorry to see this, but at least the house and business is still standing. It could've been so much worse."

"Aye, Nick, it could've been."

Nick and the Ingersolls are nearby seeking to offer some solace to the young man they've become fond of, not really knowing what to say. Dominic wears a look of defeat when he looks back at the pile of smoldering debris. Passing the empty cup back to Mrs. Ingersoll, he looks to the house to consider Nick's comment.

"Aye, I still have the business and there was no one hurt. It's all just things, isn't it? And I finished that sketch I was working on, Nick, so I'll be able to remember what it looked like at one time."

Seeing the Ingersoll's questioning look, he explains.

"I was working on a sketch of the buildings and I finished it today. I had made a fire in the stove and I think that might be what started the fire but I can't be sure. Do you think someone may have done this

Allan Hudson

intentionally?"

They're all shaking their heads, uttering denials, with Nick the loudest.

"No, no, there's no way someone would do this. It was an accident, Dominic. Maybe from the stove, like you said. But you're safe and the house too."

The Ingersolls agree and offer Dominic a place to stay if he wants to get away from this for a bit.

"No, I'm okay now. I'll deal with it. Thank you; I'm touched by your kindness. You folks should head home now, there's nothing more to be done here and I expect, like me, you're quite tired."

The Ingersolls leave and Nick remains behind a moment, concerned by the false bravado in his friend's face.

"You okay, Dominic? Really? I can stay with you if you like."

Patting Nick on the back, Dominic tries on a smile that is meant only for reassurance.

"I'm good, Nick. I'm going to take a last look and head up to bed. I'm beat. I'll be making plans in the next couple of days to get rid of this mess and I'll likely need your help if you're free."

Nick is nodding in the affirmative.

"Salter's Shipyard have hired me on for a few days next week and the regular pick-up off the train on Mondays. I could probably help you Thursday."

Heading inside, Dominic gives a limp wave to his friend.

"Good...good, I'll see ya then."

CHAPTER 2

Hanging a "Closed Due to Fire," sign in the front window, Dominic busies himself with tasks to escape from the shadows of his memories. He wakes the first morning knowing how fortunate he is in only losing the barn. It's just wood and nails. He'll deal with the loneliness it provoked one day at a time. The first thing he does is ignore the pile of ashes. An inspector has come and gone and determined nothing amiss; the fire started around the stove, burned hottest in the center. He goes to the bank, talks to Van Geist, seeking his advice regarding his expenditures. The bank manager is impressed by Alexander's willingness to get his hands dirty by suggesting he will do the clean-up himself, and reminds him of his income as a goldsmith and owner of a business. Perhaps it would be much wiser to hire the people he needs.

The coal dealer sends over a wagon with heavy sideboards, hauled by two dapple gray Percherons. Coal dust blackens every crevice. Dominic must supply the men. With the war in full swing, young and middle-aged men are not easy to come by – the workers are either very young or old, but the three men he hires, known to the Ingersolls, are as tough as the horses and able workers. By Tuesday evening the site is clean; all that remains is a circle of crust around the perimeter where the heat had melted the snow and a bare spot of leveled gravel.

That night he sits down and sketches what he wants to do. The draft is rough by Dominic's standards but shows a decent replica of what was there before, only half the size: two lofts, one room right and left, and a rejuvenated main area. Lengths, heights and width are marked upon another sheet. He does an estimate of the materials he will need. He decides to do those things in the morning and open for business in the afternoon. When Nick shows up Thursday, he'll send him for supplies and ask if he knows someone who can help him rebuild. Tucking his notes together with the pad, he drops a sheet that was folded and loose inside. Bending down to retrieve it, he sees the advertisement he penned. He'll remember to do that too.

Dominic is relieved when he rises Wednesday morning. Activity has been healing. He cleans up and shaves, liking the moustache that is beginning to take shape. Glad to finally be out of dirtier clothes, he looks forward to getting dressed up. Dressing up for Dominic is still the dark jacket and blue cotton shirts instead of the brown he wears to work. The wool pants are new, a sharp crease along the leg still visible. He has learnt how to make his own biscuits and favors them with a fried egg and lots of butter. Checking his watch, he plans on being at the saw mill at 8 a.m. It's a twenty-minute walk. Seeing the yellow gleam in the window, it roots out a slight smile. Pulling on his mitts, he heads out.

Even though the sun is shining, the air is cool and he can see his breath. When he starts along the driveway, a buggy turns in to meet him halfway. The horse is young and lithe, similar to the driver. Even with the tightened jacket or likely because of it, the lady is alluring. When she reins in beside him, all Dominic can see are her eyes. He's never imagined such a beguiling blue, like the horizon on a cloudy day just before sunset. Every move she makes exudes confidence, as does her smile.

"Are you Mr. Alexander?"

He's captivated. He can't decide whether her hair is blond or light brown. He simply notes how it frames her face perfectly. The lady reminds him of Gloria. She doesn't like it when people stare but is amused by this man who looks so innocent. She speaks a little louder.

"Excuse me. Are you Mr. Alexander?

He realizes he's been ogling and responds to her, thinking her a customer.

"Oh, sorry, you remind me of someone back home, the way your face lights up when you smile."

Cheeks go rosy.

"Well thank you, I guess. Back home must be Scotland?"

"Aye, tis. How did you know?"

The playful sarcasm produces an easy laugh. Dominic points to the sign on the front door, the dark letters visible from where they stand.

"Unless it's an emergency, I'm only going to be open at one o'clock."

Still holding the reins, she steps down from the buggy, with Dominic offering her assistance. When she faces him, she's almost as tall, if you include the hat. It's dark and follows the curve of her head, pulled low over her brow, coquettish. Her jacket is the same purple as the hat, fitting neatly over charcoal skirts. Up close her clothes are neat but expose the burden of being worn often. He's charmed by her accent.

"I'm terribly sorry about your barn burning, Mr. Alexander."

"Well, thank you, but please call me Dominic. And your name is…?"

A slight curtsy.

"Maria, Maria Desjardins. My cousin is married to Nick's cousin, so I've heard of you before Dominic."

It's his turn to blush, wondering what she might've heard.

"Good things, I hope."

"Oh yes, Nick thinks you're a real gentleman and calls you '*mon ami*' when he speaks of you."

"Aye, he's calls me that sometimes too. I'm lucky to have him as a friend. And if you're a friend of Nick's, I'll have to give you a good deal on whatever brings you here today."

Maria wears a more serious expression. Shifting the reins from one hand to the other, she points to the front door.

"Well I actually came to see you about work. Nick mentioned that you were considering hiring someone to help here."

Thinking of the note he has in his satchel, he studies her more carefully when he responds.

"Aye, I did say that. Your timing is good, I was going to place an ad in the paper today."

Checking his watch, he catches the hopeful look on her face, how pretty she is. Deciding he has enough time, he gestures towards the hitching post at the end of the driveway.

"Tie up your horse and we can go in for a moment. I'll tell you about the job."

"Thank you, Dominic"

Swinging back up into the seat with ease, overcoming the long folds of her skirt, she snaps the reins. Directing the horse to the left, she pulls up in front of the white bar Dominic has provided while he walks back towards the house admiring the way she handles the horse. The sureness in her commands. She joins him at the walkway, a small leather clutch in one hand, both joined at her waist. He waves her to follow and he goes to unlock the front door. Two steps behind him, she watches his back, how his hair curls up at the back of his hat. She likes the dark eyes and amusing accent. More than anything she hopes she can convince him to hire her. She needs to be working. Dominic pushes the door inward and with a slight bow, nods for her to enter first.

With a sharp intake of breath, she surveys the foyer, the warmth of the dark wood, the welcoming colors of the wallpaper and the sketches on the wall. Stepping in closer, she can see the main area and counter.

"How inviting; it's very nice."

Dominic tries to be modest as he leads her to the waiting area.

"Thank you, Maria. Please join me at the table."

When they are seated, she facing the window, and he to her right, Dominic places his satchel at his feet and digs out his notepad and a fresh pencil. While doing so, Maria removes her gloves and places them in her lap with her clutch. She scrutinizes the drawings on the wall. Dominic notices a small diamond in a very simple setting upon her left hand, but no wedding band.

"Let me tell you what I need and then you can tell me about yourself. Is that all right?"

Maria gives a soft nod, sits attentively, eyeing him directly. As he speaks, he has to look down at his pad; her cobalt eyes are too distracting. He had made quick notes on what tasks he might give to his helper and embellishes upon those as he explains what he needs. It takes him almost ten minutes and she's leaning forward, listening and nodding.

"…and that's pretty well what the person I hire would have to do. So, what kind of work have you done before?"

"My last job was working at The Corner Drug Store. I was a cashier and helped stock the store. I worked there for almost three years. I've also worked at…"

Relating her experience since leaving school in Grade 10 to work at home. Her mother, Beatrice, became ill and Maria is the only girl in the family of four children. Her father, Benoit, and three older brothers were fishermen. The brothers are at war now, two in the army and one in the Royal Air Corps in England. Her mother passed away two years ago. Last year her father sold his boat, unable to fish with his bad back. In the summer, he started seeing the Johnson widow from St. Thomas, so Maria moved to Moncton. She's only had two jobs since then.

"…and when I worked at Creaghans, it was only to help out for the Christmas season but that's when I realized how much I enjoyed serving people and selling things. It's a lot of fun most times. When the owner's wife wanted to come back to work at the drugstore, they didn't need me anymore, so that's why I'm looking for another job."

Dominic has been listening carefully, liking the way she uses her hands to express some points. He thinks her perfect for the job and would like having her around. She's had schooling and can read and write. She seems genuinely cheerful. He thinks people will be drawn to her because he knows how she is affecting him and chastises himself for it. He feels a pang of guilt with that thought, missing Gloria. He looks back at her left hand.

"I see that you are engaged. Do you like jewellery?"

Instead of the expected happy response, she looks seriously at the ring, toying with it on her finger. She and her fiancé had an argument this morning. He was invited to supper at her aunt's house to celebrate her birthday and had shown up drunk when everyone was leaving. Smelling like stale beer, making a fool of himself, staggering, treating everybody like his best friend, reeling, making muddy footprints through the kitchen and the parlor only to pass out on the sofa, where she had left him. It's happening too often and she is tired of his apologies. She told him she didn't want his *I'm sorry* and she didn't want to see him until he quit drinking. She's not holding out much hope.

She forces a smile when she looks back at Dominic.

"Yes…yes, I like jewellery very much, what lady doesn't? And yes, I'm betrothed."

Dominic sees he's triggered a bad memory. Wanting to change the subject, he asks her another question.

"And you live here in Moncton?"

"Yes, I live with my aunt on Church Street. My father Benoit, lives in Notre Dame."

Dominic picks that up right away. The mention of the village close to Cocagne and the coincidence causes him to grin.

"Do you know Pascal Brun from Cocagne by any chance?"

"I've heard of the Brun's but I don't know them. How do you know him?"

"He's married to my sister back in Scotland. He also told me about his home in Cocagne and Moncton and that's why I decided to move here."

He feels he's getting too personal; sure she's not interested and carries on with the interview.

"What kind of things do you like to do when you're not working?"

Sitting up straighter, a real smile, she perks up.

"I love to read books. I love ice skating and going fast. I like sleigh rides in the winter. I like the beaches and the sand by home in the summer. I want to have beehives someday. And I like birthday parties. I was at one last night, my aunt's, where I board. She turned sixty. There's good music and always too much food. *C'est un bon temp.*"

Her enthusiasm prompts her to slip into her mother tongue and she sees Dominic's puzzled look.

"That means it's a good time. Lots of fun."

He sees in her eyes these things make her happy. He's pleased to hear she's a reader. Realizing she fits the job perfectly, he sees no reason not to hire her. His hesitation is at the fact he's never done this before, never hired anyone. He doesn't want to make his decision too hastily. While he's thinking, he picks up the loose paper that he wrote his ad on.

"The work is only part time to start. From noon to 5 o'clock when I close, Tuesday to Saturday. I'm to be closed Mondays for the summer to work on the barn some. That's twenty-five hours a week and I'm willing to pay the right person forty-five cents an hour. Does the work still interest you?"

Maria is quick with numbers and almost gulps with relief, $11.25 a week is more than she was making at Creaghans. It'll do quite nicely. She remembers her father's advice, don't always take a man's first offer but he hasn't offered her anything yet. She closes her lips and it's almost like a pout. It's the first time he sees her dimples, faint creases along her cheek, it's then he finds her most becoming. They disappear when she looks up.

"Well, if I am offered this job, there is a lot of things to learn and I have a lot of experience with people. I was expecting a little more."

Dominic would probably give her the business right now if Duff's gruff voice didn't echo through his head. "Be wise and when it comes to women, don't think with your pecker." He was originally planning on forty cents an hour, possibly fifty. But that's an extra ten dollars a month. He's calculating how much more he needs to earn to cover the extra expense. She was feigning casualness glancing at the sketch between the windows, hoping she hadn't over stepped herself. She really wants to work here. He's jotting down some figures when he tosses her a random thought.

"So, what are you reading these days?"

"Oh, I forget the name, but it has a giant bear on the cover and is by a guy named Curwood."

He frowns when his head lifts.

"*The Grizzly King*?"

"Yes, that's it. Have you read it?"

Dominic doesn't answer her. He picks up the paper with the ad written on it and rips it in half, then in half again. Placing the shreds on the table, he sits back, folding his hands on his chest, eyes bright.

"Aye, fifty cents an hour then. When can you start?"

Maria is playfully clapping her hands together.

"Oh thank you, Dominic. You'll see that I'm a good worker and reliable. I can start today if you like?"

Standing he checks his watch again and offers her a hand up.

"I should be back here by eleven o'clock, can you come back then?"

"Yes certainly."

He walks her to the door and they're both very pleased. Hat and gloves back on and his bag over his shoulder, he locks up and starts out the walkway. She calls out to him as she unties the reins from the hitching post.

"I can give you a ride into the city if you're going that way."

"Aye, that would be fine."

He gets off at Hachey's Lumberyards on Main Street, deals with the yardmaster so Nick can load up the lumber tomorrow, and pays for his order. Walking west on Main, he heads to his appointment with Morley Lombroso, who, according to Van Geist, is the shrewdest bookkeeper in the city. Not much for manners, but he has a kinship with numbers. He charges fair and your records will balance to the penny. Dominic knows he's keeping track as best he can, but with the income from the business, his expenses... it gets too much not knowing how to keep a record of everything. He appealed to the bank manager for his advice, and he recommended Lombroso. Even called on Dominic's behalf.

The warming weather brings out many people. Some are gathered around the new city hall, almost finished. With bold stone and graceful columns, many agree it is striking. Ignoring it, he marches up the street, the things he wants to accomplish this morning roll through his head. He needs to get a haircut. Go to the bank. Take out some money. Go to the post office. See Mr. Allain about possibly doing his custom work and then meet Maria. Turning north from Main onto Cameron, the office is in Lombroso's house, fourth from the corner, he pauses in front of the side door, thinking about his new helper. Recalling the dimples and the enthusiastic nods, he knows his customers will like her. Satisfied with his decision, he knocks on the door and enters.

His last task for the morning is to see Mr. Allain. Now that he has help, he can take on more work. Designing and making unique pieces is his favorite. Allain's Jewelers is on St. George Street. The ten o'clock whistle at the yard can be heard over the din of the street when Dominic enters the store. The owner is showing a young man a gold necklace, likely extolling the virtues of owning or giving such a piece. When it comes to jewellery, Dominic knows that it mostly comes from the heart.

Mr. Allain acknowledges Dominic with a nod and finishes up with his customer. Dominic bids hello to the lady behind the counter to his left, where there are watches displayed telling her he is here to see Mr. Allain. He dawdles around the timepieces admiring the stylish designs. A few minutes go by and he is approached by the owner, a middle-aged man with a long forehead and happy eyes who has been a big help to Dominic in getting his business off the ground.

"Hello Dominic. How nice to see you. I was out your way recently and must say, you did a wonderful job. Your home looks splendid. I'm terribly sorry about your barn, but it's so good to see that you are okay. What brings you in today?"

Dominic is digging in his satchel, which is hanging from his shoulder, as he speaks.

"Yes, I lost the barn but I'm lucky to have my home and business intact, thank you. I dropped in today to show you a few sketches of some pieces I've done since I opened and would like to offer my custom services to you, Mr. Allain."

Passing him several sketches neatly tucked in a manila folder, Dominic offers up his most confident smile.

While reaching for them, Mr. Allain tells his visitor not to be so formal.

"Please call me Ronald or Ron like most people do. These drawings are amazing Dominic. Did you do them yourself?"

"Yes, I like sketching a lot. My Granda likes to draw too and he's shown me lots of tricks. I can usually do a rough sketch quite fast to get a feel for what folks want and then I do a drawing like these for them to give their okay."

Allain sees something most people don't. Talking of his Granda, Dominic's mien transforms to an adolescent much younger than his stature alludes to. Allain is quick to think that Dominic could be the same age as his son who turned sixteen last month. Yet, he is the owner of his own home and business. Very impressive. Thinking highly of the young Scotsman, he offers him an opportunity.

"Normally I use a company in Montreal for our custom jewellery and it's a slow process. It would be beneficial to us, of course, to have a reliable source right here. We would have to settle that our retail pricing is similar and we would be able to realize a profitable commission. Do you agree? "

"Aye, of course. I think we should…"

They settle the terms and each other's expectations. A hand shake ensues with trust in their grips. Allain asks Dominic to wait a moment. He scurries behind the counter to help an elderly man, the young lady clerk is occupied with a couple not much older than she, and a replica of the owner, has to be a son, is serving two women. It's a busy spot. Dominic is almost beside himself. The elation he feels from Ron's trust and offer of jobs, or commissions as he calls them. Tucking the sketches back in his bag, he returns to the watches and chuckles when he thinks to himself, "to kill time."

He's studying the clocks hanging on the wall when Ron Allain returns holding a parcel paper, unfolding it to expose an emerald cut ruby. The stone is the lush red of a rose, with no visible marks or inclusions, very rare. Offering it to Dominic, he smiles at his reaction, eyes wide, taking in the splendour of the gem.

"My client wants this stone set horizontally along a narrow band roughly three millimeters wide with a vine growing upward to the stone and four leaves holding each corner of the ruby. Not etched in but as an applique. Do you understand?"

"Aye, aye, I've an idea already."

"Well good. When can you get me a sketch?"

"How about this Friday, the tenth?"

"Perfect. Could we meet earlier in the morning? I'm an early riser and I could drop in at your shop to see what you've done, if you don't mind?"

Another handshake follows and a date is made for Friday morning at eight o'clock at Alexander's Jewellery Repair. With profuse thanks, Dominic leaves to meet Maria.

Almost to his driveway, he steps aside for a large wagon with a load of feed in bags that stops at the head of his entrance. The driver is a big man with wide shoulders, cap pulled tightly down. The lady who climbs down from the seat, he realizes, is Maria. There's no sign of goodbyes. No sooner than when she sets foot on the ground, the driver flicks the reins and pulls in behind an auto that passed. She sees Dominic and waves. Dominic doffs his hat and when he reaches her he points to the driveway.

"Welcome to your first day of work Maria and thank you for being on time. Come, let's go in and I'll get you familiar with what you need to start greeting customers."

"Thank you again, Dominic, I won't let you down."

"I'm sure of that."

He shows her where to hang her coat and keep a few things in the closet to the left of the stairs, the first door. He shows her where the other doors lead. The last on the left is into a small kitchen for him and the staff, a table, icebox, stove, narrow cupboards, a sink and a couch. A second door goes from the kitchen to the shop. First door on the right is a washroom, nothing special. The last room on the right is an office, or what is intended to be an office. Nothing is in much order except for the desk, chair and a box with papers in it. There's things Dominic hangs on to leaning along one wall, items he's purchased at auction that he has no use for at present, but he wanted. A weathervane with a rusted cock strutting on the top, almost full size, pointers like hunting arrows spin freely on a central rod. A writing table with a broken leg, the auctioneer called it an "*escritoire*", said it was very old. A maple desk with three side drawers and a thousand scratches. Other trinkets piled around those items.

Pointing out the table and chairs where they met earlier, he tells her that sometimes people need to wait and they can there. Taking her behind the counter, he reaches under to the open shelf and brings out the bill of sales booklet, a mandrel and a set of finger sizers. He shows her how he fills it out, asking her if she can draw a reasonable likeness. She uses her own ring as an example and draws a fair image of it, enough that it could be distinguished from others. He has her fill out a page so he can check her writing and whether she asks the right questions. More and more people are getting phones, so he reminds her to be sure to ask for a telephone number.

Because changing ring sizes is his most popular repair, he wants her to learn how to use the tools but lets her know he is just behind her in the shop until she perfects the sizing task. Using her ring again as a sample, she catches on to how it works and uses the sizing rings on all her fingers and by the fourth one she has a good idea of how simple it is. She will learn new things every day and he's always here to help her. He emphasizes for her not to be shy with her questions. He shows her where his cash drawer is and asks her to wait in the front while he opens his safe, which is at the back of the shop behind what looks like a closet door. After he opens it, he asks for her help.

"C'mon back in Maria and I'll show you where we put the jewellery. I have a box with work completed, to be picked up, and another where I put work to do."

The two boxes are placed on the counter inside the archway to the right of the workstation and to the left when you enter the room. Dominic tries to keep this area neat but loose envelopes and pencils lie about.

"So, this one has the names of each person on the top and inside is the jewellery and the sales slip. I always mark if not paid or if they give me a deposit, like I showed you. This other one is for what we get today. The box beside my desk that was in the safe too, is what I am working on. Understand all that?"

"*Ah oui*, I do. I know I'll have questions. That doesn't seem like too much. What else can I do?"

Looking at the clock over the boxes, he sees it is almost opening time. He points at the box with finished pieces in it.

"Well when you are not busy, you can start by getting these in order by alphabet and I left some scissors and heavy paper to make dividers with letters on them so it would be easier to find them, like A, then B… you know? Then after, you will find my jotting pad under the counter. Under it is a lot of loose leaves that keep numbers and addresses on but there is no order and I bought a better booklet at the stationers for keeping that stuff straight and if you could sort that out it would be good. So, I see someone at the door, it's time we open. "

He can tell she's a bit nervous from the hasty swallows. He caught how much she was paying attention to what he says and catches on quickly. He likes that. Following him, she watches as he unlocks the door and greets the gentleman.

"Good morning, Mr. Donnelly, are you here to pick up your wife's ring?"

"Yes, I am, and I see I'm the first customer today. Do I win a prize or anything?"

The three laugh at the easy banter, and Dominic introduces his new helper while escorting his customer back to the counter. Showing Maria where to find the ring, they deal with their customer together while Maria watches carefully. The charge for the work is $3.25. Donnelly offers a five-dollar bill. Maria doesn't hesitate to get his change and to write "Paid" on the customer's copy just as Dominic instructed her. Putting the ring in one of the small velvet bags stored under the counter, she passes it to the man.

"Thank you for your business, Mr. Donnelly."

After the customer leaves, Dominic pats her on the shoulder.

"Well done, Maria, you're going to do very well here."

Smiles of satisfaction grace each of their faces as they set about the day's work.

The next day Nick arrives early, having already been to the Hachey's to pick up the lumber. He has brought an older gentleman with him as well as another horse to work with his Clementine. The wagon digs ruts in the roadway from the heavy load – beams sixteen to twenty feet long for the frame stick out from the end of the wagon bed. Clementine and her partner's chest muscles strain against the leather stays attaching them to the wagon as they enter the slight rise of Dominic's driveway. They draw the load right up behind the house to the empty space where the barn will be built. They will unload the lumber close enough to use but out of the way. Dominic meets them at the end of the parking lot. Nick passes the reins to his companion and jumps down to meet Dominic. He points back at the wagon.

"That's my uncle, Omer Bourgeois. *Mon oncle*, this is Dominic Alexander."

Bourgeois is a slight man, with a face that seems to be perpetually smiling and a bright orange toque pulled down to his brow.

"Pleased to meet you, Mr. Bourgeois."

"And you as well, Mr. Alexander.

Dominic waves the greeting off.

"Call me Dominic, please, and I'll call you Omer, okay.

"*Oui*, sounds good to me, Dominic."

"So you know a bit of carpentry, Omer?"

"Worked at it most of my life with the Dunn Brothers, the housebuilders. Never had the patience for the finish stuff, but I've framed many a building. Don't do it too often now that I'm retired, but when I get bored, Nick always finds me something to do."

"That's good then, Omer. We can keep you from getting bored for sure. Now, Nick, I think if we put that load right at the edge of my yard, to the right of the old barn will be a good spot. I'll give you a hand. Can you back that wagon up with the horses?"

"*Bien*, can I back it up? Of course. Jump down, *mon oncle*, and bring the reins."

Nick walks the horses in a circle until the rear of the wagon faces the back of the house to the right, the empty hole to the left. He walks to the front and holds Clementine's cheek to his own, she whinnies at the gesture. Holding the reins tight, he speaks gently in French.

"*Recule, ma douce Clementine, recule.*" (Back up, my sweet Clementine, back up.)

Using his hand to guide her head in the way he wants her to go, the other horse following, he steers the wagon skillfully almost to the picket fence. It is the first of four loads he will deliver today. They empty the wagon. Dominic makes them tea and heats up some of his biscuits. While they take a few minutes upstairs in Dominic's kitchen, he shows them the sketches he has made, similar to a blueprint that Dominic has seen Tubs use. They talk about the framing and Dominic wants to use concrete to support the structure so they will need to begin with that. By the time they leave for the second load and Dominic hurries to change and clean up, they all agree that the building will probably take six to eight weeks.

CHAPTER 3

By the end of May, Maria has proven herself to be more than a clerk. She's a conscientious assistant. She sizes fingers perfectly, knows how much common repairs cost and only has to confirm with Dominic occasionally. She is never off by much most times. He's gotten to know more about her, especially how frustrated she is with her fiancé. They've known each other since she was thirteen. He's sworn off drinking but slips often and she has confided to Dominic that she grows weary of his promises as much as she cares about him. The worst part is that when he backslides, he gets very angry with her and aggressive. The last argument they had was only two days ago on Sunday when she was off and she vowed that it was the last time. She's even removed her ring and put it in her purse, loose on the bottom.

Dominic has come to rely on her heavily as his business grows, with him having more time behind the bench where the real money is made. She has established a system for repairs, custom pieces. In addition to her regular duties with the guests, any free time is spent organizing the office and work areas. She has taken on the cleaning duties as well when one morning she commented on the dust collecting on the sketch frames and windowsills. Dominic had told her that he did the cleaning, but with as much work as he has, he sometimes forgets to do the dusting. Now the floors always sparkle, the dust is gone and the downstairs washroom is so clean a person almost feels guilty for using it.

On the last Tuesday of the month, she's sweeping the floor in the main reception area when there are no customers and while doing so, notices how the large space seems wasted for only a waiting area. Dominic comes from the work area to retrieve his loupe and sees her, motionless, staring at the archway with a broom in her hand.

"Is something wrong, Maria?"

"Well, I was just thinking, Dominic, with so much empty space in this room, why don't you add a few counters and we could sell jewellery, maybe some watches, in addition to the repair and custom work you do? There's plenty of room and you could still keep a smaller seating area although it doesn't get used too much."

Dominic at first frowns at the idea – only because he never thought of it before. But when he looks around at the main area, he sees what she means. It is not anything he considered and yet it makes good sense.

"That's a great idea, Maria, but I don't know where I'd get the time to source out suppliers and find or build counters."

She brushes the small collection of debris into a metal dustpan as she speaks.

"I could look into it if you like. I wouldn't commit to anything of course when it comes to buying products, but I could do the searching for you."

Dominic is wiping his hands on his apron and meets her in the middle of the floor. Looking around he starts to imagine a layout for displays. He gestures toward the end of the counter where Maria and he greet the customers.

"I could add one there at the end and another at a right angle to it with lots of room in the back."

She's nodding and seeing the same thing. She moves to the left window.

"You could add one or two here where the light shines in."

"Aye, maybe just one there and we could start with three. I wonder if Ron Allain would help us. He might not like having another competitor, but he's been so helpful. Maybe you could go see him in the morning before you come to work if you have your buggy, ask him what he thinks."

"Yes, I'll have it tomorrow and I'll do that."

Dominic is overwhelmed at how smart Maria is and how she treats the business as if it were her own. He knows by now he can trust her completely and will give her key to the front door before she leaves today to show her how much he appreciates her. He returns to the work area contemplating the change. She must be too.

"You might have to make a new sign because you will be more than repairs."

He's smiling as he sits at his bench but is soon startled by the banging open of the front door, followed by a belligerent deep voice. When he looks out the window to the main area, he sees the large man who sometimes drops Maria off. He's waving a sheet of paper and angrily confronting her. Dominic soon realizes this is her fiancé, Jacques Fontaine, even though he has never met the man.

They begin to argue, with Maria telling him this is not the time or place. The man glares at her, grabs her by the arm and shakes her, almost yelling that she can't leave him. He's trying as best he can. He's still going on and on as Dominic comes from the back room and interrupts him.

"Unhand the lady, sir. You don't have to be so rough."

The man stares at Dominic. His hair, beard and clothing are disheveled. His breath reeks so bad that Dominic can smell the cheap booze from six feet away. Pointing at Dominic with a meaty finger he warns him.

"You mind your business!"

Dominic steps closer, not intimidated by the man's demeanor or size.

"This is my shop and what you do here is my business, especially when you are hurting a member of my staff. Now let her go!"

The fingers on Maria's arm dig in deeper and she yelps from the pain. Dominic realizes at that moment that she is more than an assistant; he cares for her deeply. He doesn't even give the man a chance to back off. Rushing forward, he slams his fist under the man's chin, knocking him backwards and loosening his grip on Maria. Clutching her arm, she hurries behind the counter, terrified at the outburst. Dominic steps closer and squares off. He raises one hand to protect his face, balancing on his toes and waving his other fist at the aggressor.

Jacques is rubbing his chin, amazed at the power of the punch from someone as light as Dominic. His eyes see red and anger overtakes him. He reaches back to take a swing but Dominic sees it coming and sidesteps, landing a hard fist into the man's midsection. When the man doubles over, Dominic delivers a blow to his temple, rattling the man`s brain. The swift action knocks the man upright. The eyes are glazed;

he's not even breathing, it seems, when he falls forward, slamming his heavy body on the floor.

Maria shrieks and runs from behind the counter to bend over the fallen man.

Dominic steps away, his heart beating rapidly, and looks down at Maria, who is touching her fiancé's face. He is full of doubt and thinks she's upset at what he's done. Only when she looks up at Dominic does he see the relief on her face, the look of adoration for Dominic's defense of her. Rubbing her forearm where she had been held, she stands and faces Dominic.

"Thank you. He's gotten worse lately, but this is the first time he's hurt me. We have to get him out of here, but please don't call the police. Help me get him in the wagon and I`ll take him to his house. His father will bring me back."

Dominic worries that when he comes to, he may hurt her again.

"What if he is even angrier when he wakes up? Will you be all right?"

"He's been drinking, I think he'll be out for a while. I'll be okay."

They get Jacques in the back of the wagon and cradle his head with an empty feedbag from the floor. Maria jumps up to command the two heavy horses. Dominic watches her leave. He calms down when he sees her in full control and returns to his work area. All he thinks about is the look on Maria's face when she checked to see if her fiancé was okay after Dominic knocked him out. There was something in her eyes he hadn't seen before as she had smiled at him.

Maria returns an hour later and apologizes over and over until Dominic has to tell her not to say it anymore. He understands. Changing the subject, he asks her to write down the things she thinks they will need if he decides to add items for sale – when she has time. Tending customers, repairing jewellery and carving a wax for a new design he is doing for the mayor's wife keeps them busy most of the day. At three o'clock, Dominic removes his apron and folds it over the back of his chair. Brushing the lint from his trousers, he straightens up his shirt, tucking it back in. The top drawer on his workbench is locked. He removes a key ring from his pocket to open it. Among a few personal items and loose change are several keys. He removes one of the largest, placing it in his pocket, and shuts the drawer. Looking out the open window to the main area, he sees Maria sitting at the table in the waiting area scribbling. Warm beams of mid-afternoon sun stream through the windows, shrouding her in an amber glow.

Approaching her, he studies her profile, her brow and chin so serious, eye and nose so delicate. Concentrating deeply, she doesn't hear him approach. He hates to disturb her, but he wants to get to work on the inside of the barn. It's almost done. He speaks softly.

"Maria?"

Startled by the interruption, she touches her heart with both hands, dropping her pencil.

"Oh my, Dominic, you scared me!"

"Oh, I'm… I'm sorry."

Recovering somewhat, she sees her pencil on the floor and bends to pick it up. Dominic sees the pencil also and acting like a gentleman, bends to pick it up, at the same time. Contact!

"Ouch!"

"Yeow."

They're both rubbing their head where they collided, each with a brief scowl that matches the pain. Dominic straightens up sharply and sees the look on her face. Expecting a reprimand, he sees the flutter of a smile. Thinking of the coincidence, he can't help but laugh. He leans on the table for support with one hand on his stomach, the other on the bump forming slightly above his hairline and roars. Maria is leaning forward in her seat, massaging the middle of her head. Her laughter is like chimes, delightful to hear. They carry on for a good minute until they're both grinning as widely as possible. Maria stands, straightens out her skirt and steps to one side.

"It feels nice to have a good laugh."

"Aye, it does. Made the pain go away too."

"I feel so silly"

Dominic waves the thought away, bending to pick up the pencil but not before holding out a warning hand that he is doing so, and that causes another chuckle.

"It's my fault. I shouldn't have scared you."

"Oh, you gave me such a start. I was thinking about the positioning of the counters and how we could use the natural light best."

"Aye, I could see how serious you were and hated to interrupt."

She closes her notebook to hold it in front of her with both hands. Still smiling she questions him with raised brows.

"What did you want to tell me?"

He digs the key from his pocket and holds it out to her.

"I'd like you to have a key for the front door so you can open and close if I am unable to do it. And today is a good day to start. I'd like to go change and work in the barn. The only thing left to finish is the fireplace mantle. If you feel you are ready, you can balance the receipts and money, leave it on my workbench and close up."

When she accepts the key, he can tell by her expression that she is pleased, perhaps a bit surprised. She closes her fingers over the key, regarding him with her warmest smile.

"Well *merci* for your trust, Dominic. If you show me where you keep your ledger, I can make the daily entries if you like. I've seen you do it and I like working with numbers."

"Aye, that's a grand idea, I get bored by that and don't keep it as up to date as I should. My accountant, Mr. Lombroso, is always scolding me for it. There are so many things to remember for a business; I get confused sometimes. So, sure, do the entries. the book is in the drawer under the counter where we keep the repair envelopes and I'll have a look at it later. Right now I'm going to change, and I'll be in the barn if you need me."

Back a little straighter, she moves to the doorway to the work area to retrieve the logbook wanting to familiarize herself now that they are not busy. She offers him a compliment over her shoulder.

"You and the men have done a wonderful job. I can't wait to see the inside."

"Well, come over after if you have time and I'll give you a tour."

Dominic goes out the back door, coveralls clad, and stops for a moment to admire the barn. The wide dark grey corners match the house and the lighter grey shingles are freshly painted. Two thirds the original size, it is an identical replica, a traditional country barn. Instead of tall main doors, he has opted for more windows and a regular door into each of the three sections, as well as an upper door in the left gable end to access the storage area. He loves the shrubs and flower beds that will soon expose their colors and the crushed stones in the driveway and parking. Instead of a stable, there is a paddock for horses in back. Tall white posts and rails match the picket fence.

He goes in the main door, wiping his boots on the newspapers he laid out. His tool belt lies where he left it on the temporary workbench he made for the restoration. It holds all his tools, some wood pieces and containers of nails and some screws. The walls are rough planks and wide beams. Doorways are centered on the right and left. The wall in the front is mostly window, waist high and an arms width wide. They face south, letting the sun in. The ceiling is beams and planks like the walls, filled with sawdust and seaweed for insulation. The floors are wide planks on their narrow ends, like the old one except this one has been lacquered to a high gloss.

The back wall is mostly river rock for the first eight feet, with a smaller window on each side and a wide fireplace in the center with the unfinished mantle. A tarp is spread out at the base of the wall and littered with sawdust and boot marks. A sawhorse holds down each end. In the center is another pair of sawhorses holding a temporary table. Removing his boots, he puts on a pair of tattered slippers Adairia gave him for Christmas two years ago and as usual he reflects on the image they conjure. They were all at her house Christmas Eve and she was feeling tipsy and teasing Duff he should dye his beard white to look more like Santa, making them all laugh. He can't wait for her next letter.

The mantle is almost finished when there is a soft knock on the front door and Maria enters. He guesses it's after six o'clock if she's closed up the store and is wrapped in her beige knitted shawl, carrying her purse and lunch bag. Stepping into the room, she hesitates when she catches sight of the fireplace and Dominic smiling at her. He can see the delight on her face, the wide smile where her dimples show.

"Ah, Dominic, *c'est beau, vraiment beau*! It's very nice."

"Thank you, Maria. Come in and I'll show you around."

The tour takes fifteen minutes and the last room he shows her is the space above on the right side of the building, which is mainly empty except for some leftover building material and two used couches that are going downstairs when he is finished. They're covered with a clean canvas tarp. There are three large windows facing east. Walking over to one of the windows that has a dusty film, she wipes a spot with her gloved hand to peer out. Dusk approaches.

"You can see the city and the river from here. What will this room be for?"

He's looking at her back as she gazes through the glass, watching her tilt her head to look towards the river and sees the faint indent on her cheek. He is smitten. The feeling is quickly followed by a fading image of Gloria, and guilt. He is torn by his adoration of Maria and his commitment to the young lady back in his homeland.

She turns to face him; he hasn't answered her question. Seeing the way he is staring at her, she is overcome by a sensation of deep attraction to his dark eyes, the loose bangs over his intelligent and handsome face. She wants to embrace him and feel his lips on hers, but she restrains herself, remembering him mentioning a girl back home and that he is her employer.

The silence is thick. They both know what is happening. Dominic is shy now and turns away to point at the back wall.

"I was thinking of making a studio up here for my sketching eventually, but I'm not sure yet and I'm in no hurry to do anything right now. I'm planning on…"

Interrupted by a hand on his shoulder, he turns to find Maria standing a few inches away from him. His heart races. There is no thought of anything except how beautiful this woman is and how much he wants her. Maria gives in to her impulse and reaches for his neck to pull him towards her. Their first kiss is delicious, prized with the passion of budding love. Maria is not shy when it comes to intimacy. Her tongue finds his and a rapturous sensation prickles his whole body. He's never been kissed like this before. The heat rises within them and she feels his reaction when she pushes her hips against his. Breathing heavily, she hesitates a moment, remembering how unpleasant her first and only experience was. She had offered her body to the man she thought she loved as an incentive for him to stop his wasteful drinking only to discover he was a selfish and an unrousing lover. Leaning back to look at the man in front of her, she sees only goodness, only adoration in his eyes. Taking both hands in hers, she places them on her breasts. She points at the couches.

"Take me now Dominic. Take me right here."

Maria is a grown woman, while Dominic is still an adolescent at heart. He's speechless and scared of not knowing what to do. She doesn't understand his reluctance until a new thought forms that she hadn't considered.

"Are you a virgin, Dominic?"

Nodding, he looks down at the floor, afraid she will see his embarrassment.

"Do you want me, Dominic?"

His head snaps up.

"Aye, aye Maria, more than I've ever wanted anything."

The dimpled smile. She reaches for his hand.

"*Vien*. Let's go to the house."

Curled upon his bed, their brows are still moist from their desires. She's spooned into him, her back to his chest. Engulfed within Dominic's arms, Maria holds them tight, reliving the passion of the last moments, enjoying the tingling she feels all over her body. He stares down at her profile: her eyes are shut, strands of hair lie playfully upon her cheek. He's in a fog. He had no idea that a person could experience so much pleasure, such intense pleasure. Unable to imagine anything better than the feeling of her soft and warm body so close to his, the contour of her firm breast filling one hand, the scent of something musky on her skin, he wishes this moment to never end. Enveloped in utter content, they doze.

Faint rays of light from the setting sun color the bedroom a short time later and Maria wakes to realize she has been smiling in her sleep. She feels Dominic's warm breath upon her cheek. Remembering his inexperience, she recalls the moment he entered her and the innocence on his face. It causes her to stir, squirming her behind against him. The movement awakens Dominic, and his response is the tightening of his loins as he thrusts against her. This time their lovemaking is exploratory, searching out where their efforts please each other the most, the heightened emotions caused by fingertips and tongue. This is the moment when they truly fall in love, a bond that will carry them into the future as one.

It's almost ten o'clock when they are sitting at the kitchen table, each wrapped in a blanket from the bed, nude underneath. She has the cloth wrapped like an East Indian sari just under her arms, covering her breasts. Dominic has the quilt tented over his shoulders and crumpled in his lap. Empty plates, a jar of strawberry jam, half-filled teacups and a ceramic sugar dish are on the table. Dominic burnt the first pair of toast and the scent lingers. They are laughing over the story of when Duff commented on a lady's portly stomach, asking her when she was due and finding out she wasn't pregnant. Duff sputtering and trying to cover himself, only making things worse.

They talk of their families; their intimate relationships. Who their best friends are. What colors they like. What they dream of for the future and how that might change now. Maria sheds a tear when Dominic tells her about the first time he went to live with Duff and the difficult parting with his mother. The death of his father and the demise of his brother William and the horrible ending of his uncle. The disappearance of his mother. She marvels at his fortitude and the way he describes each sibling with affection in his eyes. She is impressed by how brave he is to leave all that is familiar so far away, but sensitive to his reasons.

He listens with glee and interest when she describes her family, her best friend Denise Chiasson, her first pair of skates. He holds her hand when she shares the death of her mother and the worries of her brothers fighting in this awful war. Does Dominic know when it will end? She sips from her cold tea and tells him how fascinated she is with bees and the making of honey.

"Do you like honey, Dominic?'

"Aye, I do, a lot, and sometime I like it in my tea, but I don't always buy it."

"And don't you think it odd that something so delicious could be made by an insect? And people have honey farms and hives. I think it would be a fun hobby."

Dominic is shaking his head, sits back in the chair and pulls the quilt tighter.

"I don't like the little buggers. They can sting you."

"*Oui,* they can; but a bee dies if he does that, and I imagine he thinks twice about stinging you unless he feels the hive is threatened."

"I like quieter hobbies, like a scrapbook."

Elbows on the table with teacup poised in both hands, she speaks over the rim.

"Do you have one?"

"I do. I know it's late and I'll escort you home shortly, but would you like to see it?"

Dominic shuffles back to the bedroom, taking an extra minute to dress, eyeing her skirts laying at the foot of the bed, tangled among the blankets. He digs the scrapbook from the drawer of his night table and returns to the kitchen. She has followed him in and changes when he leaves her alone to return and clean off the kitchen table. When she returns, he has removed the dinnerware and jam and laid out several articles obviously cut from a newspaper. Seeing him arrange the items, she sees the enthusiasm in the unblemished forehead and wide grin, making him look so young. She always assumed he was close to her age, maybe a year younger but she wonders how old he really is. She'll ask him one day.

"Come, I'll show you what I'm pasting in next and then we'll head out."

Germany and Britain engage in sea battles off the Belgian Coast.
Canada and the US sign migratory bird treaty.
Montreal Canadians win the Stanley Cup, defeating the Portland Rosebuds 3 games to 2.
Germany ratifies bill becoming first country in the world to use Daylight Savings Time.
Jesse Willard and Frank Moran fight in World Boxing Championship to no decision after 10 rounds in NYC.
General Pershing and 15000 troops chase Pancho Villa back into Mexico.
Irish Republican army abandon Post Office in Dublin surrendering unconditionally to end the Easter Rising.

CHAPTER 4

The summer of 1916 is the happiest of Dominic's young life. Maria and he spend as much time together as they can. Cuddling at the movies. Long walks in the woods with birds serenading them and trees shushing in the warm breezes. Bonfires on starlit nights, the smell of smoke and the taste of cool nature upon their lips. The joy of revealing their feelings for each other to friends and her family. Sneaking kisses while at work. The first month Dominic frets over telling Gloria about Maria. He's promised Maria he will; they've talked about it. He experiences both passion and guilt when he is with Maria. Gloria is so far away, fading except for the warm feeling of a first girlfriend. He decides to write her soon and suggest she find someone else.

Two days later, on May 26, he receives a letter from Scotland. He's alone in the shop the next day sorting through the mail from the day before, the place not opened yet. A familiar white envelope has no usual return address in the upper left hand corner but from the large loops and graceful curves, he knows it's from Gloria. Dreading her words of endearment with shame coloring his cheeks, he tears off the glued edge and retrieves the pages. There are only two. When he reads the words, a slow grin reshapes his sorry face. It's not the emotion the writer expected. At the end, he tosses the sheets of paper into the air and lets out a yelp that resounds through the empty building.

"Och. I dinna need to do anything. She's met someone else and nicely told me to bugger off."

It's the first thing he tells Maria when she arrives to start work. They dance around the store holding hands and Maria flushes at the certainty of Dominic's love.

The store takes shape. Maria is a genius with numbers, percentages and profits, margins and expenses. Dominic helps select designs and quality pieces from the traveling agents but leaves the haggling to Maria. He and Maria have refused all offers of available credit with fair interest, paying only with check or in some cases cash. He picks out all the men's watches; she, the ladies'. The used cabinets he purchased have been refaced, with some new glass added. The woodwork matches the dark wainscoting. The gems and colored stones of rings, brooches, hatpins, earrings, pendants and chains sparkle when sunlight streams through the windows.

Even without advertising, sales are steady, and the business grows rich.

Maria brings Dominic to her country home to meet and have dinner with her father, Benoit, a kindly man with thinning hair and bushy eyebrows. After supper on a warm June evening, she leads him to the river near her house to follow a narrow path westward for a hundred feet to where a clearing opens and fallen logs frame a rough fire pit. Trees encompass the nest and face the water. The river is narrower here before it curves away and gurgles musically over logs and river stones. The shadows of the trees grow longer as the day ends. She has Dominic light a fire and when they sit, she removes a blanket she left earlier in the day from behind one seat. Dominic doesn't need to ask what it is for. With night approaching and the warm air from the fire, they snuggle together. Their kisses are passionate as they remove each other's clothing. Their lovemaking is slow and tender. Later when the fire begins to die and with Maria held tightly to him, he explains to her that he is not as old as he previously told her. He is three years younger.

She grows quiet, not from disappointment but from awe of someone so young having experienced so much heartbreak and so much success. When she lays her head on his shoulder, he knows his worrying was for naught.

"We'll not tell anyone yet, Dominic, and it doesn't matter to me. I love you no matter how old you are."

The old boyfriend stops at the store at the end of July and Dominic steps from the back room thinking another confrontation is coming but is relieved when Jacques explains he has joined the army and has come to say he's sorry for his past behaviour and wishes them well. It will be the last time they ever see him. Like so many others, his life will be lost in the terrible war.

CHAPTER 5

In early July, the Battle of the Somme begins. The French Sixth Army assaults the German Second Army at Foucaucourt-en-Santerre along the River Somme. The war claims thousands of lives, technology providing new ways to kill: rapid fire machine guns, poison gas and submarines. Scientists and engineers have been given the task to create a vehicle that can overcome the stalemate in the war, a way to advance over the trenches of men and their munitions. As a result, the British, French and Germany develop tanks – armored land ships.

In the victory of the Canadian Corps and its allies in the Battle of Hill 62, Corporal Raymond Desjardins dies leading his men forward into a blaze of German fire. When the war ends, he will be hailed a hero, but two months after his death he is being mourned by his family in Notre Dame. No body to honor, only a letter announcing his death and the honors to be bestowed, hand delivered. The bearer, a middle-aged man in uniform and a shared sorrow upon his face, apologizes for the late notification, blaming the extremes of the vile war. The memorial service is being held today, the second Sunday in September.

Somber clouds grace the skyline behind the church, the late morning sun not yet risen above them. Still it frosts the upper edges with a yellow tinge, softening the sad greyness below. Mourners comment on the possibility of sunshine, offering the family a little hope. The air has a tint of burning coal from the train that rolled through only moments ago, its load mainly freight. Maria crinkles her nose at it when she disembarks from her carriage, Dominic at her side. Her father pulls the buggy away from the church; being early, the parking area only has one other buggy, probably Father Hébert's.

The church was built in 1909, a simple enclosure with the basic raised nave and apse, tall paneled windows, wide front doors and hard wooden pews on each side. Candles flicker around the altar, with wisps of blackish smoke escaping from the frosted white vials containing them. In the middle of the aisle at the front, near the railing where people kneel to receive communion, is a small table covered by a crisp, linen cloth that drapes on all sides to the floor. On it sits a wreath, propped up by a wooden easel. A photo of Corporal Desjardins, issued by the Canadian Corps, is in a golden metal frame that stands beside the circle of flowers.

The church is full, men standing in the back. The Desjardins family is held in high regard and most of the village is there to pay their respects. Dominic escorts Maria to the front left pew to join her father and her brother, Private André Desjardins, who is home on bereavement leave from the Valcartier military base in Quebec. The oldest brother, Robert, remains in England. Aunts and uncles and many cousins occupy the four pews behind them.

At the end of the mass, Father Hébert invites the family to the table. Dominic remains seated while Maria, André and their father huddle around the frame, their arms about each other. The silence is so absolute you can hear the several tears from the old man splatter close to the frame. No one moves to wipe it away. Maria's stoic mien disguises both her anger and sorrow at the madness of the war, the end of her brother's life. André stares at the photo, afraid to blink, a stiffness in his chin. It could be him.

Afterwards, the family and close relatives gather at Maria's father's home. The two-storey house is similar in style to Dominic's, a bit smaller, and with a covered porch only on the front. White shingles and black trim were painted last summer and gleam with the last sun of the day. The Cocagne River weaves back and forth behind the house, close enough you can hear the trill of water. People are sitting on the porch, Benoit in his rocker. Some are still eating, with plates on their knees. A few younger men are in the back, near the woodshed, tipping from someone's bottle. A funeral is a good occasion to have a drink, a toast to the brave man. Dominic wipe's a dribble of the hard liquor off his chin, shivers at the alcohol's bite and thanks the new friends he's met.

"Aye, that's wicked stuff. Maria said some of her cousins were full of mischief, and I think she was talking of you boys."

A ripple of laughter circles the quartet. Dominic promises to remember their names when he sees them again and looks each man in the eye. His Scottish brogue has a similar rolling R as the French and pleases the men.

"Jean Marc." To the tallest one.

"Pierre." To the youngest one.

"Jerome." To the stoutest one.

Amid backslapping and jocular jesting, Dominic notices Maria in the driveway bidding farewell to her uncle Fernand, the bachelor, helping him into a buggy. He can see the fatigue in her eyes, the errant curls on her forehead, the smile he knows is forced. Reaching into his right jacket pocket, he fingers the small velvet bag. Knowing she needs a break, he catches up with her before she goes back in the house.

"Maria, Maria my dear, I can see the strain on your pretty face. You're always greeting people, serving people, comforting others, grieving yourself. Come for a walk with me, down to the fire pit. We'll sit a few moments and you can rest some. If it's like any funeral back home, this won't end soon."

She is about to protest, thinking like the woman of the house, of all the things needing to be done when there's a crowd in her home. Seeing the caring in his eyes and his caring smile, she knows she could use his strong arms around her.

"*Oui, c'est une bonne idée.* A very good idea, actually. Only for a bit, Dominic. Some people will be leaving soon – the older ones – and I'll want to thank everyone for coming. But I need a hug. Let's go now because if I go back in someone will be looking for me."

Maria and Dominic stroll hand in hand to the small enclosure along the river and are sitting on one of the logs, turned towards each other. She hangs her head, with her eyes closed, and her voice is soft and sorrowful.

"Ray was the middle brother, the referee in the family, and the one who stood up for me the most. He was so handsome, the girls all were crazy over him. He almost married a girl from Richibucto, Lynn was her name. Some Fontaine guy stole her heart. Losing her made him feel sad and short-tempered for a couple of months, until he realized she wasn't the only girl in town."

She lifts her head to look at Dominic, a half smile betraying her grief.

"He liked telling jokes too, Dominic, I don't know how he remembered them all. I'm sorry you never met him. I know you would have liked him."

"Aye, I'm sure I would. And I love a good joke."

She turns to stare at the river on her left. The water moves over a fallen log on the opposite side, churning bubbles and eddies where it falls, never changing. She nods her chin at the stream and returns her gaze to Dominic.

"No matter what happens here today, or yesterday or tomorrow, the river is always the same, always moving on. I feel we have to be like that, and I know Raymond will now be a memory."

Dominic moves closer to embrace her, offering her the comfort and support of his body and heart. Relishing the soft scent of lavender from her *eau de cologne*, he decides that now is the time.

He holds her shoulders in his hands and gently pushes her to arm's-length from him. Looking into the most perfect blue eyes, his heart starts beating fast. Reaching into the pocket again, he grasps the soft bag. Maria is looking at him with wonderment on her brow, her eyes shaded. Dominic is blushing, an awkward shyness overcomes him when being intimate and she wonders what he is up to. Surprised when he moves to kneel on strewn leaves, she gets goosebumps from what it might mean.

"Maria Desjardins, will you marry me and be my wife?"

Taking her right hand in his, he turns it face up. Opening the drawstring on the gray bag, he empties it into her palm. The oval amethyst is clear and sparkles even in the low light. The perimeter is surrounded with alternating diamonds and smaller amethysts. He knew how much she loves the purple-colored stone. She often commented when they were choosing engagement rings for the store, saying she would rather have her favorite stone than a diamond if she ever got engaged again.

"Oh Dominic, yes, yes I would be proud to be your wife and I've never seen a more beautiful ring. You made this, didn't you? You are such a talented and romantic man."

She slips the ring on her finger and has to push gently to get it over the knuckle and Dominic frets momentarily, thinking it might be too small but the rings slides on, fitting perfectly. She holds it up and away from her to admire the sparkle coming from the many facets.

"Wherever did you find such a rich purple, Dominic? It's so lovely.

I can't wait to show it to my friends and cousins. Is that okay if we tell them now?"

Still blushing and beaming, he's nodding his head.

"Aye, if you think it is the right time, Maria. And maybe we can talk about a date sometime soon."

Lowering her hand to her lap, the smile disappears. Seeing the concern on her face, Dominic wonders what is wrong.

"Oh, Dominic. I want this terrible war to end. I want my brothers to come home and for things to be like they were before. With Raymond gone now, some things are changed forever. When we get married, it will be the second happiest day of my life after today and I don't want any more bad news. Can we wait until after the war, *mon amour*?"

Feeling selfish, he nods again with a smile, knowing she is right.

"So long as you don't change your mind."

"Never!"

They embrace fiercely, love flowing through their bodies like alternating current with the sparks and intensity on the inside. She whispers in his ear.

"I will always love you, Dominic, I know that now. *Vien*, let's return to the house. I want to show my father."

When she cuddles next to Dominic and announces their engagement, Benoit is the first to react. He stands to face Dominic, grips his hand in both of his, shaking it with a look of pride on his face. Words are not necessary; he smiles at his daughter. She knows her father well enough to know he approves. Everyone surrounds Maria when she shows off her new ring.

CHAPTER 6

André Desjardins is sent to war. Fighting with the Canadian Corp attacking a German Marine Brigade, they push the enemy back 400 yards east of Courcelette. Their orders are to capture a section of the German front lines along the River Somme. Historians will refer to it as the battle of Ancre Heights. October 9 is chilly, unending rain. Both sides are dug in, defeated by the weather. Three hundred and fifty yards from an enemy machine gun pit through empty fields is a stone house – its existence measured in generations; its defeat measured in minutes when artillery shells destroyed the front half. Two bedrooms in the back have been salvaged as cover from the enemy where Corporal Desjardins and four members of his platoon are held up against the paralyzing downpour. Night approaches from the east with soldiers hoping for sunrise when the light will be in their enemy's eyes. The plan is to attack when the sun breaches the level plains around them. Tonight, the men will get some much-needed rest.

Desjardins lies his head back on a rickety bed, the mattress stained with mud from the heavy coats of other soldiers. His turn on watch is in two hours and he wants to sleep, needs to sleep. Before he nods off, he thinks of his sister, Maria. A warm smile splits his face and he hopes she's having fun, that someone is having a party for her. She loves birthday parties.

In Moncton, the ninth has a moody beginning. Sun and clouds vie for attention and push each other about. Off again, on again sunlight does nothing to dampen Maria's mood. Today she turns nineteen. Because the shop is closed on Mondays, Dominic is meeting her at

235

Creaghans in an hour when they open at nine. He's promised to buy her a new hat. She fusses with her hair, a playful look in her eyes. Her wavy hair is short and falls to her ears with the ends curling outward. The old mirror in her aunt's spare room is losing its silver and there are blotches in the reflection. She can't see what the left side is like in the back but it will have to do. She does a little spin admiring her dress in the mirror.

Almost to her ankles, the skirt is the softest cotton, the shade of lilacs. A belt of the same material gathers at the waist, emphasizing Maria's flattering figure. A bodice with a one button front is open around the neck. Wider lapels lie flat and like the two delicate pockets on the front of her dress are purple velvet. The ensemble is casual with a hint of elegance and suits Maria perfectly. It's her birthday present to herself and she can't wait to show Dominic.

She lives close enough to downtown and there is no wind today so she decides to walk. The weather is warmer than usual, with the thermometer hitting sixty-five degrees and its only 8:45. Still she wraps a beige shawl about her shoulders stopping at the entryway mirror to double check her hat. The one she is wearing this morning is beige with a black silk band around it. The brim is wide and holds a cloth rose on the left. She hopes to find one with purple trim to match her new dress.

When she turns the corner onto Main, she is only a block away from the store. Dominic is leaning against the storefront, reading a copy of the *Times*. He doesn't see her yet and she stops a moment to admire the man she is in love with. His hair is in a pompadour and she giggles knowing that by the end of the morning it will be flopping on his forehead. The thin mustache appeals to her. Dark eyes roam the paper peacefully and a half grin softens his face. He mentioned he might be looking for a hat too. She boldly steps towards him and seeing no one close by she disturbs his reading.

"Hello, lover."

Startled by the soft voice he looks about, blushing at the endearment. Young ladies usually don't talk like that in public, but that's Maria, he thinks. Tucking the paper under his arm, he turns to greet her with a full smile.

"You shouldn't call me that in public."

"Why not?"

"Well, we're not married and young ladies are supposed to be chaste and all, aren't they?"

The eyes are mischievous and match her mood when she teases him.

"There's no one around and it's my favorite way of thinking of you."

He wraps his arms around her and offers a quick peck on the cheek so as not to disturb her lipstick. Squeezing him tightly, she holds him for a moment until two elderly ladies pass by tsk-tsking. Taking his hand, she leads him into the store, reminding him of his promise. The hat shopping takes a little over an hour. She chooses a mauve, wide brimmed hat with one side raised for a jaunty look. A wide purple ribbon surrounds the bonnet and ends in a bow on the other side. The next half hour is spent laughing at poor Dominic, who looks funny in most hats. At first he feels insulted that she finds it amusing, but her laughter is infectious and he joins in with crazy faces to match each one he tries. Only when he places a black fedora upon his head, cocked forward, does she stop laughing.

"Oh, how nice, Dominic. That's the one. Makes you look mysterious and successful. You should take that one."

"If you like it, then I will. The cold weather is coming and I'm tired of always wearing the one with the big earflaps."

"*Ah oui*, that'll make me happy too."

Laughing together, they go to the cash and Dominic forks over a ten-dollar bill for the hats. Hers is the latest design and costs almost four dollars. His is three fifty. Gathering the change and the hatbox holding the hat she came with. He decides to wear his. He asks her if she would like to walk over to Benny's Diner. He knows she doesn't like to eat first thing in the morning, and she is likely hungry by now. Will she have breakfast with him? They can talk about the party tonight and make sure they have everything they need. He also has three surprises for her.

"But Dominic, the hat is more than enough and my party is costing you quite a bit. I don't need anything else."

"Aye, but these surprises have nothing to do with your birthday."

"Can't you tell me now?"

"I'm afraid not, my dear. C'mon now, let's go have a bite and then I'll tell you."

Entering Benny's, they find a booth close to the back of the restaurant and when they slide in, the older waitress, whom Dominic now knows to be Debbie from Hillsborough, brings a cup of tea and two menus.

"Good mornin', young folks. I know Dominic here likes his tea, but what will you have to drink, Miss?"

"I'd like a tea also please, but just black. Thank you."

They decide on an omelet, his with cheese and hers with cheese and ham. Both order toast as well. Debbie refills their tea cups, telling them it won't be long. Adjusting her skirts, Maria sits up and her eyes sparkle.

"Well, what is the surprise about, Dominic?"

"Well first off, I wanted to tell you about a property I own in Cocagne?"

"In Cocagne? How come you never mentioned it before?"

Dominic fidgets in his seat, uncomfortable that he hasn't told her about the house.

"To be honest Maria, there has been so much going on in our lives since I bought the old MacDougall farm and turned it into a business, then the fire and hiring you, the crazy war in Europe, worrying about family back home and well, it's just life getting away from me and it never seemed important. But now that we plan on getting married, I want to share it with you."

A bit of a frown on her face but he can see from the eyes that she is pleased. He continues.

"When I first arrived here, I knew a bit about Cocagne and Moncton from Pascal telling me about his homeland. You remember who Pascal is?"

"Yes of course, he married your sister Mary."

"When I visited the village, there was a house situated across the road from the bay and it was for sale. It looks out at the northern portion of a fairly long island, maybe a mile or so away. The sun rises over the water, or ice when I first saw it. The colors are amazing, orange like fire, yellows and pinks and a hundred shades of blue. There are many acres of land and some on the water. It was a very good deal really and I knew that someday I'd want to live there, but I had to establish my business first, so I bought it more on impulse but have not been there since last fall."

They're interrupted when Debbie brings them their breakfast. Placing the plates before them she inquires if they need anything else. Confirming that they don't, she leaves them to their meal. They dig in with relish, Dominic because he's famished. Maria questions him between bites; she wants to know more about the house. She loves to decorate and it could be hers as well someday.

"What do you plan on doing with it, Dominic?"

"I was hoping that we could go visit soon, and next spring we could start to make some changes and make it comfortable for us. Maybe as a summer home for now or maybe to move there when we get married."

"Oh, how exciting, Dominic, but how would we get back and forth. It's quite far."

"Aye, but that's surprise number two. The business is doing very well, thanks to you. And according to the last statement that my accountant gave me, I've made back all I've spent on the business. So I'd like you to help me shop for an automobile. What do you think of that?"

He can tell by the half smile she's not totally convinced. She hurriedly swallows her last bite and after a sip of tea, she nods her pretty head.

"An automobile, Dominic? Those things make such a foul smell and so much noise, but they seem to be getting very popular though."

Her face lights up with a sudden thought.

"Could you teach me to drive it?"

That's Maria, he thinks, willing to try anything new. He laughs at her suggestion. With a moue, the smile disappears, but before she can protest Dominic goes on.

"Nae, I don't know how to do that myself. But when we find something we like, we can both learn. How about that?"

"*Oui*, that makes sense. When did you want to do it?"

"How about right after our breakfast? We could go down to the Ford dealership on Main Street and take a peek. Nothing fancy and extravagant like Van Geist's new Packard. That's a beauty. I understand the Model T's are priced very reasonably, thanks to Mr. Ford's way to build them, on a production line. Can you imagine such a thing, Maria?"

"I don't understand things like that, Dominic, I only want to know where it will take us."

The possibilities of such freedom cause a dreamy look upon her brow.

"It'll be fun, yes, let's go today."

"Good, we'll walk down after we're finished here."

They finish off the eggs and order more tea. Maria opts for a piece of apple pie, exclaiming that she can't eat the whole thing but will share it with him. When they are all done and the table has been cleared except for their cups, she pushes hers away and sits back with her hands in her lap.

"What's the last surprise?

"It's not as much as a surprise, Maria, more of a request. You know how my accountant prepares my monthly statement I mentioned earlier, you've seen them of course now that you are so involved in the business. What would you think if I gave you the ten dollars each month and you keep track of everything like you do the daily balances? We could have the figures checked a couple of times a year."

"Why, Dominic, I'm flattered that you think me capable of doing that. I do love numbers. I'd need a little guidance. Do you think Mr. Lombroso would be willing to show me even though he's losing the business?"

"Aye, I'm sure he'd be interested if we offer to pay for your lessons. We'll have to ask. We could go see him later."

Now she's visualizing the extra income and is all smiles. Knowing that she and Dominic will marry when the war is over, she is still on her own and would never think of imposing upon her fiancé for extra money. She'll even be able to save some.

"*Oui*, Dominic, I'd like that very much."

"Perfect, now that that's settled, let's go shopping for a new Ford."

By midafternoon, they have decided the four seats of the Touring model would be worth the extra cost. The man selling them the car is shining the front fender where they left fingerprints, showing Dominic what is under the bonnet. The brass trim around the radiator and the Ford logo in the middle glow with a high sheen. The cloth top is up even though the sun is shining and the day is warm enough to make Dominic remove his jacket. His sleeves are rolled up above the elbow and a bead of sweat creases his brow and upper lip. He's been practicing starting the car and getting under way. There's much to remember. He feels certain of what to do and is ready to leave. Maria is sitting in the front right seat and waves at him through the windshield. Speaking loud enough for her to hear him, he points down with his thumb.

"Remember, now, when it starts, push the lever on the left side of the steering wheel down."

"*Oui, oui*, I know, I know. Hurry up, Dominic. This is so exciting."

With the crank in his hand, he's going over everything quickly in his mind.

The fuel tank has been topped up; he set the emergency brake — it'd be embarrassing to get run over by his own car. He advanced the spark adjust lever to retard, set the battery switch to the off position, adjusted the throttle to ¼, the switch is off and he doesn't need the choke because the engine is still warm. Confidently he inserts the crank and gives it a rapid spin, it only needs the one. Stepping back, he replaces the crank in its storage slot, grins at Maria and the engine is soon running smoothly. Wiping sweat away with his upper arm, he shouts out to the salesman who has stepped back from the car.

"Thanks for helping us out today, Mr. Selkirk."

"You're quite welcome. You catch on very quickly and *thank you* for your business, Mr. Alexander. We'll have all your paperwork in order tomorrow and I'll call you at your business when it's ready. Good day to you and Miss Desjardins."

Climbing up in the driver's seat, he flicks a switch to battery, he moves the brake lever into position, adds some throttle, pushes the right pedals and the car moves forward slowly, as tentative as the new driver. When Dominic is leaving the car lot he forgets to look for oncoming vehicles or buggies. In doing so he means to go left towards his home and pulls out in front of a four horse team pulling a heavy dray laden with lumber and strong beams. The lead horse closest stops short and with heavy hooves paw at the moving menace. The yardarm comes taut and the forward momentum of the wagon shoves the Clydesdale forward. Its breath warms Maria's cheek, it's that close. She screams. The lead hoof comes down on the stiff running board, and the car rocks awkwardly up and down.

Instinctively, Dominic pushes the throttle to full, pushes the left pedal to shift the car into high gear. The grinding is almost as loud as the neighing of the startled horses and the damnation of their handler. The car jerks into motion and its left rear wheel spits out a bit of dirt as it cuts into the turn. Not used to the higher speed he's soon catching up to another car in front of him that is trying to pass a buggy. Pulling back the throttle he gets the car straightened out.

When he finally looks over at Maria, she's as white as a new hankie, hands against her heart and panting.

"*Ah, mon Dieu*, that scared me Dominic."

"I'm sorry, Maria. It scared the dickens out of me too. I never even thought to look. Is there damage on the side?"

Maria bends over the door to peer down and sees a dent, scratch marks and dirt made by the prancing hoof.

"Yes, Dominic, there is a mark on the thing you stand on to get in."

"It's the running board. Damn, I haven't owned the car for more than an hour and I've already had an accident. What do you think of that?"

She's mad at him but she sees by his frown he's feeling guilty. There's a blush in his cheeks, so he's embarrassed too. Probably punishment enough. She's not going to let this ruin their afternoon.

"*Bien*, Dominic, it is only your first time. You've never driven a car before and look at you, you're doing great."

He is. The other car turns up Highfield Street, the only thing in front of him is a buggy for four, pulled by a pair of trotters, black and sleek. The horses are at a slow pace. The road leads out of the city towards Dominic's place. There is nothing coming towards them. He pulls the Model T to the left, and at ten miles per hour, he sails past the buggy. A lick of dust follows them. He can't smile any wider at the freedom he feels, the places he can go. Lots of confidence now.

"Let's drive to Salisbury and back, then we can go home. It's still a nice day and..." Pausing to check his watch. "...it's only a little after three. People won't be arriving for the party until seven o'clock. We have lots of time."

Maria is enthralled with the car, sitting watching the landscape go by. The seats are not well padded and when the road is rough she can feel the bumps. Already thinking of cushions, she wonders what color would look best in here with all the black.

"*Oui, oui*, let's do that, Dominic. This is so much fun. I can't wait for you to teach me how to drive it. And go faster."

They arrive home as the sun is setting, it's farewell a pinkish glow on the horizon. Dominic has all the gears, pedals and buttons figured out and changes them as needed with confidence. He's tired. As much fun as it's been, he will be glad to get home and start the party, everything is ready. Besides the sore bum, Maria is elated. The idea of going places so much faster fascinates her. She can't wait to go see the house in Cocagne. And she can't wait for the party to start, Nick said he was bringing his guitar and her uncle is bringing his harmonica and if Denis can come, he's bringing his fiddle.

"When can we go see the house, Dominic?"

"How about next Sunday?"

Before she can reply, the car sputters and starts to lose acceleration to finally jerk to a complete stop fifty feet from his driveway. The car lights go out. Dominic stares at the dead space and when he realizes what happens, hangs his head on the steering wheel.

"I forgot to check for fuel."

Maria can't help but grin. She pats him on the shoulder.

"So what, Dominic? Look how close we are. Better here than a few miles behind us. It could be worse, you know."

Almost in symphony with her statement, a few clouds get together and agree. The rain comes down in heavy pelts. The drops tap-tap on the roof like applause. Looking at each other, they can't help but laugh. They chuckle until they fall into each other's arms. The culmination of the day's highs and lows sweeps through them, and they share the joy. Their lips meet, kisses and soft caresses follow. Dominic is so thankful for the strong woman in his arms, his hugs almost crush her.

Maria holds him tightly, her head upon his chest. She feels the beating of his heart. She's never felt so loved.

As suddenly as it started, the patter of the rain stops abruptly and the quiet disturbs them from their embrace. Maria looks up at him.

"I love you, Dominic Alexander. I can't wait to be your wife. Now let's go get ready for our guests."

CHAPTER 7

The following Sunday, making a note that they need to set up an appointment to have the running board fixed on Monday, they leave Moncton at nine o'clock. The sky is cloudy and a gentle breeze carries the promise of warmth. The road is shouldered by trees ablaze in a multitude of colors; crows and seagulls circle above. At one time Dominic has the car up to twenty-five miles per hour, and Maria's scarf flutters in the wind. There is a smattering of rain when they travel through Shediac Bridge, but by the time they leave Grande Digue, it turns into a mist making the windshield blurry and driving difficult so they stop at the edge of the road until it ends, which only takes a few minutes. The clouds are traveling from east to west and by the time they reach Cocagne, the horizon is turning blue with rays of warmth following them.

The drive to Cocagne from Moncton takes them two hours and forty-five minutes in the Model T. Entering the community from the east, they can see the Bayview Hotel where Lover's Lane starts. Across the river mouth there is a schooner in full sail departing the wharf.

They had to bring extra gas along and the fumes sometimes escape from the closed containers in the rear seat and wrinkle Maria's nose.

"That fuel stinks."

"Aye, it does, but I wasn't sure where I could get gas along the way so I needed to bring it along in case. I know now that I can get gas in Shediac, but that's still a ways from Cocagne. I'll drop these off at the house, which is not far from here. Look out at the bay Maria, I think the sun is coming out."

Crossing the old bridge, they turn right at the corner and travel through the empty fields away from the village for eight miles. The road that follows the coastline is narrower here, rutted and slow going, with very few cars, mostly buggies and wagons. Houses and farms follow the road, sometimes over half a mile apart. When they are within view of Dominic's house, the full sun appears from the clouds and a gust of warm air pushes them along. Pointing ahead, Dominic's face lights up.

"That's the one there, Maria, close to the road."

Maria perks up when she sees the house, not so much for its features because it is like many they have seen on the trip. It is built similar to homes along the way, with a storey and a half in the front and a one-storey kitchen in the back. There's a good size shed behind the house and a smaller building that looks like it may have held chickens at one time. A field stretches behind for hundreds of feet until it runs up against a wooded area. She's excited about what it's like inside and what condition it's in. And she hopes Dominic will let her decorate.

"It looks nice Dominic, but it might need some new paint. And there's so much land. Is that field yours too?"

Concentrating on getting the car over the narrow culvert, he downshifts to low and reduces the throttle.

"Aye, and a bunch of the forest as well – almost a hundred acres."

He wears a look of accomplishment as he brings the car to a stop right by the back door, a mere three steps to a short stone walkway. Flat stones of different sizes are sunk in the sod and narrow strips of grass grow around them. As wide as the back door, it stops two steps from the house. It's the first thing she sees when she opens the door after he shuts off the car.

"Look Dominic, how nice."

Setting the brake lever, he alights from the vehicle and stands beside her, nodding.

"Aye, I understand the owner's father did this over fifty years ago when he built the house. Here's the key. You lead the way and we'll have a look."

He marvels at her gumption wearing trousers. Not many women do, and mostly women engaged in industry because of the war. Black cotton, flared hips, rolled up on the bottom, cinched tightly at the waist with a wide belt, she has paired them with a pink cotton blouse. An orange and pink flowered scarf is tied about her hair. He's thinking she could be a catalogue model. And while inserting the key in the door, she's thinking if the place hasn't been occupied for a long time, where would she start first.

The door opens with more of a groan than a squeak, like it's gotten lazy from not being used. It reveals a cookstove sitting kitty corner about ten feet away. A rough wood box is against the wall between them and the stove. Woodchips are sprinkled on the floor around the box. A few split logs stick out the top, united by cobwebs. The door opens against the end wall. A hall tree and boot mat line the rest of the wall. To their right is a pine table with three matching chairs and a stray – stiffer and darker skinned – that sits at one end. Perhaps signifying it was the head of the table. An ice box is on the right, cupboards against the lower wall, no doors but curtains covering the contents. The counter goes around to a pump and then a door that opens to other rooms.

Walking slowly through the house and commenting on what's good and what's bad and how much dust there is, they tour a small rectangular sitting room, a bedroom and a pantry downstairs and two bedrooms upstairs, with most of the furniture still in them. No closets.

"Put that number one on your list, Dominic. You need to have a closet. Where did these people keep their clothes?"

"Probably folded and in the dressers we saw in the bedrooms. Some people don't have much clothes anyway, unlike some girls I know."

She slaps him on the upper arm playfully.

"Don't you like the way I look?"

He puts his arms around here and she keeps hers defiantly by her side.

"I love the way you look. I love the way you look right now."

Warming up to him, she hugs him closely.

"We still need a closet, don't you think?"

"I'll build you twenty closets if you want, or turn the whole place into one big closet."

Warm laughter fills the old room with new sounds. Knowing her weakness for his embrace, she pushes him away.

"One will do nicely, Dominic. Now let's get busy and clean this place up. Go get the things we brought with us."

It's almost four o'clock by the time the house has been dusted, floors swept and mopped, furniture rearranged, some selected for removal, and a list made of things they need to bring when they return: sheets, pillows, blankets, plates and mugs as well as food. Dominic has roughly sketched the rooms and added dimensions; they've discussed any remodeling that should be done. The kitchen stove works, the one in the sitting room needs the chimney swept. The pump works and needs to be primed. They decide they will spend a few weekends here before winter comes, and to be safe from neighborly gossip, they will bring a third person so that Maria's reputation will not be blemished – most likely her friend Denise or maybe Nick and his girlfriend.

They lock the house and cross the road to walk the short distance to the beach on the land that is also Dominic's. The sun is behind them as it sets in the west and with the level terrain the colors along the horizon shift from pink to blue in a glorious array that is only rivaled by a sunrise. Maria is exhausted from the day's work and holds Dominic's arm when they traverse the rocky slope, six careful steps. The sand extends for several feet, turning into small pebbles where the water washes the finer grains away. The tide is coming in and wavelets spill against the shore, making a splashing sound. They stand at the water's edge and Dominic bends his head back and with eyes closed breaths deeply through his nose.

"I've never smelled anything so clean, Maria. And just above it, almost like a perfume, the brine of the bay and broken seashells reminds us where we are. I'm so lucky to be here."

Maria smiles and looks up to Dominic but frowns when she sees a forlorn look on his face. She was expecting his happy face.

"What's wrong, Dominic? What's on your mind?"

"I've been thinking of your brother André, somewhere in Europe fighting the Germans, probably scared and hungry; and your brother Robert, flying into danger. Here I am, earning a living and enjoying life. I should be doing more for the war effort."

Maria turns her back to the water and steps in front of Dominic. Eyes wide with surprise, her voice trembles.

"Oh, you can't, Dominic. You already tried and you told me they refused you because of your leg. Even now if it's humid, you comment on a dull throb in the bone. And besides, my family has given so much already to the war; I can't bear if you go too."

"Aye, you're right about your family and even more reason for me to go, there must be something I can do. There's talk of conscription and I'd probably have to go anyway."

He steps closer to hold her, her eyes the same blue as the horizon tearing up. Embracing her tightly, with her head on his shoulder, he anguishes over his decision. He thinks of Duff and his Da, knowing what they'd do in the same spot. He must at least try, bad leg or not. He's also sensitive to Maria's feelings and how difficult it would be to go. He can feel her sobbing. He owes it to her to think about it more and allay her fears of his not returning because, he swears to himself, if he goes, he's coming back.

"I'm not going tomorrow, Maria. We'll talk about it again. I just wanted you to know how I feel. I get a stab of guilt every time I walk by the recruiting station on St. George Street. And your brothers are so brave."

She steps back, wiping a tear from her cheek.

"I know you are too, Dominic. I remember you standing up for me. I see it in the way you face difficult decisions. There's no question. You have your business and even in terrible times, free people still want their shiny things. Yes, Dominic, please think really hard about going to war. I couldn't stand to lose you."

Enveloped in his arms once more, they remain there for many minutes, both fending off their own troubling thoughts and the consequences of their actions. The sun is only aglow over the forest at the back of the property, casting long shadows over the water. A flock of seagulls shriek and land, disturbing the melancholy mood. With one arm around her shoulders, he turns her towards the house.

"Let's go home and we'll worry about it tomorrow."

CHAPTER 8

The last stretch of 1916 passes quickly. Letters from Scotland, some two months old, have arrived. Mary is pregnant with her and Pascal's first child. Pascal has joined the British army and she has no idea where he is. She worries and asks Dominic to pray for him. Lilly and Ivan are madly in love. Granda has a girlfriend. Adairia still mourns for Duff but stays busy; she volunteers with the Red Cross, helping the injured and displaced. The war is fierce and bombs fall around the shipyards. Tubs is working for the British Army as a civilian and is in England on an air force base and is the supervisor for the repair and maintenance crew. Jackie Boy is with him. Esmerelda and Adairia have become good friends.

Dominic and Nick have converted one portion of the barn into a garage and the car has been covered and stowed away. Winter settles over the countryside; snow and chilly winds are ever present. Maria has moved out of her aunt's house and shares an apartment with her friend Denise. On nice days, she still walks to the store. On bad days, she hires a buggy and Dominic pays for it. The business continues to grow.

The busiest season approaches with Christmas. Dominic and Maria discuss the war, both resigned to the notion he will be going. If the war hasn't ended by the end of the year, he will try. They decide that Maria will run the business. She knows everything she needs to know. Her signature and authorization have been added to the business account. She will need to hire someone to help, another sales person. They will start telling customers there will be no repair service after December 31 until further notice. They spend as much free time together as they can, sneaking intimate moments filled with passion as if each one is the last.

Dominic gives Maria a sketch he's done for her for Christmas. It shows her in a garden full of detailed flowers with her bending to smell a rose and a cluster of bees visiting flowers around her. With the war going full tilt, he cannot send gifts back home this year nor will he receive any, but Maria gives him a Waltham pocket watch she has purchased with her own money from the sales agent who represents that brand. His name, the date and Maria's initials are engraved inside the case. They spend Christmas at her father's place in Notre Dame and celebrate with a few friends.

Later tonight they are going to a New Year's party at Maria's aunt's house and Dominic is deciding which jacket to wear. He has the last cut outs for his scrapbook and wants to paste them in before he leaves. Staring at the first headline, *French Army defeats Germany in the Battle of Verdun*, he thinks of his appointment Wednesday, January 2, with Sgt. Warren Smith at the recruiting office. He's nervous but yet confident in his decision. Thinking of seeing Maria soon has him hasten to glue the last headlines and articles into his collection.

Conscription begins in Britain.
Mary Pickford becomes the first female film star to sign a contract for over a million dollars.
Mexican troops defeat the US Expeditionary Force under General Pershing.
The Battle of Jutland, the largest naval battle of the war ends with a British victory.
Edith Wharton is appointed to Chevalier of the Legion of Honor, France's highest award.
On the first day of the Battle of the Somme, Britain and her allies lose 19,240 men.
St Louis Brown's Ernie Koob pitches the whole 17 innings in a 0-0 tie with Boston.
Margaret Sanger opens the first birth control center in New York.
Boston Red Sox beat Brooklyn Dodgers 4 games to one to win the 13th World Series.

1917

When Dominic tells the recruiter about his bad leg and how he was rejected back in Scotland, he is informed that there are shortages of many men for different efforts in the war besides the infantry, but just as dangerous. When Dominic joins up, he's assigned to the 26th Battalion (New Brunswick) under the command of Lt-Col A.E.G. McKenzie. Elements of the Battalion have recently been in the Battle of the Somme and are now being readied for a planned British offensive on the German-held French city of Arras, but that's not where Dom is going. When he arrives in England, he will be seconded to the Royal Air Corps to receive training as an observer.

During the first weeks of February, he goes on basic training in Valcartier, Quebec. It's torturous; his leg aches every night. He discovers muscles he never knew he had until they show up sore. The one thing he's exemplary at (*his trainer's words*) is marksmanship. The Ross Mk II rifle and he became close friends; they look after each other. Other recruits argue that it is too long for trench warfare, but Dominic sticks up for the rifle, proclaiming its long range precision as being significant. His rate of accuracy is the highest in his company. Training is shortened by the urgent call for men from across the ocean. He's given a four-day pass before he ships out.

The twenty-fifth of February is bitterly cold, especially just as the sun sets, which is early today at 5:20. Any time spent out of doors is an invitation to more than frost bite, more like a frost banquet. Exposed skin will freeze in twenty minutes. It's been that long since Dominic left his house. Walking into the city, he's warm inside his new

251

greatcoat. Ice crystals whiten a khaki scarf that covers his mouth. A beaver skin hat is pulled down to cover his head, ears, and the nape of his neck and forehead. The greatcoat goes to his ankles. Pure Canadian wool that keeps you warm even if it gets wet. Inside the heavy coat, Private Dominic Alexander is wearing the olive drab uniform of the Canadian Expeditionary Force: wool jacket, shirt and tie and heavy wool pants with leggings wrapped about his calf to his knees, tucked into black sturdy boots large enough for two pairs of socks. He's bundled up against the cold.

Two days from now, on Tuesday, he's to report for duty at 6:00 a.m. in Halifax, where he will embark for England on the *HMS Andania.* Dominic will depart for the war from the same wharf he arrived at a little over two years ago. Tonight, he is attending a going away party for him and today is also his birthday. When he turns up Cameron Street, Maria's aunt's house is on the next corner on Gordon Street, less than a minute away. He's familiar enough with the large house where Maria and her family tend to have their gatherings because the place is so big. *Ma tante Emma,* as she is called, is a widower whose late husband was a doctor. An addition contained his offices at one time but now they are all divided into rooms to let, providing a continuous income. She keeps the main house as it was, terribly big, bought with the expectation of many running feet when they were younger, but alas, that wasn't to be. A large open living room and adjoining parlour can hold twenty people in comfort. The kitchen has a cozy nook and small table in one corner and room for three or four cooks. With a dining room containing heavy furniture that can seat ten, there's plenty of space. No one enjoys a get together more than *ma tante Emma* and her home is the perfect spot.

People are coming over later but Emma invited him to come earlier and have supper with her and Maria, who has been there helping. She made an old family recipe especially for Dominic, an Acadian treat she told him. What she called it sounded like *Poo-tin Raw-pay.* Maria assured him they are delicious and a lot of work to make.

Dressed as warm as he is, by the time he knocks on the front door, he's starting to feel a chill. A faint command to "come in" seeps through the keyhole and he enters the foyer. Maria greets him in the hallway, standing back slightly, not recognizing the shrouded figure at first. Only when he removes the scarf away from his mouth does she know who it is.

"Hello, my beloved. Come in quick. Don't let too much of that cold in here."

Regarding the coating of frost on the scarf where it covered his mouth, her eyes widen in disbelief.

"My goodness, Dominic, did you walk from your house?"

While removing the hat, he's nodding.

"Aye I did. I didn't realize it was this cold."

She pays more attention to his clothing as he removes his greatcoat.

"Oh how wonderful, Dominic, you wore your new uniform. Here, give me that coat and let me see."

She calls out to her aunt, who is setting the table in the kitchen nook where she, Maria and Dominic will have their supper.

"*Ma tante Emma, vien voir Dominic avec sa nouvelle uniforme!*" ("Aunt Emma, come see Dominic with his new uniform").

Passing his coat and hat to Maria, Dominic removes his boots to leave them at the door and steps forward to meet Emma. She doesn't walk so much as she waddles. She's a big woman, not too tall, with open arms and a large bosom that begs to be hugged. Rosy cheeks always look like they're blushing and a perpetual smile adorns her face. Short greyish curls top her round head. An aroma of boiled potatoes follows her.

"What a handsome lad you are, Dominic. A shame that you have to go off to war. We'll have to telegram ahead to warn all those young British girls, won't we, Maria?"

She says that with a wink and engulfs Dominic in her arms. Stooping a bit to enjoy the warmth of her embrace, he takes in the lovely scent of jasmine.

"Now come, Dominic, we have some delicious poutines for you. I've made a batch for our company to enjoy later on. If it's one thing you will learn from us Acadians is that we love a good meal."

Placing Dominic's coat, scarf and hat on a hanger, Maria stows them in the closet by the front door and gives her boyfriend a quick hug, a peck on the check, and waves for him to follow. The hallway has a set of stairs on the right and extends towards the back on the left. Colorful ribbons are strung around the walls and a hand printed sign hangs over the stairway proclaiming *Bon Voyage, Happy Birthday* and *Best Wishes*. The dining room is on the immediate right and the kitchen is on the same side. A table in the corner of the kitchen is set for three and Emma invites Dominic to take the head of the table near the window and has Maria take the side seat facing the kitchen and her place setting is on the opposite end of Dominic's. She spoons out each a *poutine* on three plates and brings one to set in front of Maria and the other in front of Dominic. He stares at it and loses his appetite.

For those who've never eaten *poutine rapée*, the first time you see one can be a perplexing proposition. Dominic doesn't know what to say. The object on his plate is the size of a grapefruit, a misshapen, steaming globule that makes him think of snowballs. Emma sets her plate down and turns to get them some tea. Maria is slicing hers in half when she notices the look on Dominic's face and starts to giggle. She's seen the same look before when someone is introduced to this delicacy.

"They're much tastier than they look Dominic. Just cut it in bite size chunks and add some sugar or molasses on it. There's delicious meat in the middle and you can choose between white sugar or brown sugar. I like brown sugar on mine. Some folks just eat them with salt and pepper."

He replies hesitatingly.

"If you say so."

Not wanting to seem ungrateful, he does as she suggests. Picking up his knife, he slices the poutine down the middle. The two halves divide to expose a center of tender chunks of pork that have been salted and spiced.

"Well it certainly smells good."

After placing cups of tea down, Emma joins them.

"I prefer molasses on mine Dominic. You can try a little bite of each and see which you like best."

Slicing small tentative pieces, he sprinkles a bit of brown sugar on one, white sugar on another, a drip of molasses on the third and only salt and pepper on the fourth. Not sure about sugar on potatoes, he tries the unsweetened one first. Biting into it, he closes his eyes and his teeth sink into the firm but creamy potato mixture with tender pieces of pork that almost melt in his mouth.

"Mmmm, it is good! Certainly much better than I expected."

Maria agrees as she chews on her own piece.

"Told you so, didn't I?"

Dominic tries the sweetened pieces and a smile states how much he agrees with the flavors, but he decides he likes the natural taste of the poutine best with salt and pepper. Poutine is a heavy meal and he shares a second one with Emma, Maria is full with just one. For their dessert one of Emma's neighbors has dropped off a raisin pie for the celebration and it is another food that Dominic has not had before and he falls in love with the flaky crust and the sweetness of the dried fruit. The plates are cleared off and washed up before the trio sit at the table with their last cup of tea. People will not begin to arrive before seven o'clock. With everything ready for their guests, they broach a variety of subjects.

Dominic wonders how you make poutine. Emma fills him in.

"Well we started with about 90 potatoes because we wanted to have 60 poutine or so. After we peel them, half of them are boiled and mashed. The other half is grated, the liquid squeezed out with a cheese cloth which we call *épurer*. Salt and milk are added and the two potato mixtures are blended together, we call that part *mêler*. Then you need to be quick because if the potato mixture is left out too long, it turns gray, still as tasty but not so pretty. So you form them into balls, *rouler*, add seasoned pork in the center and put them in a pot of boiling water for two hours and *voila*, you have *poutine rapée*."

"Wow! That does seem like a lot of work"

Emma is Maria's favorite aunt and she loves the rapport and goodwill between her aunt and her boyfriend as she listens to their banter. Emma shows concern with knitted brows when she asks Dominic about going to war.

"What's going to happen when you get to England, Dominic?"

"There's a shortage of men trained in Morse code and photography for observers and that's what I will be learning to do."

Maria is all ears now as Dominic has not explained in detail what he will be doing.

"It's always from an airplane and there's several different types of missions a pilot and an observer might do, for instance…"

They chatter away. Dominic explains he's nervous of flying but is excited at the same time. He feels it will be safer in the air than in the trenches. The ladies tell him how much he will be missed, to be as carful as he can be, and to come back home. It's almost six-thirty by the time they finish their conversation. Maria explains that she will be travelling to Halifax with Dominic to say their goodbyes there. Seeing her aunt's raised eyebrows, Maria is quick to add a reassurance.

"…and my friend Denise is coming with us so I'll have company coming back on the train Tuesday afternoon. We're going to stay overnight tomorrow evening and accompany Dominic to the ship."

"Oh, she's such a lovely girl that Denise."

Glancing at the clock on the counter she sees it's close to seven o'clock.

"Folks will be arriving soon. I think we should get the punch out now and some ice from the icebox, Maria. I'll clean up these teacups. I feel a chill. Dominic, would you put more wood in the furnace downstairs for us? The steps are under the main stairway, first door on the left when you go out into the hallway."

A knock on the front door. Maria is heading to answer it for their first guest.

"I bet that's Denise. She always comes a little earlier."

She's the first of the fourteen people who show up. The O'Donnell's have come, Rosie, Nick and his girlfriend, Joanne, Ron Allain and his wife, John Bannister and his latest girlfriend (there are many), Emma's "companion" Adolph, Maria's uncle Rudy, who lives in the city also, and Emma's neighbors, Bonnie and Claude Dickson.

The party goers move around, some with punch in hand, a few with juice in their wine glasses and a few with pints tucked in their pants pocket. Emma swarms around hugging, offering tidbits to munch on, telling them the poutines will only be served at eleven, teasing the young ones who always seem to be holding hands. There's always a small group around Dominic, the ladies flirting and charming, the men talking about the war. Nick surprises everyone by informing them he will be leaving soon also. He signed up today. Even his girlfriend is astonished; she gives him the cold shoulder until the music starts later.

Rudy has brought his accordion and Nick his mandolin instead of the guitar, and Maria plays the spoons when she can be talked into it. If you're not bouncing to the music within a few moments, it's quite possible you're deaf. The tunes go on until late in the evening, no one wanting them to stop and the food can wait. The floor in the living room has all the furniture moved back and those that can show off their tap dancing skills do so. Couples swing to the music, making partners dizzy. There's no classics played tonight, just toe tapping diddies and ballads lamenting the deportation of the Acadians in the eighteenth century and forlorn love. All the girls want to dance and swing with Dominic, who's down to his shirt with sleeves rolled up.

He won't find his tie until morning. Emma breaks things up by entering from the kitchen tapping on a thick water glass with a butter knife. The tinging of her glass quiets everyone.

"Foods on. The poutines are hot, and I've put on two pots of tea. Plates and spoons are on the counter by the stove. Sit wherever you can. Now go help yourselves and then we'll sing Happy Birthday to our soldier."

Everyone eyes Dominic and applauds. Dominic reddens from the attention. A few of the tipsy guests salute him. Emma grabs him away and steers him towards the kitchen.

"You first, Dominic."

He heads to the kitchen with zeal, knowing how delicious the poutine is, and as hungry as he is. Nick brought some homemade beer with him and Dominic had several. He's not staggering, but his head is swimming a lap or two. The gang follow and spread about the rooms. Those that don't get a seat at either table take to the parlour, where they eat with their plates on their knees. Pie and chocolate cake follow and an extra pot of tea is made. It's midnight before he opens his gifts.

Emma and Adolph give him Zane Grey's latest novel, *The Border Legion*. The O'Donnell's give him a card made by their ten year old daughter with Kraft paper and dried flowers along with a small bag of homemade fudge and a new leather belt. From the Allain's he receives a gold jeweler's loupe with his initials engraved on it, "for when he gets back." Nick and Joanne chipped in to buy him a canvas duffle bag. Nick has seen Dominic's suitcase and it won't last where he's going. The Dickson's give him an Ever Ready razor and shaving brush, the newest in men's grooming. Rudy gives him a harmonica, one of his older ones.

Even though he has his father's, Maria gives him a four-inch jackknife, pearl handles, filigreed ends, the balance as he hefts it in his hand is perfect. She knows Dom won't use the one his mother gave him because it's too sentimental to use every day and every man should carry a jackknife, she's been told. The men stare at it with envy. A chrome panel is embedded in the pearl on one side. Dominic reads the inscription out loud.

"Forever yours. Maria."

The ladies ooh and aah. "That's sweet," "Oh, what a dear," "How nice," they all say.

Dominic turns to his fiancé and hugs her closely, whispering in her ear.

"I'll always be yours too, Maria. I love you."

Everyone hears it and titters and blushes and claps their hands. The men elbow each other and wink. Turning to the crowd, Dominic speaks up.

"Thank you everyone. I know that I don't say it proper but, *Mare-see*. These are all really nice gifts and I'll cherish each one. I'll ask for your prayers when I'm gone, and to keep me in mind. I hope… we all hope… this bloody war will be over soon and we'll be celebrating something else."

Back slapping, hand shaking, hugs and kisses from the ladies, the night comes to an end when everyone leaves. Emma and Denise are straightening things up and collecting stray dishes, cups and glasses. Shortly Dominique is wrapped up for the cold walk home; the only thing missing is his tie and he's holding his scarf. Maria has her hands on his shoulders and is only a few inches away. She's downcast, chin tucked into her chest. Sadness softens her words

"I wish you didn't have to go. I never want to let you go."

He tilts her chin up. A half smile on his face.

"That wouldn't look good in front of your aunt, and she'd faint if you came to my house. We'll be together tomorrow night, Maria. We'll hold each other not thinking of anything else. Let's be thankful for that, okay?"

"Yes, my darling, tomorrow then. Denise and I will meet you at the train station at ten."

"I can arrange for you to be picked up."

"No thanks, Dominic. Denise is staying here tonight and we're walking to her house in the morning. Her father is going to get us to the station. I'll see you there. Now, goodnight, my love."

She kisses him passionately, her arms tightly about his neck. When he starts to respond to her ardor, she steps away and points to the door.

"Go home or I won't let you leave."

He's laughing at that when he sets out, but he's thinking of those deep blue, unabashed eyes.

CHAPTER 2

Denise and Maria have been best friends for many years. They know each other's favorite color, the food they hate, the desserts they love, the styles preferred, and all their secrets. Denise goes to Halifax as a chaperone for Maria, but it's for show only. Maria does not have to worry about anyone finding out from Denise that she and Dominic will sleep in the same room tonight.

After a late covering of snow in the morning, the sun dominates the sky all afternoon. The fresh snow ripples with reflections as the train speeds towards Halifax. Trees make long shadows in the windows, flashing too fast to count. Dominic occupies a seat to himself with Denise and Maria across the aisle from him. He's brought a copy of the Transcript and spends a half hour or so reading. Headlines regarding the conflict in Europe take up most of the news. His ad for the store that Maria designed is in the classifieds. The girls chatter and giggle, not for once thinking of the parting to come, as if not discussing it will make it go away. Denise knows what her friend is thinking, seeing the concern in her eyes and the false smile she sometimes wears.

Dominic dozes off. Only when the conductor strolls through the coaches announcing their arrival does he wake. Wiping away the drool that has built up at the corner of his mouth, he rubs his eyes as he watches the many buildings slide by as the train reduces its speed to enter the city. On the opposite side, he can see ships of all sizes ready to move into convoy. Merchantmen await in the basin, tankers with oil and fuel, cargo ships and freighters with munitions, foodstuffs, uniforms, lumber, ropes and wire, horses, artillery and needed commodities to feed the war machine. Troop ships like the *HMS Andania* will sail in the middle. Two British war ships lie at anchor at the head of the collection, armed escorts for defense from the deadly U-boats that have been wreaking havoc upon shipping in the North Atlantic.

When the trio emerges from the train station, it is a short walk to the Hotel Nova Scotia where they have booked two rooms for the night, one for Dominic and one for the ladies in Maria's name. They've decided to check in and the ladies want to "freshen up" before going out for something to eat. Dominic agrees to meet them in the lobby at six o'clock, a half hour from now.

The ladies are all aglow when Dominic sees them approach from the stairway. True to their Acadian heritage, their hands are doing a lot of their talking. He loves the way Maria expresses herself with pointing fingers and sweeping gestures. They've kept their long dark skirts and because Halifax doesn't get near as much snow, they've changed to walking shoes and added a shawl. The finest touch of pink graces their lips. He remembers Maria telling him too much would be considered brazen. Dominic is gladdened by their shared laughter but feeling melancholy not knowing when he will hear it again. He steps towards them.

"You two look beautiful. I'm a lucky man to have such lovely companions for the evening."

Maria hugs him, flirting with her eyes. Denise's soft smile signals her approval, she likes Dominic, sweetened by his good looks. Maria takes one arm.

"We're the lucky ones, don't you think, Denise."

She takes the other arm and squeezes it.

"Yes we are, Maria. Now where you taking us, Mr. Alexander?"

"There's a small restaurant on Barrington that John Bannister told me about when he found out I was departing from Halifax. There's a family of fishermen, three brothers own boats, the fourth brother owns a restaurant and it's to be said their seafood is the freshest. The owner is the chef and only uses his ancestors' recipes. John said their seafood casserole can't be better. Are you ladies up for that?"

Nodding in agreement, the trio walk the fifteen minutes to the restaurant. It's easy to find, there are three other couples in a line outside. There is a canopy, bright blue like seawater. On the end they can see a painted fishing boat upon a choppy sea. Under the picture reads *Four Brothers Grill & Eatery* in English style script. The façade is red brick and large windows with curtains. When they take their place at the end of the line behind a soldier and a young lady, the couple tell them that the maitre'd said it would be about a half an hour. Even without the protection of the canopy, it's a mild night and they stand under a clear sky obstructed by the yellowish glow of a streetlamp across from them. The young couple have eaten there before and assure them the wait will be worth it. The world can often be a friendly place. Strangers can become friends in the shortest of gaps. The commonality of being soldiers have the five introducing themselves. The soldier and his wife are Hacheys, Clovis and Linda, also from New Brunswick but from Saint John. By the time they all get a table, they agree to share one if possible.

The restaurant accommodates them by joining two tables that are free. The evening passes too quickly for them. They discover that Clovis and Dominic are sailing on the same ship and plan to see each other on board. The two men find much in common, especially a fondness for a good beer, even with prohibition in place. By eight-thirty, a few are yawning. A full course meal of chowder, main dish and lemon pie for dessert has them sated and lazy from a full stomach. Maria teases Dominic with her feet under the table with a pleading expression on her face. He gazes at her with the same desire.

"Well, let's head back to our rooms, shall we? I'm mighty tired and morning will come early."

Everyone agrees. The bills are paid, the coats and shawls replaced. Goodbyes are said, the trio split from their new acquaintances and head back to the hotel, but not before Dominic notices that their dinner partner in uniform has a slight limp like him. When they enter the lobby proceeding into the hallway, Maria halts them at the foot of the stairs. Pointing upwards, she motions and winks to Dominic speaking in a dreamy lilt.

"I'll be right up. I just want to talk to Denise a moment, all right dear?"

With a shake of his head and a leer in his eyes, he hurries up the stairs, already undoing his coat. Turning to her friend, Maria places the room key in her hand.

"Thank you for doing this, Denise. I'd die if anyone knew what I am doing with Dominic, and I know you understand. My aunt especially and the fuddy-duddies she chums with, or worse my father. I think they'd disown me."

Denise squeezes her friend's hand.

"I can see how much you two love each other. I mean Dominic practically pants over you like a puppy and you're all funny-eyed when he's around, like I feel about your brother Yves. I would do anything for him and I don't think he knows."

Maria bobs her head.

"Oh, he does, Denise. Yves is just so shy. You're going to have to ask him out yourself when he comes home."

The statement of coming home dissolves the good feeling; frowns appear. A few seconds pass before Denise admonishes her friend.

"Never mind that for tonight, Maria. Go…go to your lover's arms and be happy. Make him promise to come back. Wake me tomorrow and we'll see him off and then catch the train back home. Good night."

Maria shuts the door to Dominic's room and leans back on it a moment to stare at the man she loves. He's standing at the end of the bed, his jacket tossed upon the dresser, tie askew, sleeves rolled up, staring at her with a lustful gaze. He strokes his moustache, a gesture she enjoys. Seconds pass, as if their situation seems too good to be true. Breaking their concentration, she hastens to his arms. Tossing her hat in the air, it becomes the first victim of their frenzy to be unhindered by their clothing. Lips pressed together, kisses full of need. Tugging at each other's garments they remove them piece by piece, popping a button on her blouse in their haste.

In the middle of the floor, they embrace in naked splendor. Kisses are not restricted to the lips. Their hands explore smooth skin, the defining curves of each other, and the sensitive differences of their anatomy. Leading Dominic by the hand, Maria pulls back the covers and lies upon the sheets. There are no thoughts of tomorrow, only the precious moments ahead of them. Dominic is captivated by her beauty, the pale skin of her shoulders, the flushing of her cheeks, the rise and fall of her sensuous breasts, the slightly parted legs, and the fervor in her eyes.

Their lovemaking is all consuming, like a fire raging in their hearts. Every sense is heightened by the uncertainty of their parting in the morning. Every touch, every kiss, every movement is meant to please. Lips and tongues linger at the crook of an elbow, the curve of the neck, an open palm; unbridled, they discover more sensitive regions. Rising to the peak of their pleasures, release comes amongst vows of unending love. The night passes with the lovers in a tight embrace.

CHAPTER 3

The next morning is overcast, still chilly but warmer than yesterday and a heavy mist hangs in the air. The profiles of the many ships in the basin are shrouded in a faint fog that favors a sneaky getaway. The *RMS Andania* is tethered to the dock in almost the same position as the *SS Missanabie* was when Dominic set foot on this wharf for the first time. The surroundings are the same, but there is more urgency. Soldiers are everywhere. The convoy leaves in four hours and the troop carriers have to form in the middle so the ship is boarding now. Soon only lovers embracing are left on the pier. Men are not the only warriors boarding the ship, there are women in uniform and nurse's outfits amongst those bidding farewell, some to spouses and others to children with tears in their eyes. Dominic, Maria and Denise stand at the foot of the gangplank, off to the side. Giving Denise a quick hug, Dominic then embraces Maria.

There are no more words to be said. They promised each other in the night there would be no goodbyes, only a farewell until they meet again. Holding his beloved in his arms, Dominic ponders his decision to leave for the war. Doubts fill his head like chafe in the wind. They are disturbed by a whistle blowing and officers issuing orders for everyone to board. When Maria backs away, she doesn't show her sorrow.

"Come back to me, my love."

Holding her upper arms in his hands, he stares at her lovingly.

"I will, Maria. I'll write as often as I can and look forward to hearing from you."

He turns to head up the walkway to the ship and calls out.

"I love you, Miss Desjardins."

Too emotional to respond, Maria watches her lover board the ship, waving briskly at him, hoping he can't see the tears. He stands at the gunwale until the ship moves from the pier to join the convoy.

CHAPTER 4

The crossing is marred only by the sinking of one of the merchantmen when the convoy encounters a U-boat two hundred nautical miles from Great Britain. The British armored cruiser, warrior class, *HMS Achilles*, sinks the submarine with all hands going to the bottom while the armed merchantman, an American built cargo ship named *Mount Shasta* only loses three men as many of its crew are picked up by other ships in the fleet. The group was slowed northeast of Newfoundland because of icebergs and it takes twelve days to cross. During the sailing Dominic and Clovis become fast friends among a handful of other soldiers that find a common bond of being from New Brunswick.

All but one of them confess to the heartbreak of leaving their families, how difficult it is. Setting himself up for a series of taunts and playful teasing, the odd man out, Don from Newcastle, said he joined up to get away from his nagging wife. Mark from Grande Anse is engaged to be married, like Dominic. Adam from Lincoln is a happily married man with three children and a husky name Alaska. Chris from Jacquet River spent the last three days on his honeymoon before sailing. They all wear the same uniform, proud of the patch that's says *Canada*. They all know how to kill men, and they all admit to being scared.

In a cold morning rain, the *HMS Andania* docks at Plymouth on March 9. Embarkation is a slow process as the men follow orders to their postings. Don and Mark are attached to 26th Battalion of the Royal New Brunswick Regiment. Chris and Adam to the 12th battalion of Royal Rifles of Canada Regiment. Dominic is reporting to the

Wireless and Observers School in Brooklands. Clovis has the same orders. The two men will be learning similar crafts but for different reasons.

The men are being directed to the trains that will carry them to their units. The men huddle one last time at the train station, shaking hands, slapping backs, wishing each other good luck and showing false bravado. Clovis and Dominic's train leaves at ten, but the four others hustle for theirs, which leave in just fifteen minutes. Clovis has a deck of cards, and because they have a couple of hours, they find a bench under a station awning and he teaches Dominic how to play forty-fives. It will be the first of many games.

Sandwiches and tea are provided by the army, with a temporary mess erected near the station. Dominic and Clovis are sharing more intimate stories of their lives now that they are alone. Clovis still has a hard time understanding Dominic sometimes even though his brogue has been softened by the time he's spent in Canada. Clovis, who has grown up in a French home where their mother tongue is still spoken, has trouble with a few English words. Clovis tells why he limps, having fallen from a tree in the back yard of his grandfather's house when he was only twelve. Dominic tells him of the antics that led to his own limp. Clovis has been married two years this coming March, has a daughter named Florence and is a carpenter and helps on a farm of fifty acres and twenty cows being looked after by his father-in-law, who is a widower and lives with him and his wife. Dominic gives a short version of how he ended up in Canada. More stories and more card games keep them busy until it is time to board the train.

The trip is almost eight hours, and by the time they store their gear and find seats, it isn't long until Clovis is snoring curled up by the window and Dominic is reading the Zane Grey novel that Emma gave him on his birthday. When they get to Brooklands and transfer to the airbase the sun is almost set, only a yellow glow on the horizon. Clovis is wide awake and Dominic trudges along.

The sergeant they report to is a gruff Englishman with a heavy moustache and deep set eyes glare dislike at everybody. His hair is on the gray side and so short it barely covers his scalp. A scar runs from the middle of his forehead extending partway down his check, just nicking his left eye. The outer edge of the eyebrow is missing. The left hand is also missing, only a scarred stump sticks out of his uniform sleeve. Grimacing at their accents when they report to him, he doesn't like them already. He frowns at each page while checking their papers. The practiced sarcasm is thick enough to paint with.

"Just what I'm needing, another bloody Scotsman and a Frenchie Canuck. Must be my lucky day!

They're told they are to call him Sgt. Cunningham, then get their "lazy arses" to C Barracks. "The last on the left when you go out if you can remember which is your left," he tells them with a smirk. He'll see them again at 0530 hours, not a second later.

"Count your blessings lads, there's a roof over your head here; you're not stuck in a tent like the infantry."

It's a five-minute walk to the barracks. The ground is wet from an earlier rain, their boots slurp noisily as they track through the muck. Approaching the barracks, their conversation is interrupted when the main door bursts open. A long gangly man tumbles out the door, clad only in long-johns and a mop of red hair. Flying off the short stoop, he lands on his ass in the largest puddle in the yard. Blood froths at his nose. Dominic and Clovis are only a few feet away and back off in surprise. The man falls on his back and the water is up to his mouth. Before he can get a handhold in the muck, he begins to choke. Chucking their bags by the steps, they wade into the wet patch and grasping the soaked man under the arms. They get him to his feet. An angry voice shouts out.

"Leave him be, the bugger's not worth the effort."

Dominic and Clovis stare up at the hairiest man they've ever seen. An exposed barrel chest and wide shoulders stands at the open door, arms at his side. The heavy brows alone would be threatening, but they match the menace in his scowl.

"Cunningham's pet. Runs blabbering whenever he has a tale to tell, something to get one of the boys in trouble. Making stuff up to get lighter duty. He's a loser. Says us Canadians are a bunch of cowards. Leave him be."

The man has his hand on his nose trying to stem the blood, he's moaning and mouthing gibberish and starting to shake from the chill, his body covered with soggy underwear, the crotch stretched halfway to his knees, his feet bare.

"It's not true, it's not true… It's… not… true!"

Turning from the doorway, the big man waves them away, like he's wasting his time. His back is equally hirsute and probably protects him from the cold. Dominic and Clovis eye the stranger and push him toward the door. Grabbing their bags, they wordlessly follow him. When they enter the barracks, the man from the puddle turns to his immediate left, where there are washroom facilities, and starts peeling his sodden trunks off. Only half of the bunks are taken, the first six on each side are occupied with a motley collection of men. All ages are present, from a young man barely shaving to a wrinkled man who looks old enough to be their grandfather and has a cigarette constantly sticking out of his mouth. A few middle-aged men like the bear who greeted them at the door and the rest probably in their twenties. Most don't speak to the duo as they select a bunk except for a few who welcome them to purgatory. The one common thing that seems to unite them all is a deformity of their person. There is one with a missing arm, some with missing fingers, a couple of peg legs and the older man only has one eye. Men unfit for the rigors of war in the field but smart enough to be trained as observers. Some will end up being spies, especially the ones who speak French. Of the twenty-six men, eleven are Canadian, seven are from Australia and the rest are British.

At 0520 hours, Cunningham bursts through the doors wailing at the men to get their arses (one of his favorite words) up and out the door. Be dressed in five minutes and meet him in the yard.

"We'll see what kind of shape you recruits are in and then you'll be told where to go after breakfast. Now get a move on!"

The training goes on for the next month. Turns out Cunningham is not so bad, just strict. The crybaby who ended up in the puddle has a run in with Clovis and this time it is Dominic that gives him a black eye and a licking. It's the last time he tattles on any of the Canadians. Parades, fitness and marksmanship routines daily, Morse code for the new wireless radios, aerial photography, geography of the war zones, conduct, severe warnings of the consequences of cowardice and desertion, and how to survive and link up with the resistance should they find themselves behind enemy lines takes up their ten-hour days. Dominic is at the top of all his classes, an accomplishment that will not allow him to finish his training completely. War does not follow a schedule, nor does it care about men and machines, it grinds them down like a scythe amongst the weeds. Aircraft and pilots are being downed at the rate of two a day. He's transferred to Gainsborough where he will meet the pilots and experience his first flight.

CHAPTER 5

Maria has moved into Dominic's upstairs apartment while he is in Europe and she has brought Denise with her. On the return trip from Halifax after seeing Dominic off, Maria offered Denise a job helping her at the store. She had been working at the hospital in the kitchen and was content with her lot, but when Maria suggested she could earn more at the store with a decent hourly wage and commission on her sales, she gladly accepted. There was a brief setback when there was no more repair work being done in January, but people still wanted their baubles, even with the war going on and rationing enforced, so sales continue to climb.

April 2 is a Monday and is a relief from the dreary weather of March, which has been days of snow and then rain, icy sidewalks, soggy streets and always gray skies. The sun rises over the cityscape in the east at six twenty-three, dissipating shadows with warm yellow rays turning long faces into smiles. Maria is already up, wrapped in her peach housecoat and slippers, sitting in the downstairs office going over the receipts for the last month, trying to decide if she should add a selection of pearls to their inventory. Her last letter to Dominic was three weeks ago, filled with longing and statements of love, of missing him so much at times it hurt. She prays for his safety, admonishing him to not take any chances, begging for his safe return. On a separate sheet, she gives him the highlights of the business and asks his opinion of the pearls but she has not heard back from him yet. Pearls are only sought after by the rich because of their rarity, making them more expensive than diamonds. Today she is meeting with the sales agent

269

and has promised him an answer.

She met with Van Geist on Friday and he complimented her on her shrewd business mind and clever accounting. Leery at first upon Dominic's request that she be allowed full signing authority to his business account and decision making during his absence, he soon came to admire her skills with purchasing, precise documenting of all that prevailed with *Alexander's Jewellery*, her accounting on a daily business correct within pennies. To say nothing of her charm and coquettish manner that he is flattered by. He advised her to perhaps start with a few simple pieces with the pearls and go from there. At the end of their meeting, the final item on Maria's small notepad was the addition of another safe. Peering at her over his glasses, he agreed.

"Yes, do that Maria. You've been quite fortunate, having such valuables so far from the city. It's wise that someone lives there and the idea of adding the lights around the building was genius. Another safe is a good investment."

At seven thirty, she can hear Denise stirring upstairs, probably starting breakfast for the two of them. Deciding to head up to join her, Maria pauses for a moment, reflecting on her good fortune, for having Dominic in her life and his providing for them with his keen business mind and talent. She realizes she's found her calling in life, the love of working with numbers, the pleasure of selecting gifts for people who want to express their love or accomplishments. At times she feels a pressure to make sure that the work Dominic has done is not wasted and she accounts for every penny she spends. She decides at that moment that when Mr. Beers calls on her this afternoon, she will go with half of her original order of the pearls. After breakfast, she will have Denise rearrange the cabinet between the windows to accommodate the new selection.

After she has dressed and eaten, she meets Nick's uncle, Omer, in the yard by the barn as Denise opens the store. He is getting the automobile ready for driving today and because of the sun shining she will take it out later when she visits the accounting offices that will do their quarterly check up on her numbers. The old man has the automobile backed out and is installing the battery before fueling it up. He has brought a gas container with him and she offers to pay him back.

"How much do I owe you this morning, Omer?"

Doffing his hat, he greets Maria with a grizzled smile.

"Fuel has gone up another penny I'm afraid Miss Maria and is at 17 cents a gallon, so it'll be 85 cents please."

Digging in her small change purse, she extracts a one dollar bill and eighty-five cents, handing it to him.

"I hope that will make up for your time this morning."

The older man is eager to take her money, a half a day's wages for effort that couldn't be called work.

"Thank you, Miss Maria. God bless ya."

Turning and pointing to the Ford, he reminds her to watch her throttle. He tightened the lever up so it moves a bit stiffer than before.

"And I cleaned off the dust from the seats and inside, polished it up a bit too."

Opening the automobile door, she smiles at the spotless interior.

"Thank you, Omer, you did a fine job."

Climbing into the driver's seat, she places her purse on the seat beside her, shifts her skirts up so she can manipulate the pedals. After Omer cranks the auto Maria moves the appropriate gears and idles out towards the road. Halting halfway, she waits for a team of horses and a wagon on her left and a convoy of three buggies on the right. She would've liked to have gotten ahead of the traffic, which seems heavy this morning. She smiles inwardly at what a commotion she could cause if she roared out the driveway towards the horses. Her good cheer makes her mischievous.

When the trio of buggies go by heading into the city, she follows slowly. Although the skies have been gray, there has been no rain for several days and the road is somewhat drier, no mud, only hard packed brown gravel. When she approaches the lot at the end of Dominic's property, which he sold to the coal dealer, there is a man huddled by the sign post, staring at her intently. His clothing and person are unkempt, as if he's spent the night in them. The only thing that isn't drab is the red toque he has pulled down to his eyebrows. When she is close enough to see him clearly, there is meanness in his glare and she feels a slight shiver. She has kept a good distance behind the traffic but steps it up until she pulls into the Ford dealership, where she parks the automobile off to the back. Shutting the vehicle off, she grabs her purse and alights from the automobile. Stopping for a few minutes, she instructs the service people that the automobile is to be made ready for the summer driving season. Deciding to walk back to the store, she tells them she will pick it up in a couple of days.

It only takes a half hour to meet with Mr. Lombroso, the accountant, who assures her that everything is up to date. Before she begins the walk home she stops at Creaghans to pick up the blouse she saw last week in their window display. It is a pink with white trim and a high collar. It's Denise's birthday soon and she knows how much she likes pink. After making her purchase, she heads home just as the clouds move apart and the first rays of sunshine cast their cheery glow. While walking, she's thinking of Dominic and how much she misses him, how she worries about his safety. She knows from his last letter three weeks ago that he is anxious to be flying, and she worries about him even more. Knowing there is nothing she can do about it, she tries to think of other things.

When she is almost to the store, she notices someone entering the front door and stops when she realizes it is the man who had been standing by the coal yard when she passed it earlier. She knows it is him from the red head covering. A sudden chill crawls up her spine, knowing something is wrong. Hiking her skirts higher, she clutches her bag tighter in one hand and dashes across the field to the right of the building where there are no windows and she can remain unseen. Behind the house she quietly enters the back stairs to Dominic's apartment and creeps upwards to the door that opens into the kitchen. What she needs is in the bedroom, under the bed. She hesitates, worrying that the man below may hear her walk across the floor when suddenly there is the sound of breaking glass and she hears Denise scream. The man is yelling, but Maria can't discern what he is saying.

Maria removes her boots, tiptoes to the bedroom, fetches a weapon from under the bed and creeps down the main stairs where she can now hear the man yelling at Denise. His voice is rough and words are slurred as if he's been drinking. When Maria steps up to the wall by the arch leading into the store she peeks around the pillar. The man is holding a knife out with the point only inches away from Denise who is sobbing and filling a dirty burlap bag with jewellery from one of the cabinet's whose glass top has been broken. In his hand he has a fist-size rock. When he steps to his left, he raises the rock to smash the top of the cabinet that hold the watches, Maria stealthily steps behind him and jams the barrel of the twelve-gauge shotgun into the back of his head. Her voice is like ice.

"Do it Mister and I'll blow the top of your head off."

Both the intruder and Denise are shocked by Maria's appearance.

Denise gasps and drops the bag on the floor. The man remains perfectly still, unsure of what he is up against. Maria pokes the gun a bit harder.

"Place that rock gently on the counter. Get your other hand in the air where I can see it."

Knowing his attacker is a woman, he goads her, thinking he can get her off guard while he slowly places the rock on the counter but doesn't let it go and lifts his other arm.

"I know who you are missy; I don't think you have what it takes to shoot an unarmed man in the back."

She ignores the sarcasm and looks at Denise, who is backed against the wall, visibly shaken from the encounter.

"Denise, go call the police."

Denise is terrified and stares at the gun in Maria's hands. She can't believe what she is seeing. Maria uses a more forceful voice.

"Denise, get moving. Go to the phone and call the police now."

Thinking his antagonist is distracted and fearing the authorities, he twists suddenly, thinking to throw the rock at her. Maria is as cool as the frost on the windows and doesn't hesitate. Lowering the gun and pulling the trigger like Dominic taught her, the blast of a hundred pellets tears through the man's calf, shredding cloth, skin, muscle and blood vessels, propelling him against the glass case where he ricochets onto the floor. Both he and Denise are screaming. The recoil from the shotgun almost breaks Maria's slender shoulder and she flies backwards, falling to the floor and the gun landing beside her. Recovering from the fall, Maria gets to her feet, disregarding the pain in her shoulder. Picking up the gun, she looks at the man on the floor while directing Denise into action.

"Denise, pull yourself together; call the police and tell them to send an ambulance. Hurry, he's bleeding badly."

Denise does as she's told, the threat that had frozen her earlier gone now. Watching the man moaning on the floor, Maria calmly breaks the gun, removes the spent shell, dropping it on the floor and replacing it with another from her jacket pocket. She steps over the man and points it at his head. He's looking at her with a hateful glare. She feels no compassion whatsoever.

"Still think I won't do it?"

An hour later the ambulance is leaving the driveway. Denise is cleaning up the glass and putting the jewellery away. Maria is on the front stoop with a police officer and Chief Harwood who is admonishing Maria even though she can see the respect in his eyes.

"You should've left and called us. Things could've gone a lot worse Maria."

"I know Chief, but I was worried about Denise and Dominic has worked too hard for someone like that lowlife to be stealing his property. I just did what I thought was right."

Her boldness causes the chief to smile.

"I remember speaking to young Alexander when he started this business and I warned him about being so far from the city – to be careful with his precious goods and to take every security measure properly. I can see though that he's left it in good hands. Nonetheless, think twice about taking the law unto yourself. I expect there will be answers needed once this criminal is in court so we may be speaking to you again."

"Thank you, Chief Harwood and Officer Kelly."

Returning to the store, Maria is overcome with what has taken place and collapses into one of the chairs in the waiting area and starts to shake from the shock of what she's been through. Only after it is all over does she think of what has happened and how close the two women were to danger. Denise approaches and sits beside her, offering words of comfort.

"You're so brave Maria. I could never have done that. I guess I need to thank you for looking after me."

The women embrace and Maria's shakes disappear after a few moments. When calm returns, the two women wordlessly survey the damage to the glass cases, the blood on the floor and the shotgun lying on the counter. Maria stands and offers her friend a smile.

"I don't think I'll tell Dominic about this in my next letter. I'm sure he has enough to worry about without wondering what kind of trouble we get into. Let's lock up and get this place cleaned up okay?"

Denise nods and offers a suggestion.

"Maybe you should put that gun away; it might make our customers nervous."

This causes a break in their grief and the two ladies, disguising their nervousness, are laughing at the absurdity of it all.

Word gets around quickly and the publicity, while notorious, only helps the business. Curiosity brings more patrons.

CHAPTER 6

The B.E.2c aircraft is a two-seater biplane originally designed and developed by the Royal Aircraft Factory as a pioneer night fighter to be used against the German airship raiders. Unsuitable for quick maneuvers, it has been withdrawn as a fighter plane, being replaced by the Airco D.H.2 and the Nieuport 11. It is a difficult plane to fly, but under the hands of a skilled pilot, it is a stable aircraft ideally suited to aerial photography and observation over and behind enemy lines. The pilot controls the plane from the back seat and the observer sits in the front. Eight of these aircraft are being ferried to Saint Omer, France, where the No.16 Squadron RAF is stationed. Dominic's training flights have been in one and he leaves today, April 9, for mainland Europe. He has been teamed up with Lieutenant Roger Selkirk, a fellow Scotsman and an able pilot with eleven sorties to his credit. The British and Canadian Expeditionary Forces have begun the Battle of Arras and tomorrow will be Dominic's first glimpse of the fighting.

The next morning, Dominic is awake early. The day has not yet dawned. Looking east from one of the windows of his barracks, there is a wink of the rising sun. Heavy clouds are moving north from a stiff breeze that brings warmer air from the south. He is sitting on the edge of his cot, half dressed, holding the last letter he received from Maria only two days ago. It is dated three weeks previous and he received it only yesterday. Scanning it last night for the first time, he rereads it now. He also received a letter from his sister Mary, which is almost six weeks old and had travelled to Canada before being sent back to England where it caught up to him at the same time as Maria's. He hasn't read that one yet.

The first page of Maria's letter contains words of love and expresses her yearning to be together again. She has the Ford out and serviced and uses it often, how much she loves the freedom it offers her. Joanne has told her that Nick has been wounded from shrapnel during the fighting in northern France and is recovering in a hospital in England. He will return to the front when he has healed enough.

She goes on to tell him of the business, how she's added a few pieces of pearls to their inventory, how well the sales are going and how Denise is adapting to the business and what a terrific saleslady she is. Her last note before she closes playfully reassures him that she is saving articles from the local papers for his scrapbook and lists them on the bottom of the last page.

Suffragette Alice Paul and the National Woman's party lead the first protest outside the White House in Washington.
Royal Bank of Canada takes over Quebec Bank.
US liner Housatonic is sunk by German U-boat.
The first synagogue in 425 years opens in Madrid Spain.
The first Jazz recording is made by the Dixieland Jazz band. (Maria notes how much she likes the new music).
The first ever NHL championship games takes place and the Toronto Arenas beat the Montreal Canadians 7-3 in their first match.

The letter from Mary doesn't contain all happy news. He sorely misses his family and wishes there was more time for him to visit while he is here in Europe, but with the war going on there is no liberty or free time for soldiers or airmen. Perhaps when it's over and if he is still alive, he will go see them before he returns to Canada.

Dear Dominic.

It pains me to tell you that Granda passed away, the doctor said it was his heart. He worked right up until the middle of the afternoon, sat down for a tea and never got up. Funny thing Dominic is that Granda didn't leave as early as he usually did that day and stayed at the breakfast table chatting and greeting all the brood we have here. He was in a jolly mood, teasing the younger ones. Sheila adored him, so did we all...

He pauses to grieve for his grandfather, the letter going limp in his hand. He'll want to visit the gravesite when he can. Stiffening up so the other men won't see him, he continues to read the letter. It goes on to tell him that Pascal is somewhere in Europe fighting the enemy. She hasn't seen Tommy or heard of him for over a year now; no one knows where he is. Lilly and Ivan see each other often and hold hands all the time they are together. Ivan has filled out and is a fine looking young man, he wants to join the navy, and Lilly tries to talk him out of it. Paul is a lovable boy but like the older brothers (*except you sweet Dom*) a little on the wild side. Sheila is a pet, no trouble with her. Everyone sends their love.

Rereading about his grandfather, he remembers him teaching him to draw and giving him his precious charcoals when they parted at Duff's house. He was stern but never mean, too shy to express his love, not much of a hugger. How he loved his horses, working with them each day. He was always kind to Dominic and he feels that pang of loss and grits his teeth so as not to cry. Other men are stirring; he folds the letter and replaces it in his locker. Remembering his mission today, both fear and excitement force all other thoughts from his head. Anticipating the battle from the air, watching the havoc like a bird, exhilarates him. The danger of anti-aircraft cannons makes him nervous, but that is quickly overcome by his trust in the pilot. Lieutenant Selkirk has always come back.

Looking out the window, he's heartened to see the sun and scattering clouds. Remembering how cold it is in the open cockpit, he dons an extra pair of long underwear. His heavy leather jacket protects his upper body and heavy mitts protect his hands when he's not sending code. Lieutenant Selkirk informed him that they would be doing an artillery run. The British eighteen pounders are bombarding Vimy Ridge, but the German fortifications are over a mile away. He and Selkirk will direct their shots. They will be flying low at 6,000 feet, making then an easy target for ground fire or another aircraft. Checking his watch, he sees he has enough time for a quick bite at the mess and some tea.

There, he sits with Selkirk, two of his pilot buddies and two other observers. Barely a moment for introductions and handshakes before the yard whistle blows. All flight personnel are to report to planes. Those that have not finished eating are stuffing their faces while rising and the men hasten to the field. Three B.E.2c are ready for flight. They will be escorted by two Sopwith Camels, the British bi-plane fighter, armed with two .303 Vickers machineguns attached just ahead of the cockpit and 4 Cooper bombs. It's a deadly menace to the enemy.

Dominic has his leather helmet pulled tight, goggles adjusted and face covered with his scarf when the plane taxies to the runway laid out on a long flat field. He loves the sensation of lift as the plane leaves the ground and everything grows smaller. From up here, the land looks as though it is in pain, muddy and cratered by the constant shelling, trenches slicing through the barren fields armed with tiny men. The Western Front contains a no-man's land, filled with mines and barbed wire, mud and thousands of puddles, defended by opposing armies and even from the air looks desolate. Nothing moves within.

The Artillery Battalion has hundreds of eighteen pounder guns dug in north of the hamlet Neuville-Saint-Vaast. Hidden in broken structures and camouflaged pits, they will shortly begin a creeping barrage and it will be Dominic's responsibility to ensure the guns stay ahead of the infantry. The lives of British and Canadian soldiers lie in the hands of professional gunners and observers that tell them where to shoot. The barrage will form a defensive wall for the advancing soldiers and, if successful, will leave their enemies dazed and confused, unprepared for the assault of men and guns.

Swinging to the west, Selkirk flies over the German fortifications near Vimy and the barrage begins a hundred yards in front of the British. Dominic can see the men crawling out of the trenches and following the barrage of shells as it raises clouds of dust and debris. Dominic sends code to a Morse operator on the ground (it might even be Clovis) and the barrage lifts and moves towards the enemy fortifications and the German front lines. The battle rages with unbelievable noise and destruction.

Shells from the German antiaircraft artillery burst close to the plane, close enough that the heat from the blast is felt as the plane rocks in the turbulence. Dominic is too busy to be scared. Selkirk keeps the plane as level as possible but takes evasive measures from the bombardment of guns on the ground. At 6,000 feet, there is danger from rifle and machine gun fire, but the plane is very difficult to hit. He studies the geography and recalls the terrain from his training as he directs the barrage to the northwest in 100-yard increments. In the next fifteen minutes the barrage from the British guns are behind the enemy lines but continue so as to discourage reinforcements from the rear.

Dominic and Selkirk fly over the battle and can see men falling, running, engaged in hand-to-hand combat – and the killing continues. At first they don't see the enemy aircraft as the German Fokkers approach from the west. Only when they hear the chatter of the machine guns and the ripping of the cloth when the bullets punch holes in the wings do they react to the menace. Selkirk dives and twists to get out of the line of fire. Close behind is a red Fokker tri-plane with the German cross in bold black and white on the fuselage. Two machine guns are mounted ahead of the cockpit and the pilot sprays a deadly stream towards them. Selkirk twists and turns, taking erratic undulations to avoid the stream of bullets when as quickly as they started, they stop. When Dominic looks back, he can see the Fokker break off with a Sopwith on his tail. The planes launch an aerial dogfight, which he doesn't get to see the end of. Selkirk points to the damaged wing and heads for the airfield. The landing is perilous as the plane yaws and shifts from the uneven distribution of airflow. When the plane comes to a stop, Dominic's heart is pounding, his fingers and arms are sore from the tenseness he is feeling and his head and face are covered with sweat. Selkirk is as calm as if he just got out of bed. He yells over the dying engine.

"Told ya I'd get ya home, laddie, didn't I?"

Dominic just nods, happy to be alive. He is beat from the efforts and exhilaration of his first encounter with battle. The fear he was feeling is gone. He joins the men at the edge of the field where they wait to see if the others return. There is just quiet as the two aircraft like his return within the next half hour but only one of the Sopwith camels comes back. The pilot informs the ground crew that he saw the other go down over Vimy and burst into flames when it hit the ground. He doesn't imagine the pilot survived. A pall is cast over the men. Those that returned are thankful for their safety, yet dread the coming days as it must be done all over again.

For the first time in the war, all four divisions of the Canadian First Army fight against three divisions of the German Sixth Army and take Vimy Ridge. The final objective is reached on April 12 when the Canadians take a fortified knoll near the village of Givenchy-en-Gohelle. The death toll is tremendous. Of the one hundred thousand soldiers, it's estimated that over 3,500 men die and 7,000 are injured. They take over 4,000 prisoners-of-war. The Germans fall back to the Oppy-Mericourt line and dig in. There is no major breakthrough and the Battle of Arras continues, with both sides reaching a stalemate.

On April 14 the Canadians lead another attack on the German trenches. Artillery observers are put into service to locate and direct the shooting where hundreds of British guns will shoot over two hundred rounds each before the day is over. Along with the other observers, Dominic and Selkirk are in the air again with the damaged wing fixed as best as possible. Selkirk curses at the instability of the aircraft, but Dominic concentrates on his mission and leaves the flying to his pilot, whom he's come to respect and trust.

Peering down at the devastation in no man's land, Dominic is shocked at what he sees. The flesh is torn from the earth; fields are swathed in mire that sticks to anything it touches. Dead animals and dead humans litter the grounds. Giant trees, scorched bare of branches and upper limbs, haphazardly poke their fractured trunks towards the skies in what was once a forest. Debris and dead wood, barbed wire and the sucking mud make a sad sight. Dominic yearns for an end to the destruction. A burst to his starboard side shocks his reverie as they pass over the German trenches. Soldiers are shooting at them with rifles and machine guns. The shooting stops when the British guns begin pounding the terrain near the trenches.

The German antiaircraft guns, however, are well within range. Selkirk jigs the plane to and fro to avoid the bursts. When their plane is 2,000 yards behind enemy lines, Selkirk sweeps to port so Dominic can relay the proper information to the ground crew when a shell from a German field howitzer detonates close to them, tearing the bottom wing, struts and over half of the top wing off. Shrapnel from the shell rips through the side of the aircraft piercing Dominic's clothing and flesh. Luckily none of it is fatal. But everyone's luck runs out sometime. Selkirk takes shrapnel to the head and is killed immediately. The plane begins a downward spiral towards a large copse of trees. Dominic thinks he is going to die and holds an image of Maria in his mind. He grips the handholds, closes his eyes and waits for the crash.

The plane hits an upward air current 100 feet above the tree line and straightens out with a forward movement and sinks. Striking a section of younger, supple trees, the tops snap off and the trees bend to cushion some of the fall. The nose of the plane crashes into the ground, buckling the undercarriage and the remaining wing. Dominic is thrown from the aircraft upon impact and lands at the edge of an adjoining field where smaller brush and abandoned hay mounds rest.

This cushions his fall. The debris is enough to save his life but not enough to save him from injury. His bad leg snaps where it had broken before, and his left arm breaks below the elbow. The flesh wound on his hip and shoulder bleed, and he's knocked unconscious.

The downed plane and its rapid descent are witnessed by hundreds of soldiers, both Germans and allies. There is very little anyone can do except for two men who are near the crash site. They wear the field grey of the German Army.

CHAPTER 7

Maria opens the door to the shop and steps outside. May 15 is promising. Sunshine struggles through the tangle of broken clouds to warm the land. The thermometer that Dominic attached to the front corner of the house reads 68 degrees and it is only eight o'clock. The tulips along the front of the building are already almost a foot tall and she can hardly wait for the first lush blooms of color. With the fields bordering the property lying fallow, the smell of new earth greets her as well as the odor of damp coal from the coal yard after yesterday's rain. She looks up the street towards the city, hoping to see Mrs. Smith. Her husband used to deliver the mail but is in Europe, fighting alongside his fellow soldiers, so she has taken over his job. Alexander's Jewellery is the first stop on her route and she is normally here by now. She is anxious to hear from Dominic. He usually writes her a letter every week and with the vagaries of war and shipping across the Atlantic, their arrival is sporadic but they always arrive. There has been no mail from him for almost a month, and she worries about him.

There are too many things on her mind to get bogged down about slow letters. Denise has taken ill and is still not well enough to work in the store, but when she checked on her earlier, she seems to be a bit better and the fever is gone. The darn flu has been spreading like crazy this spring. While she hopes to hear from Dominic soon, she reminds herself that there has been no word from the War office to make her think something bad may have happened. She's heard of the fateful moments when a soldier, usually a younger one, shows up at the door with terrible news and that hasn't happened yet. Pausing for a moment

282

of the end of the porch, she wonders why anyone would show up here unless Dominic told them she is next of kin, and she really isn't. They are only engaged, and they never talked about it before he left, but she assumes that Dominic would've told his recruiting officer to notify her if something happened to him. She rubs her hands together and talks out loud, if only to herself.

"Darn, another thing to worry about. I'll stop at the recruiter's office tomorrow if Denise is feeling better and ask."

Looking at her watch, she realizes she's been dawdling and the store opens at nine. She goes back inside and stops at the main counter where she keeps her notepad. Denise is always making fun of her lists and jokingly asks her if she makes a list of her lists. Maria writes everything down and rarely forgets any of her tasks. The most urgent matter today is Gina Amato and her husband's wedding bands. The wedding is this coming Saturday and the rings were supposed to be here last week. When they did arrive, the sizes were mixed up when Denise ordered them and Gina's ring was a nine and her husband's was a seven instead of the reverse. If Dominic was here, he would have just sized them but Maria had to send them back and reorder them. She will call the supplier later as it is an hour earlier in Montreal where the rings were made. Making a check mark on the pad she gives this task #1.

She is going through the list when she hears someone outside and goes to check. It is Mrs. Smith, who knocks at the door instead of leaving the mail in the box that Dominic made. Maria is wide eyed at the look on the post mistress's face.

"Come in please, Mrs. Smith, the door is open."

Meeting the lady at the door, Mrs. Smith wordlessly hands her an official looking letter that has the address of the War Commission of Ottawa on the outer flap.

"I wanted to be sure you received this, my dear, and didn't want to leave it in the box."

Mrs. Smith knows that these letters usually carry bad news and hesitates before leaving as she feels she should say something, especially when Maria's face goes pale.

"It might be good news, Maria. I'll pray for you."

Patting Maria on the shoulder, Mrs. Smith leaves.

With shaking hands, Maria takes the letter to the counter and puts it down, too scared to open it and yet dying for news. She takes a deep breath and searches for the small jackknife under the counter and slits the envelope open. She frowns at what looks like an official document with the second page a hand written letter in a strange hand. Unfolding them, she holds the first to the light from the window. It's from The Canadian Headquarters in London, and is dated April 20. It goes on to tell Maria that her fiancé, Dominic Alexander has been missing since April 14. According to the enclosed letter, which was received at this office, all efforts are being made to locate him. She doesn't finish the letter but drops it on the counter to read the other page. It is written hastily and in pencil.

April 17

Maria Desjardins

Dear Miss Desjardins,

My name is Hector LeGrand. I am with the French Army and my note is to let you know that we have recovered Dominic Alexander from his downed aircraft. He is not well but he is alive and through very limited speech he has asked, no he pesters me, to write and inform you of his whereabouts. You will likely receive official word from the Canadian Army but he was insistent that I write as soon as possible. I have taken great pains to get this to you. He has memory lapses and could not remember the address so I have sent this to the War Commission in England where it could possibly be censored. He is in a stable condition but requires more intense medical attention soon. The cave and fields where he is being held temporarily has fallen into German hands once more and there is too much danger in trying to move him.

He has suffered multiple fractures and we are worried about infection…

Maria faints. When her body falls to the floor, Denise hears the thud and rushes downstairs to fine her prone on the floor with the pages scattered about her.

"My goodness… Maria… Maria!"

Kneeling at her head, Denise holds her in her lap and sees her eyelids flutter.

"Maria, what happened? Are you okay?"

Sitting up with Denise's help, she holds her head in one hand and brushes the tears from her eyes.

"It's Dominic, Denise. His plane crashed over a month ago and he was badly injured."

"Oh no, is he... is he still alive Maria?"

"I don't know, Denise."

CHAPTER 8

On the same day, Dominic is in one of the 504 beds at the No. 2 Canadian General Hospital in Le Treport, France. He has a visitor today. Hector LeGrand is beside his bed with a wooden wheelchair. Pushing aside a hard backed chair, he motions for Dominic to get in. With his arm and leg still in casts, his movement is limited, but getting out of the bed sounds very good. He is able to slide to the side of the bed and sit up. Sunlight streams through the open tent flaps calling to the weary to come out and enjoy the day. The room is already getting hot at ten o'clock. It will only get worse. It smells of carbolic lotion and coal tar the doctors use to fight infection.

"Come, my friend, let me get you into the chair and I'll take you outside where we can talk and smoke, Oui?"

Feeling sorry for himself, Dominic is not very polite.

"Ach, and who would you be?"

"I'm the man, who along with my brother, saved your life."

Dominic arches his brows in surprise, then feels humbled. His face reddens. He can't remember many details after the crash. There are flashes that pop up in his head sometimes of some of the events after the plane went down, but it is mostly blank until he ended up in the Casualty Clearing Station set up by the British Field Ambulance.

"Well, I guess the first thing I need to say is thank you, which hardly seems enough."

LeGrand grins as he strives to get Dominic, who balances on his good leg, into the chair.

"Not even necessary, *mon ami*, we're all in this together."

"How did you find me? And why are you here?"

"I'll explain that all later. Let's find a spot in the shade. It's going to be a hot one today."

"Thank you. It will be a pleasure to get out of this tent."

LeGrand gets Dominic's feet on the foot rests and wheels him through the ward, around the nurses, aides, doctors and other patients who wander around the beds. Exiting through a large tied back flap, a soft breeze cools the perspiration on Dominic's face. He squints when he enters the sunlit yard. Heading towards a small copse of trees to the left of the tent, there are benches and a rough table set up under several tall skinny trees that are sprouting their first buds. Parking Dominic at the end of the table, LeGrand sits at the end waving to two other men who sit on the opposite end. Digging a worn metal flask from his hip pocket, he offers it to Dominic.

"Try some of this medicine. I guarantee that after a couple of slugs, you won't be feeling any pain."

"That'd be good right about now."

Dominic takes a small sip and after swallowing his face glows and he coughs. Expelling a deep breath, he pants from the strong liquor.

"Whoa, that stuff would likely remove paint."

LeGrand chuckles heartily and takes a wee sip himself. Grimacing, he replaces the cap and then puts the container back in his pocket. Taking a smoke from a crumpled box, he offers it to Dominic, who declines.

"Haven't acquired a taste for those yet but the liquor is damn fine. So tell me, I know that my plane went down west of the German line, how did you and your brother…what's his name?"

"Henri."

"What were you and Henri doing back there before you got me through the line with my body in such bad shape?"

Hector enjoys a story, so do his hands. Every statement has a gesture keeping Dominic enthralled throughout their conversation.

"We sneak across and see what strength our enemy is, see what armament we are up against, their weak spots, spy stuff, things you can't see from the sky. Henri and I have a German father and a French mother, so we speak both languages. We wear uniforms we stole from dead soldiers who were in no need any longer."

Hector laughs at his own joke; it comes easy.

"Using both of our shirts, we cut stripes and bound your leg and arm to your torso and put pressure on your wounds. You came to several times but passed out again, I expect from the pain. We had to make a stretcher. After a five hour hike, we got you to a rowboat we have hidden on the river north of where your plane went down. There we waited until nightfall and rowed you for several miles, and then we hid you at a safe place. It was almost twenty-four hours before anyone could pay attention to your injuries. You were lucky none of the fractured bones broke skin. It took a week before we got you over. We had a close call, let me tell you..."

Hector regales the patient with a tale of true bravado and relates it as if he does similar deeds every day. His version is full of danger, stress, and difficult moments and yet he makes his audience laugh many times. He told Dominic about the two German soldiers who came to the cabin... "only a minute to get you out and in the woods." Cognac was the only pain medicine they had. The dark cave where they stayed overnight and how cold it was with no fire. The cabin, a rotted out shell of little interest but a waterproof roof. The strange medicine lady that tended him, her voice like a man's and the hairs on her chin, a witch he thinks. Finally, the heavy bombardment of the German trenches when many of the shells found plenty of men to destroy. Whole stretches empty of any soldiers for several days with no reinforcements. The three other injured men they had hid, and how they had waited for the first opportunity to get them to the other side. The beautiful nurse at the Casualty Station where they had parted company.

"...*a plus belle*, she was a pretty lady, even when her apron was covered in blood. Huh, don't you think, Dominic?"

Dominic has been firing questions at him and ignores his sore arm, the left is limited by the sling. A half empty flask causes his legs to be numb so he doesn't feel them. The warmth of the absinthe and the mirth in the storyteller's eyes keeps his mind off his troubles. A full hour passes when Dominic grows tired and his ass is sore from sitting in the wooden chair. It's almost time for dinner as well and his stomach rumbles. Taking advantage of a lull and Hector putting out his cigarette, Dominic asks if he can be wheeled back in.

"I'm glad you came by Hector, really I am. I hope we can stay in touch. Please pass on my thank you to Henri. Thank you very, very much Hector, you're a great man. If you are ever in Canada, come see me. In Moncton, I'm easy to find."

288

With a doff of his beret, Hector LeGrand, the man who helped save Dominic's life, is swallowed by the war.

After a scolding from the nurse who saw them come back in for not telling them he was going – he's not supposed to be out of bed – Dominic is comfortable. Her brows are knitted and her upper lip stiff. She may not be tall but Dominic is afraid of her. She means business. He promises he won't do it again, and after a moment with a piercing stare, her face smooths out and a half smile appears when she hands him a letter.

"This came for you earlier. I didn't want to leave it on the bed; there's thieves in here. The hand writing looks like a lady's and you're lucky it found you; you've only been here a couple of weeks. I've slit it open for you. Do you need help getting the pages out?"

"No that's okay, Nurse Roberts, I can dig it out with my good hand. Thank you."

"Now, stay in bed… and enjoy your letter."

He can see it is from Maria and feels guilty for not being able to write. Only last week was he able to have one of the nurses write and tell her of his plight – to let Maria know he was in hospital. Unfolding the pages, he spreads the sheets on his lap.

My dearest Dominic.

You don't know how relieved I am that you are alive. I wish I was there to take care of you. When I received the letter from someone named Hector, I was afraid for the worst and I was in agony until I heard from the War Office that you had been rescued and that you were in hospital with injuries. It was the worst time of my life. I yearn for your well-being and return to my loving arms. I miss you so much my love. I…

The letter goes on to tell of her undying love, her commitment to their happiness when he returns. There is a brief note at the end of the letter about the business and how well it is doing. Dominic begins to read it for a second time when he is disturbed by a Canadian officer. Lieutenant Geoffrey Delahunt introduces himself. A tall man with protruding chin and infectious smile, he bears good news.

"Private Alexander, I'm here to inform you that you will be heading back to Canada in less than a week. A Canadian hospital ship will be sailing from Calais and you will be transported there within the next day or two. Your war service is done and you are to be awarded the Campaign Star, British War Medal, Distinguished Conduct Medal and the Military Medal. Once you are back in Canada, there will be an honourable discharge and other paperwork to be completed, but there is no hurry for that. What's important now is that we get you home and that you recover properly. Any questions?"

"Thank you, Lieutenant, that is indeed good news. Do you know how long it will be before I am actually back in Canada?"

"Well if everything goes as planned, you should dock in Halifax by the first week in June."

CHAPTER 9

Dark swirling clouds on the early morning of June 7 do nothing to dampen the spirits of those that pause inside the waiting room of Pier 23 in Halifax harbour. A hospital ship docked at night. The *SS Grand Bay*, a Canadian steamship, is ideally suited to its humanitarian role. She's fast and has ample space for doctors, nurses, medical equipment, crew and patients. The bow is white, identified by a large red cross painted on the sides. In conformity to the Hague Convention of 1907, she ran fully lighted so the enemy would know her cargo is wounded or dying soldiers, pathetic results of the violence they leave behind. The Germans don't care. Unregulated submarine warfare means the ship's purpose and mission is given no consideration; it is not immune to torpedoes. But this ship made it home.

Maria, Denise, Rosie, Emma and Adolph are talking to a uniformed man who waves his clipboard to make himself look important. Thinking Dominic immobile and requiring further hospitalization in Halifax, they want to know where Private Alexander will be taken. The rotund fellow is flipping papers. Scrunched as they are, the brows and moustache form a fuzzy trio that scrutinize the names. His voice is high pitched and sympathetic.

"Yes, well, we're not certain yet, the hospitals are full, you know. The worst cases are given the highest priority and moved as quickly as possible. Usually that takes much time. I don't see his name on the list for immediate transportation but these lists are never complete. Any patients that are mobile have to be processed and that started an hour ago at seven. They are beginning to come ashore and if you step outside and look east at the furthest walkway, if he's able to walk, you might see him there, otherwise you'll have to wait until I have more information."

Maria is at the head of the small crowd, anxiety caressing her brow. The group move to the window and see men being pushed ashore in wheelchairs, some on crutches, others on their own power, but with assistance. It has stopped raining and there is a small break in the dark clouds so that the sky emits a subtle ray of warmth. The four of them go outside and edge closer to a cordoned area. Gazing intently through diamond shaped openings in the fence, they see men hustling about everywhere. Horses and wagons, ambulances fill the empty spaces on the wharves. New motorized trucks off-load smelly garbage and hospital detritus. Ships lie at anchor nearby and undulate in the murky waters. Maria is pointing to the men coming down the gangplank.

"There he is! On the top of the walkway! He's walking on his own."

The quintet is elated, they begin waving and calling his name. Dominic doesn't see them yet. The casts were removed four days ago. He spent hours exercising the un-worked muscles and he still experiences pain in his leg. His limp is more pronounced so he takes it easy, relying on his cane. He was offered a wheelchair from the orderlies to bring him ashore but declined. Certain Maria and maybe others are here to take him home, he would rather they see him walking. He can hear his name above the crowd and noises. Looking towards the receiving building, a woman jumping up and down, both arms in the air, catches his eyes. It's Maria. His heart is almost bursting with longing.

The crowd disappears and he only has eyes for her. Like a beacon, a smile so big and bright beckons. The small duffel bag he carries and the tenderness in his leg hamper his haste. At the bottom of the gangplank he stops momentarily to catch his breath and sees the people with Maria. Denise, Rosie, Emma and Adolph are waving and cheering.

Maria can't stand it any longer and dashes past the "keep out" sign and through an unclasped gate to rush to her lover's arms. No one tries to stop her. She veers around harried workers, shies a horse and clears her way to his side. Crushing herself to his chest, his cane clatters to the floor and he bears his weight into her open arms. One hand holds his head close to hers. He breathes in the familiar scent of his lover's skin and the months apart disappear. Soft sobs in his ear exclaim how happy she is. With weak arms, he clings to her gently. The embrace lasts many moments until they stare at each other. Their first kiss is longing, deep. Follow up kisses are just as passionate but beyond lips, to necks and fluttering eyelids. Dominic pulls himself away and holds her at arm's-length.

"You're even more beautiful than I've kept in my memory. I've missed you so much, Maria."

"Oh, Dominic, I felt like a part of me was missing. You don't know how happy I am. And to see you walking and looking so fit makes me even happier. A little thin maybe, but *ma tante Emma* will fix that. I love you, you brave soldier."

Hugging her once more, he whispers words of love and promises to never leave again. She agrees, shaking her head, and squeezes him tighter. Stepping back, her eyes widen at the sadness in his, a glazed look.

"What is it Dominic?"

"You won't believe the things I saw Maria, it's a terrible waste. So much death, so much destruction, how cruel we are to each other. When I was sailing home, I was bothered by the images that are stuck in my head. I realize how lucky I am; those poor soldiers are stuck there fighting for their lives, like your brothers and Nick and Pascal. I just want to say to you before we meet the others and head home, that those memories kind of haunt me and I want to concentrate on getting back to our normal life again."

Hugging him again, her heart pounding, she reassures him.

"I will always be here for you, Dominic, always. We'll get you back to good health and there's lots of work waiting for you, and everyone asks about you. We're all so happy you're back. Everything will work out, my love. The war will be over soon, it must!"

Nodding with an uncertain smile, he shrugs and stoops to pick up his cane. Maria pats his shoulder and waves at the entrance.

"Come now; let's get you through whatever it is you have to do inside before you can leave. A stuffy Sergeant said something about papers you had to have and sign. I'll go with you and if they don't like it…well, too bad."

Maria gathers up his duffel bag and they go through the doors.

It will be a long time before Dominic gives up the cane. The arm has healed fine and he buries himself in his work. He sketches. He worships Maria. The summer passes with more rain than usual, and it's on those days that Dominic feels the melancholiest. The dreams are not as bad. People have learned that he will only speak of the war in the present tense and talks of some of the fine men he met there, but not of his involvement. The connection with his customers and the work Maria has done at the store make him happy, happy enough to enjoy the quiet of his life and to pray for those that are still fighting. His business prospers.

Nothing happens at his house in Cocagne. They are so busy and only escaped there twice over the summer. Dominic's widening waistline can be attributed mostly to eating at Emma's often. The city vibrates with wartime commerce. Ships arrive and depart regularly to sail the Petitcodiac River's red muddy waters. Trains travel through the city with war material. Women are working, the conflict in Europe hoarding the men, so far away. Their replacements are expected to do the same work but are not paid the same as the men. The inequality is not well known but that's about to change.

CHAPTER 10

The tower of the cotton mill looms menacingly, like a fist, above the small crowd gathered in the shadows of the office door. The last Friday of September has not started off peacefully in the east end of Moncton. Odors from the workings of raw cotton float in the light autumn breeze. The sun barely crests the horizon, yet a cluster of shouting women and several men are waving and demanding that the owner, Baylor Crosswaithe, treat his female employs fairly. They make a glut along the driveway so no one can exit or enter without running over them. It came to light that female weavers are making three dollars a day less than men doing the same work. Young children also labour at the mill for very low wages. The crowd is angry.

It is unlikely that Crosswaithe will show his face, mainly because he doesn't care. He has stated publicly that the mill is his business and he will run it as he sees fit. If the workers don't like their wages, they are free to look elsewhere for jobs. The truth of the matter is that the mill is in financial difficulty and Crosswaithe is scrambling to keep the business operating. There is an abundance of cotton mills throughout the country, driving the prices down.

Maria Desjardins decides that enough is enough and against Dominic's wishes that she not be involved, she makes phone calls and organizes rallies. It has a mild adverse effect on the business and it is the first heated conversation they have in their relationship. He agrees with her but wants her out of sight. Today she is at the forefront of the protestors. She is also the loudest.

"It's not fair that your ladies work so hard for wages that are unequal"

The other women, Emma included, along with twelve of their friends and acquaintances and a handful of husbands, are making a racket and waving hand drawn placards, demanding equal rights. Denise wanted to be there but had to work at the store, especially since Maria organized the rally and she hasn't told Dominic. The suffragette movement has been slow to reach Moncton, but these are the same ladies that are most vocal for equality. Other women are afraid of their husbands, or their employers, or their disagreeable families to be involved publicly. Some write letters of protest; others say and do nothing. The bunch gathered are just as verbal as their leader.

"Give woman the same money as the men!"

"Tell Crosswaithe that we demand an audience!"

"How can you sleep knowing women are treated so unfairly?"

"We want some answers!"

The commotion is being witnessed by people on the periphery, not involved but intrigued by the uncommon sight of women creating such a disturbance. Most of the protesters are in everyday wear but one is in an elegant jacket and skirts of the latest fashion – namely Mildred Van Geist. Van Geist is not as boisterous but her presence lends gravity to the cause. Much to her husband's chagrin, she too has an effect on his banking business. Men in delivery carts, people walking to work or going to the hospital up the street, are watching. Not everyone is sympathetic, especially domineering males.

At the opposite end of the building is a loose group of workers staring, lingering at the worker's entrance, fronted by three burly men glaring at the women with hateful glazes, shaking their fists at them and yelling abuse. Maria shakes her fist back at them. The men take offence and advance on the crowd, but are only a few steps away when the shift whistle blares calling them to work. More fist waves and the workers disappear in the side entrance while those ending their workday hustle away from the crowd, knowing what's going on and having been warned by their supervisors to give no heed to the disruptive behavior out front, to ignore the ideas they are spreading. The women especially are reminded of how fortunate they are to have a job. None hang around.

From the front doors comes a portly man, tie askew, trousers bagging at the knees. Angry eyes bulge from a hairless head except for a few wisps around small ears. The mouth is almost a snarl. Behind him are two ruffians who work in the warehouse. They're known for their quick temper and heavy lifting has made them strong. The mill manager, Wade Flanagan, is a misogynist and finds aggressive females annoying, especially this troublesome Desjardins woman who has been disrupting their peace. Stepping closely to Maria, he waves for attention. The crowd quiets except for their leader. Maria has arms akimbo, a folded umbrella hanging on one arm, her expression unhappy.

"Where's Crosswaithe?" she demands.

Flanagan flips his hand as if the idea is absurd. His voice is raspy and pompous.

"Mr. Crosswaithe does not have time for you troublemakers. Nor do we. I'd advise you to leave the premises at once. You are on private property. We've called the police as well and they should be here soon, so it's better you go peacefully."

Pointing his finger at Maria, his voice lowers, becomes more spiteful. She hears him quite clearly amidst the clamor of the crowd.

"I know who you are, Miss Desjardins. I'd advise you to be more careful. One can only wonder what your fiancé must think. Perhaps he should remember who buys his jewellery and pays for his services, certainly not these peasants you care so much about. Mr. Crosswaithe is a very big part of the financial community here in Moncton and can be influential. Do you know that word, influential, as in advising his associates to buy elsewhere? Hmm?"

Maria is about to let loose with a barrage of unkind words when a deeper voice calls for calm.

"Quiet, everyone, quiet. People stop your yelling. You two in the back, un-ball those fists. Stop waving that umbrella so threateningly, young lady. Mr. Flanagan, perhaps you could step back a bit and tell me what's going on here."

The police officer is thick chested and tall, authority and a shiny badge makes people stop their fidgeting and they close in to hear what is being said. Officer Melanson steps between Maria and Flanagan, who are staring darts at each other. Maria starts to complain when Melanson holds a hand out to wait her turn. Nodding at the manager, he prompts him once more.

"What's all the fuss about here now, Flanagan?"

Chin in the air he points at Maria.

"She's egging this bunch of rowdies on, Officer. It's disrupting our business and they are on private property as well. We'd like them to disperse as soon as possible. They make such foolish demands, asking for Crosswaithe of all things, as if he has time to deal with these troublemakers. I'd like it if you and your fellow officer I see over there could get this crowd moving. In fact, I demand it!"

Melanson doesn't like the manager's attitude and knows a few of the women here. He is also aware of the unfair labor practices in the factories but he must uphold the law. Turning to Maria, his eyes beg indulgence.

"Its troublemakers you are, ladies and gents? You know we can't have that. You'll need to go home now. You're holding up traffic and there are delivery carts waiting to get in and you are on someone else's property."

The group lower their cards and their shoulders, some starting to move on, wending through a crowd of gatherers, some of whom are not friendly. Maria respects the law and doesn't want any trouble, only to be listened to. She watches Flanagan beam a smug look at the thinning assembly and she sees all the rottenness in his manner.

"You'll not get away with this much longer, Mister. The indecent way you treat your women."

Flanagan can see that the police are moving people away and feels he has won. Only she can hear him.

"It's better than most deserve. Humph!"

Despising him so much, she doesn't even think. Running forward with umbrella raised, she whacks him on the head. Before Officer Melanson can contain her, she's hit him several times. One of the blows from the long stem of her weapon hits him on the nose and makes it bleed. Another to the side of the head makes it on the next day's front page of the *Transcript*. The flash from the photographer's camera catches another of Maria being escorted to the police automobile.

Flanagan rushes into the building with his blood-stained handkerchief held tightly to his nose. The two bodyguards block the entrance. Putting Maria in the back seat, the other officer drives and Melanson sits beside her, his manner abrupt, asking her questions while taking notes. What's her name? Where does she live? They take Maria home. Since Dominic has been back, she moved in with Emma, where they were going to take her but she convinces Officer Melanson that she is needed at work and he will know where she is. She promises to go directly to her aunt's place after work. Melanson can be a soft touch sometimes for a pretty girl. Taking her at her word, he does as she asks. When they arrive, before she is allowed out of the automobile, she is chastised severely by Melanson for her actions. It's possible that Flanagan may lay charges against her for assault. There's a tinge of sympathy in his voice when he reaches over to open the other automobile door so she can get out.

"You'll not be able to do any protesting if you're sitting in jail. Stay off their property. Don't go anywhere until we tell you to. You could still be in a lot of trouble. Otherwise the day is still long. I hope the rest is more peaceful, Miss Desjardins."

Maria knows enough to keep quiet. The realization of what she's done is sinking in. She begins to worry about Dominic's reaction. She hopes he's out back doing repairs. Lifting her skirts to slide out, she steps carefully onto the driveway, waving over her shoulder.

"Thank you, Officer."

Dominic frowns when he espies the police automobile coming up the driveway and wonders what trouble they are bringing. He's serving a client who can't decide on three or four small diamonds on the side of her new ring. They'll have to come in, he thinks, as he explains the symmetry of the four stones to the lady and she should spend the small extra for such a unique design. Denise is showing watches to an elderly man who is inspecting them with his monocle. Two timepieces are laid out on a black velvet cloth. He selects a gold Waltham with a black leather strap and tries it on. Denise sneaks a look at the automobile in the driveway and sees the Black Ford with an officer telling Maria something, and he looks upset. The old man almost drops the watch, startled when Denise gasps, putting her hand to her heart, hoping Maria's not hurt. Forgetting the watches, she touches the customer on the shoulder and excuses herself to hasten over to Dominic. Her abruptness causes both Dominic and Mrs. Lawson to step back with questioning looks. The man puts the watch back, leans on the counter, his curiosity piqued. Denise moves around the counter clutching Dominic's arm with both hands. Mrs. Lawson grasps her ring and moves away. They're all looking at the police automobile.

"Look who's in the automobile Dominic, maybe she's hurt."

Brows raised, he's almost laughing,

"Hurt? How could she get hurt at the accountant's office? She was going to talk to Lombroso about the receipts for last month. Is that her in the back?"

"That's not where she went."

Unfolding himself from her arm, his frown is askance.

"Where did she go?"

Denise worries about his reaction, knowing Dominic disagrees with Maria's displays in public.

"To the cotton mill; there was a rally."

Slapping himself on the forehead, he shakes his head.

"Ach, knowing her, she was probably at the front of the crowd going on about women's wages."

Dominic and Denise move around the counter. Everyone's in the middle of the store watching Maria step out of the vehicle and head up the walkway. Head up, chin out, she waves over her shoulder at the policeman. Head down now, she enters the store, but she has to step aside for Mrs. Lawson, who glares at her as she goes out the door. The Lawsons own a department store and hire mostly women. The older man is still leaning on the counter, chuckling at the whole episode. Deciding he'll come back for a watch another day, probably the gold Waltham, he bids them farewell and hobbles out. Dominic frets over the ring for Mrs. Lawson, apologizes to the man before he leaves and is furious underneath. Maria is not afraid to stand up for herself. She loves Dominic so much and wishes he could understand how she feels. But she doesn't want to make him unhappy either. She sees the displeasure on his face. Untying his apron, he chucks it on the counter.

"What have you been doing, Maria? Why were the police needed?"

"Oh Dominic, I... I was arrested for hitting that monster Flanagan over the head with my umbrella."

Dominic is startled, eyes bugging out. Denise's hands go to her mouth to stifle a laugh. Dominic sees the glee in Denise's eyes and then looks back at Maria to see the same mirth in hers.

"You women think this is funny? Did you not see two guests leave the store? Maybe the gentleman will be back, but not Mrs. Lawson. She knows we're engaged, Maria. Can't you help the workers without being in the center of it all?"

Maria steps closer to him, wanting to explain, but Dominic holds up a hand to ward her off.

"I'm too upset to discuss this any further, Maria. Now that you're here, you and Denise can watch the store and close up. I'm taking the Ford, perhaps visit Cocagne for the rest of the day. I need to think about what you've done."

Stepping aside, Maria knows that will be best. She's never seen him so angry and doesn't want an argument even though she feels she is doing the right thing.

Dominic stays away until the next day. When he returns, he holds a copy of the newspaper with her picture and confronts her once more. After an hour or so of angry words, their compassion for each other prevails as they hash out their differences. Maria agrees to keep herself behind the scenes, but will not back down from the issues that are important to her. Dominic wants to support her but worries about the affect it will have on the store.

A week goes by and Dominic receives a formal invitation to sit with the business leaders at their monthly meeting where mutual agreements are made that benefit the overall business community of Moncton and surrounding areas. When he arrives, he is put in the hot seat for his fiancée's actions. The accusations are made by Crosswaithe, supported by his cronies. Then they deliver an ultimatum that either she backs down as a leader to what they refer to as nonsense or they will do all within their power to divert business to the other jewellery stores in the city. While Dominic may have been compliant to their requests and was willing to say so, his opinion changed when Crosswaithe crossed the line.

"You've given her too much responsibility Alexander, and you know she should be in the kitchen where women belong."

Not all the gentlemen gathered there laugh even though none want to become Crosswaithe's enemy. He has too much influence with political leaders and other entrepreneurs. Dominic thinks of his sisters, Adairia, all the women in his life, and becomes red-faced with anger. Getting up from his chair, he glares at Crosswaithe, pointing a finger at him.

"You, sir, are a disgrace with that attitude. Maria is one of the kindest, most thoughtful persons I know, regardless of my own personal feelings for her. Women have every right to enjoy the benefits of life that we men take for granted. Shame on you and your gaggle of followers. From now on, I'll be at her side when she takes up her cause once more, and as far as any extra business you suggest you can drum up for me, you can stick it up your arse!"

Dominic hastily leaves the premises. Crosswaithe gapes at the insolence and is speechless as no one speaks to him in that way. A hush follows Dominic out until several men applaud and leave also. Crosswaithe's plans to sway business away from the young upstart only hurt temporarily. The store receipts falter briefly but continue to grow.

CHAPTER 11

Maria is more involved in women's issues and the few times there have been public displays, Dominic is at her side. Early December everyone is devastated by the Halifax Explosion. When the French cargo ship *SS Mont Blanc*, filled with explosives, collides with the Norwegian ship *SS IMO*. The resulting blast levels most of the city. The death toll is horrific. Christmas nears and there is little time for politics. New business comes daily in the smaller purchases from the many average buyers whom Maria and her ideals have become popular with. Letters from home arrive for Dominic. Mary tells him that Pascal is still fighting and the family is growing. They all miss him so much. Her letter has a page with scribbles from Paul and Sheila has enclosed a drawing of the flowers she and Mary have planted. There is evidence in the youngster's doodling that she might take after Granda and Dominic. Ivan sends a letter for the first time, filled with the adventures of a young man terribly in love with Dominic's younger sister. Lilly writes too. So does Adairia.

Christmas Eve is spent in Notre Dame with Maria's father and his new girlfriend. Christmas day is spent at Emma's. Everyone is presented with a framed five by seven sketch from Dominic in charcoal, except Maria. Dominic has crafted an attractive pendant shaped like a rose, which is her favorite flower, and in the center is a sparkling half carat diamond he secured from a client that was divesting himself of his deceased wife's jewellery. Everyone is stunned by the craftsmanship.

The war seems far away at times, but the devastation and killing continue. Nick has been hospitalized, suffering from injuries sustained from the German bombs. Robert Desjardins never returned from his last mission in November and is listed as missing in action, his whereabouts and condition unknown. Andre Desjardins is doing his part in France, fighting near Cambrai. The allies push towards Germany. Everyone prays for it to end, especially Maria, who wants her brothers to come home and to marry Dominic.

One of the last event's in Dominic's year is updating his scrapbooks. The latest one is only half full. The pleasure he feels are from the memories of when he started the hobby back in Scotland at his uncle's place. The actions tie him to the happiness he felt there.

First NHL game is played on artificial ice.
Jeannette Rankin is the first woman elected to Congress.
Canadian ace Billy Bishop is awarded the Victoria Cross for his successful solo mission beyond enemy lines.
US declares war on Germany.
The Quebec Bridge opens after 20 years of planning and construction.
Dutch dancer Mata Hari is executed by firing squad for spying for Germany.
Canadian troops capture the town of Passchendaele in the Third Battle of Ypres.
HMS Vanguard explodes internally at Scapa Flow, killing all 805 aboard.
Congress passes the 18th Amendment authorizing prohibition of alcohol.
Toronto Maples' Harry Cameron becomes the first NHL defenseman to score a goal.

1918

By the time Dominic celebrates his 18th birthday, people think he's twenty-one, except Maria who knows his true age. There's still an adolescent's gleam in his eyes but with the moustache and long sideburns, he acts the part quite well. Alexander's Jewellery & Repair has \$11, 667.31 in its business account. The store owns its entire product offering outright, nothing has been purchased on credit. Dominic's personal account is pennies away from where it was when he first opened his account at the Royal Bank. He sold an acre of land next to the coal yard to Clayton Bradshaw, a homebuilder, netting him a tidy sum of \$500.00. He didn't want to sell but Bradshaw's offer was too tempting. Dominic heard he's bargaining for the coal yard too, says houses will be coming this way soon. Nobody agrees with him, saying the city's growing in the north, talk of houses being built beyond Mountain Road.

All in all, Dominic's wise with his money, Duff's admonition ringing like a bell in his head each time he has to make a decision. When he wakes some mornings, he pauses at the side of the bed and wonders why he's been so lucky: a beautiful girlfriend he's going to marry, his own successful business, and many new friends. Other times he's homesick for Scotland, the smell of the shipyards, the sound of bagpipes, his family, Duff and the memories. Most days he hasn't time for melancholy, his work is in demand. His life is here.

He's feeling woozy this morning after too much homemade beer last night at his birthday party that Emma threw for him. She treats him like a son. The mirror in the bathroom seems to hold two images until they focus into his morning face. Hair askew, stubble on his cheeks, sleep poised at the edge of one eye and the other is bruised along the side of the nose and upper eyelid. A cut across the top of his nose stings like a wasp's been at it. He's a mess. Remembering the empty bottles on the table, he can still hear Adolph.

"*Autre, autre*, c'mon young man, it's only your birthday once a year…have another!"

Right! It was only when Emma said everyone had had enough and it was time to go, reminding them that tomorrow is Monday, did the party end at midnight. It was cold and slippery when he weaved along the street with Denise, escorting her home first and then making his way to his house, careful not to fall on the slick spots until he reached the back door. The light is burnt, and in the darkness, his foot found a patch of ice. Even with his hands out, he knocked his face on the bottom step. He was too drunk to realize it hurt and forgot about it until now. Gently he touches the cut.

"Ach, look at that craw. Goodness Alexander but you're ugly. Ooh, that hurts too. Better get decent, have to open up in less than an hour."

Taking a quick peek out the window, he sees rain run down the pane and frowns at the bad weather, although it reminds him of Govan, grey and damp. It's been like that all winter, a little snow and then a cold downpour. It's a few minutes after eight. Washing the cut with hot water hurts even more but soothes quickly. The shave is shaky until the stubble disappears. Moustache trimmed and combed. Never mind the hair, it lays on his forehead as always and the sides are so short, they never need grooming. Today he picks a tan cotton shirt whose collar Maria has starched, telling him the soft collars he wears makes his face look skinnier. Freshly ironed trousers of light wool, dark of course, today they're navy. When he reaches his workbench, even before he opens, he dons a clean apron. Previously he wore the same apron every day with all its stains and tiny rips. Maria made him aware that he owned the business and should dress accordingly instead of in the pauper's cloth he wore all the time. Now he has a fresh apron each day with a stylized *A* on the bib that he designed. Maria had them made for his first store anniversary last fall. He has enough for a full week.

Opening the front door, he gives a quick glance to the parking area and sees a man get out of one of White's new taxis. Approaching the bottom of the steps, the stranger holds a large black umbrella shading his face. It becomes visible when he steps under the porch and drops the rain protection. The wide face is split with a toothy smile. The eyes are set apart and seem to not trust each other. Bushy sideburns that look like small wings sit under a black fedora. Though the face is lightly lined, the strands of grey hair suggest he's close to fifty. He's about Dominic's size except for the round pot that hangs over the belt of his rich suit.

A cape-like coat of tweed hangs open, exposing jacket and vest with fine stripes to match the trousers, the fabric reeks of money. As does the large gold chain extending from a watch fob to the middle button of his vest. When he reaches out to shake Dominic's hand, the large diamond on a pinky ring gleams even in the morning haze. His cologne is strong and smells of limes. His accent is foreign, almost like Ivan's.

"You must be Mr. Alexander?"

Dominic takes his hand and can't help but notice the groomed nails and the soft palm. Not a tradesman's hand for sure, he thinks.

"Aye, I am. And you are, Sair?"

"I am Janos Horvat, people call me John."

"Please come in, I was just opening. How can I help you today…"

He pauses, not sure if he can pronounce the man's last name correctly.

"…uh, John"

The man shakes his umbrella and secures it shut. Before entering he slides out a slim leather case that is cradled between his arm and chest. He comments on Dominic's eye.

"Had a little mishap did you, Mr. Alexander?

Dominic has forgotten about the bluish tint and his cheeks redden a little.

"Aye, I met a front step last night in my travels and we didn't get along. Slipped on the ice. The weather has been so foul of late."

"Yes, yes it has but nonetheless, better days ahead I'm sure…"

The opening of the front door disturbs the men as Maria enters. Her smile turns to a frown when she sees Dominic's eye. Dropping her umbrella she gapes at his face with both hands on her cheeks. Rushing to him, in her concern, she doesn't even notice the gentleman who has stepped backed.

"Oh, my goodness, whatever happened to you, Dominic? Your eye looks terrible."

"Ah, it's nothing. A little slip out back getting home."

He swivels his eyes and gives a slight nod towards their customer.

"I can tell you about it later, but I'd like you to meet John, and John, this is Maria. She manages the store."

The man steps forward, offering a slight bow. He can't believe his good fortune. It's obvious she is in love with this man, much better for his plans as he deems women more soft-hearted than men. Reaching for her gloved hand, he sweeps it to his lips. Maria touches her chest with her free hand, unfamiliar with such flattery and her surprise turns into a smile when he addresses her.

She remains leery, however, when she sees something in his eyes — something unfriendly.

"It is a pleasure to meet such a charming young lady who is concerned for you, Mr. Alexander."

Maria takes in his appearance. Sees he is well dressed and clearly has money. She remembers her manners.

"The pleasure is mine, John. It's not often I get such a pleasant greeting. I apologize for interrupting..."

She looks to Dominic with a mock frown.

"...but someone needs to be more careful. Now that I can see he's okay, I'll let you two get on to business."

Removing her coat, she heads to the office first before setting up the cash box. Dominic invites Horvat to the waiting area in the corner. The small table and chairs are shouldered by the polished cabinets of the store's wares. Dominic has added wainscoting to the open walls with Maria adding the comforting colors. Sitting in the chair to the right, Horvat places the leather folder on the table. He reaches into the fob and peeks at the watch as if he's in a hurry. Dominic can't help but see the deep engravings and scrolls on the case, a magnificent timepiece.

"That's a beautiful watch, John."

"Thank you. It was my father's. A Model 57 made in 1881 by the American Watch Company. It's quite dear to me."

"Aye, I expect so. Now, how can I be of service? And please call me, Dominic."

"Well there are two things actually, Dominic."

He bends to the table to open the folder and removes two sketches the size of postcards picturing a ring. The paper is pasted to a heavier card. The edges are worn, the drawing is not new.

"This is a drawing I had done about ten years ago of a ring I commissioned with my father's family crest on one side and my mother's on the other. The stone is a cabochon black onyx, one of which I have in my possession at this moment. I lost the ring recently, much to my dismay. I must have another. You come highly recommended. My first request is the cost to create such a ring and how quickly it can be done for I am leaving this Wednesday to meet with other interested parties in Halifax. The terrible war calls us all to action, there is so much to do. Could you do this by Wednesday morning at the latest?"

"Give me a moment, John."

Looking at the drawing closely, he ponders the detailed design as well as the size of Horvat's ring finger. The casting, filing, setting the stone, he can do blindfolded but the engraving takes time, careful preparation, precise incisions with his sharp tools. Considering his other obligations, he would have to start it today. Calculating the costs of material and his time he offers to do it for $120.00. A huge amount for a man's ring, but a small amount for the artistic value of the craftsmanship on such short notice.

Horvat doesn't even blink.

"Good then."

Removing a wallet from an inner coat pocket, he unfolds three twenty-dollar bills. Placing the money on the table, he sits back in the chair, more relaxed.

"I'll leave that deposit and pay you the rest when I pick it up on Wednesday before noon. Now the other matter I wish to discuss can best be described as humanitarian. There are so many in Europe that need our help."

He removes a business card from the leather folder, offering it to Dominic.

Janos Horvat
President
World Aid Foundation
Toronto, Canada

Dominic holds it in his hand and looks at Horvat with compassion in his eyes. He saw the homeless, the war torn lives of the local people, the hunger on their faces, their belongings few.

"How can I help?"

Horvat didn't need the pictures he had brought of the plight so far away. He knew Dominic had been in the war; he knew he'd want to reach out. In the next ten minutes, the Hungarian ran his spiel, expounding on the fact that so many have nothing. He and other "investors" are sending stores of goods on chartered ships to Europe. Medical supplies, truckloads of bandages, blankets, canned goods, dry goods, clothing, lumber and other necessities to the liberated cities. The project can only be done by the donations of kind people. Dominic is spellbound by the oration, the seriousness in the man's countenance.

"Well yes of course, I could help. I expect I could dig up a couple hundred for such a worthy cause, and..."

He's interrupted by a wave of Horvat's hand and shaking head.

"No, no Dominic, undertakings of this magnitude take tens of thousands, we fill as many ships as we can. Many of your peers, your business associates and other owners are contributing two, three, why as much as five thousand, but of course I can't say who they are. Is there somewhere we can talk more private?"

The large amounts wake Dominic up. The reality of a ship full of goods would be costly of such amounts, he can only guess. Realizing that he lives a fruitful and safe life, he can afford to be more generous, but again Duff's warning floats through his skull. If others are helping, he doesn't want to be seen as uncaring in the business community, yet he remains cautious.

"Aye there is, my kitchen upstairs. Come, I'll tell Maria where I will be and you can tell me more."

When Horvat leaves forty-five minutes later, Dominic is convinced that he needs to help those suffering as a result of the tragedy in Europe. The only thing not settled at the time of Horvat's departure is the amount Dominic is willing to donate. Horvat is well pleased that the commitment from the young Scotsman will be substantial. They have agreed to meet in the dining room of the American Hotel on Bonaccord Street tomorrow evening at seven o'clock for dessert and gentlemen's coffees. Dominic offered to bring a check. Horvat has explained that he would not want a check made out to him but rather that the donation is made in cash to expedite the lading of the ship, which is now harbored in Montreal awaiting funds for the purchase of more goods for its hold. Horvat has assured Dominic that he will receive a receipt for the donation as well as a mention in the World

Aid Federation's monthly progress updates, for which Dominic will be added to the mailing list.

After Dominic bids Horvat farewell, Maria inquires what the meeting was about. Dominic explains briefly what he is going to do.

"I intend to donate to the Foundation but I'm not sure exactly how much I should contribute. I'm meeting Mr. Horvat tomorrow night after dinner, but I'll visit the bank first."

There was something about Horvat that Maria distrusts and she explains her feelings to Dominic.

"Oh, don't be silly Maria. He's offered me a nice commission for a custom ring and left a deposit. He is extremely well dressed, educated and a generous man to take such a task upon himself to help those in need in Europe. What would there be not to trust?"

"Well I'm just saying Dominic, be careful. And this year we will all have to pay the new temporary income tax that Borden's government is creating to help finance the war. We need to watch our expenses. Why don't you talk to Mr. Van Geist and get his opinion?"

Dominic has already made up his mind, but to soother Maria's doubts, he agrees.

"Aye, I'll do that Maria. My contribution will be from my own savings and it won't affect the business, but now I'd better finish sizing your cousin's ring we promised her today. Is there anything else that needs attention before I start on Horvat's ring?"

"Yes, there's a couple of things. Don't forget to put the new clasp on Frieda Clarkson's brooch you promised her today, other than that Mr. Mariano from Forever Diamonds is in town and wants to meet with you after lunch. Watch him; he's shifty. You can bargain this guy down. We buy a lot of diamonds from him. We absolutely need two matching sparkly 25 pointers. The rest can wait."

Van Geist listens to Dominic's intentions of donating a large sum of money. The banker is impressed and bobbing his head in agreement when Dominic's shares his own experiences in the war. The utter poverty left behind. When he's finished, he's looking down at the top of Van Geist's desk, lost in thought. Looking up from the business card, the banker studies him.

"I understand how you feel. I agree that those who can should help if they want. It is after all their hard-earned money. I could ask around about Mr. Horvat if you want. Do you feel you can trust this man, Dominic?"

It takes a few seconds for Dominic to look up as he asks himself the same question. Remembering a tear in Horvat's eye when talking about the bombed out village of Ypres, recently liberated and people with absolutely nowhere to go. The man obviously has plenty of his own money.

"Yes, yes I do. Please Mr. Van Geist, if you could arrange two thousand dollars in large bills from my personal account I would appreciate it. Thank you for your help."

Dominic is early when he walks into the dining room. It's not busy for a Tuesday night; only two other tables have patrons. He asks for a seat by the fireplace that is in the center of the back wall of the room. He can still feel the chill from outside. White linen adorns the tables, with gleaming silver and bright red napkins. Removing his jacket to place it around the top of his chair, he sets his hat on the edge of the table with his gloves. No sooner has he pulled out the chair to sit down when Horvat comes through the archway leading from the front desk. Dabbing his head with a handkerchief, Horvat looks worried. Dominic's moment of compassion is dispelled, replaced with concern. He stands to greet Horvat.

"Hello, John. Excuse me, but you look like something's bothering you?"

The waiter approaches to interrupt them, but Horvat waves and seats himself across from Dominic. He doesn't ask Dominic what he wants.

"Two of your butterscotch pies, two strong coffees, if you will."

Raised brows ask Dominic if that sounds okay.

"Aye, sounds about right."

When the coffee and pie arrive, Horvat pulls a shiny flask from an inside pocket, pours himself a generous portion into his coffee and looks askance at Dominic.

"Are you a prohibitionist Dominic?"

"Nae, it's a silly law."

Horvat furtively adds a dollop to Dominic's coffee. Before they dig into the delight on the plates, Dominic inquires again of Horvat's worried look.

"I can see you're troubled, John, tell me what bothers you."

Dabbing at the meringue stuck to his upper lip, he sips the hot mixture before speaking.

"Oh, Dominic, I've just been off the phone with my assistant in

Montreal. The chandlers at the pier are holding over four thousand dollars' worth of canned goods, flour and grains. It's the last to be loaded and they will only wait until noon tomorrow or they will return the truck loads. I need to wire them funds as soon as possible."

Pausing for another sip, another bite, he watches Dominic's look of disquiet. He waits for Horvat go on.

"Everywhere there is a hand out for what we are trying to accomplish. Prices are higher. No one trusts anyone. But the Foundation always finds the money. I've just come from another kind soul in Moncton, one of the sawmill owners, and he was very generous. That's between us now Dominic. But it is because of kind people like you we are able to help so many. Did you bring the money, by the way?"

While Dominic reaches into his inside jacket pocket to remove a white letter-size envelope, Horvat waves for more coffee and finishes his pie. Dominic is about to flick through the bills when the waiter approaches and Horvat covers the envelope with his hand. The plates are cleared, two more coffees poured and another two shots added. An official receipt is issued.

Horvat is excited by the progress on his ring and exclaims that he can't wait to see it. Dominic promises to meet Horvat in the lobby at noon with the ring. When the night ends at the ten o'clock closing time, the raw liquor takes effect and both men stagger about. Best friends. Dominic insists on paying for the meal and drinks, fumbling with his wallet. Horvat is the more lucid of the two and hires a covered cart for Dominic, sending him home. Not before he double-checks the wadded envelope in his side coat pocket.

When the cart is out of sight along Main Street, Horvat stops to study his surroundings. He's alert, not drunk. He doesn't see anyone following him. The train to Montreal leaves in twenty minutes. On the other hand, the train to Halifax, where he has already made contact with other "donors," people of wealth in the port city, leaves tomorrow at one in the afternoon. Unsure of what to do, he heads west on Main street in case he decides to stay and needs somewhere to sleep, but first he needs to retrieve his travel bag.

Regardless of the hangover and Maria admonishment of him drinking in public, he is filled with content. He's been smiling all morning. Only a half hour ago, he finished setting the black onyx and polishing the ring. It's one of his best works. The likeness to the sketch is complete, almost unimaginable. He guesses at Horvat's reaction. No doubt he'll be pleased. Maria gushes over the detail, the high gloss of the yellow metal. He calls for a hired cart, loving the new service launched by the White brothers. Placing the ring in a velvet-lined box, he places it in one of the store's paper bags before shoving it in his coat pocket.

Dominic finds a seat in the hotel lobby on the couch that faces the front windows. It's open to a hallway and both sides. Dominic can be clearly seen from either the entrance or inside the hotel. He was five minutes late but doesn't see Horvat, probably hasn't checked out yet. He brought the newspaper with him, so he reads while he waits. The news and his latest ad have him absorbed. Good news of more German defeats covers the front page. The high loss of men is the bad news, the payment for winning. He doesn't notice the time pass and when he glances at his watch, he sees it is almost one o'clock. Jumping from his seat and roughly folding the paper, he chucks it on the couch and hastens to the front desk, worried that he may have missed Horvat.

There is a middle-aged woman at the desk sorting papers who looks up at Dominic when he approaches.

"Excuse me, Ma'am, but did Mr. Horvat check out yet?"

She turns to a large open ledger on the counter.

"Hmm, Horvat doesn't sound familiar. Let me check."

A baffled look follows the names on the pages and a slight shake to her head as she scans the names.

"No, sorry, but there`s no Horvat staying with us. Are you sure you have the right hotel?"

"Yes, he told me he was staying here. Been here since Monday. Are you quite certain there's nothing there under Horvat?"

"Oh yes, that name is quite unusual and I would see it here. There's been no one registered under that name. Sorry."

Dominic stares at her in disbelief. He can't imagine that Horvat would've been lying. He was so engrossed last night when they shared stories of the war and what good the donations were doing. Remembering the train to Halifax, he thanks the woman and rushes out the door. The train station is across the street. If Horvat is still around, he'll be waiting there.

The station is full of activity. The sun is out today for the first time in many days and people are smiling and laughing. Freight is being loaded in the last cars. People are milling about, saying goodbye, boarding the train. The smell of coal burning mingles with the steam from the giant engine. Dominic enters the station and searches for Horvat but there is no one that even looks like him. He doesn't think Horvat would board and leave without his ring and desperately seeks him on the ramp by the tracks. He confronts a conductor who is helping an elderly lady board. Describing Horvat, Dominic asks if the conductor has seen a man like him. With just a shake of his head he lets Dominic know there has been no one with that description. There is nothing else to do but wait inside for Horvat to show up. Taking a seat near the front door, Dominic watches through the window while toying with the velvet box that holds Horvat's ring. The possibility that he has been conned has not entered his mind.

Only when the crowd thins and the train slowly pulls from the station does Dominic face what he doesn't want to: Horvat, or whoever he is, has taken Dominic's money and run. Laden with too many emotions, he puts the ring back in his pocket. Embarrassed, angry at his gullibility, angry at Horvat, he beats himself up by thinking of his money gone, the ring without an owner and all the time he invested in it. He knows what he must do, but has already lost hope that he will ever recover the money. With slumped shoulders and a heavy heart, he heads for the police station. What he dreads most is telling Maria. He'll be hard put to trust anyone again.

CHAPTER 2

War, war, war, will it ever end? The topmost headline reads, *The Battle of the Somme begins. The Germans bomb Paris. 256 dead.*

Standing at the kitchen table, Dominic looks down at the scattering of newspaper clippings. He had returned home last night from taking Maria to see the new *Tarzan of the Apes* movie at the Empress amazed by the way the ape man swung through the jungle just like a real monkey. Too keyed up from the excitement of the moving pictures, he had tackled the pile of pages he's torn from newspapers, saving some clippings of things that interested him. Mary sent him a copy of the *Daily Record and Mail* from home. It was a month old when he received it but what a treat to read of things back in Scotland.

The articles are arranged on the table, ready for pasting into the scrapbook. He'll do it after breakfast. He loves Sunday morning breakfasts when he's off.

Opening the side door to the icebox, the remainder of the pork waves at him, so he decides to slice some for bacon with fried eggs. Putting them on the counter he glances at the calendar tacked to the wall by the back door. May 5, a week before Mother's Day. He loves this new holiday, this new celebration. Mothers are women, women love jewellery, jewellery makes a beautiful gift. He blinks in the ray of sunlight from the eastern window, the ancient ball yellowing the roof tops like a paint brush. Another warm day he hopes. It's cool in the house with no heat from the furnace. The sun looks promising.

He eats while still in pajamas, a colorful outfit Maria gave him one day when she discovered he slept in only his underwear. She helped him pick out the quilts too and wants him comfortable because she knows he's too stingy with the heat. This May has been late in getting going. The grass is only starting to turn green, but the tulips are up and the ferns are sprouting, and the days stay warmer a little longer. While he munches on the crispy meat, he ponders over the things he might do today. He wants to finish the sketch he started; the carpenter had moved out and the rooms need to be cleaned up; he could work on Maria's wedding band; the Ford needs to be cleaned up because he's selling it and picking up his new Cadillac next week; or he might just read his new book. He'll get dressed after he's done the scrapbook with his last cup of tea and decide then.

Great Britain give women (over 30) the right to vote.
General Motors purchases the Chevrolet Motor Company.
First Red Army victory over the Kaiser`s German troops.
S.W. Thompson is first US pilot to down an enemy aircraft.
Manfred Von Richthoven, The Red Baron, in an air battle with Canadian pilots, dies the day after he downs his 79th and 80th victim.
Finland, Russia, Estonia, Latvia and Lithuania adopt the Gregorian calendar.
Twin Peaks Tunnel for street cars opens in San Francisco, one of the world's longest at over two miles.
Russian Bolshevik Party becomes the Communist Party.
Moscow becomes the capital of revolutionary Russia.
The Toronto Arenas are the first team to win the Stanley Cup in the new National Hockey League.

By the time he puts his scrap book away and gets dressed, it's shortly after nine o'clock and he's decided to go out to the barn and draw for a while. The sketch he is working on is a ring design he wants to submit to the Aberdeen High School for their graduating students. He is supposed to have it done by the end of the month. The sun is bright and he feels it warming the house so when he leaves, he doesn't bother with a jacket. He's wearing his favorite blue cotton shirt and old dungarees that Maria claims should be thrown out, but he likes the feel of the faded cotton and doesn't have to worry about stains from the charcoal. When he heads out, he notices the fields that his neighbours, the Donnellys, have plowed recently and he loves the smell of the fresh dirt. Crossing to the barn, he sees movement in the old grass by the front door. It startles him at first, thinking it might be a snake, but he relaxes when he sees it's a kitten.

The furry ball is curled up by the door, its mews exclaiming its hunger. Dominic reaches down tentatively to pick it up, not wanting to scare it. It reminds him of Pearl, same greyish body, except for a blotch of reddish fur on his chest, same white mittens on the front paws. Unlike a Scottish Fold, the ears are perky and follow every sound.

"Now where did you come from?"

The kitten responds by licking Dominic's hand, perhaps it smells the traces of the morning bacon.

"Probably from the farm next door, I bet. That's quite a stretch for such a little fellow like you. Must be lost. And are you a little fellow or a little lady?"

After lifting the tail and verifying that he is holding a girl kitten, he looks across the field knowing the Donnellys always have cats and they give away a dozen kittens every year. Perhaps he should return it after lunch, but he'll feed it first. He opens the barn door with the kitten held in his other hand. Placing it on the floor, the kitten stops mewling when it discovers the new scents and trots off, its natural curiosity piqued. Dominic closes the door and goes for a small bowl of milk and a scrap piece of bacon rind.

When he comes from the back door, he sees an auto pulling into his driveway. Recognizing it right away as Nick's uncle's, much to his delight Nick is sitting up front with him. Joanne had told him three weeks ago that Nick was coming home and he's never returning to war, his injuries are too bad. There's only been one letter from him since he was hospitalized and she wasn't sure of the extent of his condition. From the look on his friend's face, it doesn't seem good. As the vehicle approaches, Nick's countenance changes when he sees his friend.

"*Bonjour mon ami*, how wonderful to see you again."

Dominic waves to the uncle and then at Nick who is covered with a heavy blanket on his lap which seems odd because it isn't that cold.

"Aye and a happy day to you as well, Nick. What a wonderful surprise. Joanne told me you were coming home but didn't know when."

"Our ship had to dock in Saint John because of the horrible mess in Halifax and I arrived here yesterday on the train."

"Well, I'm glad you dropped by. What brings you this way?"

Nick's smile disappears and is replaced with glassy eyes and a down-turned mouth. It's a few moments before he responds.

"Well, I'm not in great shape Dominic and besides wanting to see a good friend, I could use a bit of cheering up."

"Why's that, Nick? The war is a bad thing but you always are so easy going, not much seems to bother you."

Nick throws back the covers on his lap. Dominic is shocked to see that both of Nick's legs are missing from the knees down.

"I left the rest behind somewhere in France. My walking days are over."

Dominic is speechless. Nick's face is twisted between anger and self-pity, the eyes seem to have given up. But when Dominic looks closely, he sees the eyes of yesterday. Nick laughing at his accent, his strange words. The day he told him about Joanne – he was already asking Dominic to make her a special ring after their first date. The crazy jokes about the *Anglais*, the English. They may have taken his legs, but they could never take his goodness. Dominic breaks into his widest grin.

"If you've come looking for pity, you came to the wrong place, *mon ami*. They loved ya there so much they kept parts of ya to themselves but… they never took your heart, Nick. And they'll never take your spirit. Now let me put this bowl away and I'll be right back to get you out of that damn auto and I'll make a fire in the barn and we'll talk my friend."

Nick forgets the missing limbs and laughs out loud. Dominic's forwardness never ceases to make him laugh. The uncle hee haws too. Dominic chuckles in his quiet way, takes the bowl of milk and bacon rinds to the barn. Returning, he steps on the footrest to embrace his good friend. The hug is fierce. The embrace reassuring, a release of doubts for Nick, this stretched out hand from Dominic.

Dominic wonders if he'll have to learn how to back up the horses.

The fireplace is crusted with fiery embers of the dying fire that glows on the two men sitting on the couch. The shadows from the widow are long, with the sun heading home and almost over the horizon. The sketch remains untouched. Food-stained supper dishes are stacked on the end of a low table in front of them. Two bottles of Long River red wine smuggled from Ontario are empty and a third is half full, the cork stuck in the throat. Two tea cups have served in lieu of proper glassware and sit on the same table, except one is on its side and a blotch of red is staining the wood. Nick burps over the good food. The kitten has taken a liking to the two men and is curled up asleep on the couch between them.

"That trout was delicious, Dom. Thank you for the meal and the fine drinks. The one thing about having no feet is that I can't stagger because I can't stand up."

They want to laugh at the statement, but the bittersweet agony is that he's right. Nick and Dominic have been chatting mainly about the war, reminiscing about the men they met and the friends they lost. Hopes for a quick end now that the Americans are in the war with all the allies pushing the Germans towards Berlin. They shared a sadness of the world's mess, but they shared a few jokes. They didn't talk a lot about the future. Dominic too embarrassed to ask, Nick too uncertain to bring it up. Dominic glances at his watch and knows that Nick's uncle will be returning soon.

An idea comes to him as sudden as a lightning bolt.

"What about tomorrow, Nick? What are you planning on doing?"

"Well that's just it, Dom, I'm not too sure. I could still handle the horses and the wagon, but I can't get in and out. I can't even afford one of those wheelchairs, at least not right now. Not sure about artificial legs…"

The realization sets in and Nick hangs his head. Dominic reaches over to pat his friend on the shoulder.

"I have an idea, Nick, but let me tell you something first. Maria and I are getting married when the war ends and keeping this place as our home. There's a building for sale on Main Street that we are considering. The Coppersmith building has three levels, a clothing store on the bottom that is closing, offices on the second level and apartments on the third. It'd be a good investment for us. I plan on seeing Van Geist at the bank this week and will likely put in a bid. If I'm successful, we want to move the business there and redo the house here. What we also talked about is that I need help with all the repairs we do with the business growing. I'm planning on training another goldsmith and I think you could do it."

Nick raises his eyebrows in question.

"Me? I don't know anything about jewellery. How could I help with that?"

"I didn't either when my uncle Duff taught me. I found out I was handy with my hands and he showed me the rest. I could do the same for you."

"I'm not that handy with my hands."

"Ach but you are, Nick, you're a fine carpenter with a good eye for detail. It's just another skill."

Nick is nodding his head in agreement and perhaps hope.

"Well, that's very kind of you, Dom. I think you're just feeling sorry for me though."

"Nick, you and I have been friends from the first day we met at the train station. Yes, I feel bad, but I know you're not a quitter. I need help, you need work, and I know you can do this."

"I'll have to think about this, Dom. I have to have some way to get around. How could a wheelchair work at the store?"

Dominic sees a glitter in his friend's eye, something positive. His heart goes out to Nick.

"Look, I tell you what. I'll pay for the wheelchair and new legs if that's something that can be done for you. You agree to this and we'll make sure a wheelchair can get in and out of the new store. You don't have to serve the customers if you don't want to, but I'll build you the proper work desk and you can start your training when we open."

The tears that drop from Nick's eyes are not from pain or sorrow but from the good heart of his friend.

"I can't take charity, Dom, not even from you. I need to do this on my own or at least with any government help I can get. I went and fought in the damn war and they owe me. Besides, it will be a while before you get moved. Not sure what I'll do until then if I decide to do this."

"Aye, well you know how slow the government works, there will be cobwebs on those legs before they get off their lazy arses. I'm not giving you any charity, Nick. I'll make you a loan with no interest, and you can start paying me back when we get you working. I'll front you enough money to keep you until the work starts and for the chair and whatever else you need. You're my friend, Nick, my best friend, and I want to help, so I'm not taking no for an answer."

A knock on the barn door interrupts the conversation and Nick's uncle pokes his head in the door.

"Are you ready to go now, nephew?"

"*Oui, oui, mon oncle*. I'm tired and this crazy Scotsman has me half drunk."

Turning to Dominic, Nick reaches out his right hand. Dominic shakes it with a firm grasp.

"I can't thank you enough, *mon ami*. You are too kind and yes, I'll do it. I like the idea of working with gold and silver and shiny stones."

"Good. Are you still staying with your uncle?"

"Yes, for now. He and *ma tante Diane* have given me the downstairs bedroom. When I have enough money saved, Joanne and I want to have our own place, but that won't be right away of course."

"It'll be soon enough, Nick. The first thing we can work on in the store is a ring for your bride-to-be. How's that?"

There is a moment of awkward silence until Dominic rises uncertainly to his feet, the wine making them a bit wobbly.

"I'll be off to the bank tomorrow, Nick, and I'll come see you in a day or two."

"Thank you, Dominic."

"Oh and one more thing. Will you be my best man at the wedding?"

Nick is beaming. The afternoon has brought meaning to his life. Nothing would give him more pleasure.

"*Ah oui, mon ami*, I would be proud to be your best man, but truly, you're the best man I know."

The men get Nick in the buggy and Dominic stands in the last rays of the setting sun waving goodbye. He hasn't been this happy since Maria told him she would marry him. He was a bit hesitant about buying the building but now knows it is the right thing to do, and it will be good to have Nick as part of the business. He'll go see Van Geist and his lawyer tomorrow.

CHAPTER 3

John Bannister sits across the desk from Dominic. The law office is busy this morning, and even with the rain, Dominic is in fine spirits. He had discussed the details of his plans with Maria when she came to work this morning and she is excited, already with decorating ideas for the new store. With Nick and Maria agreeing to his plans, he wants to hurry things up with the purchase of the Coppersmith building. Bannister is frowning at a document he is holding.

"I know you have an uncanny ability to make good investments Dominic, but I don't think the Strang family will take $4,200for their building, they're asking $5,500. But there have been no offers so far, according to their lawyer Mr. Flewelling. I'll run this by him and see what they say."

"Well, it's better to start a little lower, John. I am, however, willing to go as high as $5,000 so if they get back to you that they want more, you can go that high without asking me."

Bannister sits back in his chair, tapping his pencil on his desk.

"On another matter Dominic, I heard that you had a run-in with Crosswaithe last fall over the protest business. I know Maria is very outspoken in regards to equal rights for our lady friends, which I have no problem with. I mean they work as hard as we do and sometimes harder."

Dominic shifts in his seat, wishing that business was forgotten. It reminds him of some of his lost business from clients who are either cronies of Crosswaithe's or just too scared to cross him.

"Aye, tis true but matters little at this point I expect, now that the mill has closed. I hear Mr. Marvin is looking at the building for his cookie factory."

Bannister nods his head, an amused smile on his face.

"That's true, as far as I know, but these people that run the city, not the politicians, don't forget so easy. And the reason I mention it is that Penelope Strang owns the Coppersmith building and she's related to Crosswaithe's wife somehow, a cousin or something like that. Her husband passed away in January. I think that's why she wants to get rid of the building. I was wondering if there were any hard feelings between you."

Squaring his shoulders, Dominic sits forward and replies.

"There was a little lag in the business after our meeting, but in the long run I think it actually helped. The business is fine. He's an arrogant man and I care little for his ways, but I hope this doesn't affect my buying the premises on Main Street. Maria is very excited; she loves to decorate. And when I move the store, there's the house that will need re-doing. More than anything, I hate to let her down."

Bannister picks up the papers and straightens them out with a knowing look.

"Well, let's take this to Strang's lawyer and go from there."

"Thank you, John. Let me know what happens. Good day, then."

In less than twenty-four hours Dominic is working on a new ring for one of his client's when Maria tells him John Bannister wants to talk to him on the phone. Dominic thinks that was quick, hoping the news is good. Wiping his hands on his apron, he goes to the front desk where the phone is kept.

"Good morning, John."

Maria is watching Dominic with a slight smile, feeling tingly with the hopes and thoughts of moving to the new location so she can plan their new home and wedding when this foolish war ends. Her mood swings when she sees Dominic's smile turn into a frown. She is startled by Dominic's words.

"The bastard! Why would he do that?"

Dominic listens as the lawyer takes his time explaining what is going on. Dominic interjects occasionally with an "I see" or a simple nod. After a moment, he sighs and ends the call.

"Okay, John, let me think on that and I'll call you back soon."

Maria can't wait to know what's going on. She steps closer to put her hand on his arm.

"What did he say, Dominic? Why the frown?"

"That damn Crosswaithe found out I was interested in the building and offered Mrs. Strang the $5,500 she wants. John says she won't accept any more offers, says we have to start looking at other places. That was a great spot and I know how much you were looking forward to us moving there. I don't know what to do now; I'm so disappointed."

Maria has a sheepish look on her face, knowing she's the reason Crosswaithe and Dominic are at odds in the first place. Hiding her own disappointment, she reassures Dominic.

"It wasn't meant to be, Dominic. We'll look for something else. It's not the only building in the city."

"I know, Maria. What bothers me most is that Crosswaithe is being such a *scunner*."

This is a word she's not heard before, and she smiles at his idiom.

"A scunner?"

"Aye, a terrible nuisance."

"Oh, yes, he's that for sure. In French we say he's *tannant*."

"I can think of worse things to call him but not in the presence of a lady."

When they're laughing, the phone rings and a customer enters the store. Dominic is standing by the phone and nods to the man who had entered.

"I'll get this, Maria, if you want to help our guest."

Maria greets the man and Dominic answers the phone.

"Good morning. Alexander's Jewellery and Repair. How can I help you today?"

Dominic listens intently and the facial expressions change with the news, but mostly he has a satisfied look.

"Why are they selling it so cheap?"

More nods and another grin.

"Of course. Aye, I'd like to see it. Thanks, John. We'll meet you and your client there tonight."

Dominic hangs up the phone and winks at Maria who is showing the gentleman a strand of pearls she has displayed on a black velvet cloth. He loves watching Maria with the customers. She puts the pearls on and models them with her dimpled smile and no man can resist. When he decides to take them, she shows him the matching earrings and he takes those also. After she rings up the sale, she offers to gift wrap them. When the man leaves, she goes to the back room where Dominic has returned to his bench.

"What were you winking about? Who called?"

"It was John again. You know Harrison's Hardware Store on the corner of St. George Street and Lutz?"

"The one that closed after there was a fire?"

"Aye, that one. Well as it turns out, the fire was from rubbish in the back warehouse section and only damaged the rear wall, which John says can be fixed. He's Eddie Harrison's lawyer, the owner, and from what I understand, Harrison has sold off the merchandise that wasn't damaged from the smoke and water and decided to retire. He went to see John about another matter and they talked about the building. Harrison's decided to sell it but hasn't put up a sign yet. John told him he knows people looking and you and I have an appointment after we close the store."

Maria has her head tilted, a finger on her lip, thinking.

"*Oui*, that's a nice looking building, Dominic, but so much work. What's on the second floor?"

"I don't know, but we'll find out soon enough. I was thinking…"

Dominic is interrupted by Maria shrieking when the kitten creeps close enough and brushes itself against her ankle. Both frightened, Maria steps quickly to Dominic's side, taking his arm, while the kitten darts across the floor to hide under the low table where clients wait. The poor thing was only trying to be friendly. Maria's scream caused it to panic.

Maria thinks it's a rat.

"*Bien*, Dominic, did you see that? What is it?"

Looking at her face, Dominic let's go and bends over laughing. He's stuttering as he tries to tell her

"It's…it's…it's…a kitten."

Maria's scowl softens and she walks out to kneel at the table, peeking under the lower shelf. The kitten tries to dig itself deeper into the corner. Its small limbs shake.

"Oh my goodness, I must've scared the little thing. Come help me get it out."

Dominic is down to an amused smile and attempts to move the edge of the table away from the wall when the kitten scoots out right into Maria's hands. She straightens up to hold it close to her bosom and the kitten senses the tenderness of the caress. It only takes a couple of heartbeats for them to become friends.

"Where did it come from, Dominic?"

"I found her, it's a she, by the barn yesterday when I went out to work on my sketch. I fed it and she stayed with Nick and me all day. She roamed around, ate, peed and slept in that order. She really likes Nick. Says he might even get his own."

Maria gently strokes the soft gray fur.

"Are you going to keep her?"

"Haven't decided."

"Does she have a name?"

"Nae, not yet. I'm sure if I name her, I'd have to keep her."

Maria moves her cupped hands away gently so she can see the kitten's features better. Little green saucers stare back at her. The tips of her small ears are erect, topped with little fluffs of fine hairs. In the middle of its chest is a patch of orange-ish fur shaped like a raindrop. The color is uncommon and, in the sunlight, almost looks red. Maria's grandmother on her mother's side was Irish and had hair that color.

"We'll call her Scarlet."

It's not long before Scarlet becomes the lady of the house.

*

Bannister, Dominic and Maria stand in front of the Harrison Hardware Store, awaiting its owner. St. George Street is busy with carts, heavy wagons and a few autos. The sounds of horses snickering and autos changing gears add to the cacophony of voices from people strolling or hustling along and kids playing on the lawns where there are houses. The setting sun is directly in line with the street, and looking west, one has to shade their eyes. The store occupies the northwest corner. Across the street are a tailor and the fire station – one of the reasons the fire was out quickly. To the left are many homes; to its right, a vacant lot and other houses sprinkled with the odd business establishment parked between them. The trio are admiring the brickwork of the façade. Two columns of stacked bricks define the outer edges and an arched doorway with double solid oak and glass doors greet people. The second level has three wide windows spread across the top and there is a curved stone at the very crown off the building with the word *Harrison* etched in it. Dominic is rubbing his hands over the reddish bricks by the doorway.

"The masons did a fine job. This building will stand forever."

Bannister nods his head in agreement.

"It was built in 1888 by the Gould family from Leger's Corner, a father and son masonry company. They've done the stonework on many buildings in the city. They have a well-deserved reputation for good work."

Maria is standing next to the door with her head pressed closely to the glass, like a child at a candy counter.

"Look Dominic, the entrance and floor look to be about the same level. That will be good for Nick."

Dominic is pressing his head to the glass to see better through the reflections when a McLaughlin Buick with the top down pulls up in front of the building. The dark blue body gleams as if just painted. At the wheel is a cheerful looking man with a full beard and a straw boater on his head. Bannister waves to the arrival.

"There's Harrison now. Come you two and I'll introduce you."

The lawyer makes the introductions. Harrison is taken with Maria's natural charm and Dominic's Scottish accent. He's a stockier man, a bit shorter than the three of them. His voice is mellow. A slight dip towards Maria.

"Well I'm pleased to make your acquaintance Miss Desjardins and Dominic. From the old country are you? My grandmother was Scottish, an Anderson from Govan. She had a rough beginning until she married a Harrison from Bristol when she was only fourteen and he brought her to Canada. Where's your family from Dominic?"

"Well I started off in Saltcoats out on the west coast. The last few years I lived with my uncle in Govan. The pastor there is an Anderson. His sermons were often times amusing, but you never left the church without feeling guilty about something."

Harrison's thin brows shoot up.

"Oh, that can't be. I have a distant cousin who has the same name and is a pastor. I've lost touch over the years, of course, but tell me Dominic, is he a tall man, a good looking chap with a reddish birthmark on his neck?"

"Aye that would be him, on the left side, just below the chin."

"What a wonderful coincidence…"

Harrison is beaming, he clasps Dominic by the shoulder, waves to the others to follow.

"Come along then, young man, let me show you my building."

The structure is wide, thirty feet across and open inside. Tall windows, now dusty from neglect, frame the front walls. Dominic stops at the doorway, gesturing to Maria, pointing at the opening. They both know without saying that a wheelchair can get in and out quite easily. Stepping in, they are confronted by the aroma of old wood and a dead fire. The floor is a mosaic of worn paths and rectangles of glossy hardwood floors where the missing cabinets protected them for years. Dust balls claim every corner.

Six ornate round columns stretch to support the upper floor, three abreast. A wide stairway of dark wood is on the back right. Drab beige walls are pockmarked with holes from supporting nails and screws. Empty racks are pushed haphazardly against the back wall, where a lopsided door to the rear rests askew on its hinges. One side is blackened from smoke. The wispy traces of the fire have stained the wall and part of the ceiling. While Harrison is showing the damage to Dominic, Maria and Bannister look up also. Maria's response is a quick intake of breath, Bannister is more verbal.

"Goodness gracious but that's quite fantastic."

The ceiling is artfully divided in wide squares whose corners meet at each column. The center of each square has a shallow cone surrounded by smaller squares wonderfully crafted in embossed tin, painted white, which over time has faded. The detail is magnificent. Harrison brushes off the compliment.

"Oh for sure it's a work of art, but I'll be honest, it's a dratted nuisance to keep clean."

Maria steps to Dominic's side as Bannister and Harrison discuss the complexity of the tinsmith's work. She speaks low, looking him in the eye. He can see that she is already sold.

"I don't care what the rest looks like, Dominic. The entryway can be easily improved for Nick's chair and all the big windows and the ceiling...oh, the ceiling is beautiful. We can make this real nice, Dominic. And did you see how much traffic goes by here. I think you should take it. Get the best deal you can. I can see he really likes you."

Dominic squeezes her arm. As much as he agrees with her, the glow in her eyes, the happiness in her smile, he'd do anything for her.

"I think so too, Maria, but let's see the rest and we'll bargain later."

"Good. You go, I want to look around here."

"Aye, and decorate I expect."

She blushes at her transparency.

"Well, don't you like how I decorate?"

"You know I do. Just teasing."

The men journey through the rest of the premises: the warehouse that contained the fire has a warped floor and the back wall has been partially eaten by the flames. The other walls are rough boards. All that is left is a smoke-stained silhouette of where goods and merchandise were stacked. The ceiling has a five by five-foot opening in the center. Looking up, the group see the gantry for lifting goods to a storage loft above. Two solid doors on the right open to the parking lot.

The upstairs has identical windows only not as tall, but with arches. Offices and a reception area occupy the front half. Divided by a hallway, there are five rooms in all. They are totally void of furniture, not one item remains, only the blemished evidence of where they sat or where things were hung on the walls. And the smell of smoke. The back half is the storage loft.

At the back of the property, beyond the parking lot on the left, is a fenced-in yard where larger merchandise and lumber was stored. The ground there is hard-packed gravel. To the right is the carriage house where the horses and wagons were kept. A modest shingled structure with a half-storey above the stalls. The only flaw is that the white paint on the south side is peeling in spots. At the edge of the property, the three men are looking back towards St. George Street, with Harrison pointing to the right side.

"I own twenty feet on this side, all the way to the street, where I planted those elm trees. We never used this side as you can see from the dead grass and the new green shoots. It just grows wild."

Turning back to Dominic, who is gazing at the narrow field, he notices the pleasure in the young man's eyes. He's young, thinks Harrison, but he hears good things about him. Even the run-in with Crosswaithe. He admires the boy's gumption, likes his confidence.

"What do you think, Mr. Alexander, would my humble premises be of interest to you?"

Dominic comes out of his reverie of wondering how the empty strip of land could be used, changes his demeanor, not wanting Harrison to know how much he is indeed interested. Eyes squint a little harder, chin sets firm.

"I see a lot of good things, but that smell of smoke might be hard to get rid of. The whole back wall needs to be rebuilt, possibly the other walls too if we can't get rid of the odor. The main floors are not in the best of shape. Everything will need to be repainted, several coats in some places, I imagine. I will say that you've done a splendid job of cleaning up."

"Yes, I had that done recently, sold what I could, gave some away, and scrapped the rest. I've been in the hardware business most of my life, and it's time to let it go. I've enough saved up for the rest of my days, Lord willing. My only son lives in Toronto, a big lawyer, that's begging me to come visit and stay a bit. Now you seem like a good lad, so I'll make you a deal, Dominic. I'll let you have the whole thing for $4,000."

Dominic and Bannister stare at each other, astonished. The building and land are worth every bit as much as the Strang place downtown. Dominic is so pleased he's almost laughing when he reaches over to shake Harrison's outstretched hand.

CHAPTER 4

Nick gets his chair and actually supervises the workers doing the renovations. If he needs to go upstairs, they hoist him with the manual gantry in the back. Denise covers for Maria at the store and they've hired a young girl, Christine, for the two nights they are open and Saturdays. Dominic depends enormously on Maria, who has proven to be shrewd with tradespeople and suppliers, never one to waste a penny. He often chides her for using her charm to take advantage of the men she bargains with. She reminds him that it's for both of them.

The offices are repainted, the reception area perked up. Only two offices are in use at present. The former owner's, which is taken by both Dominic *and* Maria. The front office to the left of the hallway is converted to a boardroom. Maria designed both for serious business, but also for comfort with plush chairs and bright colors.

On the first level, all the repairs to the back have been made. New plastered walls. The gantry lift is removed, the opening in the ceiling closed. A lunch room for future staff is built with running water, washrooms and shelves and hooks for hanging up their coats. A huge safe, as a tall as a man and two arms wide has been installed over a re-enforced floor.

The store is outstanding. Windows gleam with some showcasing displays. The large columns have been painted a glossy olive that takes your eyes to the startling white ceiling. The floor has been sanded and shellacked many times. Cabinets are tastefully arranged around four of the columns and by the windows. A low wall separates a portion of the back left corner where Dominic and Nick have workstations open to the public. A seating area is in front of the workshop, with a couch, matching chair, and a low table. Pine wainscoting below light olive paint surrounds the room up to the windows. With new custom frames, Dominic's sketches adorn one wall. Art from local artists covers another. A grandfather clock all the way from Switzerland sits beside the doorway to the back rooms.

Nothing happens to the house in Cocagne except for the occasional getaway; all the changes over the summer are overwhelming. They take long walks on the beach and spend wakeful nights in each other's arms, making plans for their wedding. They bask in each other's company and forget about the hubbub in the city. Summer slips by like a meandering stream, constantly moving and changing. Every spare moment is given to details.

*

By September, rumours spread of the war ending soon. A concentrated effort by the allied forces crushes the stubborn German army, forcing it to retreat almost daily. Dominic sits upstairs at his place, tired and hair wet from a bath because he was so dusty and dirty from cleaning the empty rooms downstairs. He has a towel wrapped around his shoulders and his scrapbook is open before him on the table. Everything is ready for the new store opening in two days, Monday the ninth. The sign was put up today. He plans on relaxing tomorrow with one last sweep with Maria in the evening. A few friends are invited to see the premises before it officially opens.

It's late, but before he retires, he wants to paste in the news articles he's been saving since the last entry in May.

British Airship R27 is built and launched from the William Beardmore and Company yards near Glasgow, Scotland.
Canadian Ace Billy Bishop downs six enemy aircraft in three days.
US House of Representatives approves an amendment that allows women to vote.
The Second Battle of the Marne begins.
Battle of Batten Wood first US victory.
Japanese Battleship explodes in Bay of Takayama, killing 500.
Snow falls in Pennsylvania on June 15.
Farya Kapan attempts but fails to assassinate Vladimir Lenin.

The Alexanders

Longest errorless game, Cubs beat Phillies 2-1 in 21 innings.

*

The windows at Alexanders Jewellery & Repair are covered with sheets inside. From outside in the long shadows of early evening, they look like shrouds, but they keep prying eyes away. Invited guests only. Dominic is standing at the door, Maria beside him, the key inserted into the lock. A group of people taking up the boardwalk and a bit of the street go silent. He looks out at them with a face reflecting how happy he is.

"I want you all to give me half a minute. I'd like to turn the lights on."

Dominic closes the door behind him and he grins at the chatter, mostly about the sign with the sweeping letters, striking colors of black and gold with the large stylized A. The light switches are on the wall behind the counter where a new cash register sits. Flipping the three main ones, the store is awash in bright light from new overheads. Flipping another switch brightens the sconces attached to the columns over each counter. Pulling open the door, he bows jokingly to his guests.

"Welcome to Alexander's Jewellery."

Maria leads the group, Denise and Emma right behind her, Bannister and another new girlfriend, Lombroso the accountant and his wife Matilda, Mr. and Mrs. Van Geist, Nick in his new wheelchair and Joanne, the new part-time girl, Christine, and her friend Amanda, Rosie and her new man, Alonzo, the Donnellys. There is a stunned silence as everyone mills about, taking in the beautiful surroundings. Most of the display cases are empty, with all the product – which has to be taken out each morning and put away at night – in the safe.

Dominic waves everyone over to the waiting area, where there are refreshments resting in a fancy bucket full of ice that he brought over just before the guests arrived. Maria has arranged for an adequate number of glasses and begins to pour everyone a drink. Dominic helps to distribute them. Once each person is holding a full glass of juice or soda, he wraps on the counter for attention.

"Thank you all for being here tonight. It means a lot to Maria and me that we are able to share the new store with you, our friends. You've all been so kind and supportive of my work, and I appreciate it very much. I propose a toast. To a new beginning and the end of the war drawing near."

Everyone raises their glasses and cheers. The ladies sip their drinks and the men go for seconds, with some adding spirits, while Dominic explains the layout.

"This store is twice as large as the old one and Nick is joining us as many of you know. He will be working with me doing repairs and custom work..."

Rounds of applause greet the news and Nick blushes from the pats on the back and good wishes.

"...and there is a lot of new product that Maria and Denise have selected for our patrons..."

The dialogue is disturbed by a knocking on the front doors. Maria smiles and moves to open it.

"That's the folks from Benny's."

Two staff from the diner enter with plates of sandwiches and sweets, more than enough for the small group. Maria guides them to the nearest counter where the trays are deposited. After the two depart, Maria locks the doors again and waves everyone to the food, telling them to help themselves. Dominic carries on with details of the new store.

"...and we've installed the very latest of alarms systems that is wired to the local police station. The cash register is the newest three column, full keyboard from the National Cash Register Company and I hope that it will see a lot of use."

Everyone laughs at the comment and is impressed by the new innovations incorporated into the business.

"And then there are the offices upstairs, which we will be touring next and..."

The next two hours are filled with questions and people congratulating Dominic and Maria. After the tour is completed, the evening is spent with small talk, the ladies teasing Maria about when to expect the wedding, the men studying the layout and the easy access for Nick. When the night ends, Van Geist and his wife are the last to leave, with the bank manager issuing a mild but serious piece of advice to the young entrepreneur.

"Watch your future investments, Dominic. The acquisition and renovations coupled with all the new product has cost you quite a bit, and while your business account is still healthy, no new adventures should be undertaken."

"Thank you, Mr. Van Geist, I'm well aware of all the expenses, or I should say, the boss here…"

He points to Maria, who is bidding goodnight to Mrs. Van Geist.

"…is doing a fine job of keeping track of our spending, and I couldn't agree with you more. There will be some more work done on the house, but that will be from my personal account. Thank you for your help."

When Maria and Dominic are finally alone, they turn out the lights and remove all the sheets from the windows for tomorrow's opening. Before they lock up, they embrace. She whispers in his ear.

"I'm so excited, Dominic. Let's hurry back to your place. I told Emma that I'll be staying at Denise's tonight and we can be alone."

With raised eyebrows and a face-splitting smile he asks, "Is it the right time of the month, Maria? We have to be careful."

She just nods and the two are swept up in delirious delight.

CHAPTER 5

The newspapers on November 12 have huge headlines. The War Ends. An armistice was signed on November 11 ending the terror that had lasted four long years. Dominic, Maria, Denise and Nick are listening to the radio in the back room at the store before they open. It's the first time Maria hears the news; she applauds and shouts with glee. Turning to Dominic, she takes his hands in hers.

"Still want to marry me?"

"Of course. I can't wait."

Denise and Nick are cheering and the planning begins.

The wedding date is set for November 30. Nick will be the best man. Denise is maid-of-honor. Originally, Maria had planned on being married in Notre-Dame, at the church she attended as a child. Another couple are getting married the same day, however, and asked for the church first, so they decide on St. Bernard's in Moncton, on Botsford Street. It is close to most of their guests. Father Chiasson will say the mass and perform the vows.

Emma, besides planning the reception, is making the cake and promises a three-tier enchantment with icing rosettes. Maria and Denise venture to Halifax on the train in mid-November to pick out their dresses. Dominic buys a new suit at Dikeman's Men's Wear on Main Street and picks up the bill for Nick's also. They both choose red bow ties for the event. While the suits are the same, dark grey with a fine white pinstripe, Dominic's has a vest. By the last week of November, everything is ready. On November 29, it rains all day, drizzly cold.

Maria is looking out the living room window at her aunt's house. Denise and Emma returned earlier from the Minto hotel where they were making the final preparations, hanging paper ribbons, and both of them are still uncertain whether the cake should be on the left or the right of the main table. Even this late at night, she could see steady streamlets of heavy moisture slither down the panes with shiny tails distorting her view. Disappointment shows in her gaze. All she sees is water.

The gentle hand on her shoulder breaking her focus is Emma reassuring her with her usual optimism.

"Don't worry dear, we're all praying for nicer weather. Just remember, Maria, even if this foul rain doesn't stop, you're marrying a fine young man who adores you. It'll be a great day in your life, rainy day or sunny day."

Maria is uplifted by the thought of Dominic as her husband and nods at her aunt.

"You're right, *ma tante*. I'm very lucky and tomorrow will be fine. It will be the best day of my life."

"Now come, Maria, you must be tired, you've been running around all day. It's almost eleven and we need to be at the church for ten forty-five. I've put the extra blanket at the foot of your bed if you need it."

Maria lets herself be led away by her aunt. She is tired. Just talking about it has made her aware of how much she needs to lie down. Hoping she dreams of her new husband, Maria falls asleep within seconds.

Dominic on the other hand is sitting at his table, which is now downstairs in the renovated house, the one Maria is moving into permanently tomorrow. He's so excited about the wedding he hasn't even considered the weather. Nothing will ruin his wedding day. Happiness is evidenced by the constant half smile he bears. Wearing his winter pajamas he dug out today, he has a black housecoat thrown over his shoulders, open and falling to the sides. A lined scratch pad lies in front of him, a sharpened pencil in his hand. The page is filled with numbered tasks and all except one are crossed out.

4. Honeymoon? Trip to Scotland with Maria. When? New Year?

He thinks of the last week with all the preparations. They couldn't decide on a honeymoon. They decided to spend the night downtown at the Minto Hotel and then spend a week in Cocagne at the old house. It will be the first real holiday they have had. Dominic had a new wood stove installed and a cord of wood delivered. Denise, Christine and Nick will look after the store.

He wants his family back in Scotland to meet his new bride and decides that it would be best in the spring, possibly May. Things will be getting back to normal, he hopes, after the war, and it will be much safer to travel then. He makes a check mark by No. 4. Yawning, he rises from the table and shuffles to the bedroom. He checks his suit again for any wrinkles or lint. Finding none, like the last ten times, he lets the housecoat fall to the floor. Shutting off the light by the bed, he crawls in and dreams of his bride.

Dominic is an early riser, usually up by six thirty or seven o'clock at the latest. The morning of his wedding it's a little past seven thirty as he sits up and rubs the sleep from his eyes. It was well after midnight when he finally went to bed so he's feeling woozy. Hands resting on the side of the bed, he's staring at the floor trying to clear his mind. There is very little to do other than get dressed, pick up Nick and get married. Sitting straighter and stretching, he grins at the thought of him and Maria when the day ends, the warmth of her arms and naked flesh. The stirring in his loins reminds him he needs to get moving. Grabbing the housecoat from the floor, he slips it on and hurries to the bathroom.

Maria is frantic. It's already ten o'clock and Fraser's haven't delivered the flowers yet. A simple bouquet of white mums and roses were supposed to be delivered at nine o'clock and when they didn't show up she had Denise go to the shop on Main Street only to find out that the clerk had marked the wrong date. The manager apologized profusely, promising them the flowers would be ready in an hour and Fraser's would send them over.

She can't find the tube of pink lipstick she bought and doesn't want to wear the bright red. Emma is searching through the house for it, complaining that she needs to get dressed and her new shoes pinch her toes. She hopes Adolph is on time, he's supposed to drive them all to the church for ten-thirty. Thank goodness the sun is shining.

Denise is the only one not fretting. She is dressed and helping Maria arrange her veil. She keeps telling the bride not to worry so much, everything will be fine. And it is. The three of them are picked up at ten twenty-five. The lipstick has been found and applied, the flowers delivered and everyone is at the church by ten-forty.

Maria and Denise are delivered to the waiting room where her father is ready to escort his daughter down the aisle. Emma and Adolph tread softly to their regular pew, which is three from the front on the right. There are about fifty people in the front ten pews; the back of the church is empty save for the organist and the Trembley sisters, who have been asked to sing. At five to eleven, Dominic and Nick arrive. The two of them proceed to the front, where Father Chiasson directs them to the right to wait for the bride to come down the aisle. A soft murmur hovers over the gathering.

At eleven o'clock exactly, the organist begins the wedding march. Dominic steps forward into the middle of the aisle, with Nick in his chair close behind him. The crowd goes quiet and everyone turns towards the back when they hear the footsteps and the rustle of Maria's soft silks. There is a collective gasp in the crowd when Denise starts her slow march towards the front and Maria appears behind her with one arm wrapped inside her father's. Denise is wearing a peach-colored ensemble, dress just below her knees. Her long hair is swept up and she wears a matching hat with a wide brim. Her only flower is a peach rose garnished with baby's breath.

As beautiful as she is, all eyes are on the bride.

Maria wears a dress so white it appears to shimmy. Falling just below her knees, the silk folds extend from her waist where a cinched yoke separates the dress from the long sleeved blouse of the same material and finishes high on her neck. Over her top she wears an open, light petticoat of fine lace. Her veil is tulle and flows down to the small of her back. It is held in place by a silk headband that is adorned with leaves and miniature pearls that match the cuffs on her blouse. Like Denise, her hair is swept up in the back. With one arm tucked at her father's side, the other holds her white bouquet. Her happiness is expressed by the full smile that exposes her faint dimples. She stares at her future husband as she approaches the altar rail, oblivious to the whispers and adoring faces of the crowd.

Dominic is as still as marble, stunned by Maria's beauty, by the delight in her eyes. With pounding heart, he's afraid to blink, to miss one moment of bliss. Denise moves to her left, Benoit passes Maria off to Dominic. Only then does Dom move to shake Benoit's hand, catching the mischievous wink that Maria can't see. Everyone's smiling, even the dour Father Chiasson. It's his favorite sacrament.

Dominic stares at his bride and removes the veil from her face. With a sudden intake of breath, he pauses. He's never seen Maria so exquisite, so radiant. Their mutual affection pulses like a physical thing between them. She holds his gaze with her own, noting how dashing her new husband is. Dominic takes her hand and they face Father Chiasson.

The priest's *chasuble* has a crimson front with an embroidered gold cross upon the chest, very formal. He stands a bit taller than the couple, waving them to step forward, and begins the ceremony. A hushed crowd follows every word. A few sobs when they say "I do." The vestry is full of cheers when, after the final prayers, the priest tells Dominic he may kiss his bride. He then cues the couple to face the congregation, with the expected announcement.

"Ladies and Gentleman, I present Mr. and Mrs. Dominic Alexander."

The closing hymn interrupts the applause and the wedding party walks from the church. The crowd follows and the festivities begin.

Emma has arranged for a feast. In the *Petitcodiac Room* of the hotel, the main table is against one wall to the right of an impromptu stage at the back for the musicians later. Refreshments are set up on the opposite side and round tables are arranged around the room for the sixty-five guests. Laughter and gaiety dominate the conversations until the formal speeches are given after a dinner of steak and lobster, baked potato and broccoli. Desserts are lined up on a separate table near a coffee urn and teapots, three kinds of pies and wedding cake. Candles flicker on every table. An aroma hovers over the guests, with a mixture of ladies' perfumes, men's colognes, cigar and cigarette smoke, and the char of seasoned meat. Staff at the hotel enter after six o'clock to clear the tables and rearrange the furniture for dancing. The women are off to powder their noses, the men continue to sip from the ever present and illegal flasks and to tell wedding jokes and stories. Dominic and Maria open their gifts before the music begins.

Nick, Maria's uncle Rudy and two of Nick's friends supply the tunes. Guitar, accordion, mandolin, harmonica, make for a fine time with reels and jigs and waltzes. Some of the older guests are leaving after a final hug, but the rest take seats here and there or stand in pockets, the men on queasy legs and a few of the ladies too. The party finally ends at one in the morning when Dominic and Maria thank everyone and leave among winks and elbow nudges to head to their room. Tomorrow they will head to Cocagne for the week.

CHAPTER 6

Sunday morning when the newlyweds check out, it's early. The sun makes a bright path along Main Street when they leave the hotel, but there is a chill with the temperature just above forty degrees and warnings of coming frost. The wedding dress and suit have been neatly folded and packed. Both are dressed casually, with Maria wearing trousers that shock onlookers. Their car is in the parking lot and they head to their house to drop off the wedding apparel and pick up suitcases for the week in the country.

When they turn in their driveway, a man is sitting on the front steps. Beside him is a scarred suitcase and a worn duffle bag. He is wearing a tam and dark jacket. Longish hair curls from the lip of the hat. A gnarly beard frames his chin, making him look mean. Maria points to the intruder.

"Who can that be Dominic? It looks like a freeloader."

Dominic doesn't respond until they pull up closer because he can't believe what he's seeing.

"It looks like my brother Tommy, but that can't be. No one in my family has seen him for quite some time. You stay in the car and I'll go see."

Dominic is still uncertain as he approaches the house until a grin splits the visitor's face and he is startled how much the man looks like his deceased grandfather.

"Tommy, what on earth are you doing here, man?"

Standing now with arms spread, the visitor greets Dominic.

"What kind of welcome is that, laddie? Is this a surprise now?

Come give me a hug, little brother."

Tommy meets Dominic halfway down the walk and engulfs him in strong arms. Dominic gets over his wonderment and embraces his brother. He wrinkles his nose at the unwashed odor.

"Ach Tommy. It's been so long, too long in fact. Where have you been? Mary told me in her last letter that they haven't heard from you for many months, over a year in fact. How did you find me?"

Tommy backs off, holding his brother by the shoulders and looking him in the eyes.

"Well the finding wasn't hard. I saw Mary and the bunch only three weeks ago and they told me where you were. You've made quite a name for yourself here, laddie. Everyone seems to have heard of Alexander's jewellery shop, wasn't hard. I've been on the porch all night so I've not slept very well, and as you can tell from the way I smell, I need to get cleaned up and a bite to eat. But who's the pretty lady frowning at us from the car?"

Dominic doesn't know how to feel about his brother being here. He waves to Maria to join them.

"That's my new wife. I was married yesterday. We were actually heading to the country for our honeymoon."

Maria is hesitant to approach the man. She steps a few feet short and stands closer to Dominic.

"Maria, this is my brother, Tommy."

Maria extends her hand and offers a slight smile. She remembers Dominic telling her about his wayward brother and is not sure how to respond. She doesn't see a lot of delight in Dominic`s face and knows this will put a wrinkle in their plans.

Tommy takes the gloved hand and shakes it gently.

"I guess congratulations are in order, my dear. I understand you married this poor sod. Well, you made a fine choice. He's certainly the best of the crop of Alexanders. I apologize for showing up at such an awkward time without letting ya know I was coming."

Maria has a difficult time with Tommy's strong accent and while Dominic's has softened, she must pay attention. She politely takes Tommy's hand, trying not to seem standoffish, but she too catches a whiff of the odor emanating from the man, reminding her of old socks. It only adds to the unpleasantness of encountering him on the first day of her marriage and she wonders to herself why this couldn't have happened next week. But it's her husband's brother, after all, and she offers him her best smile when she replies.

"Well perhaps the timing isn't the best but welcome to Canada and our house, Tommy. Why don't we go in and you can get straightened away and tell us what brings you here."

"Aye and thank you, Maria."

Turning back to his brother, Tommy pats him on the shoulder.

"I only need to get shined up a bit, and if you can help me find a place to stay for the next week or so until I decide what I'm to do, I'd be forever grateful."

Leading them up to the front door, Dominic speaks over his shoulder.

"We've made some changes to the house, Tommy, and there's an extra bedroom here, so you'll not need a place to stay while we're in the country. Come in."

The house was remodeled after the new store opened, with the downstairs office converted to an extra bedroom. A new kitchen and dining room have been added to the back area as well as a full bathroom. The old display area is now a living room again. Dominic's old work area is where the kitchen is. The upstairs is still the same and Maria hasn't decided what to do up there yet, so the two bedrooms, small kitchen and bathroom are the same. They set Tommy up in the new bedroom downstairs, and while he is taking a bath, Maria cooks up some breakfast for them all.

When Tommy enters the dining area, he's greeted with the smell of bacon frying and the sound of eggs sizzling in fresh butter. Dominic is making toast and tea. Tommy's hair shines and is swept back from his forehead. The beard is groomed and has obviously been trimmed. He's wearing clean but wrinkled trousers and a gray plaid shirt. Dominic offers him a pair of his slippers and notices one sock has a hole in the toe. Tommy grins when he sees Dominic scrutinize the sock.

"Just like when we were kids, Dominic, our socks are always worn until there's not much left to them. When I get working, I'll have to get some new ones."

Dominic chuckles at the memory.

"Aye, I remember well enough, whenever you got some new ones or Willy's old ones, there was soon a hole or two in the toes. Seems you haven't changed. Maybe you need to trim those toenails more."

Maria hands out a full plate to each man and takes one for herself to sit at the end of the table, grimacing at the subject.

"Forget the talk of toenails and socks and eat up, you two."

While they are eating, Tommy tells them of what has taken place since he saw Dominic last.

"I got in a bit of trouble after I left, when our Mum abandoned all of us. Hanging around with the wrong bunch. Found work in Perth. We was drunk one night and me and a couple of the boys got caught stealing some liquor from a distillery. We were given the choice of prison or war. I was sent off to France in the fall of 1916. It was a terrible time, but it helped me get off the drink and I've been dry now for over a year. I visited Mary and her husband and the rest of the scamps but didn't want to stick around, especially after Granda was dead, so I scraped and borrowed enough money to come here. Had a bit of trouble when I arrived in Halifax, but I told them I was visiting kin in New Brunswick. So here I am. What about you, Dominic?"

"What about the rest of the family? We only hear what Mary sends us in her letters."

"Paul's fourteen now and as tall as I am. Quit school last year and moved to Saltcoats to work on the fishing boats with our uncle. Went and saw him too before I left. Sheila's eleven and what a looker that little one is, says she wants to be a teacher or a nurse. Lilly's a real beauty too and mad about that Russian lad. They're engaged now, ya know, and she's moved to Edinburgh to be close to him, and she's studying to be a nurse."

"Didn't know about Lilly and Ivan. He's a good fellow and he'll take care of her. I sure miss them all."

Maria cleans up the table while the men chat and after pouring more tea, the three of them talk for another hour or so, with Dominic telling Tommy what's been going on since he arrived here in January of 1915. By noon, he's telling him about Duff and why he came to Canada. Maria is quiet as she's hearing things Dominic has not told her. Tommy is sitting back in his chair, shaking his head.

"I always liked uncle Duff. That's a terrible way to go. But listen you two, it's your honeymoon, and I've taken enough of your time. Why don't you carry on and I'll be fine here for a bit. Can't thank you enough for letting me stay here for a while. Any idea where I might find some work?"

Rising from the table, Dominic tells Maria to get ready and motions for Tommy to follow him. The two of them go out and walk back towards the barn. Cloud cover has moved in and the day is chilly, with no threat of rain.

"It's getting colder these days, Tommy, and there'll be snow soon. Most of the mills close up here in the winter, except for Leblanc's cause they always a have a stockpile of logs. The river doesn't freeze up due to the high tides moving back and forth so you might try the shipyards, seems they're always looking for laborers, especially Salter's, they're the biggest. Try the sugar refinery down on Main Street. All the industry is along the river. What kind of work did you do before?"

"Well as you know, I worked with Willy at the distillery in New Lanark until he died. After that I was so torn with what happened with the family, Da gone, then Willy. Mam running off like she did. Seems I didn't have any friends or family after I took to the booze. Did a lot of nothing for a bit except drink and steal stuff. I don't have any real skills, Dom. Not sure what to tell you except I've still got me strong arms and I'm not stupid, so I can learn new things."

They enter the barn and Dominic frets over his brother. He thinks that Tommy sounds sincere, but he's not convinced that he's changed like he says. And he's leery about leaving him alone for a week, but he's family.

He enters the back rooms, which are empty now except for a pile of boards, which he points at.

"This lumber is for the fence I'm working on at the edge of my property next to where I sold the lot next to the coal yard and around the outer perimeter. You will see the posts in the field I've had a friend's uncle set up. He was supposed to put the boards on but he's taken ill with the gout and doesn't get around too good. There's a hammer and saw and a bucket of nails next to the pile there. I want three boards strung along the posts, one twelve inches from the ground, the next in the center and one four inches from the top which makes them about sixteen inches apart. Think you could handle that? It's a fair stretch and it should take you the rest of the week. We'll be back on Friday, and then we can see if we can find you something else if you don't have time to look around. I'll pay you sixty cents an hour for an eight-hour day. How's that sound?"

Tommy raises his brow. He knows how to convert pounds to dollars. He's never made that much in a week before and he's flabbergasted.

"That's mighty generous of you, Dominic. I suppose you want the boards straight too?"

Dominic catches the sarcasm in Tommy's voice and look at him to see if he's serious then realizes his brother's only joking.

"Aye that'd be nice. Now come along and I'll show you where the Donnellys live. I'll talk to him before I go, and he'll come over tomorrow with his horse and wagon. You and him can take the boards out and pile them along the edge where you'll need them."

Tommy nods with a close-lipped smile.

"Thank you for this, Dominic. I know I've been up to no good, but I'm tired of that life. I'll not let you down."

"I hope not, Tommy. I'm trusting you with my house and our belongings. I have to admit there was a time I wouldn't. You always seemed so angry with the world, but I can see that you've changed."

The men eye each other and shake hands.

CHAPTER 7

When 1918 draws to a close, Alexander's Jewellery has its busiest season ever. Scarlet is eleven months old, eight ounces from full grown and still a kitten. Maria dotes on her. Scarlet in turn responds to her human's every command. The patrons exclaim over her friendliness when the she wraps herself gently about the ankle. She's spoiled by the attention but never a pest. The house in Cocagne has been mothballed for the winter. Tommy is working at the sugar refinery in the warehouse. He has taken a room at Rosie's place, and they've hit it off just fine. He's a hard worker, and when the management realizes he has a knack for numbers, they put him in charge of shipping. He's been to the capital city of the province and applied for Canadian citizenship. The young lady at the store, Christine, has taken a liking to him, and after the staff Christmas party, they start to see each other on a regular basis even though she's only sixteen. Tommy finds out that Dominic has a forged birth certificate and jokes that even though in reality he's a year older, he's now the younger brother, which is the cause for lots of joking.

The crew celebrate Christmas at Maria and Dominic's house, with all their family and friends. Tommy is true to his word and doesn't touch the liquor. Christine seems to be a good influence for him as she hates the taste of it. More letters come from Scotland. Lilly has invited them to her wedding in June and begs for Dominic to come and bring his new wife. Mary is pregnant and expecting in February. Sheila has the best marks at school and mends everyone's injuries, saying she's practising at being a nurse like Lilly, instead of being a teacher. They don't hear much from Paul.

The year ends with a New Year's party at Emma's place, and she surprises everyone by saying she and Alonzo are going to Boston to visit his sister in the spring and getting married while they are there. Maria still gets in trouble for sticking up for women's rights. The last thing Dominic does in 1918, or rather, the first thing he does in 1919 on January 1 at two in the morning after the party, is paste in the headlines he's accumulated since September.

Due to the war, the 15th World Series starts a month earlier, which is threatened by a strike. The players saying they want $2500 each for the winners and $1000 each for the losers.

The Boston Red Sox beat the Chicago Cubs 4 games to 2.

In late September the Allied Forces make a major breakthrough at the Hindenburg Line.

American soldier Alvin York single-handedly attacks a German machine gun nest, killing 25 and capturing 132 Germans.

Cecil Chubb gives prehistoric monument Stonehenge to the British nation. On the "eleventh day of the eleventh month at the eleventh hour" an armistice is signed by Germany and the Allies, officially ending the war. Poland declares independence from Russia.

In December Jack Dempsey KO's Carl Morris in 14 seconds to become the Heavyweight Boxing Champion.

ICR and NTR merged by the Federal Government, forming the Canadian National Railway.

1919

With the war over, Moncton continues to grow as a shipping and railway center. The Intercolonial Railway of Canada (ICR) shops in Moncton become the largest locomotive repair facility for the new Canadian National Railway (CNR) in the Maritimes. The CNR also makes the city the headquarters for its Marine Division. The railway management go to Alexander's Jewellery when the need for "special gifts" arise. Mr. Jerome Campbell, the lands manager for the CNR, is considering a watch, having been *volunteered* to select one for the General Manager's retirement on Friday. At present, he's leaning towards the Hamilton. A Waltham with a burgundy leather strap and roman numerals for markers is more elegant. However, the Hamilton is just as handsome but has larger numbers, and old man Blackmore, the GM, has glasses as thick as a woman's little finger. Dominic is serving Campbell, who is partially responsible for Dominic owning his property west of the city, personally.

It's obvious to Dominic from his client's flushing cheeks that he's decided on the Hamilton, which is good for him because he gets a better deal on that brand, and he knows Campbell will want a better price. Having made pocket watches for years, Hamilton made their first wrist watch two years ago and they're becoming quite the rage. Looking up at Dominic, Campbell motions with his brows at the two timepieces on the velvet cloth.

"It'll be the Hamilton then, Dominic."

"Fine choice, Mr. Campbell. Would you like us to gift wrap it for you?"

351

"That would be wonderful, Dominic, thank you."

Dominic puts the Waltham back in the case and waves to Christine, who has finished with another client.

"Christine, can you please find the proper box for this watch and then warp it for Mr. Campbell, you always make the nicest bows. Please use the new silver paper Maria bought."

Christine takes the watch and smiles at Mr. Campbell, who is flattered by the young lady's attention.

"I'd be happy to do that."

She goes to the back room, where a desk is set up for wrapping and sorting items. Campbell follows Dominic to the cash register.

"Such a pleasant girl."

"Yes, she is, we're lucky to have her. Always so happy and carefree."

Dominic offers his guest a discount for all the business he brings the store. There are several people browsing, and Denise is helping a couple celebrating an anniversary pick out a ring for the wife. Maria is in the office with the sales agent for Regency Jewellery in Ontario who is trying to get their foot in the door. Nick is concentrating on setting a large ruby in one of their clients' rings. Even with the large amounts of snow accumulated along the sidewalks and the chilly temperatures, the sun is beaming through the front window, reflecting everyone's good mood. After Campbell has paid for the watch and pocketed the receipt, he motions Dominic to the side, where they can converse unheard.

"You know Dominic, when we sold you the property west of the city a few years back, the Intercolonial was divesting itself of properties that they deemed extra, and of course you were wise to pick up that piece. However, since the government has nationalized the railways, forming the CNR, Intercolonial is thinking about future expansions of the yards now that Moncton is the main repair center in Atlantic Canada. It is willing to make you a considerable offer to buy it back."

Dominic raises his brows in surprise. This news is totally unexpected.

"Is that so, Mr. Campbell? I've not considered selling it as it is now our home. I've invested quite a few dollars in improvements. What would they do with it?"

"Well, nothing at present, probably rent the house. They are thinking of the future, Dominic, and there are many opportunities in

Moncton. The new subway for the tracks is completed on Main Street. We hear rumors that the T. Eaton Company would like to build a distribution center here in the city. The yards are a very important part of the landscape and with the extension of the lines, there will always need to be repairs on the rolling stock. They feel it is best to acquire lands close by."

"That's interesting. What do you think they might offer?"

Campbell removes a pipe from his inside coat pocket and a bag of tobacco. Filling the pipe and tamping it down, he offers Dominic a sideways glance.

"I've been instructed to make you an offer of $3,600."

Dominic is stunned at the huge sum. They both know he paid $1,800 four years ago.

"Yes, I know what you're thinking, it's quite a bit more than you paid, and the company had originally suggested less, but I know what you've done there. I suggested the offer would have to be considerable in order to catch your attention."

"Well, you've certainly done that, Mr. Campbell. It is considerable and bears thinking about. Of course, I can't answer you right now. I'll need to discuss this with Maria."

Campbell has the pipe going and a small cloud of bluish smoke hovers over him. Rubbing his large belly, he nods in agreement.

"I understand, Dominic. When you are discussing this with your wife, please note that the company is willing to give you six months from the closing date before you would have to vacate the premises."

At that moment Christine delivers to Mr. Campbell the gift-wrapped watch and places it in one of the store's bags.

"There you go, sir. Thank you for your business."

"You're quite welcome, young lady, and thank you."

Christine leaves them with blushing cheeks. Dominic is deep in thought. Campbell tucks the bag under his arm and waves his smoking pipe.

"Let me know what you think, Dominic. If you would be so kind as to respond by the first of February, it would be most appreciated."

"Aye, that's better than a week away, so I'll be in touch. Thank you."

When Mr. Campbell leaves, Dominic's mind is swirling with the possibilities. An image of the house in Cocagne looms. He's been caught up in the store and his life in Moncton, but he yearns for the country life. The money would make for many improvements. Denise interrupts his thoughts with a question regarding the sizing of the ring the couple has picked out. He decides to talk to Maria as soon as possible.

After apologizing to the couple for not having the ring in the size needed, he assures them that he can size the smaller one to a five and have it ready by tomorrow. Maria is escorting the sales agent out, a tall skinny man with an oversized briefcase. Dominic motions her towards the office. When she joins him, Dominic is sitting in the visitor's chair and grinning from ear to ear.

"What are you smiling at, dear?"

"You remember Mr. Campbell, the man I was serving?"

"Yes, from the railway company."

"Well, the new CNR want to buy my property back, where our house is."

Maria takes a seat behind the desk, all serious. Scarlet jumps upon her lap as if she's part of the decision making and Maria strokes her back.

"They do? Did they make you an offer?"

"Yes. $3,600."

Maria's hand goes to cover her mouth. Dominic sees the surprised look in her eyes.

"That's what I thought too. The offer is so incredible that we really should think about it."

"Where would we go if we did sell?"

Let's build a new one and start fixing up the house in Cocagne? We have a reliable vehicle that we can use in the winter, and the roads have been greatly improved over the last couple of years, we could stay there on the weekends. The only time to worry is in the winter, but now that Denise has her own keys, we should make her the manager and she could be responsible if we couldn't make it to the city."

He can tell she likes the idea.

"Oh Dominic, it would be a dream to build a new house… and decorate it… and I love the idea of being in Cocagne as much as we can, but you put so much work in this house, wouldn't you miss it?"

"Ach, it's just a house. I think we need to talk about this more and decide soon. Campbell wants word back by the first of next month."

Maria glances at the large calendar on the wall, one they received from Mr. Sumner advertising his store on Main Street.

"Well, that's nine days away. Yes, let's talk about it tonight, Dominic."

On the first Monday of February, the 3rd, Dominic and Maria are sitting in John Bannister's office with Mr. Campbell. All agree that the Alexanders do not have to move until the end of August. The papers are signed and Campbell passes Dominic a check for the amount agreed upon. After hands are shaken, Dominic and Maria leave, both with a bittersweet feeling of letting the house and land go. But they are ready to start looking at land in the north end to build a new house, and both have ideas for their home in Cocagne.

CHAPTER 2

The last day of March is overcast; snow swirls around the edge of the buildings, making small drifts. The clouds are stretched thin and the sun is only a yellowish glow doing nothing to warm the day. By mid-morning the temperature has reached twenty-five degrees Fahrenheit, with the wind making it seem colder. People who come to Alexander's Jewellery are bundled in thick coats; scarves adorn their necks and hats cover their heads.

When Dominic opened the store, Christine was supposed to work with him until 10:00 a.m., when Maria would be there to help. But she has not shown up yet. Commenting to Nick, Dominic is surprised because she is always punctual. Denise has Mondays off, so Dominic and Nick are alone in the store when Christine rushes in shortly after nine-thirty. Wrapped in warm clothes, with a heavy shawl clasped around her shoulders, she has frozen tears upon her cheeks. It doesn't take Dominic long to notice the distraught look on her face. He stands and greets her by the front counter.

"What's wrong, Christine?"

"Oh Dominic, I'm worried about Tommy. He was supposed to meet me last night for a movie, but he never showed up. I didn't think much of it then because, you know Tommy, he moves on his own schedule. But Jack Preston came to our house early this morning and when my father answered the door – I was getting ready for work – he asked about Tommy. You remember Jack, don't you? The young man from Salisbury who stays at Rosie's too. He works with Tommy at the refinery; they chum around a bit."

Dominic is nodding. "Aye, the lad with the freckles and curly hair."

"Yes, that's him. Well he told me that he and Tommy and a few of the boys were playing cards yesterday, and after Tommy lost a lot of money, he was upset and started a fight with one of the Thompson twins, accused him of cheating. Well I understand he beat the man pretty bad and when he left the house he took the bottle of rum the men were drinking."

Dominic is shaking his head, rubbing his hands together. Nick hears the conversation and pauses in his work, concerned for his friend.

"I thought he was over that, Christine. I was hoping he'd never go near the liquor again. No one knows where he is? He's not at Rosie's sleeping it off?"

"No, Jack knocked at his door and when he told Rosie the story, she unlocked the door and his bed hadn't been slept in. What should I do, Dominic?"

The tears start anew and Christine is shaking when Dominic tries to comfort her. He removes his apron and glancing at the clock on the wall, he sees it is a few minutes before ten o'clock.

"If he's not at home and he's been drinking, I expect he's likely in jail, Christine. When Tommy drinks, he gets rough and loud, goes looking for trouble. You stay here, Maria will be in soon, and I'll go look for him. I'll check at the police station first, then I'll check Rosie's again. Do you know any other places he hangs out?"

Shaking her head, she brushes away a tear with her scarf.

"Maybe talk to Jack Preston; he was at the card game. Tommy's probably wearing the old army coat he loves so much."

He waves to Nick with a pointing finger.

"Can you please finish polishing the brooch I was working on, Nick. Mrs. Stern is picking it up at noon."

Nick nods and wheels over to Dominic's bench, pushing the chair out of the way. Just then Maria enters and stamps the snow off her feet on the mat placed inside the door. She sees the look on Christine's face, notices she is fully dressed in her coat and hat, and asks what's going on. Dominic leads Christine to the back while explaining to Maria what he is doing. Shocked by the news, Maria tosses her coat and scarf on the wrapping table and embraces Christine, offering her a cotton hankie from her cuff to dab at the tears.

Changing his boots, Dominic dons his winter coat, scarf and fur lined hat. Before he leaves, he gently touches Christine on the shoulder.

"We'll find him!"

He leaves to walk to the police station on Main Street. With gloved hands stuffed into his pockets and head down, the wind buffets his body and thoughts of calamity occupy his mind.

Entering the station, Dominic finds plenty of activity in the reception area. One officer is behind a desk shuffling papers and looks up when Dominic approaches him. The man is bald and has fluffy side whiskers with a bushy moustache, and a don't-bother-me attitude. Dominic removes his hat and wipes the snow from the rim.

"Pardon me, sir, but I'm missing me brother and he sometimes finds himself in a bit of trouble. I was wondering if you could check to see if he's a guest here."

The officer scrunches his forehead at the word guest.

"Well, we've got a few scalawags locked up. Seems there was a bit of a disturbance last night down at the Duke Hotel. What's your brother's name?"

"Tommy. Tommy Alexander."

The man gets up from his desk and heads towards the back. He returns a few minutes later shaking his head.

"Sorry, sir, no one here by that name. Has he been missing long?"

"Well no, not really. He was last seen yesterday afternoon around four; but he's not returned to his place and is not at work this morning, so I'm a bit worried where he might be."

Dominic doesn't mention the drinking because liquor is prohibited, or the cards. He may be putting Tommy in more trouble than he might already be in. The officer returns to his seat behind the desk and waves a pencil at Dominic.

"Give him another 24 hours and if he's not been heard of, then you might want to get us involved. He's likely at a friend's place trying to get out of that minor squall we had last night. Damn snow, eh! I've had enough of this cold. Anything else, sir?"

Dominic is not sure what to do but knows that there is nothing more to be done here. He decides to walk over to Rosie's and see if Tommy may have shown up.

"No, that's fine, Officer. Thank ye for your help."

The police officer acts tough, has to. He keeps the gate. Seeing the hurt in the Scottie's eyes softens him up a notch.

"Hold on there now, young man. What's your brother look like, just in case, and where can we get a hold of you."

Relief from a hand reaching out heartens Dominic and he describes his brother, right down to the mole at the base of his neck near his left shoulder. His crooked nose and hazel eyes like their mother's. An old army greatcoat and his shirt is likely plaid, but he can't swear to that. Don't know what's on his hands or feet. Reaching inside his coat he withdraws a calling card Maria had made up for him, offering it to the man.

"...and I can be reached at this number or address. Thank you so much, Officer."

Scanning the card, he tosses it on top of a pile of papers to his right. The scowl is back.

"It's Sargent, Sargent Peterson. I'll pass that information along..."

He glances at the card again.

"...Mr. Alexander. Good day, then."

Dominic leaves Rosie's just before noon. A cup of tea, the latest gossip and hopeful ideas of where Tommy may be take up a half hour, Dominic ever hopeful his brother would walk through the door. Stepping into the cold, Dominic has a feeling that causes him to pause on Rosie's front steps. The sun is hidden by slow moving clouds and offers no comfort from the biting chill. Dominic thinks of his brother, taking the bottle of rum, possibly out in the cold passed out somewhere. He hopes he found a warm spot to crawl into.

Heading towards Main Street, he plans on having a talk with Preston about the card game. Looking at his watch, he figures that the men at the refinery will be on their lunch hour. He walks past Leblanc's sawmill on Main, which is unusually quiet with the steam engine shut down. Horses pulling heavy sleighs of logs enter the yard where men with notched sticks measure the load. Yard hands offload other loads near the back, where the logs are stockpiled. Walking in through the office door at the refinery, Dominic asks if Jack Preston is working today. He's directed to the shipping area, where three men are sitting at a rough planked table eating lunch from shiny pails. Jack Preston sees Dominic and meets him by the entrance.

"Have you found him, Dominic?"

Dominic shakes his head.

"Nae, was hoping you might have seen him."

"No, he's not been around. When Wee Willie, that's our foreman, sent me to look for Tommy, I checked out a couple of spots I thought he might be, but no luck. Seems like he's disappeared."

Dominic rubs his chin, staring at the plank floor, thinking.

"Tell me about the card game, this man he beat up."

Preston explains the events that led up to the argument and Tommy accusing Ray Thompson of cheating when Tommy lost the last of his money.

"Now Ray's no easy man to get the best of. The Thompsons from Albert County are a tough lot. They're in trouble so much, they know most of the cops by first name. There's a rumour that their old man done in Mike Turnbull for jilting his daughter back in '09. Never been proved. No one has seen Turnbull since. Anyway, your brother is a crafty boxer and strong. Thompson was much bigger, but Tommy whipped him good. Only trouble was that when Thompson was down, Tommy wouldn't stop beating on him. We had to pull him off, and he was raging. His face was red as a beet. Took a swipe at us. I've never seen so much anger."

Preston is into the story with lots of hand motions and facial expressions. Dominic remembers Tommy as a boy with their father teaching them how to defend themselves. Tommy took to it real fast. His Da had to slap him around some to stop him from picking fights.

"Aye, that'd be Tommy. He has a terrible temper and it's caused him many a scuffle. Maybe I should go talk to the Thompsons and...."

Preston interrupts him with a wave of both hands.

"Are ya daft, man? They find out you're related to the man that beat one of them up and they'll be feeding you to their hogs. No, no, stay away from there. Don't even enter Albert County."

Dominic looks at him to see if he's joking, but the eyes are serious. With a worried look, Dominic tries to think positive.

"I understand, Jack. I'm sure Tommy's going to show up. When he does, I'll let you know. I just hope he's somewhere warm."

Preston turns to go back to work.

"Me too.

By Wednesday, there has been no sign of Tommy. The best they can surmise is that he left the city by train. Dominic checks with the police station every morning. Sargent Peterson is polite today, strange in itself. Only yesterday Dominic was told not to be a pest. Today there is a different reception. Peterson swings open a half door and lifts a section of the counter.

"Come in. Our chief, Albert Robichaud, wants to talk to you."

Dominic is led down a hallway where the last office on the left has an open door. People move from office to office, everyone seemingly in a hurry, someone's cologne scents the air. The clatter of typewriters and excited voices comes from the right. Inside the chief's office, seated in front of the desk is a short, older man. Wisps of almost white hair cross his scalp. Soft blue eyes can't mask the care in them, and Dominic knows something is wrong. The Chief sits behind the desk. Robichaud is a big man, wide shoulders and a forceful brow. The Sargent introduces Dominic and leaves, shutting the door behind him. Robichaud stands to shake Dominic's hand and points to the empty chair.

"Have a seat, Mr Alexander. Say hello to Dr. Shapiro."

The man offers a pale hand, smooth-skinned, but doesn't stand. Dominic renders his best smile.

"Pleased to meet you, Doctor."

The doctor's voice is as soft as his eyes.

"And you as well, Dominic. May I call you Dominic?"

"Aye, certainly.

It comes out *sairtinly* and the Doctor smiles at his accent. Robichaud leans ahead to fold his hands and elbows on his desk, and the movement catches Dominic's attention.

"The reason we've asked you here is confidential, and as terrible as it may seem, it must remain in this room until we say different. Do you understand, Mr. Alexander?"

Too shocked to speak, Dominic nods in agreement.

"A body has been found along the Petitcodiac River snagged in an exposed root. We have reason to believe it may be your brother. I'm sorry."

Goosebumps flare upon his arms and scalp, a shiver climbs his spine. Tommy dead? He can't believe it.

"No, not Tommy. Surely it must be someone else. Can I see him?"

Robichaud says, "That's not a good idea right now. That's why Dr. Shapiro is here. He's examined the body and has a few questions."

Sitting up, the doctor has a clipboard with a sheet of paper attached resting on his knee. Reaching to an inside pocket, he removes a thin pair of glasses, which he dons before glancing at the paper.

"I have the description of your brother you left with Sargent Peterson. There is very little here to suggest it may be him."

With a little hope Dominic is quick to look for doubt.

"What about the coat, the clothes he was wearing."

"The body was found naked."

Dominic shudders at the thought, bare flesh and freezing ice.

"What about the crooked nose, the green eyes?"

Both Robichaud and the Doctor eyeball each other until the Chief nods.

"The cause of death, Dominic, has left no facial features that are distinguishable, I regret to say, and that's why we need to talk to you. You mentioned a mole at the base of the neck."

"Aye on his left shoulder, right where the shoulder changes into the neck. It isn't big."

"The body has none, but there is a scar where something like a mole may have been. Sometimes they rub off and regrow. What about birthmarks?"

Dominic has to think about that, to remember. He remembers Willie had a round black spot on his back, and Mary has what looks like a freckle under one ear, and Tommy had...

"It's a reddish spot on his right lower leg in the back, the size of a sixpence or a quarter, that looks like a man's face sideways."

The doctor consults what he's written, nodding in the affirmative. There's nothing to say. It's confirmation that Tommy Alexander was murdered.

CHAPTER 3

The 26th of May is full of butterflies. The lilac bushes Maria has planted in front of the porch draws them to their nectar. The noon sun reflects off the drops of water that grip every surface from an early morning rain. Dominic has returned from Highfield Street where their new house is being built by the Goguen Construction Company. The foreman, Eugene, has assured them it will be ready at the end of June when they return from their vacation. He heads upstairs to finish packing for their trip to Scotland. The ship leaves in two days, on Wednesday at seven in the morning. He and Maria are taking the train at four o'clock this afternoon. The steamer trunk is shiny wood and leather, two clasps and a heavy hasp with its own key. Maria has taken the bottom and it's all packed. He has the top tray and the only thing left for him to put in is the news clippings of the trial for Tommy's murderer, Ray Thompson. The latest is from May 23, when the trial ended abruptly. After goading from the District Attorney, Thompson yelled at him that yes, he had killed the son-of-a-bitch. The bloody hammer found in Thompson's garage was evidence enough had it gone to the jury.

Dominic sits on the bed for a moment with the newspaper clippings in his lap and remembers, painfully, the details of Tommy's funeral at the last of April when the ground was soft enough to dig, a small event with only a few of Dominic's closest friends attending at the Elmwood Cemetery. He remembers the arrest of Ray Thompson three weeks after they found the body and his plea of not guilty. Dominic sighs at the relief he felt when Thompson made a fool of himself in the courtroom.

He's not written to his family regarding Tommy's death. The last news they got was how well he was doing. He couldn't bear to write the details or send a telegram. Rather he wants to tell them in person upon arrival in Scotland next week. Sheila will take it the hardest because she was Tommy's favorite and he always spoiled her when he could with cookies, treats and the odd pretty dress. When she was one year old, it was only Tommy who could put her to bed when they all lived together.

Thinking of his kin, he wonders at the changes he'll see in them, and they in him. He checks his watch and realizes that Maria will be back soon and they have to head to the train station in an hour, around three. Placing the clippings between two pieces of stiff paper, he ties a string around it and places it on top of his rain jacket before closing the lid. He has enough time to paste a few more clippings in his scrapbook before they leave. He has duplicate copies of the articles about Tommy and pastes those in first.

League of Nations formed.
Hotel Pennsylvania, the world's largest, opens in Manhattan.
The Battle of George Square in Glasgow, Scotland, takes place, troops rallied against protesters in fear of a Bolshevik uprising.
Cy Denneny of the Ottawa Senators scores a record 52 goals.
Fascist Party is formed by Italian dictator, Benito Mussolini.
British Parliament enacts 48-hour work week with minimum wages.
First parachute jump by Les Irvin of the US Army Air Corps takes place.
Pacifist and Spiritual Leader Mahatma Gandhi announces resistance to Rowlatt Act.
1919 Stanley Cup is not awarded due to flu epidemic.
In Canada, New Brunswick and Yukon women are allowed to vote.

*

It's two days before Maria comes out of the cabin. From the moment the *SS France* left the calmness of Halifax Harbour and hit rougher water, she rushed to the nearest lady's room and vomited. A severe weakness overtook her and Dominic had to assist her to their cabin, where she's remained either lying down or sitting for the last 48 hours, drinking only water and sometimes black tea. The ship has been sailing in calm seas since yesterday afternoon. Dominic has remained by her side since they left except for brief moments when he had to eat or just get some fresh air, but he never went far or for long. With tremendous relief he finds her this morning well enough to get cleaned up and dressed. She complains that she is starving.

From their room in first class, they leave together shortly before 8 a.m. Breakfast for some in the dining room is a dressy event as are all meals in first class. Many women wear hats. Maria is nonchalant with her appearance and yet the simple dress she chose, a light yellow that flows to her ankles, has a wide yoke and loose fitting, three-quarter sleeves. The waist is cinched in black silk. Pale green embroidery decorates the waist and the bottom of the skirt. Tan shoes with a heel make her as tall as Dominic. Her head is unadorned and a longish bob is the latest in style. Dominic has her hand on his arm and marvels at how beautiful she is. He is so proud to take her to meet his family.

"You are looking especially lovely today, Maria."

"*Bien merci*, Dominic."

Gripping his arm tighter, she looks at her handsome husband. She loves the thin moustache, the dark romantic eyes. He looks so slim in his beige trousers and cotton shirt. At least this one is black and not the common blue he always wants to wear. She bought him several other colors and he's taken to the white and black. He dislikes shopping for clothing, so Maria dresses him up. She loves it.

It's her first visit to the dining room and she is astonished at the fabulous decor.

"Oh goodness, Dominic, look how beautiful it is in here. No wonder they nicknamed it the *Versailles of the Atlantic*. I've read that the design is inspired by the palace of the same name close to Paris. After we eat, I'd like to go on deck, Dominic, and get some of that gorgeous sun I see. But now let's get a seat by the window."

Dominic leads her to a side table where the window opens to the south. White curtains are tied back and the sparkle from the sun reflecting off the water is almost blinding when looked at directly. They order their food and as they eat, they chat between bites. Dominic has read up on the ship and explains some of her history.

"During the war, she was commissioned by the French Navy and used for troop transport before she became a hospital ship with as many as 2,000 wounded aboard at times. Painted all white with the red cross on it, she was renamed *France IV*. Imagine this beauty being used for a hospital? Her military career was interrupted when there was a boiler explosion in the engine room and nine crew members were killed. The repairs were extensive. Her name was changed back to *France* and now she plies the seas as the beautiful liner she was meant to be."

Maria is nodding between bites as Dominic talks.

"She's fast too, with only the *Mauritania* being faster – and the *Lusitania* until it was sunk by the Germans. One of the last four stackers like the *Titanic*."

With a perplexed look Maria stops chewing.

"What do you mean, four stackers?"

"You know, the funnels that the smoke from the engines escape from."

"When we left, there was only smoke coming from three of them."

"Yes, well the builders felt that the public associate the four funnels with speed, safety and luxury."

Dabbing at her lips with a white linen napkin, she agrees.

"Well, it's certainly luxurious for sure and these eggs with the sauce are delicious."

"Aye, and it's said this ship has the best food. We can thank the French for that, right?"

She answers with a smile. They're soon finished their meal and after, Dominic escorts Maria to the walkway along the first-class section of the ship. People are about, some lying on wooden deck chairs, many leaning on the gunwales watching the ocean, some strolling about greeting people. The waters are calm and the ship sails at full speed. Maria and Dominic move to the railing by one of the lifeboats that is secured to the davits and covered with a tarp.

They talk about the store and leaving Denise in charge. Maria asks about Dominic's family again and what to expect, especially when they hear about Tommy. They talk about moving to Highfield Street when they return in three weeks, and what they want to do with the house in Cocagne. Before they retire to their cabin, Maria asks again when they will arrive in Liverpool.

"On Friday, June 6, if sailing stays smooth and we don't encounter any bad weather to slow us down."

Maria frowns at the mention of bad weather.

"Or make me sick again."

Maria gains her "sea legs" and has no sickness for the remainder of the trip. The days pass with mostly sunshine, interrupted by the odd cloud that sometimes floats by, as if lost. Except Tuesday when they bunch up and burst. The rain falls and falls hard. Not mere drops but waves from a gray sky that wants to punish the ship. It lasts all day. Dominic and Maria remain in their room. After breakfast, Maria shows her lover new ways to give each other pleasure, their lovemaking both wistful and sultry.

Dominic teaches her how to play solitaire.

Another day finds them stretched out on wooden lounge chairs, Maria with her notes from the store and things she wants to discuss about the future. Dominic with his sketch pad and pencils. They dine in splendor; the food so delicious Maria keeps exclaiming she'll never get off the ship. Dominic always asking for a second helping.

Donning good dungarees and his favorite blue cotton shirt, he mingles with the folks in steerage, hangs out where they gather, meets blacksmiths, farmers, fishmongers, miners, seamstresses, maids, and an *au pair*. Maria goes with him to listen to three Irishmen play their music one night in the cafeteria. There are many drunk people.

The next evening, they attend a ball and meet the captain of the ship. They make many new friends, exchanging addresses. Dominic learns how to play eight ball and convinces his wife that the new house must have a place for a billiards table. Nothing prepares them for the first sight of land, Dominic emotional at the return to his homeland, Maria in awe of a place she's never been.

Sailing into Liverpool harbour on Friday afternoon, the ship enters the lock system on the River Mersey. Steam engines bellow, white liners lie at berth, cranes loom in the air, smoke and chaos mix with stevedores, passengers, and workers roaming the docks. Hooting, hammering, the noise of the horses and men. The smell of the water and the rusting steel, the stench of animals, greet all. Evidence of the bombing from the German Zeppelins during the war still remains, with men rebuilding, craters being filled and ruined buildings demolished. Activity everywhere.

After several hours, Dominic and Maria are settled at a hotel, not the most luxurious but in the center of the city and a close walk to everything. Early tomorrow morning the train will take them to Glasgow. They'll arrive in time for supper and he wants to take Maria to Carmichael's for some haggis and tatties. Since it's a Saturday, the folks they wish to visit will likely be there for their usual weekend get-together. Before they departed, Dominic sent a telegram to Mary and Pascal that they would be arriving around June 8 but before he goes to see his family, he wants to see Adairia, Tubbs, the Carmichaels and the rest of Duff's friends. From there he plans on hiring transport to Kilwinning. He's anxious to show off his bride and to see everyone again. Crawling between the sheets, Maria s thinking the same as him.

"I can't wait to meet your friends, the family and your uncle's friends. Oh Dominic, I'm so excited."

Dominic is buttoning his pajama top when he looks down where she's lying. Faint dimples express her delight with the biggest smile.

"Aye, me too. It's been four years since I've left. The only one I saw was Tommy..."

A moment of quiet follows the remembrance. Maria understands that he dreads telling his family, hopes to lift his spirits.

"That's okay Dominic. I know what you're thinking, but it's important for them to know. It's really been too long."

Realizing it will be over soon, he grins and nods.

"Aye, you're right. I should've sent word, but it seemed so cold to send it in a letter or telegram. Better this way, I can answer all their questions. Enough of that, we're here to have fun, right?"

Lifting the covers to tempt him in, she moves closer to his side of the bed.

"*Oui, c'est vrai.* Now get in here and cuddle me. No fooling around, we have to get up early to catch a train."

Dousing the light, Dominic jumps in. The cuddling comes later.

*

The hansom sits at the end of the street, where Dominic has asked the driver to wait for them. The walk to the empty lot where Duff's house once stood is solemn, every step prompting a memory from his life with Duff...The man tottering from too much drink when he first met him. Learning his trade. Hiding Ivan. Duff waiting up on the porch for him. The fire.

Maria holds his hand. She sees sadness has taken the shine from his eyes; his face is long in sorrow. She wonders what he is thinking.

Dominic halts in front of an empty lot; wild flowers have taken over, waves of reds blues and so many yellows. Tall grasses, heavy at the top with seed, add a healthy dose of green. In the back is the tiny shed the firefighters were able to save. The white paint is curled, pieces of shingles have fallen off from neglect. Vines have overtaken the back section, offering a quaint view as a backdrop to the field of many hues.

The fence that was between Miss Abigale's house and Duff's place is gone, replaced with a simple rail fence, waist high, and a gate halfway back. The house next door hasn't changed. Flowers growing around make it look like someone lives there.

Dominic tries on a smile, a little forced, when he remembers. He misses Duff more than ever standing here, but he doesn't want to ruin their time together. Unable to stop the flow of memories, he envisions his uncle: shirt askew among his suspenders, beard and hair damp from exertion, tearing himself from the firefighters' grip. Pearl in the upstairs window, pawing at the glass, smoke billowing out from shattered windows in the back of the house. Duff fleeing the men's grip, running to save his precious companion.

"The house I lived in with Duff was on this lot, over to the left. If you look closely, you can see the stone walkway that led to the small porch. I remember so vividly, the first time I faced that door. My mother was bringing me to live with my uncle Duff, I hardly knew him. It changed my life, Maria, I loved the man. He was so good to me."

Maria steps closer and grasps his arm, knowing he needs to do this, to let go of this part of his past.

"I'm sure he felt the same way about you, Dominic. It changed his life too from what you told me. He did it for you and now you have all the good memories. Remember those."

"Aye, that's the truth Maria. I need to focus on those memories and there are many good ones with Duff. Just give me a few more moments here and we'll head off to Carmichaels. You must be hungry?"

"*Ah oui*, I haven't eaten since those cookies from our neighbour on the train. I'm not sure if I want to try the haggis after you told me what it is."

Maria's questioning look causes Dominic to laugh, breaking the spell of melancholy. Maria is uncertain of why he is laughing and only smiles. He hugs her.

"It's a lot tastier than it sounds. I'm sure you'll like it. At least it's not as ugly as a *poutine*."

She laughs gently with her head next to his. Returning his hug earnestly, she kisses him on the cheek before stepping back.

"All right, if you say so. Now go take a look around and I'll wait here. Then we'll go eat."

With a nod he steps into the tall grass towards the forgotten stone walkway.

CHAPTER 4

A ballad of hard times and lost love fills the air at Carmichaels when they enter. A wee lass, no more that twelve or so, is singing on the small stage, accompanied by an older lad of possibly fifteen playing the accordion. A few couples are dancing closely by the bar. It's not really a dance floor, but people make room between the long bar on the right and the tables and booths on the left. The place is full. Dominic holds Maria closely when they pause inside the door.

He sees familiar faces in the booth at the back where they've always gathered. Oddly enough, Adairia is nestling up to Tubbs as they share something amusing. When the song ends and amidst the loud applause, he takes Maria's hand to guide her through the crowd, his elation is peaking. He hasn't told them he was coming.

Before they turn into where the booths are, one of the servers come out of the kitchen bearing two steaming platters of the Saturday night specials. It's Gloria. She almost runs into him and pulls up short, balancing the two plates. Looking up to see who is blocking her path and remembering to be nice, she puts on her best smile. Recognizing her first boyfriend, she drops the platters and with hands to her mouth, she screams. The crowd around her goes quiet and all attention is on them.

Dominic can't believe his eyes, she's a beautiful woman; he's speechless. Maria is looking at the vegetables on her new shoes. In seconds the group in the back recognizes Dominic and there are more shrieks from the women and hearty hellos from the men. They all push through the bewildered patrons. Gloria beats them all to it and hugs him tightly.

"I'm so happy to see you again, Dom."

"Aye, me as well Gloria. Sorry about surprising you like that."

Gloria remembers the dropped plates. She takes his hand and gives it a squeeze.

"Aye, I'd better get more and clean this up. Here comes the gang; we'll chat soon."

Everyone is talking at once. Adairia is elbowing to be the next to embrace her favorite student, Tubbs right behind her. Maria steps back, overwhelmed at the warm greetings. The young performers can feel the mood of the crowd and play a Scottish jig. A few get up to dance, the music not too loud. All three sisters are working tonight. Shirley, Carol and June are anxious to see Dominic but clean up the dropped mess, wipe the hem of a few dresses, the cuffs of a few trousers and Maria's shiny shoes, not knowing yet who she is. Other folks go back to their meals or stories and Gloria finally makes it to the right table with no surprises. From behind the bar watching the reunion, Mr. Carmichael thinks of his full till.

Adairia holds him tight for many seconds and he remembers the security he felt when she comforted him in his loneliness for Kilwinning.

"It's such a wonderful surprise to see you, Dominic. I love the moustache, what a handsome gentleman you are."

"Thank you, Adairia. You're looking splendid as well. I've missed you so.

"Aw that's nice, Dominic. It hasn't been the same since we lost both you and Duff."

They both go quiet, but only for a few seconds as Adairia doesn't want to spoil the fun.

"Step up here, Tubbs, and say hello to our prodigal son."

Tubbs has always liked Dominic and offers his hand, ever too shy to offer a hug, but Dominic doesn't accept that and embraces the older man, much to the party's delight at seeing Tubbs blush.

"Ah lad, it's jolly good to see you. Have you come back looking for a job? Although you don't be looking too needy."

Jackie Boy and Esmeralda get their hellos in, as do the Carmichael sisters. Adairia breaks up the amusement of the last few minutes when she notices Maria standing aside watching with glee. She interrupts the clatter.

"Dominic, have you forgotten this lovely lass that is watching us? Shouldn't you be introducing us?"

"Aye, aye, thank you, Adairia."

Turning to his wife he apologizes.

"Sorry, my dear."

Taking her hand, he turns to the cluster of friends.

"Ladies and gentlemen, I'd like you to meet Mrs. Maria Alexander, my wife."

The ladies gush over her smart skirt and pink blouse, adoring the side ribbons rather than a hat. The men cheer and whistle. Everyone's welcome is warm and heartfelt. When Shirley shoos them all back to the booth, they've already responded to her charm and made her one of their own. Haggis and tatties appear and Maria doesn't like what see sees but with everyone digging in and exclaiming how delicious it is, she has no choice but to taste it... The few across from her are watching with amused smiles. Maria tentatively nibbles a small bite. A few chews later when the flavors hit her, she offers a closed mouth smile and a murmur of goodness. Those checking her response nod their heads as if to say I-told-ye-so. They laugh and carry on with their meal.

Dominic tries to answer everyone's comments without his mouth full. They all want to know about Maria... how they met, the wedding and so on. The men tease with their off-color wedding jokes, the women blushing or giggling behind hankies. Toasts and drinks appear throughout the evening. The musicians are taking requests – mostly ballads later at night. They've been playing for three hours and don't seem to be losing speed. Many diners left after they ate but the place is still three quarters full, half of them close to drunk, several tottering now and soon to be asked to leave.

Questions and answers fly back and forth, laughter abounds, the night passes much too fast. Maria is accorded her first tipsy moment, unfamiliar with the strength of the warm stout. When she dozes off on Dominic's shoulder and doesn't respond to a question from Esmeralda, everyone oohs and says how sweet. Dominic adjusts his shoulder to tuck her chin in.

"I suppose we should be heading to our room at the Fitzgerald's Inn."

Now Fitzgerald's is not a cheap place to stay. Dominic said it matter of factually, not to brag. They all know that. Adairia is nothing but pleased, knowing how Duff would feel about him. They've been avoiding the subject all night. Tears make her vision blurry. She raises her mug.

"Duff would be proud of you, Dominic. We all are."

The last toast makes Dominic somber once more. Each person is filled with their own special memories of the bearded friend – that one that always pops up when they think of Duff. He was always making them laugh and out-drinking them all. A gentleman as well. The night ends with each sharing a joke in fond memory. Adairia and Dominic escort a tired Maria to the door where they deposit her on the nearest chair. A hansom is called from Carmichael's new phone. They are told they must wait fifteen minutes. Adairia takes Dominic aside, where they can talk undisturbed. Adairia wears her serious frown.

"Dominic, you remember how fond I was… and still am… of your uncle?"

"No doubt, Adairia. I always felt that about you too. I know my uncle loved you."

"I always felt that. Duff was so kind and more than once asked me to marry him, you know?"

With a troubled brow, Dominic wonders where this conversation is going.

"No, I didn't know that, but then why would I? It's not my business. Now that you bring it up, why didn't you say yes?"

Adairia stares off for a moment, a wry smile on her face.

"We'd both been on our own for so long, I never felt it was necessary to move in with someone else, even Duff. Sometimes we argued about it, but it was never a real issue. I knew he liked his time alone as well. With you it was different. I teased him he only wanted to marry me because we would split the expenses, and you remember how Duff could cut a coin in half to save money."

She says this with a soft laugh. Dominic grins when he thinks of Duff and agrees with her.

"Well, that's true. So why did you bring this up Adairia?"

She reaches over to take Dominic's hand in hers and looks him in the eyes.

"Tubbs and I are seeing each other."

Raised brows express his surprise. That was not what he was expecting.

"You and Tubbs?"

"You sound surprised."

"Well, yes. It's just that Tubbs is always so shy about expressing his feelings. Never thought he'd ask any lady out. He's been by himself so long I don't ever remember him with anyone else. I'm surprised he got around to asking you."

This causes both to chuckle.

"I must say, I was surprised. He told me he didn't want to disrespect Duff's memory. The most astonishing thing is that he told me he's always been in love with me and no one else would do. He was satisfied at being my friend. He really is a lovely man and I hope you don't mind, Dominic."

"Mind? Goodness, Adairia, it's been four years since Duff died, and Tubbs is a good man, you couldn't do better. In fact, I'm quite happy for both of you."

Adairia is overcome with pleasure and wraps her arms around Dominic. The hug is interrupted by a stranger sticking his head in the door asking if anyone is expecting a ride. Dominic breaks away from Adairia and gestures to the man to wait one moment.

"I'm very pleased, Adairia, and I wish you both the best."

Adairia helps Dominic get Maria up from her seat, and as they head out, Dominic looks over at Tubbs and his friends. They're all chatting away except for Tubbs, who is concentrating on the group at the door. Dominic waves at him with his biggest smile. Tubbs breaks out in a huge grin, knowing that Adairia has told the news to Dominic. He'd been nervous that Dom might be upset. Feeling tremendous relief, he orders another mug of beer.

Dominic bids Adairia goodnight and promises to meet them all here tomorrow morning for breakfast at nine to say goodbye before he and Maria leave for Kilwinning on the new bus service.

CHAPTER 5

It's mid-afternoon when the bus drops several of its passengers at the depot in Kilwinning. A soft breeze from the north eliminates the smelly exhaust from the running engine. The war changed nothing in the small burg. Lacking any potential targets, it was insignificant to the German bombers. The driver has to help Dominic with the trunk. In Mary's last letter, she was excited about their new phone and Dominic uses the one in the office at the depot to call her and let her know they have arrived. She assures him that his drive wouldn't be long. Dominic and Maria are waiting on a bench outside enjoying the weather. The sun comes and goes from a gaggle of clouds and even with the northern current, the day is warm. Maria removes her light cardigan and folds it on her lap. Dominic rolls up the sleeves of his shirt and sits beside her.

"Oh, Dominic, what a nice little town. I love all the stone structures and the …"

A horn blast from an approaching vehicle disturbs the conversation as well as the horses pulling traps or wagons that are not yet comfortable with automobiles. There were many more autos than Dominic expected. The approaching vehicle reminds him of his Ford with the open windows and black cloth roof. As it nears, he recognizes Pascal and stands with an enthusiastic wave. Maria stands beside him and clasps her hands to her chest in surprise. Dominic hears her faint gasp.

"What is it, Maria?"

"I recognize that man. He used to work at the corner store in

Cocagne when I was younger. Sometimes I would go with my father to deliver eggs, and we always stopped there for a treat. I had the hugest crush on him."

"Now I have some competition? Well that's Pascal, my sister Mary's husband, so no more crushes."

Pascal pulls up by the depot, stopping his vehicle next to the two traps tied up by the edge of the lot and wonders what Dominic and the pretty lady beside him are laughing about. Jumping from the driver's seat, he rushes over to shake Dominic's hand. Most of the French accent is gone and some of the words are turning Scottish.

"Ah, Dominic, how wonderful to see you again."

"Aye, you as well, Pascal."

He turns to Maria, who is staring at Pascal with the widest smile.

"Pascal, this is my wife, Maria. Perhaps she's not a stranger, says she remembers you from when you were both younger and you were working at the general store."

Pascal doffs his hat at her and with a playful grin, he shakes her hand.

"Are you and your father still selling eggs, Maria?"

They all laugh at the remembrance.

"No Pascal, not any longer. My Dad sold his chickens when he retired. They were always more of a hobby than a money maker. My goodness, how strange to see you here after all this time."

"It is indeed. I never knew your name, but I remember how you loved the licorice."

After the pleasantries, Dominic and Pascal load the trunk in the back seat. Dominic turns to his brother-in-law.

"Were you able to reserve us a room at the Highland Inn?"

"*Ah oui.* Mary was a bit tiffed that you wouldn't stay with us but what you said in your letter made sense, better this way."

"Aye, indeed, there's not much room left at the house. Ivan is here until the wedding and Paul will be back from Saltcoats, and who knows who else might be coming."

"That's true. Jump in Dominic and we'll get you to the inn and back home, everyone's excited to see you both."

Maria sits up front with Pascal and Dominic joins the steamer in the back seat. After they are settled in the room, Maria changes and freshens up. A half hour later they bump along the dirt road out of town. Pascal tells Dominic about the car he purchased after the war, a

1914 Argyll made right here in Scotland, in Alexandria. The ten-minute ride goes quickly as they catch up on events.

When they pull into the yard, a group of excited relatives rush from the house to greet them. Dominic's last memory of his family was when everyone was four years younger and he's not sure of some of them but he immediately pinpoints Lilly. Their shared affection for each other, beyond any other members of the family, has them rushing into each other's arms. Years of missing each other dissolve in the tightness of their grip. He steps back from the loving embrace to admire his younger sister.

"Ah, Lilly, what a beauty you've become."

The mole on her cheek is faint on the fairest skin, a beauty mark of the rarest kind. Long bangs sweep down from longer strands tied in a bun. Her slender face is full of smile. She eyes him up and down.

"Aye and you're a dandy yourself. Not sure if I like that moustache, but it's good to see that twinkle in your eyes again. I've missed you so, Dom."

"Aye, me too, Lilly."

He whisper's in her ear.

"Don't tell anyone, but I've missed you the most."

Her giggles are interrupted by a burly young man, square jawed, kind eyes and blondish beard. Lilly turns to Maria, liking her right away. She takes her sister-in-law's arm to introduce her around. Dominic is elated when he recognizes his friend. A bear hug ensues with words of greeting. Ivan's unique speech is Russian-Scottish and Dominic warms to the odd accent.

"How are you, my friend? What took you so long to come home again? How long can you stay?"

"Glad to know you've not changed, Ivan, always full of questions. We're her for a while and I'll have time to answer all of them. But I won't go climbing any buildings with you."

Remembering the incident when their capers led to Dominic breaking his leg, they both agree on that, with Ivan's loud laughter. Mary elbows him out of the way for her own hug, robust with her protruding belly. The glow of coming motherhood shines on her plain face.

"My little brother, how wonderful, wonderful to see you again."

"Aye, Mary, it's been much too long."

With a soft hand he touches her swelling belly.

"Don't know much about babies, but I think this rascal's coming any minute."

"Doctor McDonald says in the next two weeks for sure. Wouldn't it be a treat if he's born while you're home.

Dominic grins.

"He?"

Mary has her hands folded over her tummy, rosy cheeks bobbing.

"Oh, for sure, I've felt that ever since I knew I was pregnant."

Pascal is behind her, nodding his head.

"I think she's going to be right. *A petit garçon*, how lucky we are."

Mary and Pascal turn their attention to Maria and with approving looks. The two women comment on having similar names. Two figures catch Dominic's attention at the back of the group and when he moves to greet them, shyness holds them back. When Dominic left, they were only children, now one is a strapping young man with a brooding look and the other is a curly-haired adolescent with freckled cheeks and a silly grin that reeks of charm.

Sheila remembers Dominic's stories and his teasing and him making her look at books. She moves to give him a hug. She doesn't look like any of the others and has her own pretty countenance. Tall for a twelve-year-old, she is only starting to develop and a rosiness graces her cheeks. Pensive eyes shine up at him.

"Well, Sheila, you're going to be the best-looking Alexander in the bunch. And I brought a new story for you."

"Aw, thank you, Dom. You know how much I love books, because of you. And guess what, I made a B+ in school and I wrote a story about you. It's not very good, but it was so much fun."

Dominic is flushed with good feelings.

"That's good news, I'm so proud of you, Sheila. I expect the story's fine. I hope you'll let me read it."

"Of course, silly. It's for you. I'm giving it to you."

This provokes another hug and he holds her close. Proud of his youngest sister.

Paul wears a self-conscious look, almost like he did something he wasn't supposed to. The spitting image of their older brother Tommy, Dominic is reminded of his morbid task but shucks it off. Paul's a bit standoffish. He doesn't want to be hugged but offers his hand to his brother. Dominic feels the calluses of a man who earns his keep from hard work. The muscular shoulders attest to the same. Shorter and wider like Mary and their grandfather, he's not as tall as the others but is far from finished growing. He's only fourteen. He feels a different respect for Paul.

"Good to see you, big brother. You're looking fit for a business man. It must keep you running."

"Aye that it does, Paul, but look at you. You remind me of our Granda, and I'll bet you're just as strong as he was."

Paul warms to the remark, proud of his physique. Fishing with his cousins in Saltcoats is grueling work: hauling lines, moving gear, working canvas and unloading the day's catch power the developing muscles.

"I don't know about that Dominic. Remember the time one of the logs rolled off his wagon and pinned his helper to the ground. He picked up that log by himself and tossed it aside. It took two men to take it into the yard. I couldn't do that."

Dominic winks at Paul.

"Not yet."

Mary has prepared the evening meal for them and everyone is famished. The table in the kitchen is the same. The stove is new, all shiny with chrome edges. A meal of roast mutton, vegetables and boats of gravy is the best time to reminisce, to discover the events in each other's lives, to get to know Dominic's bride, and she to become accustomed to them, for the sorrows of the war, for the brightness of the days ahead, laughter and silly jokes, the wedding, the new baby and news of life in Canada. It's only after strawberry pie and refilled tea cups that Dominic asks for everyone's attention. A downward frown warns everyone of something dire.

"Our brother Tommy is dead."

The men freeze, the women inhale sharply with covered mouths. Tears from Sheila starts the flood and questions fly. He's decided to hold nothing back from them and delivers the gruesome news. He shares the newspaper clipping he brought with him from Canada. Mary is upset that he didn't let them know, let them mourn then. He defends himself that he couldn't bring himself to say so in a letter or a telegram, he wanted to tell them in person. Tommy's death deserved some respect regardless of his rough past, maybe because of it.

"Wouldn't you rather know this way?"

Feeling a lonesome pang for her errant brother, Mary tries to understand how it might feel.

"We'll have a service for him here, then, at our own church."

Paul guffaws at that.

"Tommy never went to church. When we were carted off by Ma, Tommy stayed in bed. Used to be sassy with her until she left him alone."

Dominic reminds Paul that he was only six when Tommy and William went to live in Newtongate with their Uncle Robert.

"That's a long time ago, and you were just a wee thing Paul."

"Nae, doesn't matter. I remembering getting a cuff from him and told to take me arse somewhere else when Mam would send me to wake him sometimes. Nae, I remember well enough. The church will have nothing to do with Tommy."

Lilly points her finger at Paul, mouth curled in defiance.

"Well you're a fine one to talk, I doubt you even remember what a pew is. Since Mam's been gone, no one's been too anxious to wake you up either."

Paul's wears a half smile, amused by Lilly's candor. He can't argue with her.

"Well you're right. I don't want you to think I don't feel bad that Tommy's gone, but he's been away so long. Every time we heard anything about him, he was usually in trouble or drunk. You folks do as you please. And yes Lilly I know what a pew is."

Lilly waves him to never mind and turns to Mary.

"Shall I speak to Pastor Robinson or would you like to?"

Mary is picking up the empty teacups. Shelia is yawning, tears dried up, head resting on the table. Paul leans against the cupboard, hands in his dungarees. Pascal never met Tommy so is quiet on the cot by the stove, listening. Maria has her clasped hands resting on the table in front of her, watching Dominic, who is standing at the end facing everyone. She is so proud of him, how he assumes the role of head male in the family. They all look at Mary.

"I'll do it," she says. "I planned on talking with him soon anyway about naming the baby. Pascal and I have already decided on Danny but his second name, we want to name him after a saint. Haven't decided on a girl's name yet but same thing goes. I'll ask him right away so Maria and Dominic can come too. Would you like that?"

Dominic catches her gaze and feels guilty. He's not been to church much, even with Maria's coaxing. She and Denise go to mass every Sunday; he goes sometimes.

"Certainly, Mary. Maybe this Sunday coming if that's not too soon, the day after the wedding."

Everyone murmurs in agreement and Dominic nods too. Checking his watch, he pats Pascal on the shoulder.

"Back to the inn, my faithful driver. There's a big tip waiting for you there."

With a good laugh, they go about the ending of the day. Maria thanks Mary for the wonderful meal and helps get Sheila off to bed. Lilly goes to dig out some blankets and makes up a bed for Ivan, who is sleeping on the couch. Paul, Ivan, Pascal and Dominic go out into the yard. Ivan and Paul roll up a cigarette. Mary, hating the smell, won't let them smoke in the house. Pascal goes to get the car ready and turn it around. Dominic has a hand on each man's shoulder watching them roll their cigarettes.

"So, Paul, you're back fishing tomorrow?"

"Aye, I am"

"How are ye planning on going?"

"Going to take the bus, goes right to Saltcoats. Only thing is I won't make the sail tomorrow, be too late, but they know where I am."

Dominic squeezes Ivan's shoulder a little harder and speaks directly to him.

"How about I borrow Pascal's auto and you and I take Paul to Saltcoats? You heard the ladies, they're all going to be as busy as chipmunks finishing up Lilly's dress. Maria is a fine seamstress, so I know she can help. Give us a chance to chat and Paul can show us around."

"Sure, that would be good. What do you say, Paul?"

"Aye, can't work anyway. You two are not such a bad lot. I won't look too terrible in your company."

Paul delivers his sarcasm with a frown and Ivan thinks he's serious. Dominic knows better and Ivan's surprise is as funny as Paul's quip. They share a hearty chuckle when Maria joins them and Pascal has pulled up the car. Everyone bids goodnight and the car bumps along with two lamps lighting the way. Pascal is happy to give Dominic his auto and tells him about the tricky ignition sequence.

CHAPTER 6

The week before the wedding slips by like an afterthought. The trip to Saltcoats bonds the brothers and the soon to be brother-in-law. The men share jokes and catch up on the missed time. Ivan and Paul have not been close, but the trip reveals a young man with ambition and no fear of hard work. Paul sees the glaze in Ivan's eyes when he speaks of Lilly, knowing she will be in good hands. Dominic shares his adventures in Canada and they all toast from a flask that Ivan has brought. Paul only has a sip, not caring much for alcohol. They get to Saltcoats an hour later even though it's not far to the coast. The road is rutted in many places where it rained for two days last week. It's not yet been graded smooth, so the going is slow. Paul shows them the wharf they sail from. Shows them fishing boats similar to his cousin's and swears he's to have one of his own in the future. A two-master that bobs with the tide's movements, commenting that she's for sale. The owner died last month and he only had daughters that are not interested in fishing, nor are any of their husbands.

The rooming house he stays at is an older fishing captain's place, right on a bluff outside of the town with a splendid view of the rock-lined shore and the lapping waters. Driving a way up the coast, they stop at a shallow beach and throw rocks at the water like little boys. They have a late dinner at the hotel and play darts at a pub. Ivan has a few too many brews and waits sluggishly in the car. After assuring Paul that one of them will be back to pick him up Friday night, the men say good day, with Paul stepping forward to give his big brother a firm handshake.

"You're a good man, Dom. I'm glad you're back home. See ya soon."

"Aye that'll be good, Paul. And listen, how much would it cost to have your own boat?"

Paul worries his face.

"Why would you be needing to know that?"

"Well, maybe I could help with a little loan, get you started"

Paul is aglow with possibilities.

"You'd do that for me?"

"Aye, I think you'd be a good investment. From your stories, I can see you love being on the water."

"Aye, you have that right. Don't know how to explain it, but it's a feeling of being alive with the rocking of the boat and the smell of salt and the winds blowing your hair about. It's a tough way to make a living, but I can't think of doing anything else."

"Settled then. See what that floater you showed us would cost and if it needs any repairs. Do you know enough about boats to make the right decision?"

"I know quite a bit, but I'll get our cousin Billy to check it with me. He's been on boats since he was a toddler."

"Good, we'll see you soon."

The men shake hands once more. Paul stares his brother in the eyes, remembering his gentle ways when they were younger but being tough with him when he had to.

"Thanks, Dom."

"You're welcome, Paul."

Every day up to the wedding is a busy time. Caught up with preparations, the cleaning of the house, the decorations, Mary frets about the meal she's trying to organize at the church hall. With her permission, Dominic and Maria offer to host it at the Baylor instead, as a gift to the newlyweds. Lilly is agog at their generosity. Mary insists the party come back to Kilwinning for music and punch. Borrowing the auto once more in the middle of the week, Dominic takes Maria to Saltcoats to meet some of his kin. He packs a lunch and they have a picnic on a grassy knoll overlooking the Firth of Clyde. The weather has been misty for the last day and a half but the sun is bright with no clouds anywhere. Maria chats about the wonderful accents and how difficult it is to understand some folks and jokes about having her own translator.

They visit his Granda's grave and Maria leaves some wild flowers she's gathered in a nearby field. Maria and Pascal spend time together so he can practice his French, joking that there's not much use for it otherwise here in Kilwinning except for the butcher, who is originally from France. On Friday evening the men gather at one of the local pubs, McCleary's Tavern, to toast Ivan on his last day as a bachelor. The women join later and the four musicians on stage play jigs and reels and heart-breaking ballads. Ivan has to be carried to Pascal's auto to get home. Not much of a drinker, the ale went down fast and cold. When Maria and Dominic are getting ready for the wedding Saturday morning, which takes place at ten, she has no pity for his headache from too much ale. It's gone, however, by the time they reach the church.

Lilly is being given away by Dominic, and they wait at the open doors of the Presbyterian Church. She wears a modest wedding dress with a lace petticoat and shimmering silk trim. Lilly's best friend, Agnes Taylor, is the maid of honor. Mary and Sheila are bridesmaids. They are dressed in similar yellow dresses that Agnes' mother made. Each holds a bouquet of white carnations, Lilly's favorite flower. Dominic has a new suit, a light worsted wool in black, a white shirt and an ascot similar to Ivan's and Pascal's. Normally Dominic would've been the best man, but Lilly wanted him to escort her down the aisle. Pascal and Ivan have become good friends, so he has happily agreed to be best man. Paul and one of Ivan's friends from school, Blair Smith, are ushers, wearing similar suits and matching ascots, with yellowish hues to match the ladies.

The church is three quarter's full. Aunts and uncles, some cousins, crowd the right side of the isle for Lilly's family, as well as several neighbours. Ivan's adopted parents, Arthur and Christine Guthrie and their kin are on the left. Several of his friends from school are there also. None of the Pestovs have been invited. Music is provided by the church pianist, Geoffrey Riley, and his daughter sings in a beautiful tenor voice. The ceremony takes place in silence except for the minster's calming words of enduring love, unity for the rest of their lives. When told to kiss the bride, the crowd cheer and applaud. He presents Lilly and Ivan Pestov.

Pascal has the auto decorated and the newlyweds enter the back seat to be driven to the Baylor which is withing walking distance but Pascal wants to parade them around town and has the top down. Lilly and Ivan are waving to the passersby and are soon parked in front of the hotel where everyone meets up. During the meal, Dominic tells family jokes and praises Lilly for her accomplishments at school and for her work as a nurse in training. After the meal, there are several testimonials from relatives and friends, but the most touching is from Arthur Guthrie, who tells of the time Ivan came to live with them. When they adopted him, Ivan asked if he could keep his last name, not because he didn't like Guthrie, but because beyond his lost family, the ancestral Pestovs were once highly decorated soldiers and scholars of the old Russian hierarchy.

"We were so happy to have this young man in our home, never a worry and always so mindful of his manners. We are very proud of you Ivan and wish you and Lilly all the happiness in the world."

After the meal, Lilly and Ivan cut the cake and serve everyone among well wishes and laughter. Dominic hired a photographer who arrives later in the afternoon. He and his assistant set up their equipment in one corner. Pulling up several satin covered chairs — different poses, a family photo – the next hour captures the youth and jubilance of the Alexander family. The reception comes to an end with an invitation for those who want to, to head to the Alexander homestead for music and more fun. Lilly and Ivan have a room at the Baylor, again compliments of Dominic and Maria, where they will rest and freshen up to meet everyone later at Mary and Pascal's home.

Dominic and Maria arrive back at the house earlier than most to find Mary and Aunt Molly buzzing about making sure all is perfect. By seven o'clock the rooms and yard are buzzing with revelry. Many of the older relatives and the Guthrie friends are not present, but thirty or more people mill about. Dusk is approaching and the westward sky blazes in swirls of orange and pink celebration. Children play hide-and-seek in the growing shadows, shrieks and happy voices fill the background. Men stand in groups telling stories, laughing, chugging their ales, sneaking from their pints and a bit of friendly arguing. Ladies mingle in pairs with some hinting to their partners they might want to dance. Mary or Molly offer treats to their guests, the occasional tray of sweets, and traditional *fofar bridie*. Ivan and Lilly stroll about, holding hands, and mingle with all the groups in and out of the house. The chatter stops when from inside comes the first notes of an engaging waltz. Sheila waves at Lilly and Ivan to come in. They are followed by the crowd. Those that can't fit in watch from the door.

The kitchen is quite large. Furniture has been rearranged to accommodate the musicians Mary knows and have agreed to play for a free meal and maybe a pint or two. Violin, guitar and piccolo provide the entertainment. The table has been pushed back by the cupboards; people are in the living room, hallway and on the stairs looking into the kitchen as Lilly and Ivan take the middle of the floor and move to the sway of the melodies. When the song stops, Ivan and Lilly embrace to everyone's glee. The trio break into a Scottish reel. The small open space is soon full of swinging partners and those that can't contain themselves are dancing in the yard.

The gathering ends long after midnight. It's almost two o'clock when Dominic uses Pascal's car to take himself, Maria, Lilly and Ivan back to the Baylor. Tomorrow when they all recover, they agree to meet again after church and a prayer for Tommy, then back to the house to say goodbye to the newlyweds, who leave on the bus for Glasgow and then on to Whiteinch, where they will live with the Guthries until they can afford their own place. They are delaying the honeymoon because Lilly is starting at the hospital in the city as a nurse in training and Ivan returns to work with his adopted uncle who has a masonry business. The future looks bright for the new couple.

CHAPTER 7

Tuesday morning comes with an overcast sky: heavy, mean-looking clouds scurry on the horizon. The air smells like coming rain. Warm gusts follow Dominic up the street as he makes his way to the dealership for extra tanks of petrol for the Argyll. In the back is a valise he purchased an hour ago especially for this unplanned trip. A crumpled message lies on the front seat. It was given to him last evening after he and Maria returned from Mary's house. It reads "Come quickly. Ivan in hospital. Lilly"

Dominic leaves as soon as he can with the borrowed auto. Maria is staying with Mary and Pascal now that Paul is back in Saltcoats. The trip will take him several hours, but it's the fastest way. Worry and speculation burden his brow. Upon arriving, he has to ask for directions to the hospital. Parking the vehicle as close as he can, he rushes in to inquire where Ivan may be. Several ladies occupy a counter to the right. After explaining who he is, the lady with the pencil stuck in her bun points to the stairs.

"Go up to the second floor. There's a desk on the right. He will be not far from there. Just ask one of the nurses."

Upon entering the room, he sees Arthur and Gertrude and Lilly gathered around a bed in the back left – one of four in the ward. A curtain is partially drawn and he can't see Ivan. Ashen- faced, he approaches them. When Lilly notices him, she drops Ivan's hand and hastens to her brother's side.

"Thank you for coming, Dominic. It's so terrible."

At the foot of the bed, Arthur moves around by his wife and

Dominic sees his friend but barely recognizes him. The skin around both eyes is blue and pasty yellow. On the edge of sleep from the medication he's been given, he tries to focus and Dominic can see that one pupil is filled with blood and stares out like a red beacon. The nose is bandaged. The mouth is cut upon the lips and stitched in two places. Abrasions and bruises line the right swollen jaw and snake around the neck. Ivan is a terrible sight as he succumbs to the oblivion of drug-induced sleep.

Gertrude dabs at her nose with her hankie, sniffling and holding Ivan's hand. Lilly has her head on Dominic's shoulder and sobs, unable to speak. Arthur answers Dominic's questioning gaze.

"They beat him up, Dominic, those bastardly brothers of his. They beat him bad. Some broken ribs and bruises all over his body."

Dominic is stunned and full of pity when he sees the tears forming in Arthur's eyes.

"But why? They've been out of his life for years. I remember they weren't too pleased when their mother signed the papers, making sure everybody knew she was happy to be rid of him. They were warned to stay out of his life."

Arthur wipes an errant tear away with the cuff of his shirt before continuing.

"They nabbed him as he was walking home from work last night. Best he could tell us is that they deal in stolen goods and need his help. They told him there's no one else they can trust and he had no choice in the matter, he is still a Pestov. When he refused, they beat him as a warning and said they would be back, only next time it would be his new wife."

Lilly grips Dominic's arm tighter and he can feel her trembling.

"Did anyone tell the police?"

"It was a constable that found him lying in a gutter on Hathaway Court in the slums. They thought he was drunk. They sent him here when they saw what he was like. He was able to tell them who he was and about us and Lilly. Not sure what they're doing now. Said they'd send someone to talk to him, but no one came by today."

Dominic is shaking his head. Anger swells in him and he thinks of the brothers, known to him only by their names. He visualizes two ugly brutes with deep voices and no conscience.

Lilly looks up at him with glazed eyes.

"What are we going to do, Dominic? They might do this again if the police don't catch them."

He's already forming a plan in his head, thinking it might be irrational, but it might be the only immediate solution.

"How much longer must he remain here?"

Lilly responds like the nurse she is.

"The doctor wants to watch for a possible concussion even though he was conscious when they found him. His nose is broken, so they need to fix that. Maybe two or three days."

Dominic is quick to make decisions.

"Arthur and Gertrude, can you watch over them for a few days?"

They both agree readily.

"Of course, my brother Lewis says he'll help out too. Keep an eye on things. And of course, we'll take good care of your sister."

"Why, Dominic? What are you up to?" asks Lilly.

"Give me a couple of days. I'll return on Thursday and we'll talk about it."

"Can't we talk about it now, Dominic? I'm scared."

"Trust me, Lilly. Let me get the facts straight, and then we'll talk."

Lilly leans into him and nods her head. The spend the next several hours standing and sitting by the bed. Ivan sweeps in and out of his stupor. Otherwise they sit mainly in silence.

Dominic meets with Maria that evening to discuss his idea. She welcomes the solution and her calculating mind is already planning ideas for its execution because they only have six days before they sail back to Canada. The next morning they meet with government officials and gather the necessary paperwork and list of instructions. She goes with him this time to deliver the news. They meet everyone at the Guthries after Dominic discoverers that Ivan went home Thursday morning. Gertrude has made a beef stew and they are just sitting down to dinner when Dominic and Maria arrive. Ivan is talking and watches his side when he shakes Dominic's hand. The bluish tint around otherwise happy eyes is fading as are the bruises on his face and neck. Sitting around the table, Dominic offers his thoughts.

"Lilly and Ivan, we'd like you to come back to Canada with us."

The thought is totally unexpected and everyone pauses at the idea. Gertrude feels the pang of distance and Arthur does too, but they look to Ivan's bandaged and bruised face and want Lilly and their son to be safe from the Russians. Ivan sits at the end of the table, spoon paused in midair. Lilly is the first to form a smile.

"Could I continue my nursing there?"

It's Maria that answers.

"For sure Lilly. My cousin Paulette is a nurse and she always complains of not enough help. There are still casualties of the war that need medical help. I'm sure you could."

"What about Ivan?"

Now Dominic replies.

"One of my very good clients is the Gould family and they own a masonry company in Moncton and are very well thought of. I'm sure they could use an intelligent apprentice and if not, the railway yards are busy, a large distribution center for mail orders is being built in Moncton, many jobs for a good worker."

Lilly looks at Ivan with teasing smile.

"Don't know about the intelligent part."

That provokes a chuckle and Ivan is holding his side, because it hurts when he laughs. His elation is profound – away from his criminal brothers, a safe place for Lilly, near his best friend. He sees the half smiles on his adopted parents' faces and can sense their discomfort at the parting. They remain quiet because they know it's the best way. He'll miss them also but Dominic makes it seem like an adventure. If Lilly wants to go, he'll offer no resistance.

Emigrating to Canada dominates the conversation for the next hour and a half, as they drank a couple pots of tea. Dominic and Arthur both suggest they can help when Lilly points out their lack of funds. With everyone in agreement, the planning begins. The remaining five days have them occupied. A trunk for clothing – what to bring and what not to. Papers to sign and submit at the government offices in Glasgow. Lilly cancels her training and Ivan informs his employer. Purchasing tickets for the sailing on Wednesday; leaving by train on Tuesday.

Maria and Lilly spend Saturday in Glasgow shopping, armed with lists for basics that they'll need. Plus new boots for Ivan, undergarments and a new shirt or two. Maria is enchanted by her sister-in-law, who has the same easy manner as Dominic, the same stubborn determination, the same questioning eyes, and an easy laugh. It's not difficult to like her. After much pleading, Lilly accepts a gift of three new outfits for the sailing. It takes them two hours.

On the same day, Dominic, Paul and Pascal pay a visit to the Pestov brothers. They aren't hard to find with Ivan's directions. The three men wear old clothes, Dominic borrowing a pair of Pascal's coveralls. When they get to Ibrox, Dominic tells Tubbs what they're up to and he wholeheartedly gets Pepper out of the stable and hooked to the old wagon. Catching the brothers alone is a bit more difficult. The tenements in the Gorbals is a depressing area. Neglected buildings; grassless three-foot lawns; litter; leaning fences; screaming, dirty children running about; clothes hanging from the windows; and with the dry dirt on the street, there's a coat of dust most everywhere. No cars come here, only horse-drawn vehicles. The road is rutted and smeared with droppings. A dreadful smell of human waste lingers.

They spy the brothers at a shed leaning from the back of the building. Another man and a boy of about twelve are going through a wooden bin of odds and ends. An older version of Ivan is talking to the stranger in what must be Russian. The other man standing in the doorway has similar features but darker hair. That would be Anton. The one in the yard is Viktor.

In Dominic's pocket is one of his rings, which he will claim he stole.

A section of the fence has been taken down and opens to a cluttered yard. A pile of rough lumber, car lamps, tires and wheels and other castoffs; everything is for sale or trade. The better items are stored in the shed, the stolen items are not around long enough to need a place to rest.

Paul walks over by the man and boy shuffling through the opposite end of the bin, where there are a few tools. Viktor is on the other side of the man at the end of the bin. Pascal stands at the bottom of the ramp close to Viktor, checking the pile of lumber. Dominic, holding out an open hand with the ring in his palm, approaches the older brother.

"Found a gent's ring down the road. Heard you buy this kind of thing."

Anton is not as tall as Dominic, wider in the shoulders. He doesn't know this man. The hand is too soft for a thief. He's cautious when he steps forward to bend and look closer, keeping the bearer in his peripheral vision. A step-cut emerald is complemented by a linear row of brilliant-cut diamonds. The ring has recently been polished, making the gold wink in the sunlight. Dominic knows it's worth to be over thirty-five quid. Anton also knows what it is worth and raises his eyebrows. He knows where he can sell this quick. The possibility of a huge profit eases his guard.

"Can I have a closer look at it?"

Dominic is staring at him with hate when an image of Ivan in the hospital bed flashes in his mind. He's readying himself as the man approaches, staring at the glittering gem. One foot back for balance. Reach out with the ring in his left. Form a fist with his right and bring it from his hip when Anton touches the ring, when he is off guard.

Dominic steps closer with all his weight moving forward. He hits Anton right under the rib cage, a balled fist of fury to the center of the solar plexus. The solar plexus is a nerve bundle. When the blow is sufficient, the nerves fire, sending impulses to nearby organs, especially the diaphragm, causing it to spasm. Breathing is a bit difficult. Anton doubles up from the pain and when he does Dominic is braced, already swinging upward and clips the doomed man in the nose. Everyone hears it crunch. The brain bangs around like loose screws in a tin. Anton is already unconscious when he hits the floor, lucky for him. He falls face down. On his nose.

Viktor is stunned, mouth agape, eyeballs bulging, frozen to the spot. He's never seen anyone taken out that fast, let alone Anton, who never loses a fight. Anger prompts him to rush the man on the platform when he's stopped in his tracks from behind by a bear hug by Paul. Viktor's arms are pinned to his side and his chest starts to hurt. He's gasping, having a hard time to breathe, when a dark-haired man yells out.

"This is for Ivan, you bastards!"

A flat piece of board smacks the side of Viktor's head. He won't remember anything for a few days, let alone in ten minutes when he comes to. The ear will never be the same. The stranger and the boy are making dust. Dominic, Paul and Pascal rush to the wagon and depart before anyone shows up. When they are ten minutes out the Gorbals, their anger has dispersed, turning into exhilaration, making them laugh at their folly.

"That nose is going to be sore for a few weeks, I bet." says Paul.

"I hope that ear it looks like…" Pascal is searching for the right word in English, he's thinking *epinard*. "…spinach, yes like spinach."

After Dominic stops laughing, he rubs his middle knuckle, which has been skinned from the impact. For a moment his countenance is serious.

"Not sure what I'm going to tell Maria about my hand."

Agreeing the wives would be upset with their caper, it's decided they'll blame the grazed knuckle on the Argyll. The battery failed and he had to use the crank. Upon arrival in Kilwinning, they take an oath not to talk about this again. When they dock in Halifax on June 30, it will only be a scar.

The day before they leave, Mary delivers an eight-pound, four-ounce baby boy they call Daniel after their father, which also happens to be Dominic's middle name, and Michael for a saint.

CHAPTER 8

August passes like a whirlwind. Piled up custom work has Dominic regretfully at his desk while Maria does the heavy lifting of getting Ivan and Lilly settled and the house packed. Emma has a welcoming party for the newlyweds so they can meet the circle of friends. She introduces them to poutine, Acadian music and eastern hospitality. Rosie finds the couple a house to rent on Gordon Street, luckily with a few pieces of furniture left behind by the previous owner. Lilly is accepted at the Moncton Hospital on King Street, where she will finish her training. When Ivan meets one of the older Goulds at their masonry company, he impresses them with his skills and is hired on the spot to work on the new Eaton Distribution Center slated for opening in 1920. Lilly and Scarlet are immediate friends and when Lilly visits the store, Scarlet dashes for her attention, and Lilly always brings a treat for her. Everyone adores Lilly, playfully teasing her about her accent when she tries to speak French. Ivan claims he's never met such a lively and friendlier bunch.

Denise has a knack for managing the store, and sales actually increased during the month that Dominic and Maria were away. She's only ordered replacement items as directed, once saving them over $2 on a shipping charge she talked the rep out of. She suggests they add Bulova watches to their wares, as well as a collection of clocks. To show her how much they trust her, they tell her to go ahead, giving her a spending limit.

Nick is honing his skills as a goldsmith. Dominic teaches him to set stones. At the end of August, a customer brings in her own ruby from a trip overseas with a simple design idea and Dominic urges Nick to give it a try. Nick has no artistic talent but can follow a plan or picture, so Dominic still has to sketch the custom work.

Christine is working full time at the store and mourns for Tommy still.

On August 31, Nick's uncle has the wagon and team of horses in front of the house that Dominic and Maria are saying goodbye to. It's loaded as full as possible, with the table legs sticking up on the top of the load. These are all the possessions from the house; they did the barn yesterday. Dominic has a pang of melancholy as he closes the door and locks it for the last time. He scans his memory for important events and the one that pleases him the most is when Maria came looking for work after the barn burned and how it changed their lives. With glossy eyes, he puts the key in an envelope and seals it. Turning to Maria, who also has a tear to shed, they embrace. He whispers in her ear.

"Let's drop this key off and go to our new home, Maria."

The house on Highfield Street is two storeys at the very top of the street, above Mountain Road. But the way the city is growing, it won't be the last house on the street for long. The design is a newer style, with a mansard roof and dormers over the windows. The lower portion is brick and painted white. There are four rooms upstairs and a full bathroom. Only three of the rooms will have beds; the other is a sewing room for Maria. Downstairs is a modern kitchen, dining room, living room and a great room where the radio and phonograph are, and where Dominic has a pool table installed. It has a ramp in the back leading to the porch and wide doors for his friend Nick.

They spend the first weekend in September setting up their furniture, and Maria makes a list of the items they need to shop for. A carriage house has been built in the back with room for the car and a studio where Dominic can sketch. He can heat it in the wintertime. In total, he has spent almost $1,200 on the new house and he expects Maria will spend another hundred on furniture and the decorating she loves so much. He expects to spend another $800 on the place in the country. The rest of the proceeds from the sale to CNR is tucked in his personal account at the bank.

The second weekend is a housewarming party. Even though they aren't completely settled, Maria wants to share her new home with family and friends. The women all bring a dish of food, flasks are tucked in men's pockets, hugs abound. Lilly, Ivan and Denise were there all afternoon helping sort things out, hanging up photos and paintings, arranging the new curtains in the living room. The woodwork and wainscoting are a light stain and polished to a bright gleam. Lilly and Ivan have met most of the guests before except for the Dicksons and Maria's brothers Andre and Robert. Before the night is over, Andre gets up the courage to ask Denise to go to the movies with him at the Grand Opera House and she is afloat with happiness as she plans their first date.

Everyone gets a tour and the ladies all fawn over the warm colors Maria has chosen and how inviting each room looks. The men do a quick peek and head for the great room, where the men congregate and challenge each other at the pool table. Some slip out to the carriage house to smoke and empty the flasks. It's such a beautiful evening that the musicians are set up in the open doors of the carriage house and people swing on the back porch. Ivan learns to tap dance and everyone teases him in good fun. The party lasts until midnight and only a few have to stagger home.

They spend the third weekend of the month taking Lilly and Ivan to Hopewell Cape to see the Rocks. It's Dominic's first time as well. Maria packs a picnic basket and after they've walked on the ocean floor gaping at the huge rock formations chiseled away by the high tides, they find a secluded spot on the beach and Lilly shares her stories from the hospital and how much she loves caring for the older people.

Mid-month, Dominic hires two local carpenters and a labourer to build an extension on the house in Cocagne and a barn, which will be identical to the one he left in Moncton. The roads are greatly improved, and with the Cadillac, Dominic and Maria can make it back and forth to Cocagne in less than four hours if they need to. They spend all their weekends there when the weather is good and talk of living there all the time someday. They hope to have everything finished by spring.

Not everything goes as planned in their lives or those of their friends. In October, among the red and yellows leaves of fall, Maria's Uncle Rudy is laid to rest. The funeral in Notre-Dame is a solemn occasion for he was a much loved musician and storyteller.

Someone tries to break into the store, smashing the front window, but barking dogs, the new alarm system and an alert policeman prevent any theft. Dominic has to pay $40 to fix the window. Even though the precious pieces are stored in the vault and the cases are covered and locked, he hires a night watchman.

On the same weekend, their house is forcibly opened and muddy footprints are in every room. The police are called and when it is discovered that nothing is missing, the police chalked it up to mischievous youths as there were other similar incidents around the same neighbourhood and the occurrence is soon forgotten once Dominic has other security measures installed.

Maria develops bronchitis and has to spend a week in the hospital. Lilly comes frequently to nurse her back to health. By the end of the month, she's feeling fine.

Lilly's birthday is on the first of November, and Ivan's is two days later. Settled in their home, she invites a few people over to celebrate on Sunday, the day between, and cooks up a typical Scottish meal for everyone. Dominic and Maria, Denise and Andre, Nick and Joanne are the guests. Ivan arranged the furniture so that Nick can get around once he's in the house. She serves a small bowl of *Cullen skink*, a thick soup of smoked haddock, potatoes and onions, for starters. Fresh bread. Leg of mutton is served with *neeps and tatties*. For dessert she has made *apple frushie* and Denise baked a birthday cake, her mother's recipe. Among chatter and laughter, everyone praises Lilly's cooking. Empty plates and overfilled bellies prove the compliments true.

Dominic gives the couple a sketch from their wedding photo with a frame he made. The detail is fascinating, happiness emanates from the paper. Maria gives them matching watches from the new Bulova line. A pink blouse for Lilly, her favorite color, and a Hoffman brick trowel with an oak handle for Ivan from Denise and Andre. The latest novel by Grace Livingston Hill, *The Search*, for Lilly, and a handcrafted leather wallet for Ivan from Nick and Joanne. Lilly thanks everyone with a watery sparkle in her eyes. Ivan blushes when the girls kiss his cheek. Dominic couldn't be more pleased. His best friends at the table, his wife and her best friend, his favorite sister.

After tea and dessert, the men sit on the back porch. Nick and Ivan both smoke. They wear jackets as the evening cools and the sun disappears behind the buildings and trees. Ivan listens quietly when the conversation turns to the war and the men's participation. It's a chance to talk to others who know what you've been through. It's one thing they have in common, a bond from the experience only a fighting soldier could know. They recall the funnier things too, the mishaps and brotherly teasing. Politics, the Black Socks Scandal of the World Series, the building boom, favorite hockey teams, the city's mayor Hanford Price and his policies, Prime Minister Borden's Unionist party – they cover all their interests.

The ladies have their tea in cups on saucers and are in the great room listening to the new gramophone records on the Victrola Talking Machine with the volume turned low so they can talk. The latest fashions, Gloria Swanson's new movie, tea cups and babies, the right to vote, the new jewellery at the store, all are subjects that dominate the animated conversation. Work calls to everyone in the morning so the evening breaks up early. Lilly is profuse with her thank-yous. Saying goodnight, she hugs Dominic closely.

"Thank you so much for what you've done for us, how much we feel welcome. How safe I feel here. I miss our kin, of course, but we're so happy here. I love you, brother."

"I feel the same way, little sister."

Winter comes like a madman. Snow falls on the first day of December and piles up almost daily. Snowbanks grow along the roadways and people are bundled in jackets and scarves, hats with ear flaps. The odd sunny day is welcome even with the freezing temperatures. Snow crunches underfoot and the hardware stores are out of shovels. Christmas festivities are becoming an annual event at Emma's and are celebrated the week before. The numbers grow each year, but her house is so big that it never seems crowded. The food always gets better, which seems an impossibility. Prohibition has done nothing to stop the flow of liquor, and the music never stops. Gaiety abounds and goodwill. Nick proposes to Joanne, giving her a ring he made himself that is a work of art.

Maria suggests that there are those not as well off and they should do a collection to give to the church for a family who needs it. It too becomes an annual event called the Raymond Desjardins Fund in memory of her brother who died in the war. Everyone chips in generously and she's collects enough for two families. This gesture of kindness sparks something in Maria. The fund will become important to many more people than she could have ever guessed.

The end of the year finds Dominic sitting at the dining room table with his scrap book. There are only two more days until 1920. The store had a stupendous season, and Dominic closed for three days at New Years, fully paid as a bonus to the staff. Maria is visiting her brothers, Robert and Andre, who have moved to Moncton, sharing an apartment on Fleet Street. They are all making plans for the New Year's celebration at the Knights of Pythias Hall.

The scrapbook is almost full, but he thinks there is enough room for the clippings he's collected. Pasting them in, he wonders what the new year and the end of the decade will bring.

The German Naval Fleet is scuttled at Scapa Flow, Scotland.
The Treaty of Versailles is signed, officially ending the World War.
Jack Dempsey beats Jess Willard to become the World Heavyweight Champion.
British R-34 lands in New York to become the first airship to cross the Atlantic Ocean.
Chicago Race Riot claims 15 whites and 23 blacks with over 500 injured.
First scheduled passenger service by airplane begins from Paris to London.
Babe Ruth hits 29 home runs, establishing a new record as well as first time hitting in every park in the league in one season.
Lady Nancy Astor becomes first female member of the British Parliament.
A pound of butter now costs 39 cents.

1920

Dominic celebrates his twentieth birthday at home. A major snowstorm has everything closed on February 25. Looking out the living room window, he can't even see the neighbors, with the wind gusting and soft flakes swirling about. Drifts accumulate along the street like small white whales. After breakfast, Maria retreats to her sewing room to work on a quilt that she and Denise started last month. The two ladies are making one with a large heart in the center made up of remnants that are various shades of red that she has collected. The last time the friends got together, Joanne was telling the ladies of her fondness for quilts, which she uses in the winter months, and how the one she has was made by her grandmother and is getting frayed on the edges. She's a talented artist and can make lovely designs but hates messing with needles so will never do one on her own. She and Nick have planned a fall wedding in October and the ladies got busy making a quilt for a wedding present using a heart motif. Today is a perfect day to spend working at it; nothing else can be done given the weather.

Maria prepares Dominic's favorite meal that evening for his birthday: roast pork, mashed potatoes and turnip. They have a quiet meal, with forbidden champagne and her cousin's apple cider, accompanied by Marion Harris singing "But I'm Happy" on the phonograph. Maria had baked a cake yesterday when Dominic was at work – again his favorite, chocolate with boiled icing. They each have a piece with their tea, and afterwards she gives him his present, a new fishing rod. He has told her of the fishing that he and Duff did and how much he missed the solitude of a running stream and the tug on the hook. When she told him to buy one, he complained that there never seemed to be enough time, what with the business and all the building and renovations over the past few years.

"So now, you will have to make an effort, dear, to get away some mornings, no matter how busy we get. You need your alone time."

Dominic is examining the rod. It's a Marhoff steel rod with plenty of nickel and silver adornments. The Shakespeare bait casting reel is top of the line. Much heavier than the bamboo rod he had at Duff's house, but he likes the feel of it.

"This is a beauty, Maria. Wherever did you get one in the middle of winter?"

"I remembered last fall how you were lamenting missing Duff and how much your fishing trips meant to you, so I ordered one from Moncton Hardware and hid it at the store. I was going to give it you for Christmas, but that seemed funny for a Christmas present, so I decided to save it until now since it's closer to spring. Clever, aren't I?"

"Yes, you are. We'll have to get you one too."

She squirms up her face at the thought.

"Oh, no thank you. I can't imagine trying to get a squishy worm on a hook, and besides, it seems terribly cruel for the poor thing. And then torturing an innocent fish by snagging it in the mouth. You go alone or with your friends with my blessing."

She offers a smile that borders on mischievous.

"But I'll help you eat them. I love trout fried in butter."

Dominic sets the rod by the counter near the sink.

"All right then. Thank you, Maria."

She stands to give him a hug and for a few moments they relish the feeling of holding each other close. The intimacy provokes ardent kisses. The lights are doused and Maria has candles burning. Soon they are naked on the living room couch, with the curtains drawn, to spend the rest of the evening in the throes of passion and the comfort of each other's arms. The storm continues to rage. Maria becomes pregnant.

CHAPTER 2

Three weeks later, on March 17, Maria wakes early, feeling a tenderness in her breasts that confuses her. Attributing it to the way she sleeps mostly on her stomach, it bothers her most of the day and at nighttime she notices a bit of swelling. Not sure what is happening to her body, she tries to sleep on her back that night still believing the way she sleeps is responsible for her sore breasts. It's only when she vomits in the morning for the next three days that it dawns on her that she might be pregnant. She beams at herself in the bathroom mirror; her reflection bears the brightest happiness.

Her mind goes back to the night of the storm and their lovemaking, remembering that Dominic tried to pull out early but she wouldn't let him, wanting the feeling to last forever. She felt certain at the time that she was not ovulating. She can't wait to tell Dominic, hoping it makes him happy. Getting dressed, she goes downstairs to find him sitting in the back room reading his latest book – he always reads for ten or fifteen minutes every morning. An empty mug sits on the side table beside a plate littered with bread crumbs. The aroma of fried bacon wafts from the kitchen. His feet up on the ottoman, he's slouched on the leather sofa with the book propped on his stomach. He is so deep in the story, he doesn't hear her approach.

When she clears her throat, she startles him and he reacts with a sideways jerk. The book flops onto the floor, crinkling a few pages. Maria jumps back from his reaction and stares at his face. He's looking at his book. The way his jaw is set tells her she's in trouble. Sitting up, he reaches for the book resting like a small tent, the curled pages holding it. Her feeling of good cheer dissipates with the emotion in his eyes when he looks up. His voice is a lot calmer than she expects. It's sorrier than accusing.

"Look what you've made me do to my new book."

He's straightening out the bent pages, more disappointed than angry. Expecting a response, he looks up at Maria to see her holding both fists to her chin, eyes sad, a slow tear wandering down her cheek, and he regrets his harshness.

"Ah, Maria, don't fret over the book. It's just paper and it's all right now. I've made the pages flat again, took out the wrinkles. Look, it's fine"

He tries a silly grin and waves the closed book at her. She nods and responds with a small voice.

"I'm sorry, Dominic, I know how much you love your books...but...but..."

The droplets in her eyes begin to flow and she turns to run back upstairs. Dominic is bewildered and not sure what to do. He's trying to think of what he said. Or did. Her sobbing can be heard from their bedroom. Thinking to comfort her, he hastens upstairs, down the hallway and through the open door of their room. Maria is lying on the bed, face down, a hankie held to her eyes. He sits gently beside her and holds her shoulders in his hands.

"Ah Maria, forget about the book, Honey, it's not as important as you. I apologize for reacting improperly."

She speaks through the hankie, her voice muffled. He moves closer to hear.

"It's not about the book."

Frowning at the back of her head, he's surprised and becomes worried.

"What's bothering you, Maria?"

Lifting her head, she looks at him, the rouge on her tear-stained cheek is all smeared and smudges remain on the pillow. Her bangs are in disarray and Dominic thinks she's never been more beautiful.

"I wanted to tell you that I think I'm pregnant."

Mouth agape, he stares at her as if he hasn't heard right. When it sinks in, he props her up in his arms, picking her up off the bed and swings her around the bedroom. He's yahooing like a kid at a circus. Maria holds his neck tight, beaming with content. He falls back on the bed with her upon him and crushes her to his chest.

"That's the happiest news I've heard since you said *I do*. Is it true my love?"

She kisses him hard on the lips before struggling out of his grip so she can sit up. Her dimple is showing and her eyes gleam. Her hands are folded protectively over her tummy. She tells him about her breasts and other signs.

"…and I've been sick in the morning for the last three days. I'm going to make an appointment with Dr. Poirier right away. I'm so excited. Are you, Dominic?"

Sitting beside her, he pulls her closer.

"Aye, I am, more pleased than anything. Like you say, "*Ah oui!*""

They fall back on the bed, laughing. They talk about turning one of the bedrooms into a nursery. Is it a boy or a girl? What will its name be and so on until they have to get ready to go to the store. She points a finger at him when they are leaving the house.

"Don't say anything to anybody until I know for sure."

"Aye, I won't."

She'll tell Denise when she comes to work.

CHAPTER 3

By the end of April all her dresses are getting tight at the waist. The telltale bump of new life will be showing soon. Dr. Poirier estimates the birth to be in the first two weeks of October. She's already shopping for a crib. Dominic hires a painter to redo one of the bedrooms, the one across the hall from theirs. It's a bright yellow. Maria says that color works for a boy or a girl. Dominic frowns, saying it's too yellow for his son; he needs something more boyish. Maria has the last word on colors, reminding him that he'd paint everything blue and it wouldn't do if it's a girl. It's bright yellow.

One of her mother's dressers with the drawers out sits on some newspapers by the window. Several coats of white paint have been applied over the years. It was a wedding gift and it's been around for half a century. It takes a scraper Dominic fashioned with wood and a piece of steel to dig through it. A fist sized block of wood and a few scraps of sandpaper rest on its top, half of which is fresh wood.

Streaming through the bare window, mid-morning rays warm the room when she looks around, arranging furniture, hanging pictures, thinking about baby blankets. The search for the right curtain fabric is also on Maria's list today, and a new curtain rod. She needs some stretchy skirts and flared tops and she wants to look at some cribs. She promised Denise she would meet her at Sumners Department Store at ten-thirty and it's already ten. She wants to check her hair and put on her latest hat, a black cloche with a gold silk band and, in the back, a wisp of horsehair. Denise shares her friend's happiness and was thrilled when they asked her to be the godmother. She wants to buy the baby's first booties.

Maria's house is ten city blocks from the store. In the living room, she moves the curtain aside to step closer, gauging the weather. It's been raining for the last two days and there are many puddles along the street, but the sides are clear. Fat, scattered clouds cause the sun to come and go. A cleansing rain has melted the last reminders of winter. She decides to walk. Donning her leather boots with a laced front, she adds a light tan raincoat and carefully tugs the belt about her middle, ever mindful of her baby. With a pat on her tummy and a satisfied smile, she and the sun step out at the same time. It follows her down Highfield Street.

The best way to Sumners is to cross Mountain Road and continue to St. George Street with the new sidewalks. Proceed until Botsford and then to Main. Denise should be at the front door. Several automobiles putter by, a hansom full of people followed by a heavy wagon and team of horses. There is a break in the traffic on Mountain Road and she darts across to continue down Highfield. She has to walk around small pools left over from yesterday's downpour and steps carefully so as not to slip. Dr. Samuel DeGrace, the hospital administrator, has a stately home on the corner of St. George and when she reaches it, she goes east.

People are coming and going, many with a friendly greeting. Maria is tall for a lady, attractive – she draws many admiring stares. Glancing at her watch she sees it's ten twenty-five; hating to be late, she hastens her pace. Almost to Botsford Street, she sees a crowd gathered around an overturned wagon carrying milks cans that are scattered and spilled on the street. A horse is on its side, snorting and pawing at the air, trying to free itself from the stays of the wagon and the leathers of command. Several men are trying to calm the animal as others struggle with the paraphernalia that holds it captive. The small lake of milk is turning brown from the dirt. Beyond the wagon is an automobile with a broken lamp, dented fender, buckled hood and hissing engine. Two men are fighting beside it. She can't see who they are, but the smaller man seems to have an upper hand. Curiosity drags her closer. She stops at the edge of the street behind the small group of bystanders. Several policemen arrive with siren blaring. The crowd near the horse jumps out of the way when it comes free and kicks itself upright. Perhaps out of fear, it starts to buck and the young man holding its reins uses all his muscle to restrain it. Everyone is yelling advice and the police whistles are blowing. It's too much for Maria and she remembers Denise.

She decides to backtrack to Church Street and steps out in to a mostly empty street up to Church. A few nosey people have pulled over with their autos as well as several buggies. With her back to the crowd, she doesn't see the horse break free and tear away from the scene, blinded with fright. The crowd's voice charges the air with warning. Only when she hears the heavy clops of the charging horse does she turn to see it almost upon her. Automatically clutching her tummy, she tries to duck away. The horse too attempts to avoid her, but it's too close. It's right front hoof hits her in the midsection with enough force to knock her on her back several feet away. She lands with a dreadful thud. The horse continues up St. George at a full gallop.

Several people rush to her side. Maria hit her head when she fell and is unconscious. A police officer breaks through the crowd and kneels at her side. Her coat has been thrown open and he can see blood forming on the front of her dress, which is torn. When he establishes that she is still breathing, he yells to a man sitting in his auto who has stopped to see what is going on.

"Hey there, bring your vehicle around. We need to get this woman to the hospital right away!"

The man swings his auto closer. They place Maria prone in the back seat. An elderly lady who was out walking said she would go with her. The hospital is only several blocks down the street. By the time they reach the emergency doors with the horn blaring, Maria is gaining consciousness and moaning from the pain in her abdomen. She keeps repeating Dominic's name and the woman recognizes her from having been at the store only a week previously. Orderlies rush from the hospital with a gurney and get her inside to the emergency room. The lady goes to the front desk and informs them that the injured lady works at Alexander's Jewellery and that they might want to contact someone at the store.

Dominic answers the phone and after his greeting, he goes pale from the caller's news. Dropping the receiver on the desk, he tells Christine to watch the store and rushes to grab his coat from the back room. Upon leaving he tells her what is happening.

"Maria is in the hospital. She was near an accident on Botsford Street and was struck by a fleeing horse. I'll be back as soon as I can."

Christine is all business, telling him to take his time and to let them know right away what is happening. He's running along St. George and can see the commotion at Botsford where the crowd is dispersing. Police are directing traffic around the car and wagon. He avoids the scene and is at the hospital in five minutes. He is directed to a waiting room and told that doctors are working on Maria as they speak. Its several hours before a Dr. Morton motions him to a corner seat to talk to him privately.

"Your wife is resting now. There was a cut on the skin of her lower abdomen, which we had to stitch. The uterus and the bladder took a direct hit from the animal's hoof. There doesn't seem to be any other internal damage that we can detect, however…"

The doctor looks down at the floor, obviously uncomfortable. Dominic fears what's coming.

"There was heavy vaginal bleeding. Upon examination, we discovered a very early fetus had been aborted."

Dominic is distraught. His skin tightens and he goes pale.

"It's…it's dead? the baby's dead?"

The doctor just nods. Lips pursed. He sits forward a little and looks away, giving Dominic a moment for the news to sink in.

Hanging his head, Dominic can't hold back the tears. Before he can remove his handkerchief, several make large blots on his suit trousers. Rapid-fire visions of those he's lost already blur his thinking, but this moment seems the worst. Stiffening his chin, he straightens his shoulders and dries his eyes. Feeling selfish, he thinks of Maria.

"Does my wife know?"

"We had to sedate Mrs. Alexander when we tended to her injuries and she is not awake yet, so no, she doesn't. Would you prefer to tell her?"

Dominic shakes his head knowing how much she will be hurt.

"Nae, I canna do it. I want to be there when you tell her though. Has there been any more bleeding?"

"There was more bleeding but it has since stopped. We expect there could be more clots. We will need to keep her under close observation for a few days."

"I understand. Can I see her now?"

The doctor glances out one of the windows off the waiting room to check the sun's position. He looks at Dominic, seeing a determined look in his eyes, his own grief set aside.

"It's close to two o'clock. She'll still be in recovery, but I'm sure they'll move her to a ward soon. You've been here some time already. It would be best for you to have something to eat and come back at three-thirty. Ask the ladies at reception to find me."

Maria is sitting propped up on pillows. Her eyes are puffy, bloodshot from so many tears. The doctor has told her the worst and she asks the question that she knows is on Dominic's mind as well. He's beside the bed holding her hand, eyes on the doctor. Her voice is groggy, yet hopeful.

"Will I be able to have more children?"

The doctor rubs his chin, searching for the right words. It's heartbreaking enough with what they are experiencing.

"We'll know more in a few days, but with the injuries you've sustained and the damage to the uterus, my colleague, Dr. Patricia Cornwallis, and I agree that your chances are very slim. Perhaps as little as 10 percent. I'm sorry to have to tell you this."

Maria sees the empathy on the doctor's face. She realizes how difficult it must be. She's trying to be tough, find something good.

"Well that's better than 0 then, isn't it. Thank you, Dr. Morton."

With a nod he turns, leaving the couple to grieve. He looks back before he shuts the door and sees the two embrace, seeking and giving solace, tears mingling on their cheeks.

CHAPTER 4

The fourth of May is a bright day. Rotund cumulus clouds are all piled up on each other, scattered about the sky. The sun clears the horizon to remove the morning chill and it promises to be a warm day when Maria and Dominic pile their luggage in the Cadillac for the weekend in Cocagne. Maria also has a new set of pots and pans, a silver service set, a red kettle, a new wall clock, enough groceries to last them a month and Scarlet. Hidden under the back seat are two bottles of Jamaican alcohol the rum runners brought into Richibucto and four bottles of wine from the fields in Ontario that prohibition hasn't closed.

All the renovations at their house have been completed, and this is their first weekend to enjoy it with no sawdust, no lumber piled in the yard, no hammering and sawing. Dominic and a local boy had cleaned up the yard last weekend and stored the unused lumber in the new barn. Two local ladies were hired to clean the house from top to bottom and all that is left to be done is add furniture and, much to Maria's delight, decorate.

They leave Moncton at 7 a.m. on the nose. The roads have recently been graded, with no rain for the last week, so the driving is enjoyable. They arrive in Cocagne at noon, having stopped in Shediac for a late breakfast at the posh Weldon House. Maria loves the classy hotel with its fancy trim. They celebrated their first anniversary there last November filling themselves with lobster from the Bay of Funday and steak. Tourist season will soon be upon the small town. Even now, the train runs back and forth from Moncton with people coming for the day. They were lucky to find a table.

When they arrive at the house, a warm air current ruffles the water in the bay and the sun sparkles off of every tiny crest like thousands of wavering candles. The barn has a large front door that is painted bright red and can be seen for a good distance. The house has an addition in the back where the new kitchen is located as well as a pantry. The old kitchen has been changed to a sitting room and the original living room has enlarged windows to see the bay and has been divided so that there is a third room downstairs that can be a bedroom or an office. It hasn't been decided yet and remains bereft of any furnishings until Maria can decide what to do with it.

Dominic is most proud of a new covered porch on the front where they can sit to watch the sunrise or view a spectacular sunset. The land is low and the setting sun provides a vivid kaleidoscope of colors on the water: pinks, deep blues, oranges and soft yellows change every minute. The whole house has been re-shingled with local cedar and painted a gleaming white, same as the barn. The trim around the windows and doors and gable ends is a bold black with the same deep shine.

Pulling in to park in front of the barn, they have to maneuver around a truck that has brought a new electric refrigerator and wood cooking stove. Scarlet pounces from Maria's lap to explore the new territory as soon as the car stops. Dominic gets out of the car to greet the men. They start to unload the truck while Dominic unlocks the house. When they walk in, he and Maria are greeted by the scent of fresh paint, disinfectant and glue from the new linoleum floor. She drops her bags on the chair in the kitchen and waves her hand in front of her face.

"Let's open some windows, Dominic, and get some fresh air and the smell of the salt water."

"Aye, that's a good idea, Maria. Then I'm going to help the men with the appliances. All we have to do is hook the stove pipe up and plug in the refrigerator."

The house has all the modern conveniences available: electricity, running water and a new telephone – the first one in this part of the countryside all the way to Bouctouche. Everyone from Dixon Point to Grande Digue to Notre Dame is talking about it.

"A Scottish gentleman and one of our local girls."

"Indoor plumbing and a telephone too!"

"Owns a jewellery business in the city."

"Last names are Alexander, but she was a Desjardins from Notre Dame."

"Benoit's daughter, a pretty young thing."

"Lots of land went with the deal I understand, must be 100 acres or more. And a big piece across the road right on the water."

"Ah but the sunrises over the bay. The best part."

Later, after Maria and Dominic have put away all the food, unpacked their bags and stored the items they brought and made the bed with new sheets, they are standing in the middle of the kitchen looking at the stove. The men helped him level it and hook up the stove pipe. The surface is blemish free, the warmer, the oven, the fire box and the water tank all have white porcelain fronts and the rest of the stove is chrome, everything right down to the elegant legs. Maria is rubbing her hands together and smiling at her husband, one of those this-makes-me-happy smiles. With arms on his hips, he nods his chin at the stove.

"It's a beauty, isn't it, Maria? What's the first thing you're going to cook on it?"

"*Ah oui, c'est tres beau.* Tomorrow morning I'm going to make pancakes for breakfast. We have the buttermilk we bought at the corner and I remembered your molasses. Plus, I have your favorite sausages, the ones from Verhoeven Farms."

He turns to give her a hug.

"You're so thoughtful and so good to me. I love you, Mrs. Alexander."

The eyes reply before the voice when she looks at him. She responds with a lusty whisper.

"I love you too, Mr. Alexander."

Kissing him passionately, she feels his arousal. Backing away slightly, a glint sparkles in her eyes and she takes him by the hand heading towards the stairway.

"Would you like to see the new sheets I put on the bed?"

*

Shadows are growing longer in front of the house when Dominic drags two kitchen chairs to the porch with Maria right behind him carrying two plates, each holding a ham sandwich, a few pickles and a chunk of aged cheddar. Dominic places the chairs to the left, away from the steps to the ground.

"Hold a bit Maria and I'll get us a table"

She's not paying attention. The shimmering water coated with the pastels of dusk approaching has her mesmerized. Scarlet is curled up on the top of the short wall and studies the ground for field mice, which she has been chasing all afternoon. Tide is out and sandbars form islands with brown grainy complexions for hundreds of feet towards deeper water. The pools closer to shore hold several colored dories that are anchored in the still water, their upside-down reflection is flawless. A half a mile offshore to their right, a forested island, lush with greenery, complements the many blues of the water and the horizon. The setting sun tints the upper skies pink with a rim of orange. Seagulls, sandpipers and an osprey glide about searching for prey. The road is empty of traffic. Only when Dominic returns and sets a wooden box upside down with a clunk is she disturbed from her musings.

"It's so lovely here, isn't it, Dominic?"

"Aye it is. Here, set the plates down and have a seat."

He pushes a chair closer to the box, which comes up to their knees, and bends at the waist with a wave of his hand.

"Your throne awaits, my dear."

She's laughing when she sits. Her cheeks still rosy from the afternoon's pleasures.

"You make me feel like a queen."

"You're my queen."

"Aw, how sweet. Come sit beside me and let's eat. I'm starved."

Before he sits, he gets the glasses of water he brought out earlier. Pulling the chair up close, he digs into his sandwich. She starts with a piece of cheese. As they eat, they gaze at the changing vista before them, deep in their own thoughts. A half wall is in front of them with uprights at the ends that hold the roof of the porch so the view is unrestricted. Seagulls are fighting over a shell fish and their squawks are almost comical, with a scolding tone. The lightest of breezes waft through sporadically, always with the scent of the water and open country.

"It doesn't get much better than this, does it, Maria?"

She's still chewing and holds up a finger with an affirmative nod. Before she can respond, a pretty Silvery Blue rises from outside the wall, flitting about on fragile wings as if unsure which way to go. It circles the table and lands on Maria's shoulder for only a few seconds as if resting before it rises on an updraft and sails on. Eyeing each other as if the butterfly answered the question, they burst out laughing. They finish their meal in silence. The mood changes. They're both thinking of the baby. Maria sets her empty plate on the box, sweeps a few crumbs from her lap and looks back out at the bay. The water is so still that you can't tell where the horizon and the water meet. The upper sky holds smeared tints of the last light of the evening. She's never felt a more peaceful moment. She decides it's time to move on.

"I can let it go now, Dominic. I think we should make you a den where the…the nursery is."

Dominic has escaped the pang of grief by keeping busy – two houses, the business, long hours during the weeks to be free on the weekends. He's watched Maria do the same thing. What he notices now is the relief in her eyes, the assurance of her soft smile. Sensing her own unburdening, a weight lifts from his shoulders.

"Aye Maria, I'd like that."

"You can even paint it blue."

Like the butterfly, the sadness catches an updraft and sails on. Their laughter is easy. They spend the rest of the evening watching darkness approach and head to bed early.

They breakfast early the next morning and the day promises to be spectacular. The sun makes pink halos on the water and the two of them munch on their pancakes and sausages and drink their tea on the porch where they left off last night. The road is busy as people head to church in buggies piled with children and older folks. The odd automobile passes also, but traffic is light. They are making plans for the day when they are interrupted by the growing roar of an auto engine. A cloud of billowing dust with air currents pushing it towards the water follows a rushing automobile. When it gets nearer it begins to slow and they can see the body is black with dust feathering the floorboards. It turns abruptly into their driveway, spewing small stones from the wheels. Skidding to a stop, the driver shuts off the engine and sets the brake before getting out. It's a man, a big man. Maria draws closer to Dominic and takes his arm, concerned by the strange visitor's heavy frown.

When he walks around the car, they can see how big he really is. Wide shoulders, no neck, just a shirt collar and tie. His suit jacket looks too small and would never button around his barrel chest. Long wavy hair starting to gray is slicked back on top of a wide head. Heavy brows and serious eyes make him look angry. His voice is like something hollow.

"Are you Dominic Alexander?"

Dominic stands with Maria at his side.

"I am. And you are sir?"

He's moved to the bottom of the steps when he pulls a leather holder from an inside breast pocket. He flips the outer cover to expose a polished brass badge with embossed characters and dark letters that Dominic is not near enough to read.

"Detective Joseph Monaghan, City of Moncton Police Department."

Dominic's eyes widen at the thought of a policeman at his house on a Sunday morning.

"What brings you here, Detective Monaghan?"

Putting the shield back in his pocket, the detective meets Dominic at the top of the steps. Maria is waiting where they ate, with her hands folded in front of her and a curious look on her face.

"I'd like to ask you a few questions."

It isn't a request and the man is no friendlier.

"Well fine. Would you like to come in and sit?"

"No, thank you. I need to confirm that you are the same Dominic Alexander, the previous owner of the property west of Main Street where a jewellery business was established and the property sold to CNR last year."

"Well, yes, that's me. What's going on?"

Rather than answering the question, he turns to Maria.

"And you are Mrs. Alexander?"

She nods, not sure what to say. The man is an imposing figure and she feels intimidated. Even Scarlet is bothered by the man and jumps from the ledge to scurry behind the house.

"When was the last time you were on the property?"

"We moved everything out of there last year just before the end of August and moved into our new home on Highfield Street. Mr. Campbell from CNR did a walkabout with me, making sure we left nothing behind, and on the last day of the month I passed him the keys to the house."

"Have either of you been back to the property since then?"

Dominic looks back at Maria with a frustrated brow. Both answer in unison.

"No, no we haven't."

"Have you ever dealt in illegal firearms, Mr. Alexander?"

Both Dominic and Maria are astounded by the question. Both have mouths agape and fear shadows Maria's eyes.

"Of course not, detective. That's absurd. Look, you're scaring my wife. Please tell us what is going on."

Monaghan is not convinced by the statement.

"Two days ago, when the barn was being prepared to be moved, having been sold to your neighbors, men from the railway were combing the building once more for any valuables and came upon one of the back rooms with a lock on the door. They broke the hasp and entered to find two cases of Browning automatic rifles that we've discovered were stolen from an armory in Maine. They also found this."

He reaches in his pocket to remove an envelope with a piece of white linen tucked in it. Using a pair of tweezers from another pocket, he removes a handkerchief and unfolds it on the ledge. It's badly wrinkled and smudged with dirt. Maria recognizes it right away and gasps. On one corner are the Initials D.D.A. Dominic goes pale.

"Is this yours, Mr. Alexander?"

Dominic reaches for the handkerchief and the detective pulls it away with the tweezers.

"Please don't touch it."

Dominic is nodding his head.

"Yes. That looks like mine. Maria bought me half a dozen for my birthday last year, but I had nothing to do with stolen guns. Why would I?"

Putting the cloth back in the envelope, the detective says, "That's the question, isn't it? If you're innocent, then you wouldn't mind if I look around?"

Maria knows absolutely that Dominic would never have anything to do with stolen goods; he's much too honest. But she imagines the big man tearing things apart in the house. She opens the screen door and waves him in.

"Please do. We have nothing to hide, do we, Dominic? I simply ask that you don't make a mess."

"Nae, of course not. Help yourself, detective."

The three enter the house and the detective checks the whole house, moving things around on dressers and cupboards, opening drawers, looking in closets, with Dominic and Maria at his heels the entire time. After having satisfied himself that there is nothing incriminating inside, he asks to view the barn and their automobile, which they readily agree to. The barn has very little in it and the search goes quickly. The automobile takes a bit longer, and while Dominic and Maria are standing aside, the burly detective is on his knees sweeping under the front car seats. A raised brow and a smirk suggest he's found something.

When he stands up, the detective holds out a shiny key, so new the sun twinkles off of it. He watches them for a reaction. When there is none, he reaches in one of his side pockets and removes a sturdy lock that is closed. Inserting the key and giving it a twist, the lock pops open. Dominic and Maria are stunned. Dominic points at the detective's hand.

"I've never seen that key before, or that lock."

The detective has a look on his face that says he doesn't believe him.

"How come it's in your auto then?"

"I don't know, Detective Monaghan. Someone must've put it there."

The policeman has heard it all before, the claim of innocence. Pocketing the key and lock, he points at his own car.

"I think you better come with me, Mr. Alexander."

"What? Am I under arrest?"

"Not if you come along peacefully. If you are indeed innocent, then we'll get to the bottom of this. But if I was you, I'd be hiring a lawyer."

Maria can't believe what is happening. She holds Dominic and is shaking in his arms. She whispers so the detective can't hear her.

"Remember when someone came in the house Dominic? When they tried to break into the store last fall? That's when they took the handkerchief I bet. Someone is trying to frame you."

They both think of Crosswaithe, but that thought dies soon enough, knowing the man may be disagreeable but doubting he would be that devious.

"This is crazy, Maria, why would someone do this? I've never hurt anyone or cheated anyone."

"I know, dear. Don't cause any trouble. I'll follow along and get hold of Bannister. We'll meet you at the police station."

They move apart and look back at Monaghan, who is standing by his auto. He waves for Dominic to get in the front seat. The drive to Moncton is one of the longest in Dominic's life; and while the detective probes him for information, Dominic remains mute, realizing it's best to keep quiet and wait for Bannister.

By the time Bannister and Maria reach the station, Dominic has been charged with possession of stolen property and has been fingerprinted. His belongings, including his shoes, have been removed from his person and listed, for which he signed, then he was placed in a cell.

Bannister argues with Detective Monaghan and Chief Robichaud that the weapons were found on property that didn't belong to Dominic anymore, how could he be charged with possession? They both point to the key and lock and suggest that Bannister confer with the prisoner and prepare for an arraignment on Monday morning. They offer the lawyer a room in which to talk to his client but inform Maria that she will have to wait in the reception area. She is frantic, unsure of what to do. She sits, nervously rubbing her hands together, watching the clock and wearing a look of disbelief. Forty minutes pass before Bannister returns and accompanies her out.

"How is he, John?"

"He's fine, Maria. He's related what took place and with what you've told me, this won't go anywhere. It has to be a set up. We need to figure out who has something against him and point the police in the right direction. He'll have to stay in jail tonight, and we'll meet with a judge in court in the morning."

Bannister notes Maria's doubt and tries to reassure her.

"Look, Maria, we both know he had nothing to do with this. We'll sort this out."

Bannister sees that Maria makes it back to her house. He contacts Denise and she joins Maria, who is fraught with worry. She has lost her appetite and wonders how this could possibly happen. She spends a sleepless night, the longest of her life, and wakes in the morning with puffy, reddened eyes. Denise fixes her breakfast before heading to the store. Maria leaves it to get cold and sits on the back deck with a cup of tea, trying to figure out who might be behind this. Nothing comes to mind. She has to wait until nine o'clock to take Dominic fresh clothing, and they promised her she can see him.

Dominic on the other hand has slept well enough considering the lumpy mattress and the two drunks who occupy nearby cells. Their rants and moaning woke him occasionally, but with his mind at ease knowing he had nothing to do with the illegal weapons, he wakes rested. His clothing is disheveled and he smells a bit unpleasant. Odd odors of old socks and unwashed bodies permeate the cell area. The jailer's strong aftershave overlays that when he pushes a tray of lukewarm tea and dry toast in a slot at the bottom of the bars.

Dominic frowns at the bareness of the cell and hopes he doesn't have to stay here long. Looking out the barred window, he can see the grey light of early morning and guesses it must be seven or eight o'clock. Bannister told him that Maria would be over in the morning when visiting hours start at nine.

Later, dressed in the clean clothes Maria had brought him, Dominic meets Bannister in the courtroom where he will plead not guilty. A court date has been set for Thursday at nine a.m. Bail has been set at $500.00, which Maria forks over and takes him home. Dominic dreads missing his work but has been told to remain in his house. By Wednesday he's pacing the kitchen back and forth. He needs a shave and he's worried sick. Bannister had met with him yesterday and brought another lawyer as he is not a criminal attorney. Mr. Basil Hunter sat with him for several hours recapping the events of the last year since Dominic had sold the property to CNR. Hunter informed him that the prosecutor has to prove Dominic's guilt beyond a shadow of a doubt and what they have is the key in his car and the handkerchief, which is damning evidence. Hunter says he will meet Dominic Thursday morning with a plan.

At the same time that Dominic is pacing, Detective Monaghan is going over his report of finding the key and arresting Dominic, preparing himself for the trial tomorrow. He's not sure that Dominic is guilty, based on testimonials from his friends, but he's heard this all before and it's simply conjecture. He has the facts and they speak for themselves. Before finishing his preparations, he is interrupted by Sargent Peterson, who is holding a smudged white, sealed envelope with Monaghan's name printed in large letters on the front.

"Found this on my desk when I returned from the washroom a few minutes ago. Didn't see who left it and there was no one in the reception area. Don't know what it is."

Monaghan takes the envelope and rips it open. Peterson's curiosity has him loitering at the detective's desk, but when he catches the eye from Monaghan, he knows he won't be told what it is. With a shrug of his shoulders, he returns to the front. Monaghan removes a single sheet of unlined white paper. Printed in pencil are large letters.

You will find more guns at the Thompsons in Albert County.

Monaghan rubs his chin while contemplating the words. He's had run-ins with the Thompsons before, when the old man was on trial for murder. That one still bothers him to this day, because he had, and still has, a gut feeling that old man Thompson was guilty, but the alibi and lack of evidence set him free. Folding the sheet back in the envelope, he goes to see the Chief.

At four o'clock, Chief Robichaud and five other policemen, accompanied by a search warrant, raid the Thompson residence in Stony Creek. At the same time, Detective Monaghan and four other police officers raid the home of Albert Thompson, Ray's twin brother, with their own search warrant. They are met with heavy resistance and verbal threats, but the officers take control of the situation, subduing the aggressive male members of the family and locking them in the paddy wagons for resisting the police's efforts.

At 5:16 pm Monaghan and Constable Leblanc uncover six more cases of the same weapons found in the barn at Dominic's former home in the cellar of Albert Thompson's house. The boxes are covered with lumber and dried wood, but Monaghan noticed the sharp edge of one of the boxes sticking out at the bottom of the pile. Clearing some of the debris, they quickly find the additional cases. Instructing the other officers, Monaghan supervises the loading of the contraband weapons in one of the police lorries.

When Robichaud hears of the discovery, he rushes to the other house, and when the cases are removed from the cellar another police officer finds a false back in a large tool cabinet pushed up tight to a back wall. When the contents are removed and the doorway forcibly opened, they discover a darkened room with a low ceiling extending beyond the cellar housing additional contraband: other weapons, cases of motor oil, liquor, and most notably a black leather carrying case with the gold embossed letters MT on the front, encased in spiderwebs. Robichaud has goosebumps when he realizes the letters could stand for Mike Turnbull, the man who was murdered in 1909. He instructs the officers to leave it untouched and to seal off the room.

421

Thompson's wife and children are told to find other accommodations. Watched over carefully by the officers, the rest of the family gathers articles of clothing and sundries and leaves with relatives who had arrived during the search. News travels fast in small communities and a group of uncles and cousins shout abuse at the police until they are run off with the rest of the family. The house is sealed and officers placed on watch. Robichaud needs to get back to the station and have the search warrant amended or another issued for evidence of a cold murder case. He also needs to prepare a schedule for officers watching the premises.

By eight o'clock that evening Dominic is told that the charges against him have been dropped. Albert Thompson cannot deny the contents of the cellar. Threatened with many years in prison alongside his brother, he is offered a charge of a lesser degree. Like many cowards, he's tough when backed by his kin or when he's drinking; but in reality, he's weak and selfish. He tells them everything. The family was upset that Ray went to jail, blaming it all on the Alexander family, vowing to get revenge. Dominic assures his friends and family he never wants to set foot in a jail cell again. When Bannister informed him of the note, Dominic never finds out who sent it but expects it was Tommy's friend, Jack. He takes the rest of the week off, returns to Cocagne and takes his scrapbook with him.

Montreal Canadians (14) beat Toronto St. Patricks (7), establishing a record of most goals per game (21).
Silver reaches a record $1.37 per ounce.
Royal Canadian Mounted Police is formed with merger of Northwest Mounted Police and Dominion Police.
Greece adopts the Gregorian calendar.
New Canadian small cent coin is introduced.
Balfour Declaration is recognized, making Palestine a British Mandate.
US President Woodrow Wilson makes the Communist Labour Party illegal.
Joan of Arc (Jeanne D'arc) is canonized as a saint.
King George V opens the Imperial War Museum at The Crystal Palace in London.
Babe Ruth smashes his 50th MLB career home run, his first for the New York Yankees.

CHAPTER 5

When September rolls around, the house in Cocagne is full of new furniture and a few antiques Maria has collected over the summer. She's all agog by the painting Dominic gave her for her birthday in August, the latest one from an artist in Shediac, and finds a special spot for it in the living room over the sofa. More art and family photos are added to the walls. Flowers and shrubs have been planted around the property. They've had several gatherings over the summer, hiring transport to bring folks for the day and returning them to their homes in the evening when it isn't too far. The folks that came from Moncton stay the night – there's lots of room for guests.

Maria and Dominic have set up an area in the barn for Maria and it acts as another bedroom when needed. She has a sewing room there and in one corner is a sofa and easy chair for chats when her girlfriends visit. It's all full of lady things: lace, dried flowers and fresh flowers in pink and yellow vases, *Home Journal* and other fashion magazines, cushions – lots of cushions, mostly with a nautical motif, and much to her husband's delight is her growing pile of books placed neatly in a corner nook.

Dominic trades the Cadillac for a new Buick 4 door sedan in burgundy with a black roof and running boards. It's not as prestigious as the Cadillac but is not as snobbish here in the country he feels. *Dr Jekyll and Mr Hyde* starring John Barrymore is the talked-about movie. When Dominic and Maria went to see the horror show the only thing better than the movie was when Maria was clinging to him in fright. Letters keep arriving regularly from Scotland. They bring only happy news with them. The fishing has been good and Paul has sent his last payment early, and now owns the boat outright. Sheila sent him a sketch she did of their Granda from memory. The likeness is astounding, the wrinkles that crease the edges of his eyes and line the base of his neck are so real, the stubbornness in his eyes and the perpetual half grin exactly as he remembers them. Dominic encourages her in his letters and they share little tips. One letter tells of little Danny turning one year old last summer and walking. Mary has to watch him constantly and Pascal is a wonderful father.

A letter he received yesterday troubles him. It's from Don Cook of Newcastle, one of the soldiers he befriended on the sailing to Europe, the one that joined up to get away from the nagging wife, the joker of the group. They parted ways the day after their arrival in 1917, he to the front lines. There has been no other contact.

August 31, 1920

Dear Dominic.

I hope this letter finds you in good health and a happy man. I remember you from the crossing and how a few of us from New Brunswick kind of stuck together. You were always the easiest going, it was not difficult to like you. I had a hard time understanding you and the French boys, but we had a lot of laughs, helped us to forget what we were heading for even though we knew at the end of the trip we'd be shitting our underwear. We all said we'd stay in touch in that brief time of friendship, but I don't know what happened to the rest of the boys, Clovis, Adam, Mark or Chris. I hope they left the war behind them. But I haven't, Dominic.

I'm so scared to sleep, I know the bad dreams are coming. They don't always but often enough to make me think of those deadly times, the broken bodies, the screaming bombs, shrapnel and the mad Germans that only wanted to kill us. We had no choice, we had to kill them too. What's worse is the flashbacks. I lost my job because of them. The doctors say it will all go away and give me more sleeping pills. My wife left me because I wake in the night still in a daze. I think she's the enemy and she's scared of me.

I need someone to talk to Dominic, I need someone that's been there, that

424

understands, that can handle it better than me. I think that's you.

I'm not looking for a handout, Dominic, only someone to share this burden with. My address is 26 Meadowbrook Lane and I'm always home.

Don Cook.

The letter brings back his own memories of the war, the terror of the guns blasting when they flew too low, the devastation he witnessed, fallen soldiers from both sides covering battlefields like human litter, the stench of death and gunpowder and the crashing of his aircraft with the death of his pilot. It's the things he tries to forget. But he's been lucky. The support he received from his wife and friends, his work, his business to run. There were nights he awoke from bad dreams too, but they've faded over the years. It troubles him that it could affect someone for so long and so strongly. He decides to answer Don Cook's request.

Folding the letter up, he peers out the window. The sun is just starting to blink over the trees in his backyard. It's almost eight-thirty. Tucking the letter in his trousers' back pocket, he leaves his home office to go to the store. Maria reminded him earlier at breakfast that she has a checkup today at the hospital and has already left. It being Friday, they are going to Cocagne after lunch. He knows of no major plans for the weekend other than storing the wood he bought in the barn, but he can do that any time before winter. He'll show Maria the letter and ask her if she minds if he leaves today. He's never driven there but knows from people who come to the store that it's about 70 miles to Newcastle. Depending on the roads and weather, he can probably manage 20 miles an hour, so about four hours. If he leaves around ten, he can stop for lunch in Richibucto, where the scallops from *Doucet's Restaurant* are the best he's eaten.

When he arrives at the store, Denise is just opening it at nine. She opens the door and gives him an earnest smile. He still can't get over how blue her eyes are and how they shine when she's happy.

"Good morning, Mr. Alexander."

Dominic doffs his hat.

"Aye, I like the Mister part. Good morning to you also, Denise."

She points to the front desk where a package sits on the counter. "It's from Mr. Spinelli, the Waterman pen representative from

Toronto. Must be the samples you asked for. You might want to have a look. Let me know whenever you want me to dash him off a reply if it's a yes or a no."

Dominic remembers the Italian, his rants of his pens being the best in the world and how they can't make enough of them. A handsome man, but the pencil mustache made him look a little shifty. None of the other jewelers carry fountain pens and he thinks they could sell.

"What do you think, Denise? Can we sell some expensive pens?"

She waves her hand around the store.

"How much do you see here for the men? Most of what we carry is for the ladies. I think the pens will fit in nicely. We could move the men's rings and cufflinks around in the middle counter and make room there for a display."

"All right then, let's have a look."

Dominic cuts away the tape holding the box shut and removes first a folded sheet of paper and two cases with the Waterman name and logo embossed on the tops. Opening the first one, he finds a beautiful gold and black fountain pen with his name engraved along the bottom barrel. The pen has intricate scroll work on the top and the Waterman clip for holding it in a pocket. It has the innovative lever supply system. The other case holds a more feminine version with Maria's name engraved. There are two bottles of blue ink enclosed in the box as well as a catalog with wholesale and retail pricing. While Denise inspects and comments on the pens, Dominic opens the letter folded on top, which is from Spinelli. It says that the pens are gifts for allowing him to demonstrate his exclusive line of writing instruments. Dominic is impressed.

"Well, this is certainly a surprise. Such craftsmanship, don't you think, Denise?"

"Yes, it is. Do you think we should order some?"

Aye, let's do it. You talk to Spinelli, order what you think we can sell and look after the display."

"Fine then, I'll get on it right away."

Dominic greets Nick and Christine as they go about their duties. Several customers have come in the store and he goes to the back to leave his jacket and hat while removing Don Cook's letter from his pocket. Donning his apron, he goes to his workstation, where he intends to finish the pendant he is making for Mr Lutes' wife and their 35th wedding anniversary. He is placing a 2.4 carat garnet that was in her father's ring in a new setting. Glancing at his watch, he expects Maria back anytime. Her appointment was for eight-thirty.

Thirty minutes later, Maria sweeps into the store with a happy face. The news must've been good. After greeting everyone and chatting with Mrs. Bertha MacDonald, Maria's hairdresser, who is choosing a ring for her husband's birthday on the coming Sunday, she catches Dominic's eye and he nods towards the back room. He brings the letter that is sitting on his work bench and takes the finished pendant to Nick.

"Can you polish this please, Nick, when you have time and ask Christine to put it in a gift box when she's finished with Mrs. MacDonald. Have her call Mr Lutes at his office to tell him it is ready."

"Sure thing, Dominic."

"Thanks, Nick."

Joining Maria in the back, he receives the news that her check-up went well. He shows her the letter. Perusing the page, she frowns at the sad news. When she's done, she looks at Dominic directly and notes his troubled countenance.

"This is so sad, Dominic. Do you think you can help him?"

"Well, I'd like to try. I've been so fortunate to have you all when I came back from the war, but it seems like he has no one."

"You want to go today, don't you? I can see it in your eyes."

'Aye. Would you mind terribly if we passed on the country this weekend or did you have something important planned?"

"Nothing that can't wait until next week. I wanted to go to Belliveau's Orchard and pick some apples but we can do that next weekend. Would you leave today? Is the pendant done for Mr. Lutes? He wanted it for tomorrow."

"Aye, Nick's going to shine it up and Christine can wrap it up and call him. I was thinking of leaving shortly. I'd just head home first and pack a few things for overnight and be back tomorrow evening. Would that be okay?"

She smiles at him and moves closer to give him a hug.

"I don't like sleeping in an empty bed, but I guess I can suffer through one night."

Stepping back from him, her look is stern.

"Be careful on the roads. You remember when Donnie, the mailman, went there last weekend and the rain had washed away a section of the road on the other side of St. Louis and he got his car stuck."

"Aye, I will. It should be fixed by now."

She gives him a kiss and is interrupted by Denise, who is holding a broken strand of pearls on a black cloth and wants an estimate on restringing them. Maria pats Dominic playfully on the rump and heads into the store with Denise. Dominic hangs his apron and leaves.

The drive to Newcastle actually takes him five hours with a stop in Richibucto for food and to add fuel to his car. The washout has been temporarily fixed. It was slow going with heavy traffic. When he gets off the ferry that has taken him across the Miramichi River into Newcastle from Chatham, he stops at a garage to ask directions to Meadowbrook Lane. The man looks askance at Dominic, glances at the new car, and questions his intentions.

"Not to be nosey, Mister, but what would you be wanting to go there for? It's not a better part of the town as the pretty street name might suggest."

"I'm to visit a friend and his letter said he lives there."

"Well be careful. There's a bad bunch that live at the end of the street, which is a dead end."

He points west.

"Go down this road for a quarter mile and when you get to town hall turn right, it'll be the last street on the left."

"Thank you."

Dominic follows the directions and enters a dirt road that is lined with dilapidated houses that the years seem to have forgotten, looking like a mouthful of bad teeth. Junk lies around the yards, dogs run free and bark at him as he passes. Number 26 is a rundown two-storey house that might've been majestic at one time. The paint is peeling, the arches with Gothic trim are rotted, the steps up to the main door are lopsided. The only thing bright is the door to 26 which looks to have been painted white recently. Dominic parks his car on the side of the road and walks through the driveway to the graveled walkway. When he gets closer, he can see that the entry to 26 is slightly ajar. Knocking tentatively on the jamb he pushes the door open a bit. An unpleasant aroma seeps down the stairway, causing Dominic to scrunch his nose. When there is no response to his rapping, he calls out.

"Hello in there. Are you home, Don?"

No answer. Worried now, he opens the door fully to see a set of worn stairs rising to the second level. Dust balls nestle in the corners.

Steps are decorated with worn shoes, a boot, a can of paint, empty paper bags and old newspapers. Entering the small foyer, Dominic treads cautiously up. The smell of old food gets stronger as he nears the top. Even though many stairs squeak, there is no response until he gets to the top of the stairs and he hears soft snoring.

He walks into a hallway that opens to a living room on the left and a man is lying on a frayed sofa. He's not sure if it's Don as the man is terribly thin. A week's worth of whiskers cover his lower face. Strands of hair that might be a comb-over lie on his forehead. The chin, the soiled shirt, the edge of the couch and a spot on the floor are covered with dried vomit. An empty quart bottle with no label lies on the floor nearby. Looking closely, he sees the scar over the right eye that Don told them he received when he was a toddler and fell, hitting his head on a rocking chair. Shaking his head at the sad sight, Dominic decides to take a look around before he disturbs the sleeping man.

The hallway leads into a kitchen, where dishes are piled in the sink. A hand pump with the handle raised guards the mess. A cold wood stove is covered by empty pots and a frying pan that is crusted with some reddish gunk. A table sits in the middle of the floor and is covered with an empty plate, used utensils, an empty bottle of jam and more discarded newspapers. A room with a wash basin, ewer and towels is further down the hall across from a bedroom where only an unmade bed and a dresser sit. The whole house is pungent with neglect and sadness.

Dominic decides to let Don sleep off whatever has taken him under. He finds a reasonably clean pot and fills it with water from the pump. There is wood and kindling packed behind the stove. He uses some of the newspaper and dry wood to start a fire to heat the water and take the dampness away. Putting his jacket and hat on one of the kitchen chairs, he rolls up his sleeves and starts to clean up the apartment.

After doing the dishes, the kitchen and the other room, he finds a broom in a hallway closet. When he is sweeping the floors, he hears the rustling of the cushions and a raspy voice moaning and cursing from the living room.

"Oh, shit man, where am I? Who's out there?"

Dominic walks into the living room bearing a glass of cold water to see Don sitting up on the couch with his head in his hands. Strands of hair fall over his fingers as he rubs his eyes and stares up when he hears Dominic enter the room. He's blinking bloodshot eyes, trying to focus. He swishes the stray hairs back over his barren pate.

"Dominic? Is that you, Dominic?"

"Aye, it's me. You don't look too good, Don."

"I don't feel too good."

When he talks his mouth is dry and smacks when he speaks.

"Here, drink this."

Don grabs the water with a shaky hand, spilling some until he has both hands on the glass. He gulps the first half until the cold water chills his throat. Breathing deep, he looks up at Dominic, who offers a brave face.

Don's eyes go watery; tears spill upon his cheeks.

"I'm… I'm so glad you're here, Dominic. Look at me. I'm ashamed of myself. The liquor is the only thing that takes the bad feelings away."

The glass of water slips from shaking hands to splash upon the floor. It lands directly on the empty quart and both shatter with a loud crack. It startles Don, who throws himself on the floor, covering his ears with both hands, crying for the bombs to stop. Dominic reacts without hesitating and kneels at Don's side. Holding him around the shoulders, he calms the spooked man with reassuring words.

"It's all right, Don. You're safe here. You're home now. It's all right."

The shaking subsides. Knowing what he's done, Don is nodding his head. Moving away from Dominic, he tries to rise but can't do so until Dominic helps him to his feet. Embarrassed and drained of words, Don hangs his head. Dominic feels a deep sorrow for the man. He needs to help him. Holding Don steady, he steers him towards the washroom.

"Come along, I've heated lots of water. Let's go get you cleaned up and then we'll talk."

Stripping the sodden clothing from Don, Dominic points out the basin and a pot of hot water on the sideboard.

"When that bowl gets used up, I have more in the kitchen. If you need help with your razor, tell me. We don't want you ending up with a bunch of nicks on your ugly face."

It's the first smile he's seen from Don. They share a light laugh. Leaving Don to his toilet, Dominic goes in search of clean clothes. Finding unsoiled trousers, underwear, wool socks and a shirt, he gathers the garments and knocks lightly on the door.

"Clothes out here, Don, by the door."

A muffled thank you comes through the door. Dominic retreats to the living room to continue cleaning.

An hour later, Don and Dominic are sitting at the kitchen table. Don is not the same man. His fair skin shines, the comb over is glued back in place, the stubble is gone, revealing a determined chin, the eyes are more hopeful, and his aroma is more pleasing. Clean clothing makes him look like the Don Dominic knew before. The house smells of soap and disinfectant.

"I've heated a can of beans I discovered in the cupboard and fried some eggs I found in the larder. Dig in. And I've made a full pot of tea."

Don is hungry and attacks the food. Dominic shares the eggs, his are boiled and covered with pepper.

They talk as they eat, forgetting such manners between friends. Dominic prompts Don to tell him everything and anything he wants to talk about. Pausing a forkful of beans, Don stares at the middle of the table, his vision somewhere gruesome. His voice is far off when he replies.

"The gas Dominic. The gas was the scariest, just breathing could kill you. I remember my friend Jean-Paul, he…"

The words flow until the sun has set. Darkness takes over the street, quiets the dogs but doesn't stop the traffic to the dead end of the street. Bootleggers. With guns, totally off limits to strangers and undesirable locals. Many visit but no one stays long. Starlight from a clear sky makes everything blue. Dominic and Don are sitting on the stoop with their fifth cup of tea cradled in their hands. The night is cooler and both have donned jackets and Dominic his hat. When the story ended with Don sending the letter, they both ponder the memories.

Dominic is reminded of the horrors and the fear, vowing they will never conquer him. Don feels a weight lifted from his shoulders, the first time he's told anyone everything. All his fears, his haunted memories, his worries about tomorrow seem lighter thanks to Dominic's caring attitude and attentive listening. He still worries about the nights.

"The only way I sleep, Dominic, and don't have bad dreams Is by drinking myself into a stupor. Now I look for any reason for the liquor, even if it is illegal."

"Haven't the doctors suggested you see a psychologist? I've heard they can help with things like this."

Don looks at Dominic as if he asked him to go to the moon.

"I'm not crazy, Dominic! Those doctors work in asylums."

Dominic grins at his friend's naïveté.

"That's not totally true, Don. Yes, they work with people at asylums, but they also have practices where they help people understand their feelings. People you can talk to without judgment, like me only I don't have the right advice. I can't tell you how to stop having those bad dreams or the flashbacks, but I bet they can."

Don is shaking his head.

"I don't know, Dominic."

"You need someone you can go to, Don, when it gets bad. You need to get working again and stay away from the booze. I know it's easy for me to say that. I've been lucky, having people close, and I can put that all away."

Don tosses the loose tea leaves from his cup and sets it on the steps beside him. He's rubbing his hands and nodding. His mind drifts to other thoughts.

"I wonder how the rest of our little gang on the ship made out. I haven't heard from any of them and you said you haven't either."

Just then, an idea blossoms in Dominic's head. He was worried about leaving Don on his own again. He claps his hands and stands to face John.

"Let's find out. We know where they're all from. I'll take some time from the store, and either by car or train, we'll find the boys and see what they're up to. Would you like that?"

Don shares a rare smile.

"Yes… yes, I would like that, but I don't have the funds to travel Dominic. I barely have enough to pay the rent, which is already a few days behind."

Dominic waves the thought away.

"Never mind that. Let's get some sleep. I'll call my wife tomorrow from town and you and I can set off on an adventure. We'll go see Mark first because I remember he lived in Grande-Anse and that's only a few hours from here by auto. I know Clovis is in Saint John. Do you remember where Adam and Chris live?"

Don is elated.

"Yes, that would be great, Dominic. I can't thank you enough for this. Now Adam lived close to Fredericton, I think in Lincoln, and Chris lives in the northern part of the province, up towards Belldune, outside of Bathurst, but I can't remember the name of the community. Let's do it, and I'll pay you back someday, Dominic."

"Let's not worry about that now. I'm beat. We'll start out first thing in the morning."

Dominic puts his hand on Don's shoulder, looking him in the eyes. The pale glaze of the starry sky can't hide the hope in them.

"No dreams tonight, Don. I'll be here with you."

By Thursday the only man they haven't visited yet is Clovis in Saint John. They had arrived in Fredericton yesterday and spent the evening with Adam. Their first visits were with Mark and Chris in Northern New Brunswick. It took less than an hour to track Mark down when they arrived in Grande-Anse, a small and friendly community. He owns a fish packing plant and even though this is a busy season, he took them home to introduce his new wife, the lady he was engaged to when they all met on the ship. His son is a year old. Business is good, no bad dreams and he left the war in Europe. All in all, a very happy man. Mark assured Don that he'd always be around if needed.

Chris took a little longer to locate. He didn't live in Jacquet River any longer but had moved to Bathurst shortly after the war. He's an accountant and works for the city. Again, they visited his home and met his wife, but the evening was spent at one of his friends who is a bachelor. Chris called a few of his buddies together to meet Don and Dominic. One of the boys had some homemade beer, but Don stayed away from the booze. They all listened to his stories, sympathy and encouragement followed the many toasts. Chris parted with the same words as Mark: he'd be there if he was needed.

Adam still lives in Lincoln, outside of the capital city. A true family man, he brought Don and Dominic home to meet his wife and the kids. He and his wife operate a diner in Fredericton. He too had many bad moments after the war, but time has softened the memories and he dwells on how fortunate he is. His favorite saying is that he never has time to worry about what went on in the past. When they leave later in the evening, Don is feeling more positive from the visits than he has in a long time. Adam too offered his friendship and vowed he would help in any way.

The road from Fredericton to Saint John is a heavily trafficked road, not altogether in the best shape and it takes many hours to make the trip. It had rained in the night and there were numerous soft spots. When they arrive in Saint John, it is early evening and they decide to take a hotel room and wait until morning to search for their friend. Don has a bad night. Dominic wakes him from a disturbing nightmare. They talk it through. It is close to four o'clock when they get back to sleep and ten o'clock by the time they have something to eat and check out. The last Dominic heard from Clovis was that he lived on Duke Street in the east end. A year ago, one of Dominic's letters was returned, undelivered. They decide to start there and canvas the street until they find someone who knows him.

Parking the car at the top of the street, they walk from house to house. It takes them eight houses of explaining who they are and who they are searching for. The robust lady who answers the door, Ruby Horncastle, is Clovis's wife's whist partner and has been for fourteen years. They meet every month at each other's homes. The Hacheys used to live at the other end of the street, towards the inlet. They moved to Loch Lomand in July of '18. He works as a carpenter. He and his two brothers build houses. And so on.

Dominic and Don listen politely to Ruby's gushing of words, unable to get a word in because there's no gap in the chatter. They're nodding and the first time she tries to take a quick breath, Dominic interrupts her.

"How would we get to Loch Lomand, Mrs. Horncastle."

She pauses and with flirting eyes says, "It's Miss Horncastle."

Dominic reddens from the insinuation and grins. She interprets his blushing for reciprocal feelings and opens the door wider.

"Would you gentleman like to come in for some tea?"

Dominic's waving both hands. Don is trying not to laugh and waits at the bottom of the stairs.

"No, no, thank you for the offer, but we must run. How do I get to Clovis' place, please?"

Disappointment shades her face and she points east. With directions committed to memory, the men hie away as quick as they can before she starts in again. When they are back in the auto, Don lets go and has a merry laugh at Dominic's expense, who only reddens more. Waving him off, they head out of the city. It takes them to almost noon before they get to Clovis's house. It's set back from the road nestled among huge oaks. Fall flowers bloom along the front. A lady putters on the porch and notices them as they approach. She recognizes Dominic right away, even though it's been three years since they've seen each other. Waving enthusiastically, she meets them at the bottom of the steps with open arms.

Dominic returns the hug; he always liked Linda. Never met anyone as cheerful. After the how-are-yous, Dominic introduces Don. She's heard of him from Clovis, so he gets a hug too.

"My goodness, Don, you're too thin. You two are going to have to stay to dinner. I've made a chicken stew and there's lots of dumplings and chicken and new vegetables. Fresh bread. Apple pie for dessert. What do ya say, boys?"

The question is rhetorical, the front door is open and they can smell the fresh stew. Of course they'll stay. She continues.

"I expect you're looking for Clovis?"

She's smiling but the eyes sadden. Dominic suspects bad news.

"Is he okay, Linda?"

"Well, Dominic, mostly yes. But he had a bad night last night. He has bad dreams sometimes, scary stuff from the war. I got him through most of it, Dominic, but there's some I can't compete with."

She's shaking her head. Dominic and Don look sharply at each other; they're thinking the same thing. Dominic places his hand on her upper arm.

"That's why we've come, Linda. We were there, we know what he's going through. Don has had some especially bad times from the painful memories."

Don is standing slightly behind Dominic, facing the house, and he offers a nod.

"I'd like to talk to Clovis. Maybe we can help each other out."

"Well your timing couldn't be better. He meets with several others that have similar issues every other Friday afternoon, and that's where he is today. It's helped him a lot."

Once more they commit directions to their memory, apologize that they can't stay and share her dinner. She shoos them out of the yard.

"Don't you worry. I'll save you some. You come on back with Clovis, whenever, and I'll see ya all then. Now go on."

The building they're looking for is not far – less than a mile away. The Catholic Church offered the men the use of their basement, a meeting room and full use of the coffee urn, as well as Father Aloysius Crane, should his presence for support be required. No one else is in the building, the entry is in the back, where a door opens into the basement. A hallway opens with several doors but the one facing them has a handwritten note tacked to the door jamb that says "Meeting". When Dominic and Don knock on the door, the chatter dies inside. Ten seconds go by before a priest opens the door wide enough to stand in. He's a tall thin man with shallow cheeks, a long neck, a toothy smile and a white clerical collar.

"How can we help you gentlemen?"

Dominic removes his hat, holds it in both hands at his chest.

"Beggin' your pardon, Father. We were told that Clovis Hachey is here and meeting with some of his friends."

Clovis can hear the conversation and is sitting at the end of a long wooden table with his back to the door. He recognizes the voice. Leaping up he taps Father Crane on the shoulder.

"It's all right, Father. I know this man."

Taking a peek at Dominic's companion, his eyes bulge at the unexpected visitor.

"I know this scalawag too, Father!"

Don laughs at the title.

"Looks who's talking. We heard about you hiding Sargent Stamford's whistle? I think you're the scalawag."

Clovis frowns and puts a finger to his lips, a light dig in Father Crane's rib.

"Shh, don't say anything, I haven't confessed that one yet."

They crack up and Father Crane waves them in.

Clovis returns to the table where three other men sit. Pointing to the visitors he introduces them first.

"This here is two buddies from the sail over. The tallest one there is Dominic Alexander from Moncton, and he thinks we talk funny, and the other chap is Don Cook and the last I heard from Newcastle."

The two of them wave to the chuckling group and Don confirms he still lives up north. The room is painted light green and white trim. A cot is in one corner near a couch and chair. A square table in the other corner has a shiny urn upon it with mugs, sugar dish and creamer nestled around it. The long wooden table where the men sit is polished oak and in the center is a plate of doughnuts and molasses cookies with quite a few missing. Clovis points to the priest who has taken a seat at the other end.

"Father Crane you've met. The big guy at far right is Harold, but we all call him Bear and you can see why. The red-headed Irishman beside him is Lenny, and on the left is the old man of the bunch, Jean-Paul. Now what brings you two to Loch Lomand and how did you find us?"

While Dominic tells of seeing Linda, Jean-Paul pulls his chair over. Father Crane fetches two more chairs from a stack in the corner. Harold offers them coffee, which both accept, and Lenny rearranges the chairs so two more will fit around the table. They're all seated again listening and Dominic gets to the point.

"...so, Don and I are working on getting things back in order for him."

Don has his head down, hands folded in his lap. It's quiet for mere seconds as each man reflects on his own grief. The quiet is disturbed by the scratching of Harold's chair legs upon the floor. He stands and walks around to where Don is sitting. Wordlessly, as they all watch, he prompts Don to stand, whereupon he takes him in his giant arms. Don cannot hold back the tears and sobs into the man's chest. Clovis rises and hugs the two of them; Lenny stands and throws his arms around the men, then Jean-Paul, then Father Crane, who gestures for Dominic to come too. The men hold each other's backs, the sounds of a distraught heart the only echo in the room, until there is only quiet. Don is overwhelmed by the tenderness of these hard men.

The embrace breaks up with the welcomes overlapping. Pats on his back, amens and onward soldier wishes as they take their seats. Clovis is the unofficial leader of the group and keeps it informal. They had been talking about dreams before. He suggests a change as he looks at Don.

"We're all here for the same reason, Don. Talking about it is good. We know how it was. I'm sure the rest of us would like to know what's bothering you."

There's agreement all around. Don straightens his shoulders and looks each man in the eye.

"I'm not a coward but...but I was scared...frightened all the time."

More amens, more nods

"I was terrified of dying somewhere in that mud, where no one would find me. There was so much death and destruction. The worst was..."

Don shares what's heavy on his soul. He talks for over an hour. The men listen, ask clarifying questions, drink their coffee until he is quiet. Dominic had heard it before, but there's not as much pity-me in the confession this time. It's a release, a sharing of the pain the war caused. He's not alone any longer. The men take a break while Father Crane counsels Don in another room. Lenny and Jean-Paul go outside for a smoke. Harold distributes more coffee. Clovis and Dominic sit on the couch speaking in low tones.

"He didn't mention it Clovis, but he hasn't a job. He was having flashbacks at the school where he was a janitor and he hurt one of the students, a young girl."

Clovis rubs his chin.

"He's having bad luck, even the wife deserted him. Poor bugger. I might have an idea about that. Where's he living? Do you think he might move down this way?"

Dominic shrugs.

"Don't know about that, but he stays at a house he rents, doesn't own much. The wife took mostly everything, sneaked out when he was at work. He might be glad to get away. It's not in a very good part of the town."

They are interrupted when Don and the priest return to the room. Don has a happy look for a change, the priest looking content. Lenny and Jean-Paul return laughing over some joke. Clovis herds them together. A western basement window catches the first rays of the sun's descent and Clovis guesses it to be about three-thirty.

"We can gab away for another hour or so. Does anyone want to share something with Don, some advice maybe."

They all take turns giving their support, ideas for Don to try to help forget the bad stuff. It all ends around five o'clock and Clovis takes a drive back with Dominic and Don insisting that they are welcome for supper.

"Linda will be very disappointed if you don't."

When they get to the house, Linda greets them once more and Clovis tells them he'll only be a moment. He runs to the house across the road. He's back in fifteen minutes with the widest of grins. Linda, Dominic, Don and three of the Hachey children are sitting on the porch. After hustling the kids off, already fed, Linda leads them to the table. Clovis whispers in her ear on the way. No war stories or unhappy events is the rule at home. They talk of Dominic's good fortune, hoping to meet his wife again. Dominic stuns them all by saying he wants to learn to fly, how he misses the excitement of flight. They all say he's crazy, better to have both feet on the ground. Clovis tells them of his work with his brothers. Before digging into the pie, he points his fork at Don who raises his brows in a what-have-I-done fashion.

"When I ran next door, I spoke with my oldest brother. We've been looking for a reliable laborer and we'd like to offer you the job. It pays ninety cents an hour and we work nine hours a day, six days a week, except Friday afternoons. It's hard work but good wages. You'd have to move down this way if you can. What do you think, Don?"

Don is momentarily overcome by the offer. Hesitating when he thinks of the cost of moving and where he'd stay. Disappointment sets the tone of his voice. He's embarrassed when he replies.

"It's a fine idea, but I don't have the means to get here. I've nowhere to stay."

Linda likes the man, sees something honest in his eyes.

"You can stay with us for a bit, Don, until you find a place."

Dominic sees the hope on Don's face – the wide eyes and smooth forehead – and antes up.

"I'll lend you the money, Don, because I know you won't take it otherwise. You can pay me back whenever you want, with no interest."

Once more Don is flabbergasted by the generosity and unable to speak, not wanting to shed more tears even though they would be more joyful. Casting off his pride he nods his head yes. A cheer goes around the table and from the other room the children join in, not sure what's going on but caught up in the glee.

It's only after dinner, when the men are sitting on the porch as Linda puts the younger ones to bed, that Dominic tells them he will start out to Moncton soon, staying in Sussex tonight. Don is staying on so he can start work in the morning. Clovis has offered to help him retrieve his property. When Dominic's ready to leave and shares a hug with Linda. Then he asks Don to walk to the car with him. He removes a hundred dollars from his wallet and hands it to Don.

"That's about two and a half weeks' wages. Think that'll get you through? And there's no hurry. Why don't we say you take until May of next year to repay me?"

Don stands straighter. A large amount of trust has been placed in his hands and he vows to do right by their faith in him. Looking at Dominic directly, he offers his hand. Dominic holds it in both of his and shakes it eagerly.

"Thank you, Dominic. I know words aren't enough. I still can't believe how lucky I am. I'll get this back to you long before May, you can be certain of that. Thank you again."

Don steps away from the auto and waves to his benefactor.

CHAPTER 6

Maria is busy on August 9 preparing a small gathering at the house, with Denise and André, Nick and Joanne and Lilly and Ivan, in the afternoon. In the early evening Dominic treats everyone to the new seafood restaurant in Leger's Corner by the racetrack. The main topic of conversation is how Maria keeps getting in trouble with the law. It's not good enough for her and her friends that only married women are allowed to vote in New Brunswick since 1918. Asians are not allowed, Indigenous woman are not allowed, single women are not allowed. Throughout the fall she and her group of believers demand the same rights for all women, regardless of marital status, regardless of race. Dominic has to pick her up at the jailhouse more often than he likes but stands behind her and defends her stance when confronted by other men who suggest he has no control over his wife. He has a simple reply for that.

"Nae I don't. And I don't intend to."

Most of those opposed to her position look down their noses at them and usually associate with Crosswaithe. Unfortunately, they are men of power and follow their own ideals or others' opinions aligned with their way of thinking. The dissenting ladies and men have more backbone and are not ready to give up. Disheartened at times but never put off, Maria spends a good part of her spare time in planning, protesting and letter writing. He watches her sometime when she's making notes, nibbling on the end of her pencil when in deep thought. The smoothing of her brow and her defiant eyes when she has a revelation and begins frantically writing. Dominic adores her determination and lively spirit.

*

Autumn of 1920 is much warmer than usual to everyone's pleasure. The only cold snap is in the first days of October, bringing a tinge of frost which sets the trees ablaze with vibrant colors. Large oaks, maples and elm stand in vivid glory, surrounding the small church in Grande Digue where Nick and Joanne get married on the first Saturday of the month. Her father delivers the bride to her future husband and Nick is standing on artificial limbs, balancing himself with a cane of polished ebony and a silver tip. Later when the festivities reach a feverish pitch at the dance hall, a loud voice shouts for attention. The bride and groom will lead off the dancing with the first waltz. He in his tuxedo, she in white satin elegance, smothered in lace. Rosy cheeks, a slender face filled with a smile, small dainty ears and a soft chin – Joanne is a beautiful bride. The musicians play an Acadian ballad. The lady playing the accordion sings in a perfect tenor, a love song of commitment and sacrifice, of deep passion and eternity. Only at the end does Nick collapse in his wheel chair, his stumps unbearably sore. Led by his bride, all thirty guests give him a standing ovation, for many minutes.

Dominic beams with pride at his friend, who always talked about walking again. People are yakking and patting his back, shaking his hand but he catches Dominic's eye. Nick glances at the wooden limbs with shoes. There is no need for words of gratitude, Dominic can see it in his eyes. A quick nod verifies message received.

Dominic enjoys himself tremendously, chatting with friends, store staff and especially Nick's family, having met many of them today. There's food everywhere, whatever refreshments you might need; the mood is merry with loud chatter and happy tunes. Dominic dances with Maria and is popular with the other ladies because he dances so well. The celebration goes long into the evening. It's shortly after midnight when Dominic and Maria decide to leave. They have plans for tomorrow and it's already late.

The lights on the Buick are strong, the roads are dry, graded just last week, so Maria drives. Dominic is dizzy from too many hits of the proffered flasks. It's not far to the house in Cocagne. The first ten minutes of the trip under a starry sky, each is in their own quiet thoughts. She of the wedding, the gorgeous dress, the tasteful shoes, the food and the look on Joanne's face when she said I do. The strongest and most sentimental image in both their thoughts is of Nick standing and walking. The effort he made, mastering the prosthetics, the pride in his stance and confidence in his manner from looking people in the eyes. The joy that emanated from the newlyweds as they moved slowly to the love song. Only the legs give him this opportunity, the pleasure everyone takes for granted. She looks at Dominic quickly and he catches the movement. She doesn't take her eyes off the road when she speaks.

"I know what you're thinking."

"You do?"

"About Nick I bet."

Dominic responds with a wry grin.

"That's eerie. I was. About him standing at the altar and the look on his face. How happy he was."

Maria smiles at the recollection.

"Yes, I saw that too. And it's all because of you."

Dominic is bashful, and his ears turn red when reminded of his generosity.

"He did all the hard work, what he went through with fittings, the uncomfortable learning steps and the exercises. I only made the legs available sooner. Besides he's my best friend and a good man."

Maria throws him a kiss.

"So are you. I love you, Mr. Alexander."

*

The dying colors of autumn disappear in strong breezes, trees and shrubs stand unclothed with bony limbs. Cold winds, dreary rain and morning frost remind them that November is almost over. The first flakes of winter touch down on November 27, the last Saturday of the month. Large crystals that fade away as soon as they touch ground. There's not enough to cover anything. A mid-morning sun dissolves what moisture remains. Alexander's Jewellery is preparing for the Christmas season and is already busy with early shoppers.

443

Dominic knows this will be the last weekend he and Maria will have off for a while. Extra staff have been hired, Denise is an able manager and there are no urgent matters.

That same day, a B2.e aircraft, manufactured by the Royal Aircraft Factory of Great Britain, will land behind his house in Cocagne. It's similar to the type of aircraft Dominic spied from behind enemy lines. He hasn't told Maria yet. Her brother Robert is partners with him, and he hasn't told his girlfriend Faye, either. The women are not convinced flying is safe. The men want to do this without worrying the ladies, and without the ladies trying to talk them out of it. They decide to wait until they have the plane on hand before saying anything.

Dominic's on his way to Cocagne now; he should be there before Robert, who estimated he'd arrive around noon, sooner if the wind was behind him. Maria is taking the train to Bouctouche later and meeting Faye in Notre-Dame. She thinks he's gone to help André, who is adding an addition to his house in Irishtown. They plan on meeting up later.

The field that stretches towards the wooded portion of his property is long enough for landing; the stubble is short from the reaping of summer's grass. The weather has turned perfect and the ground is still firm. Maria's brother Robert is ferrying the plane from Saint John. More than an able pilot, he's an ace with the Sopwith Camel he flew in the war for the Royal Air Force. Seven aerial victories, two near strikes, losing his undercarriage once and a section of his bottom wing on another mission. Piloting skills honed from combat got him home and safely on the ground. Dominic can think of no one better to introduce the aircraft to the New Brunswick skies. Robert and the plane will be a team soon flying the same routes every day if their plans go as they hope.

Turning right at the center of the community, he heads north along the shore road, passes the church, crosses a small inlet and follows the shore. His place is only ten minutes away. The rare drone of an aircraft pulls his attention from the road even before he sees it. An airplane that can only be the B2.e, is off to his right over the bay and catches up to him. He pushes away the sudden memories of the crash that momentarily distract him. Concentrating on the pilot, Robert's bright red scarf flowing in the wind, he waves and honks his car horn. Robert recognizes the auto and dips his wing. People step from their homes to view the plane and excitedly wave at this rare sight. The plane circles the bay until Dominic reaches the house and pulls into the driveway.

The runway is outlined with red posts and makeshift flags for wind direction. Robert loops around Cocagne Island and approaches the runway from the east, into the wind. Dominic gasps as the plane drops over the barn and looks as if the wheels will catch on the weather vane, but it clears the building and drops for a shaky but safe landing on the bumpy field. From where he's standing, the plane looks like it will run right into the trees. Instead, it slows quickly, coming to rest with plenty of field left.

Robert taxis the aircraft back to the barn and stops it a hundred feet away. Neighbors and onlookers are rushing towards the house. They come by buggy, running and auto to see this marvelous sight. The wings, fuselage and rims are dull grey. The upper wing spans stiffly for thirty-six feet, the lower just a bit shorter. An empty seat up front invites the curious. A plane has never landed anywhere near Cocagne before, and it offers rare excitement. Dominic runs out to greet his brother-in-law.

"Hello, Robert. So happy you made it without any mishaps, and in such perfect weather. It's a beautiful airplane."

Robert is as tall as Dominic and reminds him of Maria. Removing his goggles, his dark eyes glitter from the rush of flying. His firm jaw and a beaming smile make him look like a poster boy. Bundled in a heavy wool jacket, the red scarf, ear-flapped hat and heavy gloves, he greets Dominic with a handshake.

"No problems at all, Dominic, other than a flock of birds over Petitcodiac that I had to avoid. The aircraft runs like a charm. The controls are a bit fussy and I can see why this was used as an observation aircraft or a bomber. It's way too sluggish for a fighter."

He points to the gathering crowd approaching.

"Looks like we caused a bit of excitement."

Dominic turns to see children running, men and women in buggies, bearing wide smiles and looks of fascination.

"Aye, I think so. I called the *Times* and the *Transcript* and I'm hoping they send a reporter. Maybe get a bit of free advertising for our new enterprise coming in the spring. The men with the tarps should be here Monday."

Robert is nodding his head in agreement.

"Yes, it would be wise to get this covered up until we build the hangar we discussed."

"Aye, lots of work ahead of us. Now go greet your admirers and tell them about the plane."

Robert shows off the delights of the aircraft, lifts the children into the cockpit, flirts with the pretty ladies and shakes hands with the men and answers questions. A well-used Model T pulls into the yard towing a smelly exhaust. The brass radiator is dull and unpolished. The upper windshield is missing, explaining the driver's hat pulled low on his head and the driver himself crouched in the seat. A second man is sitting beside him. Shutting the vehicle off, the driver straightens up and gets out. He's not too tall, wearing a bulky, navy wool jacket, dark pants tucked into black rubber boots. Curls of black and grey hair spill out the back of his hat. Dominic breaks from the crowd to greet him.

"G'day, sir."

The man is agog at the plane, wide eyes stare beyond Dominic as he talks.

"Would you be Dominic Alexander?"

"Aye, that's me."

Looking directly at Dominic, he nods to the plane.

"Do you own that beauty?"

Dominic points a finger back at Robert.

"Aye, that gentleman there and I do."

Dominic studies the visitor as he introduces himself. Middle age lines the edges of the eyes, a goatee fills out a full chin. He holds a writing pad and pencil in one hand; the other he offers to Dominic.

"Name's Robichaud, Patrick Robichaud. Do a bit of writing for the paper, the *Times*, when news is down this way. Got a call I should come out and see you. Could we take a bit of your time and tell the readers about the plane and why is it here in Cocagne?"

He points to the other man in the car.

"And some pictures perhaps?"

Dominic loves pictures, plans to own a camera someday. He glances back at Robert and points at him.

"Aye, certainly, and the pilot as well."

Robichaud waves at the other man. Getting the signal, a taller man, red-faced and eyes that glance everywhere, starts to remove equipment from the rumble seat. Tripod, camera, shroud and other gear takes two trips. A few of the people are intrigued by the photographer searching for the best spot, with his back to the sun, setting up his camera. He talks very little, concentrating on his craft, feeling important in the curious gazes. Robichaud does the talking. Both Dominic and Robert answer a set of intelligent questions, about the plane, about flying (they both refused to talk about their war experience), where they will maintain it and what they are going to do with it. They are interrupted by the photographer when he is ready.

He captures ten images. Three of the crowd with and without Dominic and Robert, two of Dominic and the plane in different poses, same for Robert and three of them together in and around the plane. When he starts to take down the camera, the folks start to lose interest and most drift home. A few children from the two farms down the road hang around. Dominic and Robert finish the interview. They elaborate on the new hangar and runway to be built next summer. Robichaud looks at his notes and asks Dominic his last question.

"What are the plans for the B2.e?

Dominic smiles widely, the question he's been waiting for.

"Well, as we said earlier, Robert and I are partners, not only in the plane but in a new business we are opening in the spring that involves this aircraft. A never before offered service to the province. But that's all I'm saying at this point. You will have to wait until spring to find out the rest."

Later, Dominic checks his watch and sees it's a few minutes after four o'clock. He reminds Robert they have to go to Bouctouche to pick up the ladies at the train station. The plan is to tell them about the plane and their business idea tonight. When they arrive back at the house, Dominic pulls up to the main door of the house, keeping the auto in the center of the barn so no one can see the plane, even though it is dark now, he's not taking any chances of ruining the surprise.

He gets a fire going in the cook stove to get rid of the chill and prepare supper. Lights the stove in the far room as well. Robert and

Faye join them in the kitchen and all four gather together around the table for a steaming bowl of *chicken fricot* with fat dumplings and some fresh baked bread. Both men go back for seconds while the ladies are stuffed after one serving. Idle chatter, politics, the hockey season, the latest fashions – they talk and laugh about many topics during their meal.

Sitting in the living room with empty dessert plates and cups of tea on a center table, Dominic leans forward to set his on the small table by his chair. The women are on the couch across from him, laughing at some point Maria made about not trusting politicians. Robert is in a chair to his left, waiting for Dominic's cue. He's grinning. He's not sure how they'll react. Maria notices Dominic trying to get their attention.

"What is it, Dominic?"

He told himself he would not tiptoe around this. With a wave to his comrade he sits forward with what he hopes is his best smile.

"Robert and I have purchased a plane."

Silence. The women stare back at him, disbelief bulging their eyes, their mouths agape. Robert shifts around in his seat, waiting for their reply, uncomfortable in this quiet. Maria starts laughing, not merely tittering but a laugh from deep inside. She's bent over with her hands on her tummy, trying to contain herself. Faye gets caught up in Maria's gaiety. Her laugh is lighter but just as rampant. Robert sits forward and looks askance at Dominic before getting swept up in their amusement. Dominic's frown levels out and he too is soon laughing. The men stop first and eye each other, questions in their eyes. The ladies soon stop.

Maria and Faye are already on the edge of the sofa, they curl their lips and glare at their respective mates. They both talk at once.

"It's not true, is it, Dominic?"

"Robert, what did you do?"

If they were dogs, the men would have their ears back, knowing they'd been caught doing something bad. It might be better if they were dogs, at least they could play dumb. Dominic puts on his most convincing smile, nodding his head.

"Yes, it's true, we did. We bought a plane from England and it's like the one I flew in."

Maria, her arms crossed, stands up and shoots him a scary look.

"*Ah oui*, just like the plane you crashed in. You don't know how to fly a plane Dominic. Whatever are you going to do with it?"

Faye rises after listening to Maria, scolds Robert with a pointing finger.

"You told me you weren't going to fly again. It's too dangerous Robert!"

They're all talking at once, objecting and scolding until the girls start to ask questions. Faye doesn't change her opinion of how she will always be worrying, but she doesn't want to argue in front of their hosts so remains quiet. Maria drills the men.

"What kind of plane is it?"

Robert is still excited, having told them what it's like in the sky, softening their negative stance, when he answers.

"It's like the one I flew in in England. A bomber."

The last word provokes disaster in the women. They respond with tiny gasps and take each other's hands in fright. Dominic jumps in to reassure them it's not just a weapon. He frowns with scrunched brows at Robert before continuing.

"It's an observation airplane, a two-seater. We used it to spy on the Germans and take pictures or direct artillery. There was a surplus of planes after the war and the Royal Air Force auctioned them off. The plane originally cost them over $1,600.00, but we acquired it for less than a quarter of that. It cost as much to have it shipped here, but it's still a fantastic deal. It's new, it's fast, and it can fly great distances with low fuel consumption. Robert's going to teach me how to fly."

Maria is shaking her head. Faye looks like she's going to cry. With a soft and confident voice, the right words and patience, Dominic carries on.

"We're going to have our own business. What we have planned is…"

The women are intrigued by the potential, starting to deal with the benefits and possibilities of the men's idea. Maria sees the excitement in Dominic's eyes. Even though she is nervous about the whole idea, she can tell how much it means to him. It's after ten o'clock, when Maria asks one last question.

"Where is it?"

Dominic stands and waves to them all to follow. Robert hurries after him. The women give in and with a shrug they follow the men who each carry a lantern they lit while the woman donned jackets and boots. It's a short walk to the back of the barn under a clear sky. In the damp air the cold brushes frost along sharp edges. They can see their breath in the halo of the yellowish light. The lanterns swing with each stride and make the shadows sway. The first edge of the left wing comes into view. Getting within twenty feet of the airplane, the two lights illuminate the whole wing, the engine cowl and the propeller. The dark grey plane looks eerie in the low light. The foursome walk around the plane with the men explaining the details of the aircraft. Faye is quiet, but Maria is fascinated by the machine. She surprises them all when they are walking back to the house.

"When can we go flying?"

They can't see the huge smile on Dominic's face.

"Tomorrow."

They never convinced Faye to get in the plane, but Maria couldn't get enough. She was actually disappointed that it had to be put away for the winter. Heavy tarps cover it. Strong ropes have it tied down. A contractor has been hired for the construction of a hangar and runway next spring. Arrangements have been made for fuel delivery and storage. Everyone for miles around is talking about it. The newspaper ran the story and Dominic continues to be queried about his plans, but reminds everyone that they will have to wait until spring.

CHAPTER 7

Alexanders Jewellery & Repair has a booming December. When Dominic meets Lombroso, his accountant, to go over the year end, he lauds Dominic on his fiscal responsibility and ingenuity. There is $28,857.66 in the company account. He owes no money, not even for the goods in the store. There is a permanent staff of five, including Maria and Dominic, as well as two part-time employees. He has nearly $10,000.00 in his personal account. He owns the building outright, as well as the houses on Highfield Street and in Cocagne. His net worth is over $57,000.00, a huge sum of money in 1920. Yet Dominic and Maria remain modest. No fancy suits, no petty baubles, no outrageous automobiles. The only extravagance is the plane, and he vows it will pay for itself many times over.

On December 31, New Year's Eve, shortly after 4 p.m., they arrived home from Halifax via the train, having accompanied Lilly and Ivan to the ship that will carry them back to Great Britain for a three-week holiday. Lilly is happy in Canada but misses her family, as does Ivan. He and Maria decide to spend the last day of the year having steak and seafood at Moncton's newest restaurant, The Bend. They decide to forego the celebrations at Emma's to spend the evening together. From one of the runners in Richibucto, Dominic purchased a case of wine from Ontario and they plan on sampling it. It's a red Merlot, Maria's favorite. Before they sit, Dominic wants to paste the last news articles into his scrapbook. He has enough clippings to fill it. He's already purchased several more scrapbooks to start the next decade.

The Transatlantic liner RMS Empress of Canada is launched at Govan, Scotland.

Scotland votes against prohibition.

US Postal Service says children cannot be sent by parcel post.

Mexican rebel Pancho Villa surrenders.

Olympic games take place in Antwerp.

Jack Dempsey KOs Billy Miske in 3 for the heavyweight boxing title — first prize fight broadcast over the radio.

Wall Street bombing occurs with a horse drawn wagon exploding on Wall Street, killing 38 and injuring 143.

Babe Ruth sets record with 53 home runs.

Warren Harding is elected President of the US.

Arthur Meighen becomes Prime Minister of Canada.

The first plane to fly across Canada lands in Richmond BC, flying from Halifax, NS.

The burial of the unknown soldier takes place simultaneously in Westminster Abbey, London, and the Arc de Triomphe in Paris.

Relaxing on the couch in the living room later, Dominic reminisces about the last decade from the time he was left with his uncle Duff. The splitting of his family. The loss of his two brothers, his father and grandfather. Learning two trades from Tubbs and Duff. Befriending Ivan and the fun they had growing up. Meeting Pascal, and his and Mary's wedding. The fire and Duff's death. His inheritance and coming to Canada. Meeting Nick for the first time. Buying the house in Cocagne and the old farm in Moncton. Opening the repair shop. Hiring Maria. (The reminiscing is interrupted by tender moments, hugs and kisses when they talk of falling in love.) The war. Nick losing his legs and the changes in him with his positive attitude. The new store. The new house and fixing up the one in Cocagne. Going home again and visiting his friends and family. Bringing Lilly and Ivan back to Canada. Crosswaithe. Him going to jail. Maria's ongoing battle with the establishment. And lastly, the new plane.

It's almost midnight when there is a lull in their conversation, both thinking of the highlights of their evening's discussion. Maria tingles with pleasure, reflecting on the love and good life Dominic has brought her. She sees a faraway look on Dominic's face. It's the same one he had when they boarded the train in Halifax earlier in the day, and how he had looked after they saw Lilly and Ivan off at the wharf. He didn't want to talk about it then. She doesn't want to spoil the mood but is concerned with the Dominic's sad look, hoping it's only melancholy from his memories.

"What's troubling you Dominic?"

His eyes are watery when he looks up at her. He pauses for the right words.

"Do you remember when we passed through the customs building and there was a group of people who had just disembarked from the other ocean liner docked next to the one Lilly and Ivan are sailing on?"

"Yes."

"I think I saw my mother."

ABOUT THE AUTHOR

Allan Hudson is the author of two Drake Alexander adventure novels. This novel is about Drake's grandfather, Dominic.

He is also the author of a collection of short stories and the newest Det. Jo Naylor adventure.

The second Jo Naylor adventure is complete and will be ready for publication in the spring of 2021

The third Darke Alexander adventure is presently in the works. Publication is targeted for late 2021.

Allan lives in Cocagne, New Brunswick, on the east coast of Canada, with his wife Gloria.

He publishes a blog called South Branch Scribbler, where he posts short stories, interviews with authors, artists, and musicians. You can also find updates on his writing, novels and events.

Manufactured by Amazon.ca
Bolton, ON

35490493R00270